ABOUT THE COMPILER

David Marcus was born in Cork, read Law at University College, Cork, and King's Inns, Dublin, and was called to the Irish Bar in 1945. The following year he founded *Irish Writing*. In 1954, shortly after the publication of his first novel, *To Next Year in Jerusalem*, he went to live in London, where he spent the next thirteen years. He then returned to Ireland and founded, in the *Irish Press*, a weekly page of short stories and poetry entitled 'New Irish Writing', which has become a national institution. He has been Literary Editor of the *Irish Press* since 1968.

David Marcus has had many short stories and poems published in Ireland, Britain and the U.S.A., has translated the eighteenth century Gaelic poem *The Midnight Court*, and edited several short anthologies of Irish writing.

Biographical details about the contributors appear at the end of the book.

Irish Short Stories

Selected and introduced by David Marcus

NEW ENGLISH LIBRARY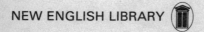

First published in Great Britain in 1980 by
The Bodley Head Ltd as *The Bodley Head Book of
Irish Short Stories*

First NEL Paperback Edition in two volumes April 1982
Reprinted in one volume May 1986

NEL Books are published by
New English Library,
Mill Road, Dunton Green,
Sevenoaks, Kent.
Editorial office: 47 Bedford Square, London WC1B 3DP

Printed and bound in Great Britain by
Cox & Wyman Ltd, Reading

British Library C.I.P.

[The Bodley Head book of Irish short stories].
    Irish short stories.
    1. Short stories, English——Irish authors
    2. English fiction——20th century
    I. Marcus, David, *1924–*
823'.01'089415[FS]   PR8876

    ISBN –0–450–39272–4

Contents

Thanks are due to the following copyright-holders for permission to reprint the stories listed:

'A Day in the Dark' by Elizabeth Bowen (Curtis Brown Ltd); 'At Night All Cats Are Grey' by Patrick Boyle (the author); 'Joy' by Daniel Corkery (Executor of the Estate of the late Daniel Corkery); 'St Patrick's Day in the Morning' by Lynn Doyle (Mrs Wyn Fisher and Duckworth Ltd); 'Foundry House' by Brian Friel (the author and Victor Gollancz Ltd); 'Two Women Waiting' by Desmond Hogan (the author and Hamish Hamilton Ltd); 'Night in Tunisia' by Neil Jordan (the author and Irish Writers' Co-Op); 'The Sisters' by James Joyce (the Society of Authors as the literary representatives of the Estate of James Joyce, the Executors of the Estate of James Joyce and Jonathan Cape Ltd); 'Lovers' by Maeve Kelly (the author and Poolbeg Press Ltd); 'The Dogs in the Great Glen' by Benedict Kiely (the author and Poolbeg Press Ltd); 'Happiness' by Mary Lavin (the author and Constable & Co. Ltd); 'The Dogs of Fionn' by Tom MacIntyre (the author); 'The Ring' by Bryan MacMahon (the author); 'The Wine Breath' by John McGahern (the author and Faber & Faber Ltd); 'The White Mare' by Michael McLaverty (the author and Poolbeg Press Ltd); 'An Occasion of Sin' by John Montague (the author and Poolbeg Press Ltd); 'A Letter to Rome' by George Moore (J. C. Medley and Colin Smythe Ltd); 'You Must Be Joking' by Val Mulkerns (the author, Poolbeg Press and A. D. Peters & Co. Ltd); 'A Sexual Relationship' by Gillman Noonan (the author and Poolbeg Press Ltd); 'Love-Child' by Edna O'Brien (the author and Weidenfeld & Nicolson Ltd); 'The Glass Wall' by Kate Cruise O'Brien (the author and Poolbeg Press Ltd); 'The Babes in the Wood' by Frank O'Connor (Hamish Hamilton Ltd and A. D. Peters & Co. Ltd); 'The Knight' by Julia O'Faolain (the author and Faber & Faber Ltd); 'The Kitchen' by Sean O'Faolain (the author and Jonathan Cape Ltd); 'The Landing' by Liam O'Flaherty (the author and Jonathan Cape Ltd); 'Ferris Moore and the

Earwig' by James Plunkett (the author, Poolbeg Press Ltd and A. D. Peters & Co. Ltd); 'Trinket's Colt' by E. Œ. Somerville and Martin Ross (John Farquharson Ltd); 'Desire' by James Stephens (the Society of Authors as the literary representatives of the Estate of James Stephens); 'A Minor Incident' by Maura Treacy (the author and Poolbeg Press Ltd); 'Teresa's Wedding' by William Trevor (the author and The Bodley Head Ltd); 'Not Isaac' by Anthony C. West (the author).

Introduction

The modern Irish short story is about as old as the century, that is, as old as the modern short story itself. Literary historians generally regard Gogol and Hawthorne as the fathers, respectively, of the short story in Russia and America (the other two countries reckoned to have been the major developers of the *genre*) yet the modern Irish short story is very seldom credited with significant parentage. But in fact it was not the immaculate conception it might appear to have been, with giants such as Liam O'Flaherty and James Joyce materialising as if by some form of literary abiogenesis: it had not only a father, but a mother as well. The father was George Moore (and it is perhaps characteristic of that smooth-tongued charmer that he was himself the first to claim fatherhood – what's more, to claim it long before there was any child on the way); the mother was (were?) that remarkable writing team of Edith Somerville and Martin Ross.

No literary parentage could have been more fruitful of promise, for father and mother emerged from the two widely-opposed cultures (Catholic and native/Protestant, or Anglo, and settler) which had become the constituents of the Irish family. Their attitude to the Irish society of their time – indeed the very areas of their concern – could not have been more divergent, but just as many of the latter's antecedents had taken on the ways and customs of the native and become 'more Irish than the Irish themselves', so did their literary descendants gradually come to write 'Irish' stories which were as germane and as committed as those being produced by the descendants of the former. Time had written off the condescensions and antagonisms, and whereas in seven centuries of history the political transplant had not yet successfully taken, in less than a single century the literary transplant was complete and both host and guest were part of the one native tradition.

The Irish pre-eminence in the field of the short story has frequently been remarked upon by commentators, both native and foreign. But what accounts for such pre-eminence? How is it that a country which boasts no notable tradition of novel-writing repeatedly throws up outstanding short story writers? The explanation can, I believe, be traced to the fortuitous correspondence between two prominent Irish characteristics and the two vital ingredients of the short story.

Words are to the writer's art much as bricks are to a house, and just as a house is not a home, a way with words will not, alone and of itself, be sufficient equipment for a short story writer. It isn't even his primary equipment. The short story writer's basic and essential gift must be his approach to the material of life, his vision of the world about him, the outlook that is exclusive to him alone by virtue of his particular emotional and intellectual chemistry: in other words, his way of seeing; if his way of seeing is sufficiently individual, sufficiently differentiated, and if to it is added a gift of expression both above average and out of the ordinary, then you have a short story writer. A way of saying and a way of seeing are the flesh and spirit of the short story.

As far as a way of saying is concerned, there is general acknowledgement of the Irish writer's – indeed the Irishman's – exceptional facility. More often than not it is phraseology that has been the Irish short story's hallmark – a phraseology heady with colour and freshness, heady, above all, with an almost intoxicated sense of release. So persuasive has been the Irish way with words that the

English language officially recognised it with a word of
its own (suggested by the Irish of course): blarney.

What can account for the phenomenon of Irish–English?
Why is it that, as H. E. Bates put it in his book *The Modern
Short Story*, 'Ireland (and America) are now the places
where the English language, both spoken and written,
shows its most vigorous and most plastic vitality'? It is
not difficult to explain the fecundity of American–English
– a country the size of the U.S.A., in which so much
regional variation is fuelled by such a hyper-competitive
ethic, is bound to find its way of speech constantly
energised by the cross-fertilisation of its society and the
need to keep abreast of that society's mania for experi-
mentation and invention. But the rhythms and scale of
the Irish way of life are so different from those of America
that such influences can hardly have contributed to the
vigour and plasticity of Irish–English. What, however, must
in large measure account for it is the fact that, as an
American commentator, Charles E. May, wrote in *Short
Story Theories*, '. . . in Ireland the English language is not
yet stale'. It is not stale because it was not until well into
the nineteenth century that the English language in Ireland
could be said to have been the only spoken language of
the vast majority of the people. Before 1800 Irish held
sway, and so when, during the ensuing hundred years, the
native population adopted English as their vernacular, they
were still thinking in Irish and consequently cobbled
together their version of English with distinctively Irish
words, inflections and constructions. And not only was
the very shape and design of their English sentence influenced, but its style and personality – its air – was determined by what I can only call the philological impetus of
the Irish language. This impetus is a direct reflection of
the speaker's culture and way of life: in America, for
instance, it is verbal (in the sense of being powered by
verbs) because American–English has to keep pace with
the go-ahead-and-get-things-done drive which its people
have inherited from their pioneering stock; but in Ireland

a traditionally near-to-standstill pace has afforded generous opportunity for the bodying forth of a bubbling Celtic imagination, and as a result simple conversation has been inflated to the status of a performance whose descriptive force has depended on its supply of adjectival lift-off. Yet this adjectival impetus is only the beginning of the Irish language's motive power: whereas in English the use of the adjective has to be restrained because it is normally placed before the noun and the noun has to be identified fairly smartly if the sense is not to be lost, in Irish the noun is placed first and so, the substantive being firmly established, there is almost no end to the number of adjectives which may be piled on it, each one adding more and more life and colour to the description. This particular adjectival balance of the Irish language would seem to me to be the major influence on the development of the English spoken in Ireland and written by Irish writers.

But what about the other – and more important – attribute of the short story writer, his special way of seeing? Is there a special Irish way of seeing? I would answer that question with the following anecdote.

Many years ago I was standing in a bus queue in the city of Cork. A station-wagon approached, its driver anxiously searching for a place to park. The area of roadway on either side of the bus-stop had, of course, to be kept clear, but there seemed to be just about a car's length free space between one of the white boundary lines of that area and the row of cars parked beyond it. Into that space the station-wagon fitted itself and out of the vehicle stepped its driver – an ageing, genial, country gentleman type, all tweeds and twinkle – who immediately proceeded to inspect his position and assure himself that he had in fact found a space, however circumscribed, which would remove from him the fear of a fine for illegal parking. What he saw made him replace his smile of self-satisfaction with a puzzled frown: certainly his four wheels had cleared the white line, but the back of the station-wagon protruded over it and into the space allocated to the bus stop. A technical infringement, at the very least? Undecided, he turned to the bus queue, and, addressing no one in particular, asked 'Do you think I'd get away with that?' For a few minutes no one in particular hazarded an answer until an ancient, wizened, diminutive type took off his cap, slowly scratched his stubbled cheek, and replied, 'Well, sir, 'tis like this: are yeh lucky?'

For me that answer encapsulates some basic elements of the Irish way of seeing as well as the pith of their way of saying – the latter, of course, being in some part a product of the former. It has a touch of fatalism – inculcated into them by centuries of religious rigour and inclement weather; a large dash of superstition – still rife in general customs and conventions, especially in rural areas; a hint of the accommodations sometimes made necessary with *force majeure* on the temporal plane – impressed upon them by the weight of their country's history; and of course the very form of the reply – a question answering a question – is the summation of the whole Irish temperament, the implicit belief that in this world, as in the world of the short story, there just are no answers; inklings and illuminations are the most one can expect.

Apart from the prowess of the Irish in the writing of short stories, there is the question of their addiction to the form. Why is the short story, rather than any other medium, the most popular Irish means of sophisticated artistic self-expression? Historical development suggests the answer. A peasant people intermittently at war – which for much of their history most of the Irish have been – is hardly likely to throw up significant painters, nor would their circumstances be conducive to the cultivation of a developing musical tradition (though in peasant peoples folk music usually flourishes and Irish folk songs are not only numerous but abound in ballads, i.e., short stories). This narrows the field down to literature, and here the importance of the *seanachie* (storyteller) as a pivotal figure in rural Irish life down to the nineteenth century must account for the predisposition of the twentieth century Irish writer towards the short story.

Every anthologist has to don, with the best grace he can, some editorial harness – most particularly the anthology's title, which is his bit and bridle. In this case I have had no problem deciding what qualifies as a short story, my standard being merely that of length rather than any academic distinction between tale, anecdote and short story proper. I have adopted 7,000 words as my upper limit – anything longer I regarded as having passed through the short story barrier into the area of the long short story – but the question 'What is an *Irish* short story?' cannot be answered by slide-rule or word count. The English critic, Walter Allen, in a recent series of articles on the Irish short story asked himself whether it was 'simply a story that happens to be written in English by an Irishman'. Wise man, he didn't attempt an answer, though he did suggest that in its early days at least the Irish short story defined itself as being in general critical of the conditions of Irish life – Moore's *The Untilled Field* and Joyce's *Dubliners* being the trend-setters – and such a comment would be no less true of the Irish short story today.

I have not attempted to conform to any special pattern or to illustrate any particular trend in making the choice for this anthology and so I have arranged the stories in chronological order of author's birth. One rule, however, I felt, could not but be observed: every story had to have an Irish context. Apart from that my concern has been to present what in my opinion are outstanding and characteristic stories by as many as possible of the authors who have given the Irish short story its high reputation, as well as those of more recent and current times who are maintaining that reputation and shaping its future course.

David Marcus
Dublin, October 1980

GEORGE MOORE
A Letter to Rome

One morning the priest's housekeeper mentioned, as she gathered up the breakfast things, that Mike Mulhare had refused to let his daughter Catherine marry James Murdoch until he had earned the price of a pig.

'This is bad news,' said the priest, and he laid down the newspaper.

'And he waiting for her all the summer! Wasn't it in February last that he came out of the poor-house? And the fine cabin he has built for her! He'll be so lonesome in it that he'll be going – '

'To America!' said the priest.

'Maybe it will be going back to the poor-house he'll be, for he'll never earn the price of his passage at the relief works.'

The priest looked at her for a moment as if he did not catch her meaning. A knock came at the door, and he said:

'The inspector is here, and there are people waiting for me.' And while he was distributing the clothes he had received from Manchester, he argued with the inspector as to the direction the new road should take; and when he came back from the relief works, his dinner was waiting. He was busy writing letters all the afternoon; and it was not until he had handed them to the post-mistress that he was free to go to poor James Murdoch, who had built a cabin at the end of one of the famine roads in a hollow out of the way of the wind.

From a long way off the priest could see him digging his patch of bog.

And when he caught sight of the priest he stuck his spade in the ground and came to meet him, almost as naked as an animal, bare feet protruding from ragged trousers; there was a shirt, but it was buttonless, and the breast-hair trembled in the wind – a likely creature to come out of the hovel behind him.

'It has been dry enough,' he said, 'all the summer; and I had a thought to make a drain. But 'tis hard luck, your reverence, and after building this house for her. There's a bit of smoke in the house now, but if I got Catherine I wouldn't be long making a chimney. I told Mike he should give Catherine a pig for her fortune, but he said he would give her a calf when I bought the pig, and I said, "Haven't I built a fine house, and wouldn't it be a fine one to rear him in?"'

And together they walked through the bog, James talking to the priest all the way, for it was seldom he had anyone to talk to.

'Now I mustn't take you any further from your digging.'

'Sure there's time enough,' said James. 'Amn't I there all day?'

'I'll go and see Mike Mulhare myself,' said the priest.

'Long life to your reverence.'

'And I will try to get you the price of the pig.'

'Ah, 'tis your reverence that's good to us.'

The priest stood looking after him, wondering if he would give up life as a bad job and go back to the poorhouse; and while thinking of James Murdoch he became conscious that the time was coming for the priests to save Ireland. Catholic Ireland was passing away; in five-and-twenty years Ireland would be a Protestant country if – (he hardly dared to formulate the thought) – if the priests did not marry. The Greek priests had been allowed to retain their wives in order to avert a schism. Rome had always known how to adapt herself to circumstances; there was no doubt that if Rome knew Ireland's need of children she would consider the revocation of the decree of celibacy, and he returned home remembering that celibacy had only been made obligatory in Ireland in the twelfth century.

Ireland was becoming a Protestant country! He drank his tea mechanically, and it was a long time before he took up his knitting. But he could not knit, and laid the stocking aside. Of what good would his letter be? A letter from a poor parish priest asking that one of the most ancient decrees should be revoked! It would be thrown into the waste-paper basket. The cardinals are men whose thoughts move up and down certain narrow ways, clever men no doubt, but clever men are often the dupes of conventions. All men who live in the world accept the conventions as truths. It is only in the wilderness that the truth is revealed to man. 'I must write the letter! Instinct,' he said, 'is a surer guide than logic, and my letter to Rome was a sudden revelation.'

As he sat knitting by his own fireside his idea seemed to come out of the corners of the room. 'When you were at Rathowen,' his idea said, 'you heard the clergy lament that the people were leaving the country. You heard the bishop and many eloquent men speak on the subject. Words, words, but on the bog road the remedy was revealed to you.

'That if each priest were to take a wife about four thousand children would be born within the year, forty thousand children would be added to the birthrate in ten years. Ireland can be saved by her priesthood!'

The truth of this estimate seemed beyond question, and yet, Father MacTurnan found it difficult to reconcile himself to the idea of a married clergy. 'One is always the dupe of prejudice,' he said to himself and went on thinking. 'The priests live in the best houses, eat the best food, wear the best clothes; they are indeed the flower of the nation, and would produce magnificent sons and daughters. And who could bring up their children according to the teaching of our holy church as well as priests?'

So did his idea unfold itself, and very soon he realised

that other advantages would accrue, beyond the addition
of forty thousand children to the birthrate, and one advantage that seemed to him to exceed the original advantage would be the nationalization of religion, the forma-
tion of an Irish Catholicism suited to the ideas and needs
of the Irish people.

In the beginning of the century the Irish lost their
language, in the middle of the century the characteristic
aspects of their religion. It was Cardinal Cullen who had
denationalized religion in Ireland. But everyone recognised
his mistake. How could a church be nationalised better than
by the rescission of the decree of celibacy? The begetting
of children would attach the priests to the soil of Ireland;
and it could not be said that anyone loved his country
who did not contribute to its maintenance. The priests
leave Ireland on foreign missions, and every Catholic
who leaves Ireland, he said, helps to bring about the very
thing that Ireland has been struggling against for centuries
– Protestantism.

His idea talked to him every evening, and, one evening,
it said, 'Religion, like everything else, must be national,'
and it led him to contrast cosmopolitanism with parochial-
ism. 'Religion, like art, came out of parishes,' he said. He
felt a great force to be behind him. He must write! He
must write. . . .

He dropped the ink over the table and over the paper,
he jotted down his ideas in the first words that came to
him until midnight; and when he slept his letter floated
through his sleep.

'I must have a clear copy of it before I begin the Latin
translation.'

He had written the English text thinking of the Latin
that would come after, very conscious of the fact that he
had written no Latin since he had left Maynooth, and that
a bad translation would discredit his ideas in the eyes of
the Pope's secretary, who was doubtless a great Latin
scholar.

'The Irish priests have always been good Latinists,' he murmured, as he hunted through the dictionary.

The table was littered with books, for he had found it necessary to create a Latin atmosphere, and one morning he finished his translation and walked to the whitening window to rest his eyes before reading it over. But he was too tired to do any more, and he laid his manuscript on the table by his bedside.

'This is very poor Latin,' he said to himself some hours later, and the manuscript lay on the floor while he dressed. It was his servant who brought it to him when he had finished his breakfast, and, taking it from her, he looked at it again.

'It is as tasteless,' he said, 'as the gruel that poor James Murdoch is eating.' He picked up *St Augustine's Confessions*. 'Here is idiom,' he muttered, and he continued reading till he was interrupted by the wheels of a car stopping at his door. It was Meehan! None had written such good Latin at Maynooth as Meehan.

'My dear Meehan, this is indeed a pleasant surprise.'

'I thought I'd like to see you. I drove over. But – I am not disturbing you. . . . You've taken to reading again. St Augustine! And you're writing in Latin!'

Father James's face grew red, and he took the manuscript out of his friend's hand.

'No, you mustn't look at that.'

And then the temptation to ask him to overlook certain passages made him change his mind.

'I was never much of a Latin scholar.'

'And you want me to overlook your Latin for you. But why are you writing Latin?'

'Because I am writing to the Pope. I was at first a little doubtful, but the more I thought of this letter the more necessary it seemed to me.'

'And what are you writing to the Pope about?'

'You see Ireland is going to become a Protestant country.'

'Is it?' said Father Meehan, and he listened, a little while. Then, interrupting his friend, he said:

'I've heard enough. Now, I strongly advise you not to send this letter. We have known each other all our lives. Now, my dear MacTurnan –'

Father Michael talked eagerly, and Father MacTurnan sat listening. At last Father Meehan saw that his arguments were producing no effect, and he said:

'You don't agree with me.'

'It isn't that I don't agree with you. You have spoken admirably from your point of view, but our points of view are different.'

'Take your papers away, burn them!'

Then, thinking his words were harsh, he laid his hand on his friend's shoulder and said:

'My dear MacTurnan, I beg of you not to send this letter.'

Father James did not answer; the silence grew painful, and Father Michael asked Father James to show him the relief works that the Government had ordered.

But important as these works were, the letter to Rome seemed more important to Father Michael, and he said:

'My good friend, there isn't a girl that would marry us; now is there? There isn't a girl in Ireland who would touch us with a forty-foot pole. Would you have the Pope release the nuns from their vows?'

'I think exceptions should be made in favour of those in Orders. But I think it would be for the good of Ireland if the secular clergy were married.'

'That's not my point. My point is that even if the decree were rescinded we shouldn't be able to get wives. You've been living too long in the waste, my dear friend. You've lost yourself in dreams. We shouldn't get a penny. "Why should we support that fellow and his family?" is what they'd be saying.'

'We should be poor, no doubt,' said Father James. 'But not so poor as our parishioners. My parishioners eat yellow meal, and I eat eggs and live in a good house.'

'We are educated men, and should live in better houses than our parishioners.'

'The greatest saints lived in deserts.'

And so the argument went on until the time came to say good-bye, and then Father James said:

'I shall be glad if you will give me a lift on your car. I want to go to the post-office.'

'To post your letter?'

'The idea came to me – it came swiftly like a lightning-flash, and I can't believe that it was an accident. If it had fallen into your mind with the suddenness that it fell into mine, you would believe that it was an inspiration.'

'It would take a good deal to make me believe I was inspired,' said Father Michael, and he watched Father James go into the post-office to register his letter.

At that hour a long string of peasants returning from their work went by. The last was Norah Flynn, and the priest blushed deeply for it was the first time he had looked on one of his parishioners in the light of a possible spouse; and he entered his house frightened; and when he looked round his parlour he asked himself if the day would come when he should see Norah Flynn sitting opposite to him in his armchair. His face flushed deeper when he looked towards the bedroom door, and he fell on his knees and prayed that God's will might be made known to him.

During the night he awoke many times, and the dream that had awakened him continued when he had left his bed, and he wandered round and round the room in the darkness, seeking a way. At last he reached the window and drew the curtain, and saw the dim dawn opening out over the bog.

'Thank God,' he said, 'it was only a dream – only a dream.'

And lying down he fell asleep, but immediately another dream as horrible as the first appeared, and his house-keeper heard him beating on the walls.

'Only a dream, only a dream,' he said.

He lay awake, not daring to sleep lest he might dream. And it was about seven o'clock when he heard his house-keeper telling him that the inspector had come to tell him they must decide what direction the new road should take. In the inspector's opinion it should run parallel with the old road. To continue the old road two miles further would involve extra labour; the people would have to go further to their work, and the stones would have to be drawn further. The priest held that the extra labour was of secondary importance. He said that to make two roads running parallel with each other would be a wanton humiliation to the people.

But the inspector could not appreciate the priest's arguments. He held that the people were thinking only how they might earn enough money to fill their bellies.

'I don't agree with you, I don't agree with you,' said the priest. 'Better go in the opposite direction and make a road to the sea.'

'You see, your reverence, the Government don't wish to engage upon any work that will benefit any special class. These are my instructions.'

'A road to the sea will benefit no one. . . . I see you are thinking of the landlord. But there isn't a harbour; no boat ever comes into that flat, waste sea.'

'Well, your reverence, one of these days a harbour may be made. An arch would look well in the middle of the bog, and the people wouldn't have to go far to their work.'

'No, no. A road to the sea will be quite useless; but its futility will not be apparent — at least, not so apparent — and the people's hearts won't be broken.'

The inspector seemed a little doubtful, but the priest assured him that the futility of the road would satisfy English ministers.

'And yet these English ministers,' the priest reflected, 'are not stupid men; they're merely men blinded by theory and prejudice, as all men are who live in the world. Their folly will be apparent to the next generation, and so on and so on for ever and ever, world without end.'

'And the worst of it is,' the priest said, 'while the people are earning their living on these roads, their fields will be lying idle, and there will be no crops next year.'

'We can't help that,' the inspector answered, and Father MacTurnan began to think of the cardinals and the transaction of the business in the Vatican; cardinals and ministers alike are the dupes of convention. Only those who are estranged from habits and customs can think straightforwardly.

'If, instead of insisting on these absurd roads, the Government would give me the money, I'd be able to feed the people at a cost of about a penny a day, and they'd be able to sow their potatoes. And if only the cardinals would consider the rescission of the decree on its merits, Ireland would be saved from Protestantism.'

Some cardinal was preparing an answer – an answer might be even in the post. Rome might not think his letter worthy of an answer.

A few days afterwards the inspector called to show him a letter he had just received from the Board of Works. Father James had to go to Dublin, and in the excitement of these philanthropic activities the emigration question was forgotten. Six weeks must have gone by when the postman handed him a letter.

'This is a letter from Father Moran,' he said to the inspector who was with him at the time. 'The Bishop wishes to see me. We will continue the conversation tomorrow. It is eight miles to Rathowen, and how much further is the Palace?'

'A good seven,' said the inspector. 'You're not going to walk it, your reverence?'

'Why not? In four hours I shall be there.' He looked at his boots first, and hoped they would hold together; and then he looked at the sky, and hoped it would not rain.

There was no likelihood of rain; no rain would fall today out of that soft dove-coloured sky full of sun; ravishing little breezes lifted the long heather, the rose-coloured hair of the knolls, and over the cut-away bog wild white cotton was blowing. Now and then a yellow-hammer rose out of the coarse grass and flew in front of the priest, and once a pair of grouse left the sunny hillside where they were nesting with a great whirr; they did not go far, but alighted in a hollow, and the priest could see their heads above the heather watching him.

'The moment I'm gone they'll return to their nest.'

He walked on, and when he had walked six miles he sat down and took a piece of bread out of his pocket. As he ate it his eyes wandered over the undulating bog, brown and rose, marked here and there by a black streak where the peasants had been cutting turf. The sky changed very little; it was still a pale, dove colour; now and then a little blue showed through the grey, and sometimes the light lessened; but a few minutes after the sunlight fluttered out of the sky again and dozed among the heather.

'I must be getting on,' he said, and he looked into the brown water, fearing he would find none other to slake his thirst. But just as he stooped he caught sight of a woman driving an ass who had come to the bog for turf, and she told him where he would find a spring, and he thought he had never drunk anything so sweet as this water.

'I've got a good long way to go yet,' he said, and he walked studying the lines of the mountains, thinking he could distinguish one hill from the other; and that in another mile or two he would be out of the bog. The road ascended, and on the other side there were a few pines. Some hundred yards further on there was a green sod. But the heather appeared again, and he had walked ten miles before he was clear of whins and heather.

As he walked he thought of his interview with the Bishop, and was nearly at the end of his journey when he stopped at a cabin to mend his shoe. And while the woman was looking for a needle and thread, he mopped his face with a great red handkerchief that he kept in the pocket of his threadbare coat – a coat that had once been black, but had grown green with age and weather. He had outwalked himself, and would not be able to answer the points that the Bishop would raise. The woman found him a scrap of leather, and it took him an hour to patch his shoe under the hawthorn tree.

He was still two miles from the Palace, and arrived foot-sore, covered with dust, and so tired that he could hardly rise from the chair to receive Father Moran when he came into the parlour.

'You seem to have walked a long way, Father MacTurnan.'

'I shall be all right presently. I suppose his Grace doesn't want to see me at once.'

'Well, that's just it. His Grace sent me to say he would see you at once. He expected you earlier.'

'I started the moment I received his Grace's letter. I suppose his Grace wishes to see me regarding my letter to Rome.'

The secretary hesitated, coughed, and went out, and Father MacTurnan wondered why Father Moran looked at him so intently. He returned in a few minutes, saying that his Grace was sorry that Father MacTurnan had had so long a walk, and he hoped he would rest awhile and partake of some refreshment. . . . The servant brought in some wine and sandwiches, and the secretary returned in half an hour. His Grace was now ready to receive him. . . .

Father Moran opened the library door, and Father MacTurnan saw the Bishop – a short, alert man, about fifty-five, with a sharp nose and grey eyes and bushy eye-brows. He popped about the room giving his secretary many orders, and Father MacTurnan wondered if the Bishop would ever finish talking to his secretary. He seemed to have finished, but a thought suddenly struck him, and he followed his secretary to the door, and Father MacTurnan began to fear that the Pope had not decided to place the Irish clergy on the same footing as the Greek. If he had, the Bishop's interest in these many various matters would have subsided: his mind would be engrossed by the larger issue.

As he returned from the door his Grace passed Father MacTurnan without speaking to him, and going to his

writing-table he began to search amid his papers. At last
Father MacTurnan said:

'Maybe your Grace is looking for my letter to Rome?'

'Yes,' said his Grace, 'do you see it?'

'It's under your Grace's hand, those blue papers.'

'Ah, yes,' and his Grace leaned back in his armchair,
leaving Father MacTurnan standing.

'Won't you sit down, Father MacTurnan?' he said
casually. 'You've been writing to Rome, I see, advocating
the revocation of the decree of celibacy. There's no doubt
the emigration of Catholics is a very serious question. So
far you have got the sympathy of Rome, and I may say of
myself; but am I to understand that it was your fear for
the religious safety of Ireland that prompted you to write
this letter?'

'What other reason could there be?'

Nothing was said for a long while, and then the Bishop's
meaning began to break in on his mind; his face flushed,
and he grew confused.

'I hope your Grace doesn't think for a moment that – '

'I only want to know if there is anyone – if your eyes
ever went in a certain direction, if your thoughts ever said,
"Well, if the decree were revoked – " '

'No, your Grace, no. Celibacy has been no burden to
me – far from it. Sometimes I feared that it was celibacy
that attracted me to the priesthood. Celibacy was a gratifi-
cation rather than a sacrifice.'

'I am glad,' said the Bishop, and he spoke slowly and
emphatically, 'that this letter was prompted by such im-
personal motives.'

'Surely, your Grace, His Holiness didn't suspect – '

The Bishop murmured an euphonious Italian name, and
Father MacTurnan understood that he was speaking of
one of the Pope's secretaries.

'More than once,' said Father MacTurnan, 'I feared if
the decree were revoked, I shouldn't have had sufficient
courage to comply with it.'

And then he told the Bishop how he had met Norah

28

Flynn on the road. An amused expression stole into the Bishop's face, and his voice changed.

'I presume you do not contemplate making marriage obligatory; you do not contemplate the suspension of the faculties of those who do not take wives?'

'It seems to me that exception should be made in favour of those in Orders, and of course in favour of those who have reached a certain age like your Grace.'

The Bishop coughed, and pretended to look for some paper which he had mislaid.

'This was one of the many points that I discussed with Father Michael Meehan.'

'Oh, so you consulted Father Meehan,' the Bishop said, looking up.

'He came in the day I was reading over my Latin translation before posting it. I'm afraid the ideas that I submitted to the consideration of His Holiness have been degraded by my very poor Latin. I should have wished Father Meehan to overlook my Latin, but he refused. He begged of me not to send the letter.'

'Father Meehan,' said his Grace, 'is a great friend of yours. Yet nothing he could say could shake your resolution to write to Rome?'

'Nothing,' said Father MacTurnan. 'The call I received was too distinct and too clear for me to hesitate.'

'Tell me about this call.'

Father MacTurnan told the Bishop that the poor man had come out of the workhouse because he wanted to be married, and that Mike Mulhare would not give him his daughter until he had earned the price of a pig. 'And as I was talking to him I heard my conscience say, "No one can afford to marry in Ireland but the clergy." We all live better than our parishioners.'

And then, forgetting the Bishop, and talking as if he were alone with his God, he described how the conviction had taken possession of him – that Ireland would become a Protestant country if the Catholic emigration did not

29

cease. And he told how this conviction had left him little peace until he had written his letter.

The priest talked on until he was interrupted by Father Moran.

'I have some business to transact with Father Moran now,' the Bishop said, 'but you must stay to dinner. You've walked a long way, and you are tired and hungry.'

'But, your Grace, if I don't start now, I shan't get home until nightfall.'

'A car will take you back, Father MacTurnan. I will see to that. I must have some exact information about your poor people. We must do something for them.'

Father MacTurnan and the Bishop were talking together when the car came to take Father MacTurnan home, and the Bishop said:

'Father MacTurnan, you have borne the loneliness of your parish a long while.'

'Loneliness is only a matter of habit. I think, your Grace, I'm better suited to the place than I am for any other. I don't wish any change, if your Grace is satisfied with me.'

'No one will look after the poor people better than yourself, Father MacTurnan. But,' he said, 'it seems to me there is one thing we have forgotten. You haven't told me if you have succeeded in getting the money to buy the pig.'

Father MacTurnan grew very red. . . . 'I had forgotten it. The relief works – '

'It's not too late. Here's five pounds, and this will buy him a pig.'

'It will indeed,' said the priest, 'it will buy him two!'

He had left the Palace without having asked the Bishop how his letter had been received at Rome, and he stopped the car, and was about to tell the driver to go back. But no matter, he would hear about his letter some other time. He was bringing happiness to two poor people, and he could not persuade himself to delay their happiness by one minute. He was not bringing one pig, but two pigs, and now Mike Mulhare would have to give him Catherine and a calf; and the priest remembered that James Murdoch

had said – 'What a fine house this will be to rear them in.'
There were many who thought that human beings and
animals should not live together; but after all, what did it
matter if they were happy? And the priest forgot his
letter to Rome in the thought of the happiness he was
bringing to two poor people. He could not see Mike
Mulhare that night; but he drove down to the famine
road, and he and the driver called till they awoke James
Murdoch. The poor man came stumbling across the bog,
and the priest told him the news.

E. Œ. SOMERVILLE
AND MARTIN ROSS
Trinket's Colt

It was Petty Sessions day in Skebawn, a cold, grey day of February. A case of trespass had dragged its burden of cross summonses and cross swearing far into the afternoon, and when I left the bench my head was singing from the bellowings of the attorneys, and the smell of their clients was heavy upon my palate.

The streets still testified to the fact that it was market day, and I evaded with difficulty the sinuous course of carts full of soddenly screwed people, and steered an equally devious one for myself among the groups anchored round the doors of the public-houses. Skebawn possesses, among its legion of public-houses, one establishment which timorously, and almost imperceptibly, proffers tea to the thirsty. I turned in there, as was my custom on court days, and found the little dingy den, known as the Ladies' Coffeeroom, in the occupancy of my friend Mr Florence McCarthy Knox, who was drinking strong tea and eating buns with serious simplicity. It was a first and quite unexpected glimpse of that domesticity that has now become a marked feature in his character.

'You're the very man I wanted to see,' I said as I sat down beside him at the oilcloth-covered table; 'a man I know in England who is not much of a judge of character has asked me to buy him a four-year-old down here, and as I should rather be stuck by a friend than a dealer, I wish you'd take over the job.'

Flurry poured himself out another cup of tea, and dropped three lumps of sugar into it in silence.

Finally he said, 'There isn't a four-year-old in this country that I'd be seen dead with at a pig fair.'

This was discouraging, from the premier authority on horseflesh in the district.

'But it isn't six weeks since you told me you had the finest filly in your stables that was ever foaled in the County Cork,' I protested; 'what's wrong with her?'

'Oh, is it that filly?' said Mr Knox with a lenient smile; 'she's gone these three weeks from me. I swapped her and six pounds for a three-year-old Ironmonger colt, and after that I swapped the colt and nineteen pounds for that Bandon horse I rode last week at your place, and after that again I sold the Bandon horse for seventy-five pounds to old Welply, and I had to give him back a couple of sovereigns luck-money. You see I did pretty well with the filly after all.'

'Yes, yes – oh, rather,' I asserted, as one dizzily accepts the propositions of a bimetallist; 'and you don't know of anything else – ?'

The room in which we were seated was closely screened from the shop by a door with a muslin-covered window in it; several of the panes were broken, and at this juncture two voices that had for some time carried on a discussion forced themselves upon our attention.

'Begging your pardon for contradicting you, ma'am,' said the voice of Mrs McDonald, proprietress of the tea-shop, and a leading light in Skebawn Dissenting circles, shrilly tremulous with indignation, 'if the servants I recommend you won't stop with you, it's no fault of mine. If respectable young girls are set picking grass out of your gravel, in place of their proper work, certainly they will give warning!'

The voice that replied struck me as being a notable one, well-bred and imperious.

'When I take a barefooted slut out of a cabin, I don't expect her to dictate to me what her duties are!'

Flurry jerked up his chin in a noiseless laugh. 'It's my grandmother!' he whispered. 'I bet you Mrs McDonald don't get much change out of her!'

'If I set her to clean the pigsty I expect her to obey me,' continued the voice in accents that would have made me clean forty pigsties had she desired me to do so.

'Very well, ma'am,' retorted Mrs McDonald, 'if that's the way you treat your servants, you needn't come here again looking for them. I consider your conduct is neither that of a lady nor a Christian!'

'Don't you, indeed?' replied Flurry's grandmother. 'Well, your opinion doesn't greatly distress me, for, to tell you the truth, I don't think you're much of a judge.'

'Didn't I tell you she'd score?' murmured Flurry, who was by this time applying his eye to a hole in the muslin curtain. 'She's off,' he went on, returning to his tea. 'She's a great character! She's eighty-three if she's a day, and she's as sound on her legs as a three-year-old! Did you see that old shandrydan of hers in the street a while ago, and a fellow on the box with a red beard on him like Robinson Crusoe? That old mare that was on the near side – Trinket her name is – is mighty near clean bred. I can tell you her foals are worth a bit of money.'

I had heard of old Mrs Knox of Aussolas; indeed, I had seldom dined out in the neighbourhood without hearing some new story of her and her remarkable *ménage*, but it had not yet been my privilege to meet her.

'Well, now,' went on Flurry in his slow voice, 'I'll tell you a thing that's just come into my head. My grandmother promised me a foal of Trinket's the day I was one-and-twenty, and that's five years ago, and deuce a one I've got from her yet. You never were at Aussolas? No, you were not. Well, I tell you the place there is like a circus with horses. She has a couple of score of them running wild in the woods, like deer.'

'Oh, come,' I said, 'I'm a bit of a liar myself – '

'Well, she has a dozen of them anyhow, rattling good colts too, some of them, but they might as well be donkeys, for all the good they are to me or any one. It's not once in three years she sells one, and there she has them walking after her for bits of sugar, like a lot of dirty lapdogs,' ended Flurry with disgust.

'Well, what's your plan? Do you want me to make her a bid for one of the lapdogs?'

'I was thinking,' replied Flurry, with great deliberation, 'that my birthday's this week, and maybe I could work a four-year-old colt of Trinket's she has out of her in honour of the occasion.'

'And sell your grandmother's birthday present to me?'

'Just that, I suppose,' answered Flurry with a slow wink.

A few days afterwards a letter from Mr Knox informed me that he had 'squared the old lady, and it would be all right about the colt'. He further told me that Mrs Knox had been good enough to offer me, with him, a day's snipe shooting on the celebrated Aussolas bogs, and he proposed to drive me there the following Monday, if convenient. Most people found it convenient to shoot the Aussolas snipe bog when they got the chance. Eight o'clock on the following Monday morning saw Flurry, myself, and a groom packed into a dogcart, with portmanteaus, gun-cases, and two rampant red setters.

It was a long drive, twelve miles at least, and a very cold one. We passed through long tracts of pasture country, fraught, for Flurry, with memories of runs, which were recorded for me, fence by fence, in every one of which the biggest dog-fox in the country had gone to ground, with not two feet – measured accurately on the handle of the whip – between him and the leading hound; through bogs that imperceptibly melted into lakes, and finally down and down into a valley, where the fir-trees of Aussolas clustered darkly round a glittering lake, and all but hid the grey roofs and pointed gables of Aussolas Castle.

'There's a nice stretch of a demesne for you,' remarked Flurry, pointing downwards with the whip, 'and one little old woman holding it all in the heel of her fist. Well able to hold it she is, too, and always was, and she'll live twenty years yet, if it's only to spite the whole lot of us, and when all's said and done goodness knows how she'll leave it!'

'It strikes me you were lucky to keep her up to her promise about the colt,' I said.

Flurry administered a composing kick to the ceaseless striving of the red setters under the seat.

'I used to be rather a pet with her,' he said, after a pause; 'but mind you, I haven't got him yet, and if she gets any notion I want to sell him I'll never get him, so say nothing about the business to her.'

The tall gates of Aussolas shrieked on their hinges as they admitted us, and shut with a clang behind us, in the faces of an old mare and a couple of young horses, who, foiled in their break for the excitements of the outer world, turned and galloped defiantly on either side of us. Flurry's admirable cob hammered on, regardless of all things save his duty.

'He's the only one I have that I'd trust myself here with,' said his master, flicking him approvingly with the whip; 'there are plenty of people afraid to come here at all, and when my grandmother goes out driving she has a boy on the box with a basket full of stones to peg at them. Talk of the dickens, here she is herself!'

A short, upright old woman was approaching, preceded by a white woolly dog with sore eyes and a bark like a tin trumpet; we both got out of the trap and advanced to meet the lady of the manor.

I may summarise her attire by saying that she looked as if she had robbed a scarecrow; her face was small and incongruously refined, the skinny hand that she extended to me had the grubby tan that bespoke the professional gardener, and was decorated with a magnificent diamond ring. On her head was a massive purple velvet bonnet.

'I am very glad to meet you, Major Yeates,' she said with an old-fashioned precision of utterance; 'your grandfather was a dancing partner of mine in old days at the Castle, when he was a handsome young aide-de-camp there, and I was — You may judge for yourself what I was.'

She ended with a startling little hoot of laughter, and I was aware that she quite realised the world's opinion of her, and was indifferent to it.

Our way to the bogs took us across Mrs Knox's home farm, and through a large field in which several young horses were grazing.

'There now, that's my fellow,' said Flurry, pointing to a fine-looking colt, 'the chestnut with the white diamond on his forehead. He'll run into three figures before he's done, but we'll not tell that to the old lady!'

The famous Aussolas bogs were as full of snipe as usual, and a good deal fuller of water than any bogs I had ever shot before. I was on my day, and Flurry was not, and as he is ordinarily an infinitely better snipe shot than I, I felt at peace with the world and all men as we walked back, wet through, at five o'clock.

The sunset had waned, and a big white moon was making the eastern tower of Aussolas look like a thing in a fairy tale or a play when we arrived at the hall door. An individual, whom I recognised as the Robinson Crusoe coachman, admitted us to a hall, the like of which one does not often see. The walls were panelled with dark oak up to the gallery that ran round three sides of it, the balusters of the wide staircase were heavily carved, and blackened portraits of Flurry's ancestors on the spindle side stared sourly down on their descendant as he tramped upstairs with the bog mould on his hobnailed boots.

We had just changed into dry clothes when Robinson Crusoe shoved his red beard round the corner of the door, with the information that the mistress said we were to stay for dinner. My heart sank. It was then barely half-past five. I said something about having no evening clothes and having to get home early.

'Sure the dinner'll be in another half hour,' said Robinson Crusoe, joining hospitably in the conversation; 'and as for evening clothes – God bless ye!'

The door closed behind him.

'Never mind,' said Flurry, 'I dare say you'll be glad

enough to eat another dinner by the time you get home.'
He laughed. 'Poor Slipper!' he added inconsequently, and
only laughed again when I asked for an explanation.

Old Mrs Knox received us in the library, where she was
seated by a roaring turf fire, which lit the room a good
deal more effectively than the pair of candles that stood
beside her in tall silver candlesticks. Ceaseless and implacable growls from under her chair indicated the presence
of the woolly dog. She talked with confounding culture
of the books that rose all round her to the ceiling; her
evening dress was accomplished by means of an additional
white shawl, rather dirtier than its congeners; as I took
her in to dinner she quoted Virgil to me, and in the same
breath screeched an objurgation at a being whose matted
head rose suddenly into view from behind an ancient
Chinese screen, as I have seen the head of a Zulu woman
peer over a bush.

Dinner was as incongruous as everything else. Detestable
soup in a splendid old silver tureen that was nearly as dark
in hue as Robinson Crusoe's thumb; a perfect salmon, perfectly cooked, on a chipped kitchen dish; such cut glass
as is not easy to find nowadays; sherry that, as Flurry
subsequently remarked, would burn the shell off an egg; and
a bottle of port, draped in immemorial cobwebs, wan with
age, and probably priceless. Throughout the vicissitudes of
the meal Mrs Knox's conversation flowed on undismayed,
directed sometimes at me – she had installed me in the
position of friend of her youth and talked to me as if I
were my own grandfather – sometimes at Crusoe, with
whom she had several heated arguments, and sometimes
she would make a statement of remarkable frankness on the
subject of her horse-farming affairs to Flurry, who, very
much on his best behaviour, agreed with all she said, and
risked no original remark. As I listened to them both, I
remembered with infinite amusement how he had told
me once that 'a pet name she had for him was "Tony
Lumpkin", and no one but herself knew what she meant by
it'. It seemed strange that she made no allusion to Trinket's

colt or to Flurry's birthday, but, mindful of my instructions, I held my peace.

As, at about half-past eight, we drove away in the moonlight, Flurry congratulated me solemnly on my success with his grandmother. He was good enough to tell me that she would marry me to-morrow if I asked her, and he wished I would, even if it was only to see what a nice grandson he'd be for me. A sympathetic giggle behind me told me that Michael, on the back seat, had heard and relished the jest.

We had left the gates of Aussolas about half a mile behind when, at the corner of a by-road, Flurry pulled up. A short squat figure arose from the black shadow of a furze bush and came out into the moonlight, swinging its arms like a cabman and cursing audibly.

'Oh murdher, oh murdher, Misther Flurry! What kept ye at all? 'Twould perish the crows to be waiting here the way I am these two hours –'

'Ah, shut your mouth, Slipper!' said Flurry, who, to my surprise, had turned back the rug and was taking off his driving coat, 'I couldn't help it. Come on, Yeates, we've got to get out here.'

'What for?' I asked, in not unnatural bewilderment.

'It's all right. I'll tell you as we go along,' replied my companion, who was already turning to follow Slipper up the by-road. 'Take the trap on, Michael, and wait at the River's Cross.' He waited for me to come up with him, and then put his hand on my arm. 'You see, Major, this is the way it is. My grandmother's given me that colt right enough, but if I waited for her to send him over to me I'd never see a hair of his tail. So I just thought that as we were over here we might as well take him back with us, and maybe you'll give us a help with him; he'll not be altogether too handy for a first go off.'

I was staggered. An infant in arms could scarcely have failed to discern the fishiness of the transaction, and I begged Mr Knox not to put himself to this trouble on my account, as I had no doubt I could find a horse for my friend elsewhere. Mr Knox assured me that it was no trouble at all, quite the contrary, and that, since his grandmother had given him the colt, he saw no reason why he should not take him when he wanted him; also, that if I didn't want him he'd be glad enough to keep him himself; and finally, that I wasn't the chap to go back on a friend, but I was welcome to drive back to Shreelane with Michael this minute if I liked.

Of course I yielded in the end. I told Flurry I should lose my job over the business, and he said I could then marry his grandmother, and the discussion was abruptly closed by the necessity of following Slipper over a locked five-barred gate.

Our pioneer took us over about half a mile of country, knocking down stone gaps where practicable and scrambling over tall banks in the deceptive moonlight. We found ourselves at length in a field with a shed in one corner of it; in a dim group of farm buildings a little way off a light was shining.

'Wait here,' said Flurry to me in a whisper; 'the less noise the better. It's an open shed, and we'll just slip in and coax him out.'

Slipper unwound from his waist a halter, and my colleagues glided like spectres into the shadow of the shed, leaving me to meditate on my duties as Resident Magistrate, and on the questions that would be asked in the House by our local member when Slipper had given away the adventure in his cups.

In less than a minute three shadows emerged from the shed, where two had gone in. They had got the colt.

'He came out as quiet as a calf when he winded the sugar,' said Flurry; 'it was well for me I filled my pockets from grandmamma's sugar basin.'

He and Slipper had a rope from each side of the colt's head; they took him quickly across a field towards a gate. The colt stepped daintily between them over the moonlit grass; he snorted occasionally, but appeared on the whole amenable.

The trouble began later, and was due, as trouble often

is, to the beguilements of a short cut. Against the maturer judgment of Slipper, Flurry insisted on following a route that he assured us he knew as well as his own pocket, and the consequence was that in about five minutes I found myself standing on top of a bank hanging on to a rope, on the other end of which the colt dangled and danced, while Flurry, with the other rope, lay prone in the ditch, and Slipper administered to the bewildered colt's hind quarters such chastisement as could be ventured on.

I have no space to narrate in detail the atrocious difficulties and disasters of the short cut. How the colt set to work to buck, and went away across a field, dragging the faithful Slipper, literally *ventre à terre*, after him, while I picked myself in ignominy out of a briar patch, and Flurry cursed himself black in the face. How we were attacked by ferocious cur dogs, and I lost my eye-glass; and how, as we neared the River's Cross, Flurry espied the police patrol on the road, and we all hid behind a rick of turf while I realised in fullness what an exceptional ass I was, to have been beguiled into an enterprise that involved hiding with Slipper from the Royal Irish Constabulary.

Let it suffice to say that Trinket's infernal offspring was finally handed over on the high road to Michael and Slipper, and Flurry drove me home in a state of mental and physical overthrow.

I saw nothing of my friend Mr Knox for the next couple of days, by the end of which time I had worked up a high polish on my misgivings, and had determined to tell him that under no circumstances would I have anything to say to his grandmother's birthday present. It was like my usual luck that, instead of writing a note to this effect, I thought it would be good for my liver to walk across the hills to Tory Cottage and tell Flurry so in person.

It was a bright, blustery morning, after a muggy day. The feeling of spring was in the air, the daffodils were already in bud, and crocuses showed purple in the grass on either side of the avenue. It was only a couple of miles to Tory Cottage by the way across the hills; I walked fast, and it was barely twelve o'clock when I saw its pink walls and clumps of evergreens below me. As I looked down at it the chiming of Flurry's hounds in the kennels came to me on the wind; I stood still to listen, and could almost have sworn that I was hearing again the clash of Magdalen bells, hard at work on May morning.

The path that I was following led downwards through a larch plantation to Flurry's back gate. Hot wafts from some hideous cauldron at the other side of a wall apprised me of the vicinity of the kennels and their cuisine, and the fir-trees round were hung with gruesome and unknown joints. I thanked heaven that I was not a master of hounds, and passed on as quickly as might be to the hall door.

I rang two or three times without response; then the door opened a couple of inches and was instantly slammed in my face. I heard the hurried paddling of bare feet on oil-cloth, and a voice, 'Hurry, Bridgie, hurry! There's quality at the door!'

Bridgie, holding a dirty cap on with one hand, presently arrived and informed me that she believed Mr Knox was out about the place. She seemed perturbed, and she cast scared glances down the drive while speaking to me.

I knew enough of Flurry's habits to shape a tolerably direct course for his whereabouts. He was, as I had expected, in the training paddock, a field behind the stable yard, in which he had put up practice jumps for his horses. It was a good-sized field with clumps of furze in it, and Flurry was standing near one of these with his hands in his pockets, singularly unoccupied. I supposed that he was prospecting for a place to put up another jump. He did not see me coming, and turned with a start as I spoke to him. There was a queer expression of mingled guilt and what I can only describe as divilment in his grey eyes as he greeted me. In my dealings with Flurry Knox, I have since formed the habit of sitting tight, in a general way, when I see that expression.

'Well, who's coming next, I wonder!' he said, as he shook hands with me; it's not ten minutes since I had two of your d – d peelers here searching the whole place for my grandmother's colt!'

'What!' I exclaimed, feeling cold all down my back; 'do you mean the police have got hold of it?'

'They haven't got hold of the colt anyway,' said Flurry, looking sideways at me from under the peak of his cap, with the glint of the sun in his eye. 'I got word in time before they came.'

'What do you mean?' I demanded; 'where is he? For heaven's sake don't tell me you've sent the brute over to my place!'

'It's a good job for you I didn't,' replied Flurry, 'as the police are on their way to Shreelane this minute to consult you about it. *You*!' He gave utterance to one of his short diabolical fits of laughter. 'He's where they'll not find him, anyhow. Ho ho! It's the funniest hand I ever played!'

'Oh yes, it's devilish funny, I've no doubt,' I retorted, beginning to lose my temper, as is the manner of many people when they are frightened; 'but I give you fair warning that if Mrs Knox asks me any questions about it, I shall tell her the whole story.'

'All right,' responded Flurry; 'and when you do, don't forget to tell her how you flogged the colt out on to the road over her own bounds ditch.'

'Very well,' I said hotly, 'I may as well go home and send in my papers. They'll break me over this – '

'Ah, hold on, Major,' said Flurry soothingly, 'it'll be all right. No one knows anything. It's only on spec the old lady sent the bobbies here. If you'll keep quiet it'll all blow over.'

'I don't care,' I said, struggling hopelessly in the toils; 'if I meet your grandmother, and she asks me about it, I shall tell her all I know.'

'Please God you'll not meet her! After all, it's not once in a blue moon that she – ' began Flurry. Even as he said the words his face changed. 'Holy fly!' he ejaculated, 'isn't that her dog coming into the field? Look at her bonnet over the wall! Hide, hide for your life!' He caught me by the shoulder and shoved me down among the furze bushes before I realised what had happened.

'Get in there! I'll talk to her.'

I may as well confess that at the mere sight of Mrs Knox's purple bonnet my heart had turned to water. In that moment I knew what it would be like to tell her how I, having eaten her salmon, and capped her quotations, and drunk her best port, had gone forth and helped to steal her horse. I abandoned my dignity, my sense of honour; I took the furze prickles to my breast and wallowed in them.

Mrs Knox had advanced with vengeful speed; already she was in high altercation with Flurry at no great distance from where I lay; varying sounds of battle reached me, and I gathered that Flurry was not – to put it mildly – shrinking from that economy of truth that the situation required.

'Is it that curby, long-backed brute? You promised him to me long ago, but I wouldn't be bothered with him!'

The old lady uttered a laugh of shrill derision. 'Is it likely I'd promise you my best colt? And still more, is it likely that you'd refuse him if I did?'

'Very well, ma'am.' Flurry's voice was admirably indignant. 'Then I suppose I'm a liar and a thief.'

'I'd be more obliged to you for the information if I hadn't known it before,' responded his grandmother with lightning speed; 'if you swore to me on a stack of Bibles you knew nothing about my colt I wouldn't believe you! I shall go straight to Major Yeates and ask his advice. I believe *him* to be a gentleman, in spite of the company he keeps!'

I writhed deeper into the furze bushes, and thereby discovered a sandy rabbit run, along which I crawled, with my cap well over my eyes, and the furze needles stabbing me through my stockings. The ground shelved a little, promising profounder concealment, but the bushes were very thick, and I laid hold of the bare stem of one to help my progress. It lifted out of the ground in my hand, revealing a freshly cut stump. Something snorted, not a yard away; I glared through the opening, and was confronted by the long, horrified face of Mrs Knox's colt, mysteriously on a level with my own.

Even without the white diamond on his forehead I should have divined the truth; but how in the name of wonder had Flurry persuaded him to couch like a woodcock in the heart of a furze brake? For a full minute I lay as still as death for fear of frightening him, while the voices of Flurry and his grandmother raged on alarmingly close to me. The colt snorted, and blew long breaths through his wide nostrils, but he did not move. I crawled an inch or two nearer, and after a few seconds of cautious peering I grasped the position. They had buried him.

A small sandpit among the furze had been utilised as a grave; they had filled him in up to his withers with sand, and a few furze bushes, artistically disposed around the pit, had done the rest. As the depth of Flurry's guile was revealed, laughter came upon me like a flood; I gurgled and shook apoplectically, and the colt gazed at me with serious surprise, until a sudden outburst of barking close to my elbow administered a fresh shock to my tottering nerves.

Mrs Knox's woolly dog had tracked me into the furze, and was now baying the colt and me with mingled terror and indignation. I addressed him in a whisper, with perfidious endearments, advancing a crafty hand towards him the while, made a snatch for the back of his neck, missed it badly, and got him by the ragged fleece of his hind quarters as he tried to flee. If I had flayed him alive he could hardly have uttered a more deafening series of yells, but, like a fool, instead of letting him go, I dragged him towards me, and tried to stifle the noise by holding his muzzle. The tussle lasted engrossingly for a few seconds, and then the climax of the nightmare arrived.

Mrs Knox's voice, close behind me, said, 'Let go my dog this instant, sir! Who are you – '

Her voice faded away, and I knew that she also had seen the colt's head.

I positively felt sorry for her. At her age there was no

knowing what effect the shock might have on her. I scrambled to my feet and confronted her.

'Major Yeates!' she said. There was a deathly pause. 'Will you kindly tell me,' said Mrs Knox slowly, 'am I in Bedlam, or are you? And *what is that*?'

She pointed to the colt, and that unfortunate animal, recognising the voice of his mistress, uttered a hoarse and lamentable whinny. Mrs Knox felt around her for support, found only furze prickles, gazed speechlessly at me, and then, to her eternal honour, fell into wild cackles of laughter.

So, I may say, did Flurry and I. I embarked on my explanation and broke down; Flurry followed suit and broke down too. Overwhelming laughter held us all three, disintegrating our very souls. Mrs Knox pulled herself together first.

'I acquit you, Major Yeates, I acquit you, though appearances are against you. It's clear enough to me you've fallen among thieves.' She stopped and glowered at Flurry. Her purple bonnet was over one eye. 'I'll thank you, sir,' she said, 'to dig out that horse before I leave this place. And when you've dug him out you may keep him. I'll be no receiver of stolen goods!'

She broke off and shook her fist at him. 'Upon my conscience, Tony, I'd give a guinea to have thought of it myself!'

LYNN DOYLE

St Patrick's Day
in the Morning

In my early and unreflective days in the North of Ireland green was to me an ominous and threatening colour. I looked on the ceremonial wearers of it with suspicion and distaste. It suggested secret combination for unlawful ends, rebellion, non-payment of rent, and a tendency towards over-sleeping in the mornings.

It was, however, only the last of these strongly-asserted failings of that body of the population which flaunted the abominable hue at 'set times' that came prominently before my childish attention.

My aunt's servant-maid, Bridget Keefe, the first of our servant-maids that emerges from the mists of my childhood, was a faithful creature, hardworking, and incurably cheerful even on washing days; with good hands for delph, china, and even glass.

I have heard my aunt declare – not to Bridget, for she didn't believe in giving her servants 'too big a notion of themselves' – that during her nine years of service Bridget broke only four cups, two plates, a vegetable dish, and five tumblers.

But there was a green streak in Bridget, or such my aunt esteemed it. One serious imperfection she suffered from. Bridget was not a beauty – a good maid seldom is – but she was a fabulous sleeper, noiseless, but profound. Unfortunately, her accomplishment reached its most

abysmal depth of oblivion about the time when she ought
to have been getting up.

My aunt, who was wakerife herself, and possibly a little
envious of Bridget's gift of slumber, used to fume and
occasionally rage about it. But, in spite of some small
asperities of manner and speech, my aunt was at heart kind
and long-suffering; and besides, good maids were hard to
get in the country. She forgave Bridget unto seventy times
seven; or, to be rigidly accurate, unto nine times three
hundred and thirteen.

It wasn't the three hundred and thirteen mornings in the
year that Bridget had to be divorced from bed as the
patient sculptor disinters a human figure from its block
of marble. No; what broke my aunt's heart, was, that fifty-
two Sunday mornings in the year, Bridget, entirely without the assistance of the alarm clock, rose from her
somewhat defective mattress like a lark springing on eager
wings from dew-impearled grass. My aunt used to follow
the green ribbons to the corner of the road, as Bridget
went off to first Mass; and set down the miraculous accomplishment to sheer bigotry.

Yet my aunt suffered patiently for nine years. She considered herself broadminded; and, indeed, according to her
lights, so she was. In her heart she respected and approved
Bridget's religious devotion. It was through a secular offend-
ing, though of the same nature, that we parted with Bridget
in the end.

On the sixteenth of a certain March, my aunt had set her
mind on travelling to Belfast to buy a Spring hat. By that
time of year Spring hats were beginning to nest in the
imaginations of farmers' wives in our neighbourhood; and
there was no telling when such a portent might hatch out
and flutter into church at morning service, causing one of
the seven deadly sins to sit up and open her eyes.

My aunt had determined to be in the very first flight;
and nothing but a Belfast hat would content her. It was a
matter of the first train, an early start on a stormy morning, with over four miles to drive. But three-and-sixpence

was three-and-sixpence; and one sacrificed at least nine-pence worth of the day by waiting for the second train.

I was not present to see all that happened on that fateful morning (for it was no less), but I was a tolerably observant child, and I think I can reconstruct it: how Bridget, anxious, and interested in hats herself, sat up in bed untimely, yawned, stretched herself, then, looking at the pale square of window, decided that the hour was not yet come, threw herself, as it were, on the bosom of that Cassandra, the alarm clock, and sank back into the blankets and slumber.

Then, my aunt's frantic knuckles on Bridget's door, incautiously seconded, for one time only, by her naked toes; Bridget's conscience-stricken moan and leap for her clothing; the lighting of the range fire, with sticks, newspaper and coal fighting for supremacy in the grate, and Bridget growing more like a negress than an Irishwoman with every dab at her tumbling hair; my aunt's exits and entrances, almost simultaneous, during this performance, until, finally, she remained long enough away – probably through some difference of opinion with whalebone – for Bridget to get at the paraffin oil jar; a match with a head as unstable as Bridget's own; a friendly blending of warm air and paraffin during the delay; then a whap! of an explosion that rattled the very shelves of the oven, and made charcoal of Bridget's St Patrick's Day fringe.

Then, there was the breakfast: the diversely cooked bacon, compounded of the three better-than-half-cooked slices, the slice that tumbled over the edge of the frying-pan and missed complete cremation by seconds, and the slice that fell on the kitchen floor and lay there half-a-dozen inches from the muzzle of a cat far too scared to put out a paw towards it. That would be the slice that my uncle (an irascible man) turned over by fortunate accident and straightway threw out of the window, along with his fork.

There was the tea, floating half-soaked on water that the kettle had been very much surprised to hear was boiling; the plateful of butter hastily quarried with the handle of a tablespoon. Bridget found her thumb-mark, with the adjoining territory of butter, sticking on the wall after my uncle had dashed off with my aunt in the trap, at a canter.

There was the electricity charged journey to B — station, with my aunt, her fingers to her ears, only kept from crying by her desperate resolve to look her best when she was trying on the new hat; the too-distant prospect of the station and a motionless but very ebullient-looking train; the change of canter into gallop; my uncle's climax of language, and my aunt's ultimate disregard of her soul in the effort to keep her body in the trap; the slow, inexorable 'Woof! Woof! Woof!' of the engine; the placid balloons of white smoke floating up from behind the goods-shed.

My aunt travelled to Belfast by the second train. It was too late. The train that had skipped from one to another of her tears that morning had borne to Belfast a neighbour of ours – a faithful wife who kept her house spotless, but my aunt didn't like her. And just as my aunt reached J – 's – 'the shop with style' – and unwontedly perceived that the very first hat her eyes lighted on in the window was the hat of the world, it was reverently lifted from its perch and taken inside.

It did not come out again. My aunt couldn't bear to go in. She waited long, then turned away. There were other head coverings in the window, but no hats. Later in the day she met her enemy, who had a large paper bag in her hand. 'Something told me,' my aunt said afterwards; though she went to church next Sunday hoping against hope, and came home at least outwardly resigned.

You will not be surprised to learn that Bridget quitted our service at the expiration of due legal notice. But you will be wrong in another conclusion. She was not given notice because she overslept on the sixteenth of March; but for quite a different reason.

For almost a year she had been in love with the leading kettle-drummer in the Patrick Sarsfield Flute Band. I always thought the green coats and white knee breeches had something to do with it; though Bridget denied this, and said he was a quare nice fellow, anyway. But on this particular St Patrick's Day the Sarsfield Flute Band was to go past our house on its way to the first train to Belfast. Perhaps the leading kettle-drummer knew the reason; for it was a good quarter of a mile out of their route.

I can only guess what passed through my aunt's mind that morning. She was a kindly woman, as I have said, and sympathetic to young love; and she knew of Bridget's affair of the heart, and favoured it, though she didn't like the green uniform. And though she had been sorely tried, I think that if Bridget had slept-in that morning as well, my aunt would have looked on it as expiation of the previous day's fault, and would have awakened her, in time at least to run after the band and her drummer.

But Bridget did not sleep-in, but rose twenty minutes before the alarm clock sounded, and was dressed in time to go off with the band, and had found leisure amazingly to contrive a fresh fringe.

I do not know what St Patrick himself would have thought of the business. I'm inclined to think he would have sided with Bridget, for he had been a slave himself, and may sometime – before he became a saint, that is – have stolen forty winks on the sides of Slemish. But, anyhow, he wasn't there to intervene on Bridget's behalf; and so we exchanged her for another servant who rose earlier, but might, according to my aunt, just as well have stayed in bed.

Bridget married the drummer later, and went to live with him many miles away; so that I don't know how the pair got on together. But I hope the Sarsfield bandsmen made her husband a wedding present of an old kettle-drum, for the mornings.

SEAMUS O'KELLY
The Rector

The Rector came round the gable of the church. He walked
down the sanded path that curved to the road. Half-way
down he paused, meditated, then turning gazed at the
building. It was square and solid, bulky against the background of the hills. The Rector hitched up his cuffs as he
gazed at the structure. Critical puckers gathered in little
lines across the preserved, peach-like cheeks. He put his
small, nicely-shaped head to one side. There was a pro-
prietorial, concerned air in his attitude. One knew that he
was thinking of the repairs to the church, anxious about
the gutters, the downpipe, the missing slates on the roof,
the painting of the doors and windows. He struck an
attitude as he pondered the problem of the cracks on the
pebble-dashed walls. His umbrella grounded on the sand
with decision. He leaned out a little on it with deliberation, his lips unconsciously shaping the words of the
ultimatum he should deliver to the Select Vestry. His
figure was slight, he looked old-world, almost funereal,
something that had become detached, that was an outpost,
half-forgotten, lonely; a man who had sunk into a parish
where there was nothing to do. He mumbled a little to
himself as he came down to the gate in the high wall that
enclosed the church grounds.

A group of peasants was coming along the yellow, lonely
road, talking and laughing. The bare-footed women stepped
with great active strides, bearing themselves with energy.
They carried heavy baskets from the market town, but

were not conscious of their weight. The carded-wool petticoats, dyed a robust red, brought a patch of vividness to the landscape. The white 'bauneens' and soft black hats of the men afforded a contrast. The Rector's eyes gazed upon the group with a schooled detachment. It was the look of a man who stood outside of their lives, who did not expect to be recognised, and who did not feel called upon to seem conscious of these peasant folk. The eyes of the peasants were unmoved, uninterested, as they were lifted to the dark figure that stood at the rusty iron gate leading into the enclosed church grounds. He gave them no salutation. Their conversation, voluble, noisy, dropped for a moment, half through embarrassment, half through a feeling that something alive stood by the wayside. A vagueness in expression on both sides was the outward signal that two conservative forces had met for a moment and refused to compromise.

One young girl, whose figure and movements would have kindled the eye of an artist, looked up and appeared as if she would smile. The Rector was conscious of her vivid face, framed in a fringe of black hair, of a mischievousness in her beauty, some careless abandon in the swing of her limbs. But something in the level dark brows of the Rector, something that was dour, forbade her smile. It died in a little flush of confusion. The peasants passed and the Rector gave them time to make some headway before he resumed his walk to the Rectory.

He looked up at the range of hills, great in their extent, mighty in their rhythm, beautiful in the play of light and mist upon them. But to the mind of the Rector they expressed something foreign, they were part of a place that was condemned and lost. He began to think of the young girl who, in her innocence, had half-smiled at him. Why did she not smile? Was she afraid? Of what was she afraid? What evil thing had come between her and that impulse of youth? Some consciousness – of what? The Rector sighed. He had, he was afraid, knowledge of what it was.

And that knowledge set his thoughts racing over their accustomed course. He ran over the long tradition of his grievances – grievances that had submerged him in a life that had not even a place in this wayside countryside. His mind worked its way down through all the stages of complaint until it arrived at the *Ne Temere* decree. The lips of the Rector no longer formed half-spoken words; they became two straight, tight little thin lines across the teeth. They would remain that way all the afternoon, held in position while he read the letters in the *Irish Times*. He would give himself up to thoughts of politics, of the deeds of wicked men, of the transactions that go on within and without governments, doping his mind with the drug of class opiates until it was time to go to bed.

Meantime he had to pass a man who was breaking stones in a ditch by the roadside. The hard cracks of the hammer were resounding on the still air. The man looked up from his work as the Rector came along; the grey face of the stone-breaker had a melancholy familiarity for him. The Rector had an impulse – it was seldom he had one. He stood in the centre of the road. The *Ne Temere* decree went from his mind.

'Good-day, my man,' he said, feeling that he had made another concession, and that it would be futile as all the others.

'Good-day, sir,' the stone-breaker made answer, hitching himself upon the sack he had put under his haunches, like one very ready for a conversation.

There was a pause. The Rector did not know very well how to continue. He should, he knew, speak with some sense of colloquialism if he was to get on with this stone-breaker, a person for whom he had a certain removed sympathy. The manner of these people's speech was really a part of the grievances of the Rector. Their conversation, he often secretly assured himself, was peppered with Romish propaganda. But the Rector made another concession.

'It's a fine day, thank God,' he said. He spoke like one who was delivering a message in an unfamiliar language. 'Thank God' was local, and might lend itself to an interpretation that could not be approved. But the Rector imported something into the words that was a protection, something that was of the pulpit, that held a solemnity in its pessimism.

'A fine day, indeed, glory be to God!' the stone-breaker made answer. There was a freshness in his expression, a cheerfulness in the prayer, that made of it an optimism.

The Rector was so conscious of the contrast that it gave him pause again. The peach-like colourings on the cheeks brightened, for a suspicion occurred to him. Could the fellow have meant anything? Had he deliberately set up an optimistic Deity in opposition to the pessimistic Deity of the Rector? The Rector hitched up the white cuffs under his dark sleeves, swung his umbrella, and resumed his way, his lips puckered, a little feverish agitation seizing him.

'A strange, down-hearted kind of a man,' the stone-breaker said to himself, as he reached out for a lump of limestone and raised his hammer. A redbreast, perched on an old thorn bush, looking out on the scene with curious eyes, stretched his wing and his leg, as much as to say, 'Ah, well,' sharpened his beak on a twig, and dropped into the ditch to pick up such gifts as the good earth yielded.

The Rector walked along the road pensive, but steadfast, his eyes upon the alien hills, his mind travelling over ridges of problems that never afforded the gleam of solution. He heard a shout of a laugh. Above the local accents that held a cadence of the Gaelic speech he heard the sharp clipped Northern accent of his own gardener and general factotum. He had brought the man with him when he first came to Connacht, half as a mild form of colonisation, half through a suspicion of local honesty. He now saw the man's shaggy head over the Rectory garden wall, and outside it were the peasants.

How was it that the gardener got on with the local

people? How was it that they stood on the road to speak with him, shouting their extravagant laughter at his keen, dry Northern humour?

When he first came the gardener had been more grimly hostile to the place than the Rector himself. There had been an ugly row on the road, and blows had been struck. But that was some years ago. The gardener now appeared very much merged in the life of the place; the gathering outside the Rectory garden was friendly, almost a family party. How was it to be accounted for? Once or twice the Rector found himself suspecting that at the bottom of the phenomenon there might be all unconscious among these people a spirit of common country, of a common democracy, a common humanity, that forced itself to the surface in course of time. The Rector stood, his lips working, his nicely-shaped little head quivering with a sudden agitation. For he found himself thinking along unusual lines, and for that very reason dangerous lines – frightfully dangerous lines, he told himself, as an ugly enlightenment broke across his mind, warming it up for a few moments and no more. As he turned in the gate at the Rectory it was a relief to him – for his own thoughts were frightening him – to see the peasants moving away and the head of the gardener disappear behind the wall. He walked up the path to the Rectory, the lawn dotted over with sombre yew trees all clipped into the shape of torpedoes, all trained directly upon the forts of Heaven! The house was large and comfortable, the walls a faded yellow. Like the church, it was thrown up against the background of the hills. It had all the sombre exclusiveness that made appeal to the Rector. The sight of it comforted him at the moment, and his mental agitation died down. He became normal enough to resume his accustomed outlook, and before he had reached the end of the path his mind had become obsessed again by the thought of the *Ne Temere* decree. Something should, he felt convinced, be done, and done at once.

He ground his umbrella on the step in front of the

Rectory door and pondered. At last he came to a conclusion, inspiration lighting up his faded eyes. He tossed his head upwards.

'I must write a letter to the papers,' he said. 'Ireland is lost.'

DANIEL CORKERY

Joy

Again Nora Kelly rose from the table, at which she had been eating, looked through the window, turned from it, and spoke to her sister, who was busy at the fire:

'When the train was passing Kilcully I said to him, "Look out the window, father, you might never see Cork city again," and he turned on me and said, "Do I want to see it? How did I come into it? What was I thinking of all these years and I walking the streets of it? Tell me that? Little care if I never see it again" – that's what he said, and no, he wouldn't look out.'

Margaret, to whom she had spoken, then came to the window from the fire and said:

'Look at him now, God help us, he don't know where to rest; that's the tenth time he's after examining that cowshed.' And she called out: 'Father, come in; there's a sup of tea here for you, come in or it will be cold on you; haven't you to-morrow or the day after to look at them, they'll be there to-morrow as well as to-night.'

The old man turned around; as will happen in strange surroundings he did not at once spy out the window where the voice had come from; when, however, his eyes rested on it, on his two daughters, it suddenly struck him, as if he had been thinking unwonted thoughts of her, that there was something wanting in Margaret's voice. It was a strong voice, with the hard, firm consonants, the pure vowels of the Irish language in it. She was now a middle-aged woman, and although she had lived thirty of her years in the city of Cork, where English is not spoken with

any sort of firmness at all, her speech was still full of the
strength that would carry up far hillsides, herding cattle
or calling to a neigbouring homestead. She was already a
full-grown girl when her father's house in Carrignadoura
in rock-strewn Iveleary was levelled with the ground on a
terrible night of wind and fire, bloodshed and marching
men. Perhaps it was that one night, rather than the previous
years of growth in that dis-peopled land, which had fixed
the temper of her mind, hardening it, making it incapable of
being wrought upon by the dilly-dally of the city. Curious,
then, that now, heard by him for the first time in thirty
years in rural surroundings, the voice struck her father
as being somewhat rough and hard; its accent did not
chime with his thoughts. But it was only a passing fancy.
She had always been the love of his heart, and was that
now more than ever. He smiled back at the two women
brightly; they were so happy-looking in the fresh-painted
window-frame of the brand-new house that the Estate
Commissioners had built for him – he smiled back at them,
waving his stick and quaintly doffing his hat, as he had seen
the grand folk in the city do. But he had no intention of
going in to them. Half the farmyard he had not yet examined. Many of the beasts were still unfamiliar to him;
he knew he was mixing them up, one with another. The
boundaries of the farm were laid along a ridge of trees;
and as yet he had not got near that ridge. He could
scarcely tear himself away from the yard. Better to him
than the drinking of wine were the smell and the sight of
the beasts as they lurched, almost fiercely, into the milking
stalls, or stood around outside, their nostrils spreading
with expectancy, their hoofs stamping impatiently on the
hard ground. He had been so long away from all that, cooped
up in the city, separated from every one of the intimate
sounds, smells, sights, that had helped to create him what
he was on that night of passion when he lashed out against
armed men! A long exile it had been, and in exile would
his days have ended only for the grit of this strong-voiced,
middle-aged woman, his daughter. All these years she had

been watching the twistings and turnings of the many new laws that were being made from time to time dealing with the land and landlordism; she made her own of them, clause by clause, judgment by judgment. And her task had been her own, no one helping. Nora, her sister, had yielded herself up to the city's influence; she was a young thing when it gripped her; both she and her brothers, one elder, one younger, soon lost whatever hope they had brought with them from Carrignadoura that they would ever again be rooted in the soil. Perhaps they did not greatly care.

No one had helped her then, unless it was the old man; and his help had been fitful, now he would be all brightness, quoting old poems of the Gaelic bards, old prophecies of the Gaelic saints, but at another time he would chide her or laugh at her: 'Rooted in the soil again – we will, child, and there'll be Kings in Tara!'

When at last the farm did come to them it was beyond even Margaret's expectations: eighty acres of prime land watered by the Blackwater, so rich, so kind, that the old man asked himself as he surveyed it whether he would now go back to Carrignadoura if choice were given him. As he went about he was contrasting the two countries – the meagre soil of the west, which had the colour, the smell, the texture of turf, and this deep, well-fattened soil which ran over with prodigality – the condition of the eighteen head of cattle was sufficient to show what it was. While he gazed at these sleek, lazy-looking animals, his inner eye was full of the skinny, wiry, daring cattle of the hills. He could hardly believe these cattle were his own; such beasts called up to vision a big house, rich acres, a family of long descent. But this they were, his own – and the rich acres as well, and a house that seemed very big to him when he remembered the dark little hovel in Carrignadoura over which blood had been spilled. And all would be his and his children's and his children's children's forever! He glowed with a solemn joy. He could not understand why he felt like sitting down in some quiet place and weeping. To banish the thought he would begin reckoning his riches once again; and so sure as

he began, the past would once more become alive. He would
recall the names, the appearance of the others who were
evicted with him on that far-off night of marching men, of
blazing roofs and stampeding cattle. None of them, so far
as he knew, had been reinstated. They had no daughter
like his Margaret. They were scattered to the four winds.
It had been like a second Famine to them — child had
drifted away from father, husband from wife, brother from
sister. What he would give to be able to gather round him
now even a few of these lost companions! But they were
gone forever. He turned to where the hedge skirted the
bohereen. There, to his astonishment, a dark-featured man
was staring at him, staring steadily, with meaning and
wonder it seemed. He stared in return. It was Tadhg
Kearney from Tooreenanean! — a man he had not seen
even once since that far-off night of struggle. 'Tadhg!
Tadhg' he called — 'Is it you?' But he couldn't wait for an
answer. 'Look,' and his stick swept round the bawn fields —
'all mine, and these yonder as well — and the cattle!' How
would Tadhg Kearney, proud man, take that? He
turned to watch him. But. . . . He went forward. What he
had taken for a dark-featured man was nothing but an old
stump of a tree that stood up from the brosna of the hedge.
He went right up to it. 'God leave me the senses,' he said,
and he poked at the trunk with the tip of his stick, as one
does to a beast at a fair. And he smiled. But almost immediately he grew solemn and anxious again. 'I'm after
thanking You, O Christ, on my bended knees,' he muttered,
his hat in his hand, 'O Christ, King of Sunday, and you
too, Mother of the Son of God, Mary of the Graces.'

More quietly, more contained than before, he wandered
from place to place; he did not now look at one thing more
than another, yet all the time he was deeply conscious of
the peace that was around him, the fatness, the well-being,
the golden evening, the peace.

Under far-spreading boughs of great beechen boles he
wandered; the ash-grey trunks were stouter than the great
pillars he had seen in the big churches in the city. Low

gleams of red sunshine shooting wilfully here and there turned the deep grass and the flowers and the brushwood to a rich golden colour – the colour of altar vessels. It was a fairy land to one who had grown up in Iveleary, where few trees are to be seen except the birch, the rowan, the holly – shrunken trees, meagre of foliage. Suddenly he stopped. He had heard merry voices; he listened; the air was full of them – a call, a cry, a ringing cheer, overtaking one another, mingling, separating. He crept slyly nearer. He came upon a well-kept path – it was dappled with sun and shadow. Almost as he discovered it, two Dominicans, very tall, very stately in their long robes of white and black, swept swiftly by, their hands were hidden in their sleeves, their voices were low, their faces earnest. They were gone! They had not seen him, although he had clutched his hat from his head and bowed with reverence. He felt a little dazed. Perhaps he had not seen them at all – he remembered the tree-trunk, how he had taken it for Tadhg Kearney. He caught hold of a slender ash-bole and leaned out into the pathway. Yes, there were the two figures, with the sun and shadow playing upon their backs as they went along the wide avenue. And others were coming. He withdrew into the shade. Looking beyond the path, he saw wide, level fields, crowded with brightly-clad youthful figures: they were hurling. It was from these the merry cries had come. To his right, through a screen of thin foliage, he caught sight of sun-white walls, buttresses, carved stones – many buildings, one of them a church: the windows were tipped with fire. It was all very unexpected, beautiful, radiant. Old poems swept into his mind, poems that were written in the darkest years of the eighteenth century when nothing except hope was left the Gael. Such an Ireland as this he had come upon to-day they had prophesied. 'The laws of Rome will be in practice – religion without blemish' – would be a literal rendering of two of the lines that swept upon him; over and over he recited them, for the Irish words were full of bright music and deftness. But a bell clanged with authority, and the

figures went from the fields; he saw the priests crossing the playing field diagonally. And then it seemed to him that a band of music had suddenly ceased!

Excited, he turned to retrace the way he had come. He felt he needed to rest; he had had too many impressions in too short a time. He would sit quietly by the hearth and take out his beads. That would be best. He drew as swiftly as he could towards the farmyard. But again he was perplexed. And he began to fear for himself. There, too, were merry voices, seemingly a host of them – not in the farmyard, the farmyard was deserted. Through it he went. A door opened: he heard a ringing voice giving out fine words and phrases: 'To the Gaelic race the riches of the air above it, the soil within it, the seas around it!' He could hear no more for the shout of approval. 'Rooted in the soil for ever, as the love of Ireland in our hearts!' was the next phrase he caught up. He hastened on. In other years he had heard such phrases, only instead of ringing with the pride of victories gained, they had rung with the hatred of dispossessed people. 'Who shall rule us but ourselves – who is fit for it?' His heart gave a leap; he made to enter the house. It was crowded with men. He then went around to the front. On the roadway, mounted on a car which had been roughly decked with green boughs, was the orator – a man with a shining forehead, and eyes full of the pride of race. Everywhere were green boughs; everywhere, too, green flags with inscriptions in red gold upon them. He saw a crowd of golden instruments. And all the time the high-hearted phrases were ringing in his ears – the myriad love-names of Ireland were invoked. Each had its own association – the Little Dark Rose, the Sean Bhean Bhocht, the Silk of the Kine, Innisfail, the Plain of Conn, Fodla, Banba – they were as so many stops on an organ. Not one of them but set old songs of the Gael stirring in his memory. He trembled with excitement. Only his anxiety to hear everything, to understand everything, kept him alive, he felt. And his thought renewed to him the priests walking in the avenue, the brightly-clad figures on the green, the

sun-tipped windows. And the rich underfoliage, the great
boles, the wide branches. He clutched his forehead: his
name had been put into the discourse, he heard the words
'His fight at Carrignadoura!' He was being seized and
dragged forward – but his daughter Margaret and his
daughter Nora were near him, and his son John was helping him – and all the faces about him were those of men
who had fought and won. As if by an afterthought, somebody took the hat from his head: there was a deafening
outburst of cheering, it was more like a roar – his locks
were unexpectedly white. It was as if the people thought
of those grey locks as spoil from that distant battle field.
The roar redoubled; it would never end. There was confusion too. His thoughts were going astray. A young man
stood before him: he was speaking in Irish: he had never
seen a young man look so handsome, so proud. He looked
like a king's son. The old man wouldn't dare to reply; his
limbs were quivering, he turned away, he drew down his
daughter's head. 'What is it?' she said. 'Are there Kings
in Tara?' he whispered, in an excited voice, breathy, warm,
husky.

When the triumph was over, when the music had died
away along the road, and no one remained in the house
except the old man and his children, they began to chaff
him on the great reception he had had. He struggled with
them good-humouredly.

'You haven't it right,' he said, 'you haven't it right at
all.'

'Haven't we now? Haven't we now?' his son kept tormenting him.

'No; you haven't; that isn't what I was thinking about
at all.'

'Isn't it now; maybe 'twas something grander then?'

'It wasn't.'

'What was it?'

'I asked Margaret here about the Kings – '

'You did – '

'Well, and if she said "Yes" instead of "No" what was it I had in my mind, do you think?'

They stood up and laughed – his head was thrust out so earnestly.

'Well, what had you in your mind?'

'You won't understand.'

'We'll try – '

He gestured with his stick.

'The best of them beasts outside – I'd send him the road to Tara – 'tis long since I had anything to give anybody.'

He took out his beads and they knelt for the night prayers.

It was a rich night in autumn; the earth was fruiting.

JAMES STEPHENS

Desire

I

He was excited, and as he leaned forward in his chair and told this story to his wife he revealed to her a degree or a species of credulity of which she could not have believed him capable.

He was a level-headed man, and habitually conducted his affairs on hard-headed principles. He had conducted his courtship, his matrimonial and domestic affairs in a manner which she should not have termed reckless or romantic. When, therefore, she found him excited, and over such a story, she did not know how just to take the matter.

She compromised by agreeing with him, not because her reason was satisfied or even touched, but simply because he was excited, and a woman can welcome anything which varies the dull round and will bathe in exclamations if she gets the chance.

This was what he told her.

As he was walking to lunch a motor car came down the street at a speed too dangerous for the narrow and congested thoroughfare. A man was walking in front of him, and, just as the car came behind, this man stepped off the path with a view to crossing the road. He did not even look behind as he stepped off. Her husband stretched a ready arm that swept the man back to the pavement one second before the car went blaring and buzzing by.

'If I had not been there,' said her husband, who liked

slang, 'you would have got it where the chicken got the axe.'

The two men grinned at each other; her husband smiling with good-fellowship, the other crinkling with amusement and gratitude.

They walked down the street and, on the strength of that adventure, they had lunch together.

They had sat for a long time after lunch, making each other's acquaintance, smoking innumerable cigarettes, and engaged in a conversation which she could never have believed her husband would have shared in for ten minutes; and they had parted with a wish, from her husband, that they should meet again on the following day, and a wordless smile from the man.

He had neither ratified nor negatived the arrangement.

'I hope he'll turn up,' said her husband.

This conversation had excited her man, for it had drawn him into an atmosphere to which he was a stranger, and he had found himself moving there with such pleasure that he wished to get back to it with as little delay as possible.

Briefly, as he explained it to her, the atmosphere was religious; and while it was entirely intellectual it was more heady and exhilarating than the emotional religion to which he had been accustomed, and from which he had silently lapsed.

He tried to describe his companion; but had such ill success in the description that she could not remember afterwards whether he was tall or short; fat or thin; fair or dark.

It was the man's eyes only that he succeeded in emphasising; and these, it appeared, were eyes such as he had never before seen in a human face.

That also, he amended, was a wrong way of putting it, for his eyes were exactly like everybody else's. It was the way he looked through them that was different. Something, very steady, very ardent, very quiet and powerful, was using these eyes for purposes of vision. He had never met anyone who looked at him so . . . comprehendingly; so agreeably.

'You are in love,' said she with a laugh.

After this her husband's explanations became more explanatory but not less confused, until she found that they were both, with curious unconsciousness, in the middle of a fairy-tale.

'He asked me,' said her husband, 'what was the thing I wished for beyond all things.

'That was the most difficult question I have ever been invited to answer,' he went on; 'and for nearly half an hour we sat thinking it out, and discussing magnificences and possibilities.

'I had all the usual thoughts; and, of course, the first of them was wealth. We are more dominated by proverbial phrases than we conceive of, and, such a question being posed, the words "healthy, wealthy, and wise" will come, unbidden, to answer it. To be alive is to be acquisitive, and so I mentioned wealth, tentatively, as a possibility; and he agreed that it was worth considering. But after a while I knew that I did not want money.'

'One always has need of money,' said his wife.

'In a way, that is true,' he replied, 'but not in this way; for, as I thought it over, I remembered that we have no children; and that our relatively few desires, or fancies, can be readily satisfied by the money we already have. Also we are fairly well off; we have enough in the stocking to last our time even if I ceased from business, which I am not going to do; and, in short, I discovered that money or its purchasing power had not any particular advantages to offer.'

'All the same!' she murmured; and halted with her eyes fixed on purchasings far away in time and space.

'All the same!' he agreed with a smile.

'I could not think of anything worth wishing for,' he continued. 'I mentioned health and wisdom, and we considered these; but, judging myself by the standard of the world in which we move, I concluded that both my health and knowledge were as good as the next man's; and I thought also that if I elected to become wiser than my contemporaries I might be a very lonely person for the rest of my days.'

'Yes,' said she thoughtfully, 'I am glad you did not ask to be made wise, unless you could have asked it for both of us.'

'I asked him in the end what he would advise me to demand, but he replied that he could not advise me at all. "Behind everything stands desire," said he, "and you must find out your desire."

'I asked him then, if the condition were reversed and if the opportunity had come to him instead of to me, what he should have asked for; not, as I explained to him, in order that I might copy his wish, but from sheer curiosity. He replied that he should not ask for anything. This reply astonished, almost alarmed me at first, but most curiously satisfied me on considering it, and I was about to adopt that attitude – '

'Oh,' said his wife.

'When an idea came to me. "Here I am," I said to myself, "forty-eight years of age: rich enough; sound enough in wind and limb; and as wise as I can afford to be. What is there now belonging to me, absolutely mine, but from which I must part, and which I should like to keep?" And I saw that the thing which was leaving me day by day; second by second; irretrievably and inevitably; was my forty-eighth year. I thought I should like to continue at the age of forty-eight until my time was up.

'I did not ask to live for ever, or any of that nonsense, for I saw that to live for ever is to be condemned to a misery of boredom more dreadful than anything else the mind can conceive of. But, while I do live, I wish to live competently, and so I asked to be allowed stay at the age of forty-eight years with all the equipment of my present state unimpaired.'

'You should not have asked for such a thing,' said his

wife, a little angrily. 'It is not fair to me,' she explained. 'You are older than I am now, but in a few years this will mean that I shall be needlessly older than you. I think it was not a loyal wish.'

'I thought of that objection,' said he, 'and I also thought that I was past the age at which certain things matter; and that both temperamentally and in the matter of years I am proof against sensual or such-like attractions. It seemed to me to be right; so I just registered my wish with him.'

'What did he say?' she queried.

'He did not say anything; he just nodded; and began to talk again of other matters – religion, life, death, mind; a host of things, which, for all the diversity they seem to have when I enumerate them, were yet one single theme.

'I feel a more contented man to-night than I have ever felt,' he continued, 'and I feel in some curious way a different person from the man I was yesterday.'

Here his wife awakened from the conversation and began to laugh.

'You are a foolish man,' said she, 'and I am just as bad. If anyone were to hear us talking this solemn silliness they would have a right to mock at us.'

He laughed heartily with her, and after a light supper they went to bed.

2

During the night his wife had a dream.

She dreamed that a ship set away for the Polar Seas on an expedition in which she was not sufficiently interested to find out its reason. The ship departed with her on board. All that she knew or cared was that she was greatly concerned with baggage, and with counting and going over the various articles that she had brought against arctic weather.

She had thick woollen stockings. She had skin boots all hairy inside, all pliable and wrinkled without. She had a great skin cap shaped like a helmet and fitting down in a cape over her shoulders. She had, and they did not astonish her, a pair of very baggy fur trousers. She had a sleeping sack.

She had an enormous quantity of things; and everybody in the expedition was equipped, if not with the same things, at least similarly.

These traps were a continuous subject of conversation aboard, and, although days and weeks passed, the talk of the ship hovered about and fell continually into the subject of warm clothing.

There came a day when the weather was perceptibly colder; so cold that she was tempted to draw on those wonderful breeches, and to fit her head into that most comfortable hat. But she did not do so; for, and everybody on the ship explained it to her, it was necessary that she should accustom herself to the feeling, the experience, of cold; and, she was further assured that the chill which she was now resenting was nothing to the freezing she should presently have to bear.

It seemed good advice; and she decided that as long as she could bear the cold she would do so, and would not put on any protective covering; thus, when the cold became really intense, she would be in some measure inured to it, and would not suffer so much.

But steadily, and day by day, the weather grew colder.

For now they were in wild and whirling seas wherein great green and white icebergs went sailing by; and all about the ship little hummocks of ice bobbed and surged, and went under and came up; and the grey water slashed and hissed against and on top of these small hillocks.

Her hands were so cold that she had to put them under her armpits to keep any warmth in them; and her feet were in a worse condition. They had begun to pain her; so she decided that on the morrow she would put on her winter equipment, and would not mind what anybody said to the contrary.

'It is cold enough,' said she, 'for my arctic trousers, for my warm soft boots, and my great furry gloves. I will put them on in the morning,' for it was then almost night and she meant to go to bed at once.

She did go to bed; and she lay there in a very misery of cold.

In the morning, she was yet colder; and immediately on rising she looked for the winter clothing which she had laid ready by the side of her bunk the night before; but she could not find them. She was forced to dress in her usual rather thin clothes; and, having done so, she went on deck.

When she got to the side of the vessel she found that the world about her had changed.

The sea had disappeared. Far as the eye could peer was a level plain of ice, not white, but dull grey; and over it there lowered a sky, grey as itself and of almost the same dullness.

Across this waste there blew a bitter, a piercing wind that her eyes winced from, and that caused her ears to tingle and sting.

Not a soul was moving on the ship, and the dead silence which brooded on the ice lay heavy and almost solid on the vessel.

She ran to the other side, and found that the whole ship's company had landed, and were staring at her from a little distance of the ship. And these people were as silent as the frozen air, as the frozen ship. They stared at her; they made no move; they made no sound.

She noticed that they were all dressed in their winter furs; and, while she stood, ice began to creep into her veins.

One of the ship's company strode forward a few paces and held up a bundle in his mittened hand. She was amazed to see that the bundle contained her clothes; her broad furry trousers; her great cosy helmet and gloves.

To get from the ship to the ice was painful but not impossible. A rope ladder was hanging against the side, and she went down this. The rungs felt hard as iron, for they were frozen stiff; and the touch of those glassy surfaces bit into her tender hand like fire. But she got to the ice and went across it towards her companions.

Then, to her dismay, to her terror, all these, suddenly, with one unexpressed accord, turned and began to run away from her; and she, with a heart that shook once and could scarcely beat again, took after them.

Every few paces she fell, for her shoes could not grip on the ice; and each time that she fell those monsters stood and turned and watched her, and the man who had her clothes waved the bundle at her and danced grotesquely, silently.

She continued running, sliding, falling, picking herself up, until her breath went, and she came to a halt, unable to move a limb further and scarcely able to breathe; and this time they did not stay to look at her.

They continued running, but now with great and greater speed, with the very speed of madmen; and she saw them become black specks away on the white distance; and she saw them disappear; and she saw that there was nothing where she stared but the long white miles, and the terrible silence, and the cold.

How cold it was!

And with that there arose a noiseless wind, keen as a razor.

It stung into her face; it swirled about her ankles like a lash; it stabbed under her armpits like a dagger.

'I am cold,' she murmured.

She looked backwards whence she had come, but the ship was no longer in sight, and she could not remember from what direction she had come.

Then she began to run in any direction.

Indeed she ran in every direction to find the ship; for when she had taken an hundred steps in one way she thought, frantically, 'This is not the way,' and at once she began to run on the opposite road. But run as she might she could not get warm; it was colder she got. And then, on a steel-grey plane, she slipped, and slipped again and went sliding down a hollow, faster and faster; she came to the brink of a cleft, and swished over this, and down into a hole of ice and there she lay.

'I shall die!' she said. 'I shall fall asleep here and die. . . .'

Then she awakened.

She opened her eyes directly on the window and saw the ghost of dawn struggling with the ghoul of darkness. A greyish perceptibility framed the window without, but could not daunt the obscurity within; and she lay for a moment terrified at that grotesque adventure, and thanking God that it had only been a dream.

In another second she felt that she was cold. She pulled the clothes more tightly about her, and she spoke to her husband.

'How miserably cold it is!' she said.

She turned in the bed and snuggled against him for warmth; and she found that an atrocity of cold came from him; that he was icy.

She leaped from the bed with a scream. She switched on the light, and bent over her husband –

He was stone dead. He was stone cold. And she stood by him, shivering and whimpering.

JAMES JOYCE
The Sisters

There was no hope for him this time: it was the third
stroke. Night after night I had passed the house (it was
vacation time) and studied the lighted square of window:
and night after night I had found it lighted in the same
way, faintly and evenly. If he was dead, I thought, I would
see the reflection of candles on the darkened blind, for I
knew that two candles must be set at the head of a corpse.
He had often said to me: 'I am not long for this world,' and I
had thought his words idle. Now I knew they were true.
Every night as I gazed up at the window I said softly to
myself the word paralysis. It had always sounded strangely
in my ears, like the word gnomon in the Euclid and the
word simony in the Catechism. But now it sounded to me
like the name of some maleficent and sinful being. It filled
me with fear, and yet I longed to be nearer to it and to look
upon its deadly work.

Old Cotter was sitting at the fire, smoking, when I came
downstairs to supper. While my aunt was ladling out my
stirabout he said, as if returning to some former remark of
his:

'No, I wouldn't say he was exactly . . . but there was
something queer . . . there was something uncanny about
him. I'll tell you my opinion . . .'

He began to puff at his pipe, no doubt arranging his
opinion in his mind. Tiresome old fool! When we knew
him first he used to be rather interesting, talking of faints
and worms; but I soon grew tired of him and his endless
stories about the distillery.

'I have my own theory about it,' he said. 'I think it was one of those . . . peculiar cases . . . But it's hard to say . . . '

He began to puff again at his pipe without giving us his theory. My uncle saw me staring and said to me:

'Well, so your old friend is gone, you'll be sorry to hear.'

'Who?' said I.

'Father Flynn.'

'Is he dead?'

'Mr Cotter here has just told us. He was passing by the house.'

I knew that I was under observation, so I continued eating as if the news had not interested me. My uncle explained to old Cotter.

'The youngster and he were great friends. The old chap taught him a great deal, mind you; and they say he had a great wish for him.'

'God have mercy on his soul,' said my aunt piously.

Old Cotter looked at me for a while. I felt that his little beady black eyes were examining me, but I would not satisfy him by looking up from my plate. He returned to his pipe and finally spat rudely into the grate.

'I wouldn't like children of mine,' he said, 'to have too much to say to a man like that.'

'How do you mean, Mr Cotter?' asked my aunt.

'What I mean is,' said old Cotter, 'it's bad for children. My idea is: let a young lad run about and play with young lads of his own age and not be . . . Am I right, Jack?'

'That's my principle, too,' said my uncle. 'Let him learn to box his corner. That's what I'm always saying to that Rosicrucian there: take exercise. Why, when I was a nipper, every morning of my life I had a cold bath, winter and summer. And that's what stands to me now. Education is all very fine and large . . . Mr Cotter might take a pick of that leg of mutton,' he added to my aunt.

'No, no, not for me,' said old Cotter.

My aunt brought the dish from the safe and put it on the table.

'But why do you think it's not good for children, Mr Cotter?' she asked.

'It's bad for children,' said old Cotter, 'because their minds are so impressionable. When children see things like that, you know, it has an effect . . .'

I crammed my mouth with stirabout for fear I might give utterance to my anger. Tiresome old red-nosed imbecile!

It was late when I fell asleep. Though I was angry with old Cotter for alluding to me as a child, I puzzled my head to extract meaning from his unfinished sentences. In the dark of my room I imagined that I saw again the heavy grey face of the paralytic. I drew the blankets over my head and tried to think of Christmas. But the grey face still followed me. It murmured; and I understood that it desired to confess something. I felt my soul receding into some pleasant and vicious region; and there again I found it waiting for me. It began to confess to me in a murmuring voice and I wondered why it smiled continually and why the lips were so moist with spittle. But then I remembered that it had died of paralysis and I felt that I too was smiling feebly, as if to absolve the simoniac of his sin.

The next morning after breakfast I went down to look at the little house in Great Britain Street. It was an unassuming shop, registered under the vague name of *Drapery*. The drapery consisted mainly of children's bootees and umbrellas; and on ordinary days a notice used to hang in the window, saying: *Umbrellas Re-covered*. No notice was visible now, for the shutters were up. A crape bouquet was tied to the door-knocker with ribbon. Two poor women and a telegram boy were reading the card pinned on the crape. I also approached and read:

1st July, 1895

The Rev. James Flynn (formerly of St Catherine's Church, Meath Street), aged sixty-five years.

R. I. P.

The reading of the card persuaded me that he was dead

and I was disturbed to find myself at check. Had he not been dead I would have gone into the little dark room behind the shop to find him sitting in his arm-chair by the fire, nearly smothered in his great-coat. Perhaps my aunt would have given me a packet of High Toast for him, and this present would have roused him from his stupefied doze. It was always I who emptied the packet into his black snuff-box, for his hands trembled too much to allow him to do this without spilling half the snuff about the floor. Even as he raised his large trembling hand to his nose little clouds of snuff dribbled through his fingers over the front of his coat. It may have been these constant showers of snuff which gave his ancient priestly garments their green faded look, for the red handkerchief, blackened, as it always was, with the snuff-stains of a week, with which he tried to brush away the fallen grains, was quite inefficacious.

I wished to go in and look at him, but I had not the courage to knock. I walked away slowly along the sunny side of the street, reading all the theatrical advertisements in the shop-windows as I went. I found it strange that neither I nor the day seemed in a mourning mood and I felt even annoyed at discovering in myself a sensation of freedom as if I had been freed from something by his death. I wondered at this for, as my uncle had said the night before, he had taught me a great deal. He had studied in the Irish college in Rome and he had taught me to pronounce Latin properly. He had told me stories about the catacombs and about Napoleon Bonaparte, and he had explained to me the meaning of the different ceremonies of the Mass and of the different vestments worn by the priest. Sometimes he had amused himself by putting difficult questions to me, asking me what one should do in certain circumstances or whether such and such sins were mortal or venial or only imperfections. His questions showed me how complex and mysterious were certain institutions of the Church which I had always regarded as the simplest acts. The duties of the priest towards the Eucharist and towards the secrecy of the confessional seemed so grave to me that I wondered how anybody had ever found in himself the courage to undertake them; and I was not surprised when he told me that the fathers of the Church had written books as thick as the *Post Office Directory* and as closely printed as the law notices in the newspaper, elucidating all these intricate questions. Often when I thought of this I could make no answer or only a very foolish and halting one, upon which he used to smile and nod his head twice or thrice. Sometimes he used to put me through the responses of the Mass, which he had made me learn by heart; and, as I pattered, he used to smile pensively and nod his head, now and then pushing huge pinches of snuff up each nostril alternately. When he smiled he used to uncover his big discoloured teeth and let his tongue lie upon his lower lip – a habit which had made me feel uneasy in the beginning of our acquaintance before I knew him well.

As I walked along in the sun I remembered old Cotter's words and tried to remember what had happened afterwards in the dream. I remembered that I had noticed long velvet curtains and a swinging lamp of antique fashion. I felt that I had been very far away, in some land where the customs were strange – in Persia, I thought . . . But I could not remember the end of the dream.

In the evening my aunt took me with her to visit the house of mourning. It was after sunset; but the window-panes of the houses that looked to the west reflected the tawny gold of a great bank of clouds. Nannie received us in the hall; and, as it would have been unseemly to have shouted at her, my aunt shook hands with her for all. The old woman pointed upwards interrogatively and, on my aunt's nodding, proceeded to toil up the narrow staircase before us, her bowed head being scarcely above the level of the banister-rail. At the first landing she stopped and beckoned us forward encouragingly towards the open door of the dead-room. My aunt went in and the old woman, seeing that I hesitated to enter, began to beckon to me again repeatedly with her hand.

I went in on tiptoe. The room through the lace end of

the blind was suffused with dusky golden light amid which
the candles looked like pale thin flames. He had been
coffined. Nannie gave the lead and we three knelt down at
the foot of the bed. I pretended to pray but I could not
gather my thoughts because the old woman's mutterings
distracted me. I noticed how clumsily her skirt was hooked
at the back and how the heels of her cloth boots were
trodden down all to one side. The fancy came to me that
the old priest was smiling as he lay there in his coffin.

But no. When we rose and went up to the head of the
bed I saw that he was not smiling. There he lay, solemn
and copious, vested as for the altar, his large hands loosely
retaining a chalice. His face was very truculent, grey and
massive, with black cavernous nostrils and circled by a
scanty white fur. There was a heavy odour in the room –
the flowers.

We crossed ourselves and came away. In the little room
downstairs we found Eliza seated in his arm-chair in state.
I groped my way towards my usual chair in the corner
while Nannie went to the sideboard and brought out a
decanter of sherry and some wine-glasses. She set these on
the table and invited us to take a little glass of wine. Then,
at her sister's bidding, she filled out the sherry into the
glasses and passed them to us. She pressed me to take some
cream crackers also, but I declined because I thought I
would make too much noise eating them. She seemed to be
somewhat disappointed at my refusal and went over quietly
to the sofa, where she sat down behind her sister. No one
spoke: we all gazed at the empty fireplace.

My aunt waited until Eliza sighed and then said:

'Ah, well, he's gone to a better world.'

Eliza sighed again and bowed her head in assent. My
aunt fingered the stem of her wine-glass before sipping a
little.

'Did he . . . peacefully?' she asked.

'Oh, quite peacefully, ma'am,' said Eliza. 'You couldn't
tell when the breath went out of him. He had a beautiful
death, God be praised.'

'And everything . . . ?'

'Father O'Rourke was in with him a Tuesday and anointed him and prepared him and all.'

'He knew then?'

'He was quite resigned.'

'He looks quite resigned,' said my aunt.

'That's what the woman we had in to wash him said. She said he just looked as if he was asleep, he looked that peaceful and resigned. No one would think he'd make such a beautiful corpse.'

'Yes, indeed,' said my aunt.

She sipped a little more from her glass and said:

'Well, Miss Flynn, at any rate it must be a great comfort for you to know that you did all you could for him. You were both very kind to him, I must say.'

Eliza smoothed her dress over her knees.

'Ah, poor James!' she said. 'God knows we done all we could, as poor as we are – we couldn't see him want anything while he was in it.'

Nannie had leaned her head against the soft-pillow and seemed about to fall asleep.

'There's poor Nannie,' said Eliza, looking at her, 'she's wore out. All the work we had, she and me, getting in the woman to wash him and then laying him out and then the coffin and then arranging about the Mass in the chapel. Only for Father O'Rourke I don't know what we'd done at all. It was him brought us all them flowers and them two candlesticks out of the chapel, and wrote out the notice for the *Freeman's General* and took charge of all the papers for the cemetery and poor James's insurance.'

'Wasn't that good of him?' said my aunt.

Eliza closed her eyes and shook her head slowly.

'Ah, there's no friends like old friends,' she said, 'when all is said and done, no friends that a body can trust.'

'Indeed, that's true,' said my aunt. 'And I'm sure now that he's gone to his eternal reward he won't forget you and all your kindness to him.'

'Ah, poor James!' said Eliza. 'He was no great trouble to

us. You wouldn't hear him in the house any more than now. Still, I know he's gone and all to that . . .'

'It's when it's all over that you'll miss him,' said my aunt.

'I know that,' said Eliza. 'I won't be bringing him in his cup of beef tea any more, nor you, ma'am, send him his snuff. Ah, poor James!'

She stopped, as if she were communing with the past, and then said shrewdly:

'Mind you, I noticed there was something queer coming over him latterly. Whenever I'd bring in his soup to him there, I'd find him with his breviary fallen to the floor, lying back in the chair and his mouth open.'

She laid a finger against her nose and frowned; then she continued:

'But still and all he kept on saying that before the summer was over he'd go out for a drive one fine day just to see the old house again where we were all born down in Irishtown, and take me and Nannie with him. If we could only get one of them new-fangled carriages that makes no noise that Father O'Rourke told him about, them with the rheumatic wheels, for the day cheap — he said, at Johnny Rush's over the way there and drive out the three of us together of a Sunday evening. He had his mind set on that . . . Poor James!'

'The Lord have mercy on his soul!' said my aunt.

Eliza took out her handkerchief and wiped her eyes with it. Then she put it back again in her pocket and gazed into the empty grate for some time without speaking.

'He was too scrupulous always,' she said. 'The duties of the priesthood was too much for him. And then his life was, you might say, crossed.'

'Yes,' said my aunt. 'He was a disappointed man. You could see that.'

A silence took possession of the little room and, under cover of it, I approached the table and tasted my sherry and then returned quietly to my chair in the corner. Eliza seemed to have fallen into a deep reverie. We waited respectfully for her to break the silence: and after a long pause she said slowly:

'It was that chalice he broke ... That was the beginning of it. Of course, they say it was all right, that it contained nothing, I mean. But still ... They say it was the boy's fault. But poor James was so nervous, God be merciful to him!'

'And was that it?' said my aunt. 'I heard something...'

Eliza nodded.

'That affected his mind,' she said. 'After that he began to mope by himself, talking to no one and wandering about by himself. So one night he was wanted for to go on a call and they couldn't find him anywhere. They looked high up and low down; and still they couldn't see a sight of him anywhere. So then the clerk suggested to try the chapel. So then they got the keys and opened the chapel, and the clerk and Father O'Rourke and another priest that was there brought in a light for to look for him ... And what do you think but there he was, sitting up by himself in the dark in his confession-box, wide-awake and laughing-like softly to himself?'

She stopped suddenly as if to listen. I too listened; but there was no sound in the house: and I knew that the old priest was lying still in his coffin as we had seen him, solemn and truculent in death, an idle chalice on his breast.

Eliza resumed:

'Wide-awake and laughing-like to himself ... So then, of course, when they saw that, that made them think that there was something gone wrong with him ...'

LIAM O'FLAHERTY
The Landing

Two old women were sitting on the rocks that lay in a
great uneven wall along the seashore beyond the village
of Rundangan. They were knitting. Their red petticoats
formed the only patch of colour among the grey crags
about them and behind them. In front of them stretched
the sea, blue and calm. It sparkled far out where the sun
was shining on it. The sky was blue and empty and the
winds were silent. The only noise came from the sea, near
the shore, where it was just low tide. The water babbled
and flopped along the seaweed on the low rocks that lay
afar out, black strips of rocks with red seaweed growing
on them. It was a spring evening and the air was warm
and fresh, as if it had just been sprinkled with eau de
cologne or something. The old women were talking in low
voices sleepily as they knitted woollen stockings. 'Ah yes',
said one of them called Big Bridget Conlon, an old woman
of seventy, a woman of great size and strength, with big
square jaws like a man, high cheekbones, red complexion
and wistful blue eyes that always seemed to be in mourning
about something. She made a wedge of a corner of the
little black shawl that was tied around her neck and cleaned
out her right ear with it. 'I don't know', she said, 'why it
is, but I always get a pain in that ear when there's bad
weather coming. There it is now, just as if there was a
little stream running along inside in it. My grandmother,
God have mercy on her, suffered the same way.'

'Yes', said the other woman, with a lazy and insincere
sigh, 'there is no going against tokens that are sent that

way.' The other woman, Mary Mullen, was only sixty-five and her reddish hair had not yet turned very grey. She had shifty grey eyes and she was very thin about the body. She was greatly feared in the fishing village of Rundangan for her slandering tongue, and her habit of listening by night at other people's doors to eavesdrop on their conversation.

'Heh, heh', said Big Bridget, looking out mournfully at the sea, 'sure, we only live by the Grace of God, sure enough, with the sea always watching to devour us. And yet only for it we would starve. Sure, many a thing is a queer thing, sure enough.' She stuck the end of a knitting needle against her teeth and leaned her head against it. With brooding eyes she looked out at the sea that way, as if she were trying to explain something to herself.

The two old women lapsed into silence again and knitted away. The tide turned and it began to flow. From where the women sat the land stretched out on either side into the sea. To the east of them, it stretched out in high cliffs, and to the west it ran along almost level with the sea for about a mile, a bare stretch of naked grey rock strewn with boulders. Farther west it rose gradually into high cliffs. Now a light breeze crept along the crags in fitful gusts, here and there, irregularly. The women did not notice it.

Then suddenly a sharp gust of wind came up from the sea and blew the old women's petticoats in the air like balloons. It fluttered about viciously for a few moments and then disppeared again. The old women sniffed anxiously and rolled up their knitting by a common impulse before they spoke a word. They looked at one another with furrowed brows.

'What did I say to you, Mary?' said Big Bridget in an awed whisper, in which however there was a weird melancholy note of intense pleasure. She covered her mouth with the palm of her right hand and then made a motion as if she were throwing her teeth at the other woman. It was a customary gesture with her. 'That pain in my ear is always right', she continued; 'it's a storm sure enough.' 'God between us and all harm', said Mary Mullen, 'and that man of mine is out fishing with my son Patrick and Stephen Halloran. Good mother of mercy,' she whimpered uneasily as she got to her feet, 'they are the only people out fishing from the whole village and a storm is coming. Amn't I the unfortunate woman? Drowned, drowned they will be.' Suddenly she worked herself into a wild frenzy of fear and lamentation and she spread her hands out towards the sea. Standing on the summit of the line of boulders with her hands stretched out and wisps of her grey hair flying about her face, while the rising and whistling wind blew her red petticoat backwards so that her lean thighs were sharply outlined, she began to curse the sea and bemoan her fate.

'Oh, God forgive you, woman of no sense', cried Big Bridget, struggling to her feet with difficulty on account of the rheumatic pains she had in her right hip; 'what is this you are saying? Abandoned woman, don't tempt the sea with your words. Don't talk of drowning.' There was a sudden ferocity in her words that was strangely akin to the rapid charges of the wind coming up from the sea about them, cold, contemptuous and biting, like bullets flying across a battlefield fired by unknown men against others whom they have never met, the fierce and destructive movement of maddened nature, blind, and rejoicing in madness. And Mary Mullen, with her hands outstretched, paid no heed to Big Bridget, but shrieked at the top of her voice, 'Drowned, drowned they will be.' She also seemed to be possessed with a frenzy in which sorrow and joy had lost their values and had intermingled in some emotion that transcended themselves. The sea began to swell and break its back with rivulets of foam.

People came running down to the beach from the village as the storm grew in intensity. They gathered together on the wall of boulders with the two old women. Soon there was a cluster of red petticoats and heads hooded in little black shawls, while the men stood about talking anxiously and looking out to sea towards the west. The sea was getting rougher with every wave that broke along the rocky beach. It began to growl and toss about and make noises as if monstrous teeth were being ground. It became alive and spoke with a multitude of different yells that inspired the listeners with horror and hypnotised them into feeling mad with the sea. Their faces set in a deep frown and their eyes had a distant fiery look in them. They shouted when they spoke to one another. Each contradicted the other. They swore angrily. They strutted about on the boulders with their hands behind their backs, looking at the sea suspiciously as if they thought it was going to rush up each minute and devour them.

Stephen Halloran's wife squatted down on a boulder beside Mary Mullen, and the two women, whose men were out fishing, became the centre of interest. They arrogated to themselves a vast importance from the fact that their men were in danger of death from a common enemy, the sea. Their faces were lengthened with an expression of sorrow, but there was a fierce pride in their sharp eyes that looked out at the sea with hatred, like the wives of ancient warriors who watched on the ramparts of stone forts while their men fought in front with stone battleaxes against the enemy. Stephen Halloran's wife, a weak-featured, pale-faced woman with weak eyes that were devoid of eyelashes and were red around the rims, kept rolling her little head from side to side, as she searched the sea to the west, looking out from under her eyebrows and from under the little black shawl that covered her head.

'Ah yes', she was saying, as she rocked her head, 'I told him this morning when he was setting his hooks in order, not to attempt going out, on account of the day that was in it, because it was this day twenty year ago, if anybody remembers it, that my grandfather died of pneumonia.'

'Drowned, drowned they will be', shrieked Mary Mullen. She had gone on her two knees on a boulder and she had put on a man's frieze waistcoat. She looked like a diver in it, the way it was buttoned up around her neck and three sizes too big for her.

The crashing of the waves against the cliffs to the east was drowning the wind. The wind came steadily, like the rushing of a great cataract heard at a great distance, but the noises of the sea were continually changing, rising and falling, with the stupendous modulations of an orchestra played by giants. Each sound boomed or hissed or crashed with a horrid distinctness. It stood apart from the other sounds that followed and preceded it as menacing and over-whelming as the visions that crowd on a disordered mind, each standing apart from the others in crazy independence.

Then the curragh with the three men rowing in it hove into sight from the west. A cliff jutted out into the sea, forming a breakwater where its sharp wedge-shaped face ended. Around that cliff the curragh appeared, a tiny black dot on the blue and white sea. For a moment the people saw it and they murmured in an awed loud whisper, 'There they are.' Then the curragh disappeared. It seemed to those on the beach that a monstrous wave surmounted it cal-lously and that it had been engulfed and lost for ever, swallowed into the belly of the ocean. The women shrieked and threw their hands across their breasts and some said, 'Oh Blessed Virgin, succour us.' But the men simply said to one another, 'That was the "Wave of the Reaping Hook" that came down on them.' Still the men had their mouths open and they held their breaths and their bodies leaned forward from the hips watching for the curragh to appear again. It did appear and there was an excited murmur: 'Hah, God with them.'

From the promontory where the curragh had just passed there was a lull in the water for a long way and the people could see the curragh coming along it all the time without losing sight of it. They could see the men rowing in it. They said, 'That's Stephen Halloran in the stern. It's a mistake to have him in the stern. He's too weak on his oars for a rough day.' They began to move cautiously down to the brink of the sea, where the curragh would have to

effect a landing. As the moment when the curragh would
have to risk the landing and the black rocks, on which
the three men might be dashed to pieces by the ferocious
sea, came near, the men on the beach grew more excited
and some shivered. The women began to wail. A great
babble of voices rose from the beach, harsh and confused,
like the voices of demented people. All gave advice and
none took heed of the advice given.

The place where the curragh would have to effect a
landing was in the middle of the little cove. It was a jagged
rock with a smooth space at the brink of the left-hand
corner, where a slab had been cut out of it by a thunder-
clap a few years before. In calm weather the sea just reached
level with the rock at half tide and it was easy to land a
curragh there. But now the waves were coming over it
like hills that had been overturned and were being rolled
along a level plain speedily. The men on the beach stood
at the edge of the rock and the line of boulders, fifty yards
away from the edge of the sea. Yet the waves were coming
to their feet when the sea swelled up. They shook their
heads and looked at one another.

Peter Mullen's brother, a lanky man with a lame leg,
made a megaphone of his hands and shouted to the men
in the curragh, 'Keep away as long as ye can, ye can't
come through this sea', but he couldn't be heard ten yards
away on account of the noise of the sea and of the wind.
The curragh approached until it was within two hundred
yards of the landing-place. The people on the beach could
see the faces of the rowers distinctly. Their faces were
distorted and wild. Their bodies were taut with fear and
they moved jerkily with their oars, their legs stiff against
the sides of the boat, their teeth bared. Two hundred
yards away they turned their boat suddenly sideways and
began to row away from the landing-place. Silence fell on
those on the beach. The men looked eagerly out at the
boat. The women rose to their feet and clasped one another.
For half a minute there was silence that way while the men
in the boat manoeuvred for position.

Then simultaneously a cry arose from the men on the beach and from the men in the boat. With a singing sound of oars grating against the polished wet wood of the gunwale the curragh swung around to the landing. The singing sound of the oars and the ferocious snapping of the men's breath as they pulled could be heard over the roar of the sea, it came so suddenly. The boat swung in towards the rocks. In a few moments the rowers would be smashed to pieces or in safety.

Then the women standing on the boulders became mad with excitement. They did not shrink in fear from looking at the snaky black canvas-coated boat, with three men in her, that was cutting the blue and white water, dashing in on the rocks. They screamed and there was a wild, mad joy in their screams. Big Bridget's eyes were no longer mournful. They were fiery like a man's. All the women except Mary Mullen and Stephen Halloran's wife looked greedily at the curragh, but at the same time they tore their hair and screamed with pretended fear. Mary Mullen fell on her face on the boulder and, resting her chin on her hands, she kept biting her little finger and saying in a whisper to herself, 'Oh noble son of my womb.' Stephen Halloran's wife rolled herself in her shawl low down between two boulders and went into hysterics.

And the men in the rapidly advancing boat yelled too, a mad joyous yell, as if the rapidity of their movement, the roaring of the sea, the hypnotic power of the green and white water about them and the wind overhead screaming had driven out fear. In the moment of delirium when their boat bore down on death they no longer feared death.

The boat, the crew, the men on the beach, the women on the boulder were all mingled together for a wild moment in a common contempt of danger. For a moment their cries surmounted the sound of the wind and sea. It was the defiance of humanity hurled in the face of merciless nature. And then again there was a strained pause. The noise of voices vanished suddenly and silence came.

On the back of a wave the boat came riding in, the oars

stretched out, their points tipping the water. Then the oars dipped. There was a creak, a splash, a rushing sound, a panting of frightened breath, a hurried mumble of excited voices rose from the men on the beach. The men on the beach waited in two lines with clasped hands. The foremost men were up to their waist in water. The boat rushed in between the two lines. They seized the boat. The wave passed over their heads. There was a wild shriek and then confusion. The boat and the foremost men were covered by the wave. Then the wave receded. The boat and the crew and the men holding the boat were left on the rock, clinging to the rock and to one another, like a dragged dog clings to the earth.

They rushed up the rock with the boat. They had landed safely.

ELIZABETH BOWEN
A Day in the Dark

Coming into Moher over the bridge, you may see a terrace
of houses by the river. They are to the left of the bridge,
below it. Their narrow height and faded air of importance
make them seem to mark the approach to some larger
town. The six dwellings unite into one frontage, colour-
washed apricot years ago. They face north. Their lower
sash windows, front steps and fanlit front doors are
screened by lime trees, making for privacy. There are area
railings. Between them and the water runs a road with a
parapet, which comes to its end opposite the last house.

On the other side of the bridge picturesquely rises a
ruined castle – more likely to catch the tourist's eye. Woods,
from which the river emerges, go back deeply behind the
ruin: on clear days there is a backdrop of Irish-blue
mountains. Otherwise Moher has little to show. The little
place prospers – a market town with a square, on a main
road. The hotel is ample, cheerful, and does business.
Moreover Moher is, and has been for ages, a milling town.
Obsolete stone buildings follow you some way along the
river valley as, having passed through Moher, you pursue
your road. The flour-white modern mills, elsewhere, hum.

Round the square, shops and pubs are of many colours –
in the main Moher looks like a chalk drawing. Not so the
valley with its elusive lights.

You *could*, I can see, overlook my terrace of houses –
because of the castle, indifference or haste. I only do not
because I am looking out for them. For in No. 4 lived Miss
Banderry.

She was the last of a former milling family – last, that is, but for the widowed niece, her pensioner. She owned the terrace, drew rents also from property in another part of the town, and had acquired, some miles out of Moher, a profitable farm which she'd put to management. Had control of the family mills been hers, they would not have been parted with – as it was, she had had to contend with a hopeless brother: he it was who had ended by selling out. Her demand for her share of the money left him unable to meet personal debts: he was found hanged from one of the old mill crossbeams. Miss Banderry lived in retirement, the more thought of for being seldom seen – now and then she would summon a Ford hackney and drive to her farm in it, without warning. My uncle, whose land adjoined on hers, had dealings with her, in the main friendly – which was how they first fell into talk. She, a formidable reader, took to sending him serious magazines, reviews, pamphlets and so on, with marked passages on which she would be dying to hear his views. This was her way of harrying him. For my uncle, a winning, versatile and when necessary inventive talker, fundamentally hated to tax his brain. He took to evading meetings with her as far as possible.

So much I knew when I rang her doorbell.

It was July, a sunless warm afternoon, dead still. The terrace was heavy with limes in flower. Above, through the branches, appeared the bridge with idlers who leaned on the balustrade spying down upon me, or so I thought. I felt marked by visiting this place – I was fifteen, and my every sensation was acute in a way I recall, yet cannot recall. All six houses were locked in childless silence. From under the parapet came languidly the mesmeric sound of the weir, and, from a window over my head, the wiry hopping of a bird in a cage. From the shabby other doors of the terrace, No. 4's stood out, handsomely though sombrely painted red. It opened.

I came to return a copy of *Blackwood's*. Also I carried a bunch of ungainly roses from my uncle's garden, and a request that he might borrow the thistle cutter from Miss

Banderry's farm for use on his land. One rose moulted petals on to her doorstep, then on to the linoleum in the hall. 'Goodness!' complained the niece, who had let me in. 'Those didn't travel well. Overblown, aren't they!' (I thought that applied to her.) 'And I'll bet,' she said, '*he* never sent those!' She was not in her aunt's confidence, being treated more or less like a slave. Timed (they said) when she went errands into the town – she dare not stay talking, dare not so much as look into the hotel bar while the fun was on. For a woman said to be forty, this sounded mortifying. Widowed Nan, ready to be handsome, wore a cheated ravenous look. It was understood she would come into the money when the aunt died: she must contain herself till then. As for me – how dared she speak of my uncle with her bad breath?

Naturally he *had* never thought of the roses. He had commissioned me to be gallant for him any way I chose, and I would not do too badly with these, I'd thought, as I unstrangled them from the convolvulus in the flowerbed. They would need not only to flatter but to propitiate, for this copy of *Blackwood's* I brought back had buttery thumb-marks on its margins and on its cover a blistered circle where my uncle must have stood down his glass. 'She'll be mad,' he prophesied. 'Better say it was you.' So I sacrificed a hair ribbon to tie the roses. It rejoiced me to stand between him and trouble.

'Auntie's resting,' the niece warned me, and put me to wait. The narrow parlour looked out through thick lace on to the terrace, which was reflected in a looking-glass at the far end. Ugly though I could see honourable furniture, mahogany, had been crowded in. In the middle, a circular table wore a chenille cloth. This room felt respected though seldom entered – however, it was peopled in one way: generations of oil-painted portraits hung round the walls, photographs overflowed from bracket and ledge even on to the centre table. I was faced, wherever I turned, by one or another member of the family which could only be the vanished Banderrys. There was a marble clock, but it had stopped.

Footsteps halted heavily over the ceiling, but that was all for I don't know how long. I began to wonder what those Banderrys saw – lodging the magazine and roses on the table, I went to inspect myself in the glass. A tall girl in a sketchy cotton dress. Arms thin, no sign yet of a figure. Hair forward over the shoulders in two plaits, like, said my uncle, a Red Indian maiden's. Barbie was my name.

In memory, the moment before often outlives the awaited moment. I recollect waiting for Miss Banderry – then, nothing till she was with me in the room. I got over our handshake without feeling. On to the massiveness of her bust was pinned a diamond-studded enamelled watch, depending from an enamelled bow : there was a tiny glitter as she drew breath. – 'So he sent *you*, did he?' She sat down, the better to take a look at me. Her apart knees stretched the skirt of her dress. Her choleric colouring and eyeballs made her appear angry, as against which she favoured me with a racy indulgent smile, to counteract the impression she knew she gave.

'I hear wonders of you,' said she, dealing the lie to me like a card.

She sat in reach of the table. 'My bouquet, eh?' She grasped the bundle of roses, thorns and all, and took a long voluptuous sniff at them, as though deceiving herself as to their origin – showing me she knew how to play the game, if I didn't – then shoved back the roses among the photographs and turned her eyes on the magazine, sharply. 'I'm sorry, I – ' I began. In vain. All she gave was a rumbling chuckle – she held up to me the copy of *Blackwood's* open at the page with the most thumbmarks. 'I'd know *those* anywhere!' She scrutinised the print for a line or two. 'Did he make head or tail of it?'

'He told me to tell you, he enjoyed it.' (I saw my uncle dallying, stuffing himself with the buttered toast. 'With his best thanks.'

'You're a little echo,' she said, not discontentedly.

I stared her out.

'Never mind,' she said. 'He's a handsome fellow.'

I shifted my feet. She gave me a look.

She observed: 'It's a pity to read at table.'

'He hasn't much other time, Miss Banderry.'

'Still, it's a poor compliment to you!'

She stung me into remarking: 'He doesn't often.'

'Oh, I'm sure you're a great companion for him!'

It was as though she saw me casting myself down by my uncle's chair when he'd left the room, or watching the lassitude of his hand hanging caressing a dog's ear. With him I felt the tender bond of sex. Seven, eight weeks with him under his roof, among the copper beeches from spring to summer turning from pink to purple, and I was in love with him. Such things happen, I suppose. He was my mother's brother, but I had not known him when I was a child. Of his manhood I had had no warning. Naturally growing into love I was, like the grass growing into hay on his uncut lawns. There was not a danger till she spoke.

'He's glad of company now and then,' I said as stupidly as I could.

She plucked a petal from her black serge skirt.

'Well,' she said, 'thank him for the thanks. And you for the nice little pleasure of this visit. – Then, there's nothing else?'

'My uncle wants – ' I began.

'You don't surprise me,' said Miss Banderry. 'Well, come on out with it. What this time?'

'If he could once more borrow the thistle cutter . . . ?'

' "Once more"! And what will he be looking to do next year? Get his own mended? I suppose he'd hardly go to that length.'

His own, I knew, had been sold for scrap. He was sometimes looking for ready money. I said nothing.

'Looking to me to keep him out of jail?' (Law forbids one to suffer the growth of thistles.) 'Time after time, it's the same story. It so happens, I haven't mine cut yet!'

'He'd be glad to lend you his jennet back, he says, to draw the cutter for you.'

'*That* brute! There'd be nothing for me to cut if it wasn't for what blows in off his dirty land.' With the flat of her fingers she pressed one eyeball, then the other, back into her head. She confessed, all at once almost plaintively: 'I don't care to have machinery leave my farm.'

'Very well,' I said haughtily, 'I'll tell him.'

She leaned back, rubbed her palms on her thighs. 'No, wait – this you may tell my lord. Tell him I'm not sure but I'll think it over. There might be a favourable answer, there might not. If my lord would like to know which, let him come himself. – That's a sweet little dress of yours,' she went on, examining me inside it, 'but it's skimpy. He should do better than hide behind *those* skirts!'

'I don't know what you mean, Miss Banderry.'

'He'd know.'

'Today, my uncle *was* busy.'

'I'm sure he was. Busy day after day. In my life, I've known only one other man anything like so busy as your uncle. And shall I tell you who that was? My poor brother.'

After all these years, that terrace focuses dread. I mislike any terrace facing a river. I suppose I would rather look upon it itself (as I must, whenever I cross that bridge) than be reminded of it by harmless others. True, only one house in it was Miss Banderry's, but the rest belong to her by complicity. An indelible stain is on that monotony – the extinct pink frontage, the road leading to nothing but those six doors which the lime trees, flower as they may, exist for nothing but to shelter. The monotony of the weir and the hopping bird. Within that terrace I was in one room only, and only once.

My conversation with Miss Banderry did not end where I leave off recording it. But at that point memory is torn across, as might be an intolerable page. The other half is missing. For that reason my portrait of her would be incomplete if it *were* a portrait. She could be novelist's

material, I daresay – indeed novels, particularly the French
and Irish (for Ireland in some ways resembles France), are
full of prototypes of her: oversized women insulated in
little provincial towns. Literature, once one knows it,
drains away some of the shockingness out of life. But when
I met her I was unread, my susceptibilities were virgin. I
refuse to fill in her outline retrospectively: I show you only
what I saw at the time. Not what she was, but what she did
to me.

Her amorous hostility to my uncle – or was it hostility
making use of a farce? – unsheathed itself when she likened
him to the brother she drove to death.

When I speak of dread I mean dread, not guilt. That
afternoon, I went to Miss Banderry's for my uncle's sake,
in his place. It could be said, my gathering of foreboding
had to do with my relation with him – yet in that there
was no guilt anywhere, I could swear! I swear we did each
other no harm. I think he was held that summer, as I was,
by the sense that this was a summer like no other and
which could never again be. Soon I must grow up, he must
grow old. Meanwhile we played house together on the
margin of a passion which was impossible. My longing
was for him, not for an embrace – as for him, he was glad
of companionship, as I'd truly told her. He was a man tired
by a lonely house till I joined him – a schoolgirl between
schools. All thought well of his hospitality to me. Convention was our safeguard: could one have stronger?

I left No. 4 with ceremony. I was offered raspberry cordial.
Nan bore in the tray with the thimble glasses – educated
by going visiting with my uncle, I knew refusal would
mark a breach. When the glasses were emptied, Nan
conducted me out of the presence, to the hall door – she
and I stopped aimlessly on the steps. Across the river
throve the vast new mills, unabashed, and cars swished
across the tree-ridden bridge. The niece showed a reluc-
tance to go in again – I think the bird above must have

been hers. She glanced behind her, then conspiratorially at me. 'So now you'll be going to the hotel?'

'No. Why?'

' "Why?" ' she jibed. 'Isn't he waiting for you? Anyway, that's where he is: in there. The car's outside.'

I said: 'But I'm taking the bus home.'

'Now, why ever?'

'I said I would take the bus. I came in that way.'

'You're mad. What, with his car in the square?'

All I could say was: 'When?'

'I slipped out just now,' said the niece, 'since you want to know. To a shop, only. While you were chatting with Auntie.' She laughed, perhaps at her life, and impatiently gave me a push away. 'Get on – wherever you're going to! Anybody would think you'd had bad news!'

Not till I was almost on the bridge did I hear No. 4's door shut.

I leaned on the balustrade, at the castle side. The river, coming towards me out of the distances of woods, washed the bastions and carried a paper boat – this, travelling at uncertain speed on the current, listed as it vanished under the bridge. I had not the heart to wonder how it would fare. Weeks ago, when first I came to my uncle's, here we had lingered, elbow to elbow, looking up-river through the green-hazed spring hush at the far off swan's nest, now deserted. Next I raised my eyes to the splendid battlements, kissed by the sky where they were broken.

From the bridge to the town rises a slow hill – shops and places of business come down to meet you, converting the road into a street. There are lamp posts, signboards, yard gates pasted with layers of bills, and you tread pavement. That day the approach to Moher, even the crimson valerian on stone walls, was filmed by imponderable white dust as though the flourbags had been shaken. To me, this was the pallor of suspense. An all but empty theatre was the square, which, when I entered it at a corner, paused between afternoon and evening. In the middle were parked cars, looking forgotten – my uncle's was nearest the hotel.

The hotel, glossy with green creeper, accounted for one end of the square. A cream porch, figuring the name in gold, framed the doorway – though I kept my back to that I expected at any moment to hear a shout as I searched for the independence of my bus. But where *that* should have waited, I found nothing. Nothing, at this bus end of the square, but a drip of grease on dust and a torn ticket. 'She's gone out, if that's what you're looking for,' said a bystander. So there it went, carrying passengers I was not among to the scenes of safety, and away from me every hope of solitude. Out of reach was the savingness of a house empty. Out of reach, the windows down to the ground open upon the purple beeches and lazy hay, the dear weather of those rooms in and out of which flew butterflies, my cushions on the floor, my blue striped tea mug. Out of reach, the whole of the lenient meaning of my uncle's house, which most filled it when he was not there . . . I did not want to be bothered with him, I think.

'She went out on time today, more's the pity.'

Down hung my hair in two weighted ropes as I turned away.

Moher square is oblong. Down its length, on the two sides, people started to come to the shop doors in order to look at me in amazement. They knew who I was and where he was: what should *I* be wanting to catch the bus for? They speculated. As though a sandal chafed me I bent down, spent some time loosening the strap. Then, as though I had never had any other thought, I started in the direction of the hotel.

At the same time, my uncle appeared in the porch. He tossed a cigarette away, put the hand in a pocket and stood there under the gold lettering. He was not a lord, only a landowner. Facing Moher, he was all carriage and colouring: he wore his life like he wore his coat – though, now he was finished with the hotel, a light hint of melancholy settled down on him. He was not looking for me until he saw me.

We met at his car. He asked: 'How was she, the old terror?'

'I don't know.'

'She didn't eat you?'

'No,' I said, shaking my head.

'Or send me another magazine?'

'No. Not this time.'

'Thank God.'

He opened the car door and touched my elbow, reminding me to get in.

SEAN O'FAOLAIN
The Kitchen

It was there again last night; not, I need hardly say, deliberately. If I had my own way I would never even think of that house or that city, let alone revisit them. It was the usual pattern. I was in Cork on some family business, and my business required that I should walk past the house and, as usual, although it was the deep middle of the night the kitchen window upstairs was dimly lit, as if by a lamp turned low, the way my mother used always to fix it to welcome my father home from night duty. She usually left a covered saucepan of milk beside the lamp. He would put it on the stove to heat while he shook the rain from his cape on the red tiles of the kitchen, hung his uniform on the back of the door and put on a pair of slippers. He welcomed the hot milk. It rains a lot in Cork and the night rain can be very cold. Then, as happens in dreams, where you can walk through walls like a pure spirit and time gets telescoped, it was suddenly broad daylight, I was standing in the empty kitchen and that young man was once again saying to me with a kindly chuckle, 'So this is what all that was about?' It was five past three in the morning when I sat up and groped wildly for the bedside light to dispel the misery of those eight dismissive words that I am apparently never going to be allowed to forget, even in my sleep.

It is a graceless lump of a house, three storeys high, rhomboidal, cement-faced, built at the meeting point of a quiet side street curving out of an open square and a narrow, noisy, muddy, sunless street leading to one of the busiest parts of the city. Every day for over twenty years I used to look down into this narrow street from the kitchen window – down because of the shop beneath us on the ground floor, occupied in my childhood by a firm of electrical contractors named Cyril and Eaton. Theirs was a quiet profession. Later on, when the shop was occupied by a bootmaker, we could hear his machines slapping below us all day long.

My guess is that the house was built around 1870; anyway, it had the solid, ugly, utilitarian look of the period. Not that my father and mother ever thought it ugly. They would not have known what the word meant. To them, born peasants, straight from the fields, all the word 'beautiful' meant was useful or prolific; all 'ugly' meant was useless or barren – a field that grew bad crops, a roof that leaked, a cow that gave poor milk. So, when they told us children, as they often did, that we were now living in a beautiful house all they meant was that it suited our purposes perfectly. They may also have meant something else: because they had been told that the house had originally been put up by a builder for his own use they considered it prime property, as if they had come into possession of land owned by a gentleman farmer for generations. Few things are more dear to the heart of a peasant than a clean pedigree. It keeps history at bay. Not, of course, that they owned the house, although they sometimes talked dreamily about how they would buy it someday. What a dream! Landless people, in other words people of no substance, they had already gone to the limit of daring by renting it for twenty-six pounds a year, a respectable sum in those days for a man like my father – an ordinary policeman, rank of constable, earning about thirty bob a week.

Their purpose in renting so big a place was to eke out his modest income by taking in the steady succession of lodgers who were ultimately to fill the whole house with the sole exception of the red-tiled kitchen where the six of us lived, cooked, idled or worked. I do not count as rooms the warren of attics high up under the roof where we all, including the slavey (half a crown a week and her keep), slept with nothing between us and the moon but the bare slates. Still, we were not really poor. Knowing no better life, we were content with what we had.

During some forty years this was my parents' home; for even after my brothers and I grew up and scattered to the corners of the compass, and my mother grew too old to go on keeping lodgers, and my father retired, they still held on to it. So well they might! I was looking at my father's discharge papers this morning. I find that when he retired at the age of fifty his pension was £48 10s. 8d. a year. Fortunately he did get a part-time job as a caretaker of a garage at night which brought him in another £25 5s. 5d. a year. Any roof at ten bob a week was nicely within his means. It must also have been a heartbreak to his landlord, who could not legally increase the rent.

One day, however, about a year before I left home – I was the last of us to go – my father got a letter which threatened to end this agreeable state of affairs. When he and my mother had painstakingly digested its legal formalities they found to their horror that the bootmaker downstairs had, as the saying goes, quietly bought the house 'over their heads', and was therefore their new landlord. Now, forty-odd years in a city, even in so small a city as Cork, can go a long way towards turning a peasant into a citizen. My father, as a lifelong member of the Royal Irish Constabulary, then admiringly called the Force, had over the years imbibed from his training and from the example of his officers, who were mostly Protestants and Gentlemen, not only a strong sense of military, I might even say of imperial, discipline but a considerable degree of urban refinement. My mother had likewise learned her own proper kind of urban ways, house-pride, such skills as cooking and dressmaking and a great liking for pretty clothes. At times she even affected a citified accent. When they read this letter and stared at one another in fright, all this finery fell from their backs as suddenly as Cinderella's at the stroke of midnight.

They might at that moment have been two peasants from Limerick or Kerry peering timidly through the rain from the door of a thatched hovel at a landlord, or his agent, or some villainous land-grabber driving up their brambled boreen to throw them out on the side of the road to die of cold and starvation. The kitchen suddenly became noisy with words, phrases and names that, I well knew, they could not have heard since their childhood – evictions, bum bailiffs, forcible entry, rights-of-way, actions for trespass, easements, appeals, breaches of covenant, the Land Leaguers, the Whiteboys, Parnell and Captain Boycott, as if the bootmaker downstairs slept with a shotgun by his bed every night and a brace of bloodhounds outside his shop door every day.

Nothing I said to comfort them could persuade them that their bootmaker could not possibly want to evict them; or that, far from being a land-grabber, or even a house-grabber, he was just an ordinary, normal, decent hard-working, city-bred businessman, with a large family of his own toiling beside him at his machines, who, if he wanted anything at all, could not conceivably want more than, say, one extra room where he could put another sewing machine or store his leather. And, in fact, as he patiently explained to my father, that was all he did want; or perhaps a little more – two rooms, and access for his girls to our private W.C. on the turn of the stairs. He must have been much surprised to find himself thrown headlong into the heart of a raging rural land war.

I left home that year, so I cannot tell if there was or was not litigation at this first stage of the battle. All I know for certain is that after about a year and a half of argufying, both parties settled for one room and access to the W.C. The rest I was to gather and surmise from their letters to me. These conveyed that some sort of growling peace descended on everbody for about three years, towards the end of which my father died, my mother became the sole occupant and the bootmaker, seeing that he now had only one tenant over his head, and that with expanding business he was even more cramped for space than before, renewed his request for a second room.

At once, the war broke out again, intensified now by the fact that, as my mother saw it, a bloody villain of a land-grabber, and a black Protestant to boot, was trying to throw a lonely, helpless, ailing, defenceless, solitary poor widow woman out on the side of the road to die. The bootmaker nevertheless persisted. It took him about two more years of bitter struggle to get his second room. When he got it he was in possession of the whole of the second floor of his house with the exception of the red-tiled kitchen.

Peace returned, grumbling and growling. Patiently he let another year pass. Then, in the gentlest possible words, he begged that my mother might be so kind, and so under-standing, as to allow one of his girls, and only one to enter the kitchen once a day, and only once, for the sole purpose of filling a kettle of water from the tap of her kitchen sink. There was, to be sure, he agreed, another tap downstairs in his backyard – a dank five-foot-square patch of cement – but it stood outside the male workers' outdoor W.C., and she would not, he hoped and trusted, wish any girl to be going out there to get water for her poor little cup of tea? I am sure it was the thought of the girl's poor little cup of tea that softened my mother's heart. She royally granted the humane permission, and at once began to regret it.

She realised that she had given the black villain a toe-hold into her kitchen and foresaw that the next thing he would want would be to take it over completely. She was right. I can only infer that as the bootmaking business went on expanding, so did the bootmaker's sense of the value of time. At any rate he was soon pointing out to my mother that it was a dreadful expense to him, and a hardship to his staff, to have to close his shop for an hour and a half every day while his workers, including his family, trudged home, in all weathers, some of them quite a long distance, for their midday meal. If he had the kitchen they could eat their lunch, dryshod and in comfort, inside half an hour. He entered a formal request for the kitchen.

Looking back at it now, after the passage of well over a quarter of a century, I can see clearly enough that he thought he was making a wholly reasonable request. After all, in addition to her kitchen my mother still possessed the third floor of the house, containing three fine rooms and a spacious bathroom. One of those rooms could become her kitchen, another remain her bedroom and the third and largest, which she never used, would make a splendid living room, overlooking the square's pleasant enclosure of grass and shrubs, and commanding an open view up to the main thoroughfare of the city – all in all as desirable an apartment, by any standards, as thousands of home-hungry Corkonians would have given their ears to possess.

Unfortunately, if I did decide to think his request reasonable, what I would have to forget, and what he completely failed to reckon with, was that there is not a peasant widow woman from the mountains of west Cork to the wilds of Calabria who does not feel her kitchen as the pulse and centre of her being as a wife and a mother. That red-tiled kitchen had been my mother's nest and nursery, her fireside where she prayed every morning, her chimney corner where she rested every night, the sanctum sanctorum of all her belongings, a place whose every stain and smell, spider-web and mousehole, crooked nail and cracked cup made it the ark of the covenant that she had kept through forty years of sweat and struggle for her lost husband and her scattered children.

Besides, if she lost her kitchen what would she do when the Bottle Woman came, to buy empty bottles at a half-penny apiece? This was where she always brought her to sit and share a pot of tea and argue over the bottles and talk about the secret doings of Cork. Where could she talk with the Dead Man, collecting her funeral insurance at six-pence a week, if she did not have her warm, red-eyed range where he could take off his damp boots and warm his feet in the oven while she picked him dry of all the gossip of the narrow street beneath her window? She had never in her life locked the front door downstairs except at night. Like the door of any country cottage it was always on the latch for any one of her three or four cronies to shove open and call out to her, 'Are ye there, can I come up?' – at which she would hear their footsteps banging on the brass edgings of the stairs while she hastily began to poke the fire in the range, and fill the kettle for the tea, or stir the pot of soup on the range in preparation for a cosy chat. All her life her neighbours had dropped like that into her kitchen. They would be insulted if she did not invite them into her kitchen. She would not have a crony in the world without her kitchen. Knowing nothing of all this, the bootmaker could argue himself hoarse with her, plead and wheedle with her to accept the shiniest, best-equipped, most modern American-style kitchenette, run by electricity, all white and gleaming chromium. Even if it was three storeys up from the hall door it seemed to him a marvellous exchange for this battered old cave downstairs where she crouched over a range called the Prince Albert, where the tiles were becoming loose, where he could see nothing to look at but a chipped sink, one chair, a table, one cupboard, a couple of old wooden shelves and a sofa with the horsehair coming out of it like a moustache. He might just as well have said to a queen, 'Give me your throne and I'll leave you the palace.' While as for proposing as an alternative that she could keep her old kip of a kitchen if she would only let him make a proper kitchen upstairs for himself, his family and his workers . . .

'Aha, nah!' she would cry at me whenever I visited her; and the older and angrier she became the more did her speech revert to the flat accent of her flat west Limerick, with its long vanishing versts of greasy limestone roads, its fields of rusty reeds, its wind-rattling alders and its low rain clouds endlessly trailing their Atlantic hair across the sodden plain. 'Is it to take me in the rear he wants to now? To lock me up in the loft? To grind me like corn meal between the upstairs and the downstairs? A room? And then another room? And after that another? And then what? When he'd have me surrounded with noise, and shmoke, and shmells, and darkness and a tick-tack-turro-

rum all day long? Aha. My mother, and my grandmother
before her, didn't fight the landlords, and the agents, and
the helmeted peelers with their grey guns and their black
battering rams for me to pull down the flag now! It's a
true word, God knows it, them Protestants wouldn't give
you as much as a dry twig in a rotten wood to light your
pipe with it. Well and well do I remember the time ould
foxy-whiskers, Mister Woodley the parson, died of the
grippe away back in Crawmore, and my uncle Phil stole
out the night after his funeral to cut a log in his wood!
While he was sawing it didn't the moon come out from
behind a cloud, and who do you think was sitting on the
end of the log looking at him out of his foxy eyes? Out of
my kitchen I will not stir until ye carry me out on a
board to lie in the clay beside my poor Dinny. And not
one single minit before.'

Which was exactly what happened, six years later.

All in all, from start to finish, my mother's land war must
have lasted nearly fourteen years. But what is fourteen
years to an old woman whose line and stock clung by their
fingernails to their last sour bits of earth for four centuries?
I am quite sure the poor bootmaker never understood to
the day of his death the nerve of time he had so unwittingly
touched.

After the funeral it was my last task to empty the house,
to shovel away – there is no other word for it – her life's
last lares and penates to a junk dealer for thirty shillings.
When it was all done I was standing alone in the empty
kitchen, where I used to do my homework every evening
as a boy, watching her cooking or baking, making or mend-
ing, or my father cobbling a pair of shoes for one of us, or
sitting at his ease, smoking his pipe, in his favourite straw-
bottomed chair, in his grey constabulary shirt, reading the
racing news in the pink *Cork Evening Echo*.

As I stood there I suddenly became aware that a young
man was standing in the doorway. He was the bootmaker's
son. Oddly enough, I had never spoken to his father, al-

though years ago I had seen him passing busily in and out
of his shop, always looking worn and worried, but I had
once met this son of his in the mountains of west Cork —
fishing? shooting? — and I had found him a most friendly
and attractive young fellow. He came forward now, shook
hands with me in a warm, manly way and told me how
sorry he was for me in my bereavement.

'Your mother was a grand old warrior,' he said, in
genuine admiration. 'My father always had the greatest
respect for her.'

We chatted about this and that for a while. Then, for a
moment, we both fell silent while he looked curiously
around the bare walls. He chuckled tolerantly, shook his
head several times and said, 'So this is what all that was
about?'

At those eight words, so kindly meant, so good-
humoured, so tolerant, so uncomprehending, a shock of
weakness flowed up through me like defeat until my head
began to reel and my eyes were swimming.

It was quite true that there was nothing for either of us
to see but a red-tiled floor, a smoke-browned ceiling and
four tawny distempered walls bearing some brighter patches
where a few pictures had hung and the cupboard and the
sofa used to stand. The wall to our right had deposited
at its base a scruff of distemper like dandruff. The wall to
our left gaped at us with parched mouths. He smiled up
at the flyspotted bulb in the ceiling. He touched a loose
tile with his toe and sighed deeply. All that! About this?
And yet, only a few hours before, when I had looked down
at her for the last time, withdrawn like a snail into her
shrivelled house, I had suddenly found myself straining,
bending, listening as if, I afterwards thought, I had been
staring into the perspective of a tunnel of time, much as I
stared now at him, at one with him in his bewilderment.

I thought I had completely understood what it was all
about that morning years ago when they read that letter and
so pathetically, so embarrassingly, even so comically re-

vealed their peasants' terror at the power of time. I had
thought the old bootmaker's mistake had been his failure
to understand the long fuse he had so unwittingly lighted.
But now – staring at this good-humoured young man who,
if I had said all this to him, would at once have understood
and have at once retorted, 'But even so!' – I realised that
they, and that, and this, and he and I were all caught in
something beyond reason and time. In a daze I shook hands
with him again, thanked him again for his sympathy and
handed him the keys of victory. I was still dazed as I sat
in the afternoon train for Dublin, facing the mile-long
tunnel that burrows underneath the city out to the light
and air of the upper world. As it slowly began to slide into
the tunnel I swore that I would never return.

Since then I must have gone back there forty times,
sometimes kidnapped by her, sometimes by my father,
sometimes by an anonymous rout of shadowy creatures out
of a masked ball and sometimes it is not at all the city I
once knew but a fantastically beautiful place of great
squares and pinnacled, porphyry buildings with snowy ships
drawing up beside marble quays. But, always, whatever
the order of my guides, captors or companions, I find myself at the end alone in a narrow street, dark except
for its single window and then, suddenly, it is broad daylight and I am in our old kitchen hearing that young man
say in his easy way, 'So this is what all that was about?'
and I start awake in my own dark, babbling, clawing for
the switch. As I sit up in bed I can never remember what it
was that I had been babbling, but I do understand all over
again what it was all about. It was all about the scratching
mole. In her time, when she heard it she refused to listen,
just as I do when, in my turn, I hear her velvet burrowing,
softer than sand crumbling or snow tapping, and I know
well whose whispering I had heard and what she had been
saying to me.

She was a grand old warrior. She fought her fight to a
finish. She was entirely right in everything she did. I am

all for her. Still, when I switch on the bulb over my head I do it only to banish her, to evict her, to push her out of *my* kitchen, and I often lie back to sleep under its bright light lest I should again hear her whispering to me in the dark.

FRANK O'CONNOR
The Babes in the Wood

Whenever Mrs Early made Terry put on his best trousers and gansey he knew his aunt must be coming. She didn't come half often enough to suit Terry, but when she did it was great gas. Terry's mother was dead and he lived with Mrs Early and her son, Billy. Mrs Early was a rough, deaf, scolding old woman, doubled up with rheumatics, who'd give you a clout as quick as she'd look at you, but Billy was good gas too.

This particular Sunday morning Billy was scraping his chin frantically and cursing the bloody old razor while the bell was ringing up the valley for Mass, when Terry's aunt arrived. She came into the dark little cottage eagerly, her big rosy face toasted with sunshine and her hand out in greeting.

'Hello, Billy,' she cried in a loud, laughing voice, 'late for Mass again?'

'Let me alone, Miss Conners,' stuttered Billy, turning his lathered face to her from the mirror. 'I think my mother shaves on the sly.'

'And how's Mrs Early?' cried Terry's aunt, kissing the old woman and then fumbling at the strap of her knapsack in her excitable way. Everything about his aunt was excitable and high-powered; the words tumbled out of her so fast that sometimes she became incoherent.

'Look, I brought you a couple of things – no, they're fags for Billy' – ('God bless you, Miss Conners,' from

Billy) – 'this is for you, and here are a few things for the dinner.'

'And what did you bring me, Auntie?' Terry asked.

'Oh, Terry,' she cried in consternation, 'I forgot about you.'

'You didn't.'

'I did, Terry,' she said tragically. 'I swear I did. Or did I? The bird told me something. What was it he said?'

'What sort of bird was it?' asked Terry. 'A thrush?'

'A big grey fellow?'

'That's the old thrush all right. He sings in our back yard.'

'And what was that he told me to bring you?'

'A boat!' shouted Terry.

It was a boat.

After dinner the pair of them went up the wood for a walk. His aunt had a long, swinging stride that made her hard to keep up with, but she was great gas and Terry wished she'd come to see him oftener. When she did he tried his hardest to be grown-up. All the morning he had been reminding himself: 'Terry, remember you're not a baby any longer. You're nine now, you know.' He wasn't nine, of course; he was still only five and fat, but nine, the age of his girlfriend Florrie, was the one he liked pretending to be. When you were nine you understood everything. There were still things Terry did not understand.

When they reached the top of the hill his aunt threw herself on her back with her knees in the air and her hands under her head. She liked to toast herself like that. She liked walking; her legs were always bare; she usually wore a tweed skirt and pullover. Today she wore black glasses, and when Terry looked through them he saw everything dark; the wooded hills at the other side of the valley and the buses and cars crawling between the rocks at their feet, and, still farther down, the railway track and the river. She promised him a pair for himself next time she came, a small pair to fit him, and he could scarcely bear the thought of having to wait so long for them.

'When will you come again, Auntie?' he asked. 'Next Sunday?'

'I might,' she said and rolled on her belly, propped her head on her hands, and sucked a straw as she laughed at him. 'Why? Do you like it when I come?'

'I love it.'

'Would you like to come and live with me altogether, Terry?'

'Oh, Jay, I would.'

'Are you sure now?' she said, half ragging him. 'You're sure you wouldn't be lonely after Mrs Early or Billy or Florrie?'

'I wouldn't, Auntie, honest,' he said tensely. 'When will you bring me?'

'I don't know yet,' she said. 'It might be sooner than you think.'

'Where would you bring me? Up to town?'

'If I tell you where,' she whispered, bending closer, 'will you swear a terrible oath not to tell anybody?'

'I will.'

'Not even Florrie?'

'Not even Florrie.'

'That you might be killed stone dead?' she added in a bloodcurdling tone.

'That I might be killed stone dead!'

'Well, there's a nice man over from England who wants to marry me and bring me back with him. Of course, I said I couldn't come without you and he said he'd bring you as well . . . Wouldn't that be gorgeous?' she ended, clapping her hands.

' 'Twould,' said Terry, clapping his hands in imitation. 'Where's England?'

'Oh, a long way off,' she said, pointing up the valley. 'Beyond where the railway ends. We'd have to get a big boat to take us there.'

'Chrisht!' said Terry, repeating what Billy said whenever something occurred too great for his imagination to grasp, a fairly common event. He was afraid his aunt, like

Mrs Early, would give him a wallop for it, but she only laughed. 'What sort of a place is England, Auntie?' he went on.

'Oh, a grand place,' said his aunt in her loud, enthusiastic way. 'The three of us would live in a big house of our own with lights that went off and on, and hot water in the taps, and every morning I'd take you to school on your bike.'

'Would I have a bike of my own?' Terry asked incredulously.

'You would, Terry, a two-wheeled one. And on a fine day like this we'd sit in the park – you know, a place like the garden of the big house where Billy works, with trees and flowers and a pond in the middle to sail boats in.'

'And would we have a park of our own, too?'

'Not our own; there'd be other people as well; boys and girls you could play with. And you could be sailing your boat and I'd be reading a book, and then we'd go back home to tea and I'd bath you and tell you a story in bed. Wouldn't it be massive, Terry?'

'What sort of story would you tell me?' he asked cautiously. 'Tell us one now.'

So she took off her black spectacles and, hugging her knees, told him the story of the Three Bears and was so carried away that she acted it, growling and wailing and creeping on all fours with her hair over her eyes till Terry screamed with fright and pleasure. She was really great gas.

2

Next day Florrie came to the cottage for him. Florrie lived in the village so she had to come a mile through the woods to see him, but she delighted in seeing him and Mrs Early encouraged her. 'Your young lady' she called her and Florrie blushed with pleasure. Florrie lived with Miss Clancy in the post office and was very nicely behaved; everyone admitted that. She was tall and thin, with jet-black hair, a long ivory face, and a hook nose.

'Terry!' bawled Mrs Early. 'Your young lady is here for you,' and Terry came rushing from the back of the cottage with his new boat.

'Where did you get that, Terry?' Florrie asked, opening her eyes wide at the sight of it.

'My auntie,' said Terry. 'Isn't it grand?'

'I suppose 'tis all right,' said Florrie, showing her teeth in a smile which indicated that she thought him a bit of a baby for making so much of a toy boat.

Now, that was one great weakness in Florrie, and Terry regretted it because he really was very fond of her. She was gentle, she was generous, she always took his part; she told creepy stories so well that she even frightened herself and was scared of going back through the woods alone, but she was jealous. Whenever she had anything, even if it was only a raggy doll, she made it out to be one of the seven wonders of the world, but let anyone else have a thing, no matter how valuable, and she pretended it didn't even interest her. It was the same now.

'Will you come up to the big house for a pennorth of goosegogs?' she asked.

'We'll go down the river with this one first,' insisted Terry, who knew he could always override her wishes when he chose.

'But these are grand goosegogs,' she said eagerly, and again you'd think no one in the world but herself could even have a gooseberry. 'They're that size. Miss Clancy gave me the penny.'

'We'll go down the river first,' Terry said cantankerously. 'Ah, boy, wait till you see this one sail – sssss!'

She gave in as she always did when Terry showed himself headstrong, and grumbled as she always did when she had given in. She said it would be too late; that Jerry, the under-gardener, who was their friend, would be gone and that Mr Scott, the head gardener, would only give them a handful, and not even ripe ones. She was terrible like that, an awful old worrier.

When they reached the riverbank they tied up their

clothes and went in. The river was deep enough, and under the trees it ran beautifully clear over a complete pavement of small, brown, smoothly rounded stones. The current was swift, and the little sailing-boat was tossed on its side and spun dizzily round and round before it stuck in the bank. Florrie tired of this sport sooner than Terry did. She sat on the bank with her hands under her bottom, trailing her toes in the river, and looked at the boat with growing disillusionment.

'God knows, 'tisn't much of a thing to lose a pennorth of goosegogs over,' she said bitterly.

'What's wrong with it?' Terry asked indignantly. ' 'Tis a fine boat.'

'A wonder it wouldn't sail properly so,' she said with an accusing, schoolmarmish air.

'How could it when the water is too fast for it?' shouted Terry.

'That's a good one,' she retorted in pretended grown-up amusement. ' 'Tis the first time we ever heard of water being too fast for a boat.' That was another very aggravating thing about her – her calm assumption that only what she knew was knowledge. ' 'Tis only a cheap old boat.'

' 'Tisn't a cheap old boat,' Terry cried indignantly. 'My aunt gave it to me.'

'She never gives anyone anything only cheap old things,' Florrie replied with the coolness that always maddened other children. 'She gets them cost price in the shop where she works. Everyone knows that.'

'Because you're jealous,' he cried, throwing at her the taunt the village children threw whenever she enraged them with her supercilious airs.

'That's a good one too,' she said in a quiet voice, while her long thin face maintained its air of amusement. 'I suppose you'll tell us now what we're jealous of?'

'Because Auntie brings me things and no one ever brings you anything.'

'She's mad about you,' Florrie said ironically.

'She is mad about me.'

'A wonder she wouldn't bring you to live with her so.'

'She's going to,' said Terry, forgetting his promise in his rage and triumph.

'She is, I hear!' Florrie said mockingly. 'Who told you that?'

'She did; Auntie.'

'Don't mind her at all, little boy,' Florrie said severely. 'She lives with her mother, and her mother wouldn't let you live with her.'

'Well, she's not going to live with her any more,' Terry said, knowing he had the better of her at last. 'She's going to get married.'

'Who is she going to get married to?' Florrie asked casually, but Terry could see she was impressed.

'A man in England, and I'm going to live with them. So there!'

'A man in England?' Florrie repeated, and Terry saw he had really knocked the stuffing out of her this time. Florrie had no one to bring her to England, and the jealousy was driving her mad. 'And I suppose you're going?' she asked bitterly.

'I am going,' Terry said, wild with excitement to see her overthrown; the grand lady who for all her airs had no one to bring her to England with them. 'And I'm getting a bike of my own. So now!'

'Is that what she told you?' Florrie asked with a hatred and contempt that made him more furious still.

'She's going to, she's going to,' he shouted furiously.

'Ah, she's only codding you, little boy,' Florrie said contemptuously, splashing her long legs in the water while she continued to fix him with the same dark, evil, round-eyed look, exactly like a witch in a storybook. 'Why did she send you down here at all so?'

'She didn't send me,' Terry said, stooping to fling a handful of water in her face.

'But sure, I thought everyone knew that,' she said idly, merely averting her face slightly to avoid the splashes.

'She lets on to be your aunt but we all know she's your mother.'

'She isn't,' shrieked Terry. 'My mother is dead.'

'Ah, that's only what they always tell you,' Florrie replied quietly. 'That's what they told me too, but I knew it was lies. Your mother isn't dead at all, little boy. She got into trouble with a man and her mother made her send you down here to get rid of you. The whole village knows that.'

'God will kill you stone dead for a dirty liar, Florrie Clancy,' he said and then threw himself on her and began to pummel her with his little fat fists. But he hadn't the strength, and she merely pushed him off lightly and got up on the grassy bank, flushed and triumphant, pretending to smooth down the front of her dress.

'Don't be codding yourself that you're going to England at all, little boy,' she said reprovingly. 'Sure, who'd want you? Jesus knows I'm sorry for you,' she added with mock pity, 'and I'd like to do what I could for you, but you have no sense.'

Then she went off in the direction of the wood, turning once or twice to give him her strange stare. He glared after her and danced and shrieked with hysterical rage. He had no idea what she meant, but he felt that she had got the better of him after all. 'A big, bloody brute of nine,' he said, and then began to run through the woods to the cottage, sobbing. He knew that God would kill her for the lies she had told, but if God didn't, Mrs Early would. Mrs Early was pegging up clothes on the line and peered down at him sourly.

'What ails you now didn't ail you before?' she asked.

'Florrie Clancy was telling lies,' he shrieked, his fat face black with fury. 'Big bloody brute!'

'Botheration to you and Florrie Clancy!' said Mrs Early. 'Look at the cut of you! Come here till I wipe your nose.'

'She said my aunt wasn't my aunt at all,' he cried.

'She what?' Mrs Early asked incredulously.

'She said she was my mother – Auntie that gave me the boat,' he said through his tears.

'Aha,' Mrs Early said grimly, 'let me catch her around here again and I'll toast her backside for her, and that's what she wants, the little vagabond! Whatever your mother might do, she was a decent woman, but the dear knows who that one is or where she came from.'

3

All the same it was a bad business for Terry. A very bad business! It is all very well having fights, but not when you're only five and live a mile away from the village, and there is nowhere for you to go but across the footbridge to the little railway station and the main road where you wouldn't see another kid once in a week. He'd have been very glad to make it up with Florrie, but she knew she had done wrong and that Mrs Early was only lying in wait for her to ask her what she meant.

And to make it worse, his aunt didn't come for months. When she did, she came unexpectedly and Terry had to change his clothes in a hurry because there was a car waiting for them at the station. The car made up to Terry for the disappointment (he had never been in a car before), and to crown it, they were going to the seaside, and his aunt had brought him a brand-new bucket and spade.

They crossed the river by the little wooden bridge and there in the yard of the station was a posh grey car and a tall man beside it whom Terry hadn't seen before. He was a posh-looking fellow too, with a grey hat and a nice manner, but Terry didn't pay him much attention at first. He was too interested in the car.

'This is Mr Walker, Terry,' his aunt said in her loud way. 'Shake hands with him nicely.'

'How're ye, mister?' said Terry.

'But this fellow is a blooming boxer,' Mr Walker cried, letting on to be frightened of him. 'Do you box, young Samson?' he asked.

'I do not,' said Terry, scrambling into the back of the

car and climbing up on the seat. 'Hey, mister, will we go through the village?' he added.

'What do you want to go through the village for?' asked Mr Walker.

'He wants to show off,' said his aunt with a chuckle. 'Don't you, Terry?'

'I do,' said Terry.

'Sound judge!' said Mr Walker, and they drove along the main road and up through the village street just as Mass was ending, and Terry, hurling himself from side to side, shouted to all the people he knew. First they gaped, then they laughed, finally they waved back. Terry kept shouting messages but they were lost in the noise and rush of the car. 'Billy! Billy!' he screamed when he saw Billy Early outside the church. 'This is my aunt's car. We're going for a spin. I have a bucket and spade.' Florrie was standing outside the post office with her hands behind her back. Full of magnanimity and self-importance, Terry gave her a special shout and his aunt leaned out and and waved, but though Florrie looked up she let on not to recognise them. That was Florrie all out, jealous even of the car!

Terry had not seen the sea before, and it looked so queer that he decided it was probably England. It was a nice place enough but a bit on the draughty side. There were whitewashed houses all along the beach. His aunt undressed him and made him put on bright blue bathing-drawers, but when he felt the wind he shivered and sobbed and clasped himself despairingly under the armpits.

'Ah, wisha, don't be such a baby!' his aunt said crossly.

She and Mr Walker undressed too and led him by the hand to the edge of the water. His terror and misery subsided and he sat in a shallow place, letting the bright waves crumple on his shiny little belly. They were so like lemonade that he kept on tasting them, but they tasted salt. He decided that if this was England it was all right, though he would have preferred it with a park and a bicycle. There were other children making sandcastles and he decided to do the same, but after a while, to his great annoyance, Mr Walker came to help him. Terry couldn't see why, with all that sand, he wouldn't go and make castles of his own.

'Now we want a gate, don't we?' Mr Walker asked officiously.

'All right, all right, all right,' said Terry in disgust. 'Now, you go and play over there.'

'Wouldn't you like to have a daddy like me, Terry?' Mr Walker asked suddenly.

'I don't know,' replied Terry. 'I'll ask Auntie. That's the gate now.'

'I think you'd like it where I live,' said Mr Walker. 'We've much nicer places there.'

'Have you?' asked Terry with interest. 'What sort of places?'

'Oh, you know – roundabouts and swings and things like that.'

'And parks?' asked Terry.

'Yes, parks.'

'Will we go there now?' asked Terry eagerly.

'Well, we couldn't go there today; not without a boat. It's in England, you see; right at the other side of all that water.'

'Are you the man that's going to marry Auntie?' Terry asked, so flabbergasted that he lost his balance and fell.

'Now, who told you I was going to marry Auntie?' asked Mr Walker, who seemed astonished too.

'She did,' said Terry.

'Did she, by jove?' Mr Walker exclaimed with a laugh. 'Well, I think it might be a very good thing for all of us, yourself included. What else did she tell you?'

'That you'd buy me a bike,' said Terry promptly. 'Will you?'

'Sure thing,' Mr Walker said gravely. 'First thing we'll get when you come to live with me. Is that a bargain?'

'That's a bargain,' said Terry.

'Shake,' said Mr Walker, holding out his hand.

'Shake,' replied Terry, spitting on his own.

He was content with the idea of Mr Walker as a father. He could see he'd make a good one. He had the right principles.

They had their tea on the strand and then got back late to the station. The little lamps were lit on the platform. At the other side of the valley the high hills were masked in dark trees and no light showed the position of the Earlys' cottage. Terry was tired; he didn't want to leave the car, and began to whine.

'Hurry up now, Terry,' his aunt said briskly as she lifted him out. 'Say night-night to Mr Walker.'

Terry stood in front of Mr Walker, who had got out before him, and then bowed his head.

'Aren't you going to say goodnight, old man?' Mr Walker asked in surprise.

Terry looked up at the reproach in his voice and then threw himself blindly about his knees and buried his face in his trousers. Mr Walker laughed and patted Terry's shoulder. His voice was quite different when he spoke again.

'Cheer up, Terry,' he said. 'We'll have good times yet.'

'Come along now, Terry,' his aunt said in a brisk official voice that terrified him.

'What's wrong, old man?' Mr Walker asked.

'I want to stay with you,' Terry whispered, beginning to sob. 'I don't want to stay here. I want to go back to England with you.'

'Want to come back to England with me, do you?' Mr Walker repeated. 'Well, I'm not going back tonight, Terry, but if you ask Auntie nicely we might manage it another day.'

'It's no use stuffing up the child with ideas like that,' she said sharply.

'You seem to have done that pretty well already,' Mr Walker said quietly. 'So you see, Terry, we can't manage it tonight. We must leave it for another day. Run along with Auntie now.'

'No, no, no,' Terry shrieked, trying to evade his aunt's arms. 'She only wants to get rid of me.'

'Now, who told you that wicked nonsense, Terry?' Mr Walker said severely.

'It's true, it's true,' said Terry. 'She's not my auntie. She's my mother.'

Even as he said it he knew it was dreadful. It was what Florrie Clancy said, and she hated his auntie. He knew it even more from the silence that fell on the other two. His aunt looked down at him and her look frightened him.

'Terry,' she said with a change of tone, 'you're to come with me at once and no more of this nonsense.'

'Let him to me,' Mr Walker said shortly. 'I'll find the place.'

She did so and at once Terry stopped kicking and whining and nosed his way into Mr Walker's shoulder. He knew the Englishman was for him. Besides he was very tired. He was half asleep already. When he heard Mr Walker's step on the planks of the wooden bridge he looked up and saw the dark hillside, hooded with pines, and the river like lead in the last light. He woke again in the little dark bedroom which he shared with Billy. He was sitting on Mr Walker's knee and Mr Walker was taking off his shoes.

'My bucket,' he sighed.

'Oh, by gum, lad,' Mr Walker said, 'I'd nearly forgotten your bucket.'

4

Every Sunday after, wet or fine, Terry found his way across the footbridge and the railway station to the main road. There was a pub there, and men came up from the valley and sat on the wall outside, waiting for the coast to be clear to slip in for a drink. In case there might be any danger of having to leave them behind, Terry brought his bucket and spade as well. You never knew when you'd need things like those. He sat at the foot of the wall near the men, where he could see the buses and cars coming from both directions. Sometimes a grey car like Mr Walker's appeared from around the corner and he waddled up the road towards

it, but the driver's face was always a disappointment. In
the evenings when the first buses were coming back he
returned to the cottage and Mrs Early scolded him for
moping and whining. He blamed himself a lot because all
the trouble began when he broke his word to his aunt.

One Sunday, Florrie came up the main road from the
village. She went past him slowly, waiting for him to speak
to her, but he wouldn't. It was all her fault, really. Then
she stopped and turned to speak to him. It was clear that
she knew he'd be there and had come to see him and make
it up.

'Is it anyone you're waiting for, Terry?' she asked.

'Never mind,' Terry replied rudely.

'Because if you're waiting for your aunt, she's not coming,' Florrie went on gently.

Another time Terry wouldn't have entered into conversation, but now he felt so mystified that he would have
spoken to anyone who could tell him what was keeping his
aunt and Mr Walker. It was terrible to be only five, because
nobody ever told you anything.

'How do you know?' he asked.

'Miss Clancy said it,' replied Florrie confidently. 'Miss
Clancy knows everything. She hears it all in the post office.
And the man with the grey car isn't coming either. He went
back to England.'

Terry began to snivel softly. He had been afraid that Mr
Walker wasn't really in earnest. Florrie drew closer to him
and then sat on the grass bank beside him. She plucked a
stalk and began to shred it in her lap.

'Why wouldn't you be said by me?' she asked reproachfully. 'You know I was always your girl and I wouldn't tell
you a lie?'

'But why did Mr Walker go back to England?' he asked.

'Because your aunt wouldn't go with him.'

'She said she would.'

'Her mother wouldn't let her. He was married already.
If she went with him he'd have brought you as well. You're
lucky he didn't.'

'Why?'

'Because he was a Protestant,' Florrie said primly. 'Protestants have no proper religion like us.'

Terry did his best to grasp how having a proper religion made up to a fellow for the loss of a house with lights that went off and on, a park and a bicycle, but he realised he was too young. At five it was still too deep for him.

'But why doesn't Auntie come down like she always did?'

'Because she married another fellow and he wouldn't like it.'

'Why wouldn't he like it?'

'Because it wouldn't be right,' Florrie replied almost pityingly. 'Don't you see, the English fellow have no proper religion, so he wouldn't mind, but the fellow she married owns the shop she works in, and Miss Clancy says 'tis surprising he married her at all, and he wouldn't like her to be coming here to see you. She'll be having proper children now, you see.'

'Aren't we proper children?'

'Ah, no, we're not,' Florrie said despondently.

'What's wrong with us?'

That was a question that Florrie had often asked herself, but she was too proud to show a small boy like Terry that she hadn't discovered the answer.

'Everything,' she sighed.

'Florrie Clancy,' shouted one of the men outside the pub, 'what are you doing to that kid?'

'I'm doing nothing to him,' she replied in a scandalised tone, starting as though from a dream. 'He shouldn't be here by himself at all. He'll get run over ... Come on home with me now, Terry,' she added, taking his hand.

'She said she'd bring me to England and give me a bike of my own,' Terry wailed as they crossed the tracks.

'She was only codding,' Florrie said confidently. Her tone changed gradually; it was becoming fuller, more scornful. 'She'll forget all about you when she has other kids. Miss Clancy says they're all the same. She says there isn't one of them worth bothering your head about, that

127

they never think of anyone only themselves. She says my father has pots of money. If you were in with me I might marry you when you're a bit more grown-up.'

She led him up the short cut through the woods. The trees were turning all colours. Then she sat on the grass and sedately smoothed her frock about her knees.

'What are you crying for?' she asked reproachfully. 'It was all your fault. I was always your girl. Even Mrs Early said it. I always took your part when the others were against you. I wanted you not to be said by that old one and her promises, but you cared more for her and her old toys than you did for me. I told you what she was, but you wouldn't believe me, and now, look at you! If you'll swear to be always in with me I'll be your girl again. Will you?'

'I will,' said Terry.

She put her arms about him and he fell asleep, but she remained solemnly holding him, looking at him with detached and curious eyes. He was hers at last. There were no more rivals. She fell asleep too and did not notice the evening train go up the valley. It was all lit up. The evenings were drawing in.

PATRICK BOYLE
At Night All Cats Are Grey

Unwillingly he drifted up from sleep, burrowing deeper into the blankets, pulling around him the tattered fabric of his dream, clutching vainly at the urgent, embracing, anonymous arms that were slipping away into oblivion.

It was no use. The throbbing head, the parched and gritty palate drove him relentlessly awake. Soon nothing remained of the fierce demanding fingers tearing at his neck but an irritation below one ear.

He touched the spot. It was sore all right. Cautiously he explored elbows and knees. Nothing the matter there, thank God. Though it would be no surprise to find them bruised and cut. The whiskey that the publicans were dishing out these days was young enough to give you falling sickness. A few glasses and there you were – plunging around like a bee in a bottle. And, of course, the memory gone. Except for the inevitable glimpse of disaster. The close-up of a man's astonished face, streaked and frothed with porter. An uptilted shot of the underside of a lavatory cistern framed in what appeared to be the wooden seat of a W.C. The slow dissolve of a lower set of dentures grinning from a pool of puke. Just enough information to warn you of worse to come.

He rubbed his neck gently, trying to trace the outline of the injury. Barbed wire, perhaps? Or a thorn hedge? Could there have been a police raid on the last pub you were in? Maybe you were pushed out the back door, to stagger round blindly in the darkness, blundering against porter barrels, sheets of zinc, clothes-lines, empty bottles, in an effort to make a getaway? Were you caught? And questioned?

At this thought he squeezed his closed eyes tighter shut to dam up the flood of memories that might burst upon him.

It was all the fault of that wretched little mouse-about, Quigley – the curse of Christ on his hungry carcase. Serving up a bottle of stout that was no better than porter swill.

'Impossible to get the stout in condition this cold weather, Master James,' he whines, trying to raise a top on it by playing yo-yo with the bottle.

All because he's too mean to provide enough heat in his bar to condition the stout and warm his customers. By the time you've dealt with the flat, teeth-chattering brew you're just about ready to throw back a few whiskeys to warm your petrified stomach.

'A whiskey? I've a nice drop of Irish here. Ten year old. A large tumbler, as usual? And up to the top with aqua!'

When a publican elects to water your whiskey for you, it's time to watch out. But, of course, you know better. What matter if it smells like linoleum and tastes like first-run poteen? Drink enough of it and you don't notice. By closing time . . .

What time did you leave anyway? The last remembered sequence is of a foggy distorted Quigley mopping up the counter, from which all customers have, for some reason or other, retreated. Quigley is speaking but, due to faulty dubbing, the words do not synchronise with the movements of his mouth.

'That will be twelve shillings, Master James. And three shillings for the broken glasses.'

This scene, shot in blinding unforgettable Technicolour, ends abruptly with the sound of a heavy body falling.

After that, a jumble of vague impressions. A distant light, bobbing and swaying (a lantern?) in the darkness. A woman's voice (whose?) calling out: 'Who's there?' The loud ticking of a wag-o'-the-wall (in the name of God, where?). A hand (your own?) twisting the knob of a locked door.

What hell time did you get home last night? What shape were you in? Only one person could answer that. He ran a tongue round dry and tacky lips.

'Jeannie!' he called softly.

The shallow rapid breathing from the pillow beside him never faltered.

He turned over on his back, eyes still closed.

'Jeannie!' he called again. 'Are you awake?'

He reached out an exploratory, an appeasing hand, to ruffle gently the tangled mop of blonde silky hair. The breathing changed to a steady purr. It was that bloody Siamese ruffian, Wong!

Well, that was one mystery solved. The locked door. He must have got home so late that the wife had taken avoiding action. This must be the spare room he was in. Another spell of banishment had commenced. And the ruddy cat had followed him into exile.

Obstinately he kept his eyes closed. What reason was there to open them anyway? The window would be in the usual place, looking out on the tiny cluttered yard. The birds had hardly migrated from the absurd and lurid wallpaper. The waxen-faced Christ, with scooped-out incandescent heart, would still stare down on him morosely from the far wall. On the mantelpiece the framed photograph of old Uncle Moneybags, singular vessel of devotion and long-awaited comforter of the afflicted, would still occupy the place of honour, though the old bastard will probably leave all his money to the Foreign Missions.

Did it really matter what time he was home last night? Or what time it was now? Or even what day, for that matter? There was no chance of change, even for the worse, in the monotony of his days. His life stretched out ahead of him – undeviating – settling deeper and ever deeper into the contented rut of happily married constancy. Gone for ever the hope of the unexpected, the

certainty that round the very next corner lurks the fate
that awaits you. Let it bring fear, delight, misery, enchantment – it is all one. The stimulus of change is what really
matters.

Wong's purring had become intermittent. It was now
laced with tiny sighs and moans. Shudders and twitchings
racked his body as he sank back into sleep and, in shallow
dream, stalked and killed, fought and rutted.

There was the life of Reilly! Owing no allegiance to
anyone. Irresponsible. Receiving only gentle chidance for
its sexual gluttony. Above all – discontented and disreput-
able.

The fog of second-rate contentment that fills this house
. . . Ugh! You can hardly see out of the windows for the
happiness clouding the glass. Like a bloody byre on a
frosty night. Gum-chewing cows misting the air with their
placid breath. Sweet-smelling dung-fragrant contentment!
Small wonder a fellow would tear the coupon occasionally.
Like yourself. Eh, Wong!

He reached out from under the clothes and stroked the
unseen furry warmth. A burst of purring broke out. Sensuous claws were flexed on crinkling eiderdown.

Ha-ha, you blackguard! Are you getting notions? Pam-
pering doesn't keep you at home either, does it?

At the sound of her step on the stairs, he pulled the
clothes over his head and commenced breathing loudly and
deeply. The door opened.

'Oh!' she said. 'Are you there too, Wong? Were you
out on the tiles with His Lordship? You lucky males have
all the fun.'

He heard her uncork the bottle.

'Two spoonfuls?' she asked.

He tried to breathe as sluggishly as possible.

'You're codding no one, you big baboon,' she said.
'Come out of hiding and take your liver salts.'

Spoon tinkled on glass. Fizzing sounds. He groaned.

'Sit up now, home-wrecker, before it goes flat.'

She tugged at the bedclothes.

Heaving himself up, he reached blindly for the glass. Why open his eyes? She would be standing there, a fond and stricken Madonna, oozing love and pity and anxiety. And soapy good health and sanity and main drainage and all the other Christian virtues. He heeled up the last of the salts and, gasping, sank back on the pillow, his nostrils still stinging with the spray.

'Hey, wait a minute!' she said, as he wriggled back under the clothes. 'Do I see lipstick?'

He groaned. Surely she didn't think he'd fall for *that* lure.

Throatily she growled:

'Who's been eating out of my bowl?'

Her breath fanned his cheek as she stooped to look. A moistened finger rubbed his neck.

'It's blood, you poor lamb! Were you in the wars again?'

He focused bleary eyes on her. Tall, slender, fair-skinned, blonde hair tucked into a scarf, she stood nervously twisting round her fingers the sash of her dressing-gown. Twisting the blade of remorse into his soul. It was so bloody unfair. She should have married a plaster saint and reared a plaster family somewhere in the Holy Land.

'Go away, Jeannie,' he said, 'and stop teasing me.'

'I'm not teasing you, Jim. I'm just trying to pretend I'm not worried.'

She soaked her handkerchief from the water carafe.

'I'll clean away the blood and see what it looks like,' she said.

Gently she dabbed at his injured neck.

'You know, darling, you frightened the life out of me last night. Kicking and battering the bedroom door. I thought you were going to burst it in. And the dreadful language. You were never like that before.'

He winced.

'Sorry, darling,' she said. 'The blood's badly caked.'

'I couldn't possibly have been as bad as you make out,' he said. 'I wasn't all that drunk.

'And why do you lock the bedroom door anyway?' he said.

'It was and you were,' she said. 'And you know perfectly well I hate sleeping in an empty house. That's why I lock the door.'

'You should . . .'

'It was Wong!' she said triumphantly. 'Didn't I always tell you it was dangerous to have him in the bed?'

Bewildered, he rubbed his throbbing temples. He said:

'What on earth are you talking about, Jeannie?'

'The cat. Some time during the night you rolled over on Wong. And he scratched your neck. You're just lucky he didn't injure one of your eyes.'

As if he understood the conversation, the Siamese got up and, yawning, arched his back, stretching upwards on stiff bunched-together legs like the tentacles of a swimming jelly-fish. With tail erect and delicate grace he stalked, shaking the sleep from each paw as he went. At the bottom of the bed he stretched out, staring at them with disinterest from bleak blue eyes.

'Look at him!' she said. 'The picture of guilt.'

'The cat's not to blame, Jeannie. It was the floor of Quigley's bar. It reared up and bit me on the side of the head.'

She laughed.

'Poor lamb. Always the victim of circumstance.'

She pinched his cheek.

'You're a brute,' she said. 'A callous, cantankerous, guzzling brute. But you're the only brute I've got. So I must put up with you.'

Stooping, she kissed him and whispered against his closed lips:

'Get well, honey. Try to snap out of it.'

Desperately he floundered in the treacly flood that threatened to engulf him. His breathing quickened. The throbbing in his head took on a new, an urgent note. Weakly he pushed her away.

'I must smell like a sewer,' he said.

She pulled away, sniffing.

'Phew! Not exactly Chanel 5. Still, a hot bath and a good scrubbing out of your poor stomach-lining with Cascara and you'll be my sweet little baa-lamb again.'

He groaned.

'Beat it, will you?' he said.

She straightened up, grinning.

'Well, if it wasn't Wong scratched you, it was the claws of my hated rival.'

'Here!' she said, picking up a hand-mirror from the dressing-table. 'Look for yourself!' She threw it on the bed.

At the door, she turned. He was gazing into the mirror, a look of incredulity on his face.

She intoned softly:

> *'Mirror, mirror, on the wall,*
> *Who is the fairest of them all?'*

Through the clink of the closing door she called:

'Don't go to sleep again, lazybones. I'm bringing up your breakfast directly.'

He heard nothing. He was staring at his scored neck. At the three parallel furrows reaching back from jawbone to God knows where on his neck. He screwed his head sideways but could not see where the scratches began.

These were never the claw-marks of a cat. They were much too far apart.

Painfully he tried to piece together the fragmented memories of last night. Had he really fallen in Quigley's? Could he have been in some sort of tussle? Did he stagger against anything on the way home? A fight or a fall would have left a permanent impression on his memory. Of that he was sure. Besides there would be tell-tale bruises.

No! It was something else.

Did he go straight home after leaving Quigley's? (He should have wormed out of Jeannie what time he had come home.) Could he have knocked up some other pub for more drink? Not impossible, but it rang no bell. What about a private house? Could he have staggered in somewhere on the way home and made a bloody nuisance of himself? Been flung out on his ear perhaps? Still no alarm bell.

Wait a moment! What was this nagging memory of a wag-o'-the-wall? Ticking away remorselessly. Where had he run into one of those antediluvian yokes? There weren't many of them around any more. But hold on now! Someone had spoken of one. With a bottle of water used as a driving weight. Regulated by the pouring out or in of a few drops of water. A real leery effort!

He put down the hand-mirror, closed his eyes and tried to concentrate.

Where in the village was there a bottle-driven clock? Patiently he put the question to the blob of colour floating across his eyelids. Like a pendulum it swung, drawn back and forth by his quivering jittery eyeballs. As the clock face began to take shape above the pendulum, he remembered.

Caroline, Jeannie's friend, had bought a wag-o'-the-wall recently at an auction.

Caroline Wentworth! Oh, God stone the crows! No matter how filthy rotten stinking drunk you were, you surely never burst in on the Wentworths – that pair of strait-laced, intolerant, sterilised snobs – to bore them with one of your open-confession-is-good-for-the-soul acts? Wallowing in your own filth so that Michael the Mealy-mouthed could punctuate your disclosures with dry censorious coughs and Caroline be given the opportunity of gazing at you with an expression of irony on her well-bred flawless features.

The images, flickering in vague merciful outline, sprang into focus. A long deserted street, in darkness but for a ground-floor light too many stumbling steps away. Towards this beacon you are making your way, groping along housewalls, doorways, windows, gateways. Bewildered when an entry or laneway sends you lurching into hollow darkness. Watching the solitary light grow nearer and brighter. Beckoning. It promises company. Talk, friendship, warmth, are at the core of its beam.

Then abreast of the window – halted. Listening. The wind, the river, the pounding blood, drowning out the murmuring voices. The fingernail tapping the glass – gently at first – but persisting until a woman's voice calls out: 'Who's there?'

Mewing impatiently, Wong prowled around the bed, padding across his motionless body, eventually coiling up once more on the pillow beside him. Abstractedly he stroked the bubbling throat, his thoughts swinging to the warm, lighted kitchen, the kettle purring on the range.

Caroline is making coffee. Very graceful in an ivory dressing-gown, dark hair gleaming, cheeks fire-flushed. As she moves around, telling in lowered voice of children lightly sleeping overhead: of Michael not yet back from the city; of the need to wait up for his return: of how glad she is to have company to shorten the night: of the sobering properties of coffee when taken piping hot: of Jeannie's kindness to her which could never, never be repaid.

The soft voice murmurs on, settling into the steady drone of the Siamese who was now sprawled out, in abandon, across his chest. He lay on his belly, hind paws outstretched, a front paw shielding his eyes. Like a beckoning finger, the tip of his tail kept twitching spasmodically. At last it ceased and the purring dribbled into silence.

It is a silence with explosive qualities. Caroline is gazing at you oddly. As though something startling has been said. Her parted lips have surely this moment questioned: 'Why?' Or: 'Who?' Or even: 'Me?' Something must be done to shatter this perilous hush.

The halting tick of the wall-clock gives you your clue. Up with you on your feet. Finger pointing dramatically at the poor old wag that is just doing a job of work and minding its own business. 'There's the enemy! That bloody one-legged trickster! Ticking away like an arthritic old tortoise. But God help the hare that gets in its path. It'll get short shrift. It's no use, I tell you. It's too late.' Then, gripping the pendulum in one hand and the bottleweight in the other: 'I've a right to tear its guts out!'

All a lot of old hat. Angling for sympathy.

The next thing Caroline has jumped up. She is beside you whispering: 'Maybe it's not too late, Jim!' You stand facing each other with the click ticking away goodoh, until someone (who?) sways forward.

A sight for sore eyes, surely. The pair of you, locked in each other's arms, bolt upright in the middle of the kitchen floor, the lights full on, the children probably ear-wigging overhead, a scandalised Michael due to open the door any moment and Caroline . . .

Caroline clutching at you as if you were the last tattered fragment of a dream, slipping inexorably into oblivion. Caroline pleading: 'Don't, Jim, please! Please don't!' as if she really meant it. Caroline shivering as you slide a tentative hand along her smooth flanks. Caroline grinding her body against you and moaning: 'Darling! Darling! Darling!' Caroline's fingernails raking your neck before you manage to untangle yourself, soothing her with a promise . . .

'Did you go to sleep again, you loafer?'

Jeannie's voice, from the open door, startled him.

'And, good heavens, look at Wong! Get away, you treacherous brute!'

She pushed the Siamese roughly aside with rim of the breakfast tray.

'He shouldn't be allowed up on the bed. Sit up straighter, Jim, or you'll dribble tea on the bedclothes. It's a bad habit to give a cat.'

Wong, sprawled where he had fetched up, watched with cold, feral, unblinking eyes, as she settled the tray in place.

'That cat gives me the creeps. He looks at me as if I'm a mouse or a bird.'

She sat on the edge of the bed.

'How's your poor stomach, darling? I didn't do a fry. I thought tea and toast might be better. Don't take too long over it. You've only got an hour to go before Mass time.

And you know how sharp Father John is. He hates people coming in late . . .'

Gingerly he swallowed a mouthful of orange juice and battled with his quaking stomach to keep it down. He closed his eyes. Jeannie's voice rippled on – soft, drowsy, meaningless.

'Beautiful day . . . sun splitting the trees . . . quick lunch . . . away early . . . golf date . . . Caroline . . .'

'Wha'sat?' he asked sharply, opening his eyes

'You dozed off, you wretch. You didn't hear a word I said!'

'Sorry, Jeannie. I'm spun out about proper. More sleep's the only cure. What were you saying about golf?'

'Caroline and I are playing golf after lunch. Instead of wallowing in your bed, you should root out your clubs and come along.'

Racked by a violent fit of coughing, he put down his teacup. With streaming eyes and wheezing breath, he coughed and spluttered into his handkerchief.

'We shouldn't have too much trouble gathering up another male for a foursome. The bit of exercise would make a man of you. Was the tea too hot, dear?'

'I . . . I . . . I . . .' He broke out coughing again.

'It's the same old excuse, I suppose. You're in bad form. Couldn't swing a club without your head bursting. But that's not the real reason. I know perfectly well what's wrong.'

Over the masking handkerchief his startled eyes queried her.

'You don't like Caroline. You think she's a snob. Well, she's not. She's just shy and quiet. Why don't you try to be nice to her? After all, she's my friend.'

Slowly he diced and buttered the fingers of toast. Without looking up, he said:

'I never thought I was anything else but nice to her.'

'You treat her as if she were some sort of a . . . what do you call that thing . . . that insect . . . that eats its husband?'

'The mantis,' he prompted. 'The praying mantis.'

'That's it. Like a praying mantis. That's how nice you are to her. And take that superior smile off your face, Mister Superman. You're going to treat her different from now on, or you'll have *me* to contend with.'

She glanced at her wrist and jumped up.

'Look at the time. We'll be late if we don't hurry.'

She rushed off, slamming the door. He heard her call from the head of the stairs:

'I'll run a bath for you and give a shout when it's ready.'

He pushed the breakfast tray to the side of the bed, grabbed up the Siamese and buried his face in the grassy fragrance of neck-fur.

'How's that for service, Wong?' he whispered.

He rolled the cat over on its back. Supine it lay, paws outstretched, purring ecstatically while he tickled its belly.

'Things are beginning to pick up around here, Cattypuss. Eh?'

And indeed things were. The wallpaper was gay with flamingoes, pink and white absurdities, sleeping one-legged with heads wing-tucked: grazing in shallow water, spare sections of their hosepipe necks buckled inward: flying, neck and legs outstretched, like exotic coathangers. From the wall, Christ smiled down on him indulgently. Uncle Moneybag's photograph seemed to promise the certainty of honourable mention in his last will and testament. The sunlit window opened up on a new world – a world of excitement, anxiety, intrigue, enchantment. A world of tip-and-run delight. Where desire prowls its path with breath sucked in and pounding heart. Where sleep is an enemy and daybreak disaster. A world of blanket-smothered coughs: of creaking bedsprings: of faces lit by pulsing cigarettes. A world of lies and cheating and fret and fear where love mushrooms up all-powerful only to creep away on stocking soles, parched and shivering.

Who would ever have thought that a few hours would have wrought such a change in his destiny? One moment faced with a lifetime of boring happiness: the next . . .

He stroked Wong's chops, flattening the cat's ears back, driving little squeaks of frenzy from its bared teeth.

'We'll have to make plans, Wong. Cunning, cat-like stratagems. What would you suggest, my friend?'

The first item on the agenda was to fill in last night's blank patches – where his mind had blacked out. Only Caroline could do that. It would require probing indeed to draw out significant memories without revealing that, for him, they had passed into oblivion. But it would have to be done. Without knowing where he had broken off, he would not know where to recommence.

But how to go about it? One false move and the delicate dream-like fabric of seduction would be ripped to tatters.

'Jim!' The call came faintly.

The Siamese was gnawing noisily at the pads of a hind paw. He pulled its head around gently by one ear.

'Did you hear that, Whiskers?' he said. 'There's the answer to our prayers!'

Jeannie! Of course! She was the solvent that would loosen Caroline's tongue. An evening spent in their company could well be a profitable one. After Jeannie's insistence on his being pleasant to her friend, she was hardly likely to suspect his sudden interest in Caroline and the innocent-seeming questions he would ply her with. And what woman, in the presence of the betrayed one, could resist the temptation of answering with the sly, ambiguous prattle of betrayal?

From the staircase well the call came again, louder:

'Jim!'

The cat cocked its ears, faced towards the door and made to rise.

'Stand your ground, gutless!' he said, flattening the struggling body against the counterpane. 'A little moral support, if you don't mind. We can pretend we're asleep. See!'

She was talking as she mounted the stairs:

'There's a poor way on a man when he's forced to talk to himself for lack of company. Though, of course, if he's

getting hard of hearing he mightn't know he's speaking
out loud,' and opened the door:

'Don't tell me you didn't hear me. I called you often
enough,' and stood by the bed:

'Is that wretched creature still here?' and tossed what
felt like his dressing-gown across his length:

'Come on now, my old hunker-slider! Don't pretend
you're sleeping. You tried that already this morning. Up
you get! Your bath's drawn,' and lifted away the breakfast
tray:

'If there's no harm in a lady asking, what's the significance of the smirk that's cracking your face in half,' and
blew on his closed eyes until he was forced to open them:

'Out with it!' she said, grinning down at him. 'Whose
saucer of milk did you lap up?'

She looked so vulnerable, so young and giddy and innocent, that the thought of betraying her was inconceivable.
He said:

'I was just thinking I might make a few shillings of beer
money by taking yourself and Caroline. A three-ball. Dollar
a hole. And a dollar for dykes.'

'Would you concede a stroke a hole?'

'What do you think, Wong?' he said, running a finger
gently up and down the cat's spine. 'Could we do it?'

The Siamese stretched out a paw and laid it delicately
on his bare forearm. It was a gesture of trust and he was
curiously moved by the pressure of the sponge-rubber pads.
He continued to tickle the cat's spine whilst it squeaked
and cried in slit-eyed ecstasy.

'We may take it that Wong thinks a stroke a hole
reasonable,' he said.

'Perhaps we might have a meal somewhere afterwards.
And a few drinks. Just the three of us,' he said.

She ruffled his hair.

'There are times, Jim, when you become almost human.
Promise me only one thing and I'll sponsor you for husband
of the year.'

'We know what she's after, don't we, pal?' he said,

quickening the stroking pulse. 'We've not to guzzle more than two bottles of whiskey and a case of stout. Nor will we.'

Her hands fluttered in a small gesture of dismay.

'It's not that at all, darling. You can drink as much as you like. You know I never object. All I want you to do is to be nice to Caroline.'

His heart missed a beat. The stroking hand bore down convulsively on the cat's back.

Wong squealed. The velvet paw resting so innocently on his bare arm fanned out, claws exposed. With a swift movement it raked his arm from elbow to wrist.

'Jeeeesus!' he exclaimed, shoving the cat away roughly.

Still squealing and purring fervently, Wong retreated to the bottom of the bed where, with stiff legs and arched back, it danced ceremoniously on the bedclothes.

He stared at his scored arm in dismay. The three furrows, parallel and widely spaced, were just beginning to sprout blood. He watched as it spread, trickling through the hairs on his arm with little spurts like the zigzagging course of raindrops on a window pane.

'Oh, Jim, I told you so!' she wailed, grabbing up his handkerchief to staunch the blood. 'I warned you not to allow him in the bed. You know I did!'

He looked at her with eyes cold, implacable, sick with hatred.

'I told you so! I told you so!' he mimicked, in a cracked high-pitched voice.

He brushed her hand away. Wearily, bitterly, emphasising each word with upturned shaking head he told the stricken tallow-faced Christ:

'God almighty, how I loathe people who say: "I told you so!"'

MICHAEL McLAVERTY
The White Mare

'What about Paddy, Kate? He'll be raging if we let him
lie any longer and it such a brave morning.'

'Och, let him rage away, Martha. He'll know his driver
before night if he ploughs the field.'

' 'Deed that's the truth, and with an old mare that's done
and dropping off her feet.'

'He'll get sense when it's too late. And to hear him gab-
bling you'd think he was a young man and not the spent
old thorn that he is. But what's the use of talking! Give
him a call.'

Kate, seated on a stool, blew at the fire with the bellows,
blew until the flames were spurting madly in and out
between the brown sods. Martha waited until the noise of
the blazing fire had ceased, and then rapped loudly at the
room door off the kitchen. The knocking was answered by
a husky voice.

Paddy was awake, sitting up in the bed, scratching his
head with his two hands and blinking at the bare window
in the room. His face was bony and unshaven, his
moustache grey and straggly. Presently he threw aside the
blankets and crawled out backwards on to the cold cement
floor. He stood at the window. In the early hours of the
morning it had rained, but now it was clear. A high wind
had combed the white hair of the sky, and on the bare
thorn at the side of the byre shivered swollen buds of rain.
Across the cobbled street was his stubble field, bounded on
one side by a hedge and a hill, and on the other sides by
loose stones. Two newly-ploughed furrows ran down the

centre and at the top of them lay his plough with a crow
swaying nervously on one of the handles. Last evening
when the notion took him he had commenced the ploughing, and today, with the help of God, he'd finish it. He
thought of the rough feel of the handles, the throb of the
coulter cutting the clay, and the warm sweaty smell from
his labouring mare.

With difficulty he stretched himself to his full height, his
bony joints creaking, and his lungs filling with the rain-
washed air that came through the open window; he drew
in great breaths of it, savouring it as he would savour the
water from a spring well. As he was about to turn away,
the crow rose up suddenly and flew off. At that moment
Kate was crossing to the byre, one hand holding a can, and
the other a stick. Paddy watched, trying to guess from her
movements the kind of temper she was in this morning.
But he noted nothing unusual about her. There was the
same active walk, the black triangle of shawl dipping down
her back, and the grey head with the man's cap on it. To
look at her you wouldn't think she was drawing the pension
for over six years. No, there wasn't another house in the
whole island with three drawing the pension – not another
house! We're a great stock and no mistake; a great pity
none of us married!

Kate's voice pierced the air as she shouted at a contrary
cow. Oh, a good kind woman, but a tartar when you stirred her. He'd hold his tongue this morning till he had the
mare tackled and then they could barge away. Anyway
what do women know about a man's job, with their milking
cows, and feeding hens, and washing clothes? H'm! a field
has to be ploughed and it takes a man to plough it.

When he came from the room Kate was just in from
milking and Martha moved slowly about the table arranging the mugs and the farls of bread. Paddy stooped and took
his clay-caked boots from below the table. He knew by the
look of his sisters that he'd have to lace them himself this
morning. It always caused him pain to stoop, but what

matter, he'd soon be out in the quiet of the fields where no one would say a word to him.

They all sat at the table together, eating silently and with the slow deliberation that comes with the passing years. Now and again as Paddy softened his bread in the tea, Kate would give him a hard little look. It was coming, he knew it. If only they'd keep silent until he had finished. But it was coming; the air was heavy with stifled talk.

'I suppose you'll do half the field today,' began Kate.

' 'Deed and I'll do it all,' he replied with a touch of hardness in his voice knowing he must be firm.

'Now, Paddy, you should get Jamesy's boys over to help you,' said Martha pleadingly.

'Them wee buttons of men! I'd have it done while they'd be thinkin' about it. I wouldn't have them about the place again, with their ordering this and ordering that, and their tea after their dinner, and wanting their pipes filled every minute with good tobacco. I can do it all myself with the help of God. All myself!' and with this he brought his mug down sharply on the table.

'If you get another attack of the pains it's us'll have to suffer,' put in Kate, 'attending you morning, noon and night. Have you lost your wits, man! It's too old you're getting and it'd be better if we sold the mare and let the two bits of fields.'

Paddy kept silent; it was better to let them fire away.

'The mare's past her day,' Kate continued. 'It's rest the poor thing wants an' not pulling a plough with a done man behind it.'

'Done, is it? There's work in me yet, and I can turn a furrow as straight as anyone in the island. Done! H'm, I've my work to be doing.'

He got up, threw his coat across his shoulder, and strode towards the door. His two sisters watched him go out, nodding their heads. 'Ah, but that's a foolish, hard-headed man. There's no fool like an old fool!'

Paddy crossed to the stable and the mare nickered when she heard his foot on the cobbled street. Warm, hay-scented air met him as he opened the door. Against the wall stood the white mare. She cocked her ears and turned her head towards the light. She was big and fat with veins criss-crossing on her legs like dead ivy roots on the limbs of a tree. Her eyes were wet-shining and black, their upper lids fringed with long grey lashes. Paddy stroked her neck and ran his fingers through her yellow-grey mane.

A collar with the straw sticking out of it was soon buckled on, and with chains rattling from her sides he led her through the stone-slap into the field. He looked at the sky, at the sea with its patches of mist, and then smilingly went to his plough. Last evening the coulter was cutting too deep and he now adjusted it, giving it a final smack with the spanner that rang out clear in the morning air. The mare was sniffing the rain-wet grass under the hedge and she raised her head jerkily as he approached, sending a shower of cold drops from the bushes down his neck. He shivered, but spoke kindly to the beast as he led her to be tackled. In a few minutes all was ready, and gripping the handles in God's name, he ordered the horse forward, and his day's work began.

The two sisters eyed him from the window. His back was towards them. Above the small stone fence they could see his bent figure, his navy-blue trousers with a brown patch on the seat of them, his grey shirt sleeves, the tattered back of his waistcoat, and above his shabby hat the swaying quarters of the mare.

'Did you ever see such a man since God made you! I declare to goodness he'll kill that mare,' said Martha.

'It's himself he'll kill if he's not careful. Let me bold Paddy be laid up after this and 'tis the last field he'll plough, for I'll sell the mare, done beast and all as she is!' replied Kate, pressing her face closer to the window.

Paddy was unaware of their talk. His eyes were on the sock as it slid slowly through the soft earth and pushed the gleaming furrows to the side. He was living his life. What call had he for help! Was it sit by and look at Jamesy's boys ploughing the field, and the plough wobbling to and fro like you'd think they were learning to ride a bicycle?

'Way up, girl,' he shouted to the mare, ''way up, Maggie!' and his veins swelled on his arms as he leant on the handles. The breeze blowing up from the sea, the cold smell of the broken clay, and the soft hizzing noise of the plough, all soothed his mind and stirred him to new life.

As the day advanced the sun rose higher, but there was little heat from it, and frosty vapours still lingered about the rockheads and about the sparse hills. But slowly over the little field horse and plough still moved, moved like timeless creatures of the earth, while alongside their shadows followed on the clay. Overhead and behind swarmed the gulls, screeching and darting for the worms, their flitting shadows falling coolly on Paddy's neck and on the back of the mare. At the end of the ridge he stopped to take a rest, surveying with pleasure the number of turned furrows, and wondering if his sisters were proud of him now. He looked up at the house: it was low and whitewashed, one end thatched and the other corrugated. There seemed to be no life about it except the smoke from the chimney and a crow plucking at the thatch. Soon it flew off with a few straws hanging from its bill. It's a pity he hadn't the gun now, he'd soon stop that thief; at nesting-time they wouldn't leave a roof above your head. But tomorrow he'd fix them. He spat on his hands and gripped the handles.

At two o'clock he saw Kate making down at the top of the field and he moved to the hedge. She brought him a few empty sacks to sit on; a good kind girl when you took her the right way. She had the real stuff in the eggpunch, too, nothing like it for a working man.

When he had taken his first swig of tea she said quietly, 'It's time you were quitting, Paddy.'

He must be careful. 'Did you see that devil of a crow on the thatch?'

'I didn't, thank God. But I've heard it said that it's the sure sign of a death.'

'Did you now?' he replied with a smile. 'Isn't that queer, and me always thinking that it was the sign of new life and them nesting?'

It's no use trying to frighten him, she thought, no use talking to him; he'll learn his own lesson before morning. Up she got and went off.

'Give the mare a handful of hay and a bucket of water,' he called after her.

He lay back, smoking his pipe at his ease, enjoying the look of the ribbed field and the familiar scene. To his right over the stone fence lay the bony rocks stretching their lanky legs into the sea; and now and again he could hear the hard rattle of the pebbles being sucked into the gullet of the waves. Opposite on a jutting headland rose the white column of the East Lighthouse, as lonely-looking as ever. There never was much stir on this side of the island anyway. It was a mile or more from the quay where the little sailing boats went twice a week to Ballycastle. But what little there was of land was good. As he looked down at the moist clay, pressing nail-marks in it with his toe, he pitied the people in the Lower End with their shingly fields and stunted crops. How the news would travel to them tonight about his ploughing! Every mouthful of talk would be about him and the old white mare. He puffed at his pipe vigorously and a sweet smile came over his wrinkled face. Then the shouts of the children coming from school made him aware of the passing time.

He must get up now for the sun would set early. He knocked out his pipe on the heel of his boot. When he made to rise he felt stiff in the shoulders, and a needle of pain jagged one of his legs making him give a silly little laugh. It's a bad thing to sit too long and the day flying. He walked awkwardly over to Maggie, and presently they were going slowly over the field again. The yellow-green bands at each side of the dark clay grew narrower and narrower as each new furrow was turned. Soon they would disappear.

The sky was clear and the sun falling; the daylight might hold till he had finished.

The coulter crunched on a piece of delph and its white chips were mosaiced on the clay. 'Man alive, but them's the careless women,' he said aloud. 'If the mare cut her feet there'd be a quare how-d'ye-do!' At that moment Kate came out to the stone fence and gathered clothes that had been drying. She stood with one hand on her cheek, looking at the slow, almost imperceptible, movement of the plough. She turned, shooshed the hens from her feet, and went in slamming the door behind her.

Over the rock heads the sun was setting, flushing the clay with gold, and burnishing the mould-board and the buckles on the horse. Two more furrows and the work was done. He paused for a rest, and straightened himself with difficulty. His back ached and his head throbbed, but what he saw was soothing. On the side of a hill his three sheep were haloed in gold and their long shadows sloped away from them. It was a grand sight, praise be to God, a grand sight! He bent to the plough again, his legs feeling thick and heavy. 'Go on, Maggie!' he ordered. 'Two more furrows and we're done.'

The words whipped him to a new effort and he became light with excitement. One by one the gulls flew off and the western sky burned red. A cold breeze sharp with the smell of salt breathed in the furrows. And then he was finished; the furrows as straight as loom-threads and not a bit of ground missed. A great piece of work, thanks be to God; a great bit of work for an old man and an old mare. He put on his coat and unyoked her. She felt light and airy as he led her by the head across the cobbles. Gently he took the collar from her, the hot vapour rising into the chilled air, and with a dry sack wiped her sides and legs and neck. A great worker; none better in the whole island. He stroked her between the ears and smiled at the way she coaxingly tossed her head. He put her in the stable; later on he'd be back with a bucket of warm mash.

It was semi-dark when he turned his back on the stable

and saw the orange rectangle of light in the kitchen window. It was cold, and he shivered and shrugged his shoulders as he stood listening at the door.

In the kitchen it was warm and bright. The turf was piled high, and Martha and Kate sat on opposite sides of the hearth, Kate knitting and Martha peeling potatoes. He drew a chair to the fire and sat down between them in silence. The needles clicked rapidly, and now and then a potato plopped into the bucket. He must get out his pipe; a nice way to receive a man after a day's ploughing. The needles stopped clicking and Kate put her hands on her lap and stared at him from behind her silver-rimmed spectacles. Paddy took no notice as he went slowly on cutting his plug and grinding it between his palms. Then he spat in the fire, and Kate retorted by prodding the sods with her toe, sending sparks up the chimney. The spit hissed in the strained silence. The kettle sang and he rose to feed the mare.

'Just leave that kettle alone, Mister MacNeil,' said Martha.

'The mare has to be fed!'

'It's little you care about the poor dumb beast, and you out killing yourself and her, when it would suit you better to be in peeling these spuds.'

'It's little you do in the house but make the few bits of meals, and it's time you were stirring yourself and getting a hard-worked man a good supper.'

'If you're hard-worked, who's to blame, I ask you?' flared Kate.

He was done for now. He could always manage Martha; if he raised his voice it was the end of her. But Kate – he feared her though he wouldn't admit it to himself.

'Do you hear me, Paddy MacNeil? Who's to blame? Time and again we have told you to let the fields and have sense. But no; me bold boy must be up and leppin' about like a wild thing. And what'll the women in the island be talking about, I ask you? Ah! well we know what they'll be saying. "It's a shame that Paddy MacNeil's mean old sisters wouldn't hire a man to work the land. There they have poor Paddy and his seventy years, out in the cold of March ploughing with the old white mare. And the three of them getting the pension. I always knew there was a mean streak in them MacNeils." That's what they'll be saying, well we know it!'

'Talk sense, Kate, talk sense. Don't I know what they'll be saying. They'll be putting me up as an example to all and sundry. And . . .'

'But mark my words,' interrupted Kate, shaking a needle at him, 'if you're laid up after this you can attend to your pains yourself. I'm sick, sore and tired plastering and rubbing your shoulder and dancing attendance on you, and God knows I'm not able. I'm a done old woman myself, slaving from morning to night and little thanks I get for it.' Her voice quavered; crying she'll be next. It was best to keep silent.

'Get him his supper, Martha, till we get to bed – another day like this and I'm fit for nothing.' She lifted her hands from her lap and the needles clicked slowly, listlessly.

In silence he took his supper. He was getting tired of these rows. When he had finished he went out with a bucket of warm mash for the mare. He felt very weary and sleepy, but the cold night braced him a little. The moon was up and the cobbles shone blue-white like scales of a salmon. Maggie stirred when she heard the rasping handle of the bucket.

He closed the half-door of the stable, lit the candle, and sat on an upturned tub to watch the mare feeding. It was very still and she fed noisily, lifting her head now and again, the bran dripping from her mouth. Above the top of the door he could see the night-sky, the corrugated roof of the house, and the ash tree with its bare twigs shining in the moon. A little breeze blew its wavering pattern on the roof, and looking at it he thought of the gulls on the clay and the cool rush of their wings above his head. He shivered, and got up and closed the top half of the door. It was very still now; the mare had stopped feeding, her tail swished gently, and the warm hay glowed in the candle-light. There was great peace and comfort here. Under the closed door stole the night-wind, the bits of straw around the threshold rising gently and falling back again. A mouse came out from under the manger, rustled towards the bucket blinking its little eyes at the creature on the tub. Paddy squirted a spit at it and smiled at the way it raced off. He looked at the mare, watching slight tremors passing down her limbs. He got up, stroked her silky neck and scratched her between the ears. Then he gave her fresh hay and went out.

It was very peaceful with the moon shining on the fields and the sea. He wondered if his sisters were in bed. He hesitated at the stone fence looking at the cold darkness of the field and the bits of broken crockery catching the moonlight. Through the night there came to him clear and distinct the throb, throb of a ship's engine far out at sea. He held his breath to listen to it and then he saw its two unsteady mastlights, rounding the headland and moving like stars through the darkness. It made him sad to look at it and he sighed as he turned towards the house. He sniffed the air like a spaniel; there'd be rain before long: it would do a world of good now that the field was ploughed.

His sisters were in bed; the lamp was lowered and the ashes stirred. He quenched the lamp and went up to his room. The moonlight shone in the window so he needn't bother with a candle. He knelt on a chair to say his prayers; he'd make them short tonight, for he was tired, very tired. But his people couldn't be left out. The prayers came slowly. His mind wandered. The golden shaft of the lighthouse swept into the room, mysteriously and quietly – light – dark – light – dark. For years he had watched that light, and years after when he'd be dead and gone it would still flash, and there'd be no son or daughter to say a prayer for him. It's a stupid thing for a man not to get married and have children to pray for him; a stupid thing indeed! It was strange to be associating death with a lighthouse in the night, but in some way that thought had come to him now that he was old, and he knew that it would always come. He didn't stop to examine it. He got up and sat on the chair, fumbling at his coat.

He climbed into bed, the straw mattress rustling with his weight. He lay thinking of his day's work, waiting for sleep to fall upon him. He closed his eyes, but somehow sleep wouldn't come. The tiredness was wearing off him. He'd smoke for a while, that would ease his mind. He was thinking too much; thinking kills sleep. The moonlight left the room and it became coldly dark. He stretched out his hand, groping for his pipe and matches. The effort shot a pain through his legs and he stifled a groan. At the other side of the wooden partition Kate and Martha heard him, but didn't speak. They lay listening to his movements. Then they heard the rasp of the match on the emery, heard him puffing at the pipe, and saw in their minds its warm glow in the cold darkness. There would be a long interval of silence, then the creak of his bed, and another muffled groan.

'Do you hear him?' whispered Kate. 'We're going to have another time of it with him. He has himself killed. But this is the last of it!'

'He'll be harrowing the field next,' said Martha.

'Harrow he will not. Tomorrow, send a note to the horse-dealer in Ballycastle.'

'Are you going to sell the mare, Kate?' Martha asked incredulously.

'Indeed I am. There's no sense left in that man's head while she's about.'

'Will you tell Paddy?'

'I'll tell him when she's sold, and that's time enough. So off with the note first thing in the morning.'

A handful of rain scattered itself on the tin roof above their heads. For a while there was silence, deep and dark and listening. Then with a tree-like swish the rain fell, fell without ceasing, filling the room with cold streaks of noise.

Paddy lay listening to its hard pattering. He thought of

the broken field soaking in the rain, and the disturbed
creatures seeking shelter under the sod, rushing about
with weakly legs clambering for a new house, while down
in the sea the fish would be hiding in its brown tangled
lair disturbed by no plough. It's strange the difference
between the creatures; all the strange work of God, the
God that knows all. Louder and louder fell the rain. 'It's
well the mare's in that night,' he said to himself, 'and it's
well the field's ploughed.' He pictured the sheep pressing
into the wet rocks for shelter, and the rabbits scuttling to
their holes. Then he wondered if he had closed the stable
door; it was foolish to think that way; he closed it, of
course he closed it. His thoughts wouldn't lie still. The
crow on the thatch flew into his mind. He'd see to that
villain in the morning and put a few pickles in her tail.
Some day he'd have the whole house corrugated. Maybe
now the kitchen'd be flooded. He was about to get up,
when the rain suddenly ceased. It eased his mind, and
listening now to the drip-drop of water from the eaves,
he slipped into sleep.

But in the morning he didn't get up. His shoulders, arms
and legs were stiff and painful. Martha brought him his
breakfast, and it was a very subdued man that she saw.

'Give me a lift up, Martha, on the pillows. That's a good
girl. Aisy now, aisy!' he said in a slow, pained voice.

'Do you feel bad, Paddy?'

'Bravely, Martha, bravely. There's a wee pain across
me shoulder, maybe you'd give it a rub. I'll be all right
now when I get a rest.'

'You took too much out of yourself for one day.'

'I know, I know! But it'd take any other man three days
to do the same field. Listen, Martha, put the mare out on
the side of the hill; a canter round will do her a world of
good.'

And so the first day wore on with his limbs aching,
Martha coming to attend him, or Kate coming to counsel
him. But from his bed he could see the mare clear as a
white rock on the face of the hill, and it heartened him to

watch her long tail busily swishing. On the bed beside him was his stick and on the floor a battered biscuit tin. Hour after hour he struck the tin with his stick when he wanted something – matches, tobacco, a drink, or his shoulder rubbed. And glad he was if Martha answered his knocking.

Two days passed in this way, and on the morning of the third the boat with the dealer was due. Time and again Martha went out on a hill at the back of the house, scanning the sea for the boat. At last she saw it and hurried to Kate with the news. Kate made a big bowl of warm punch and brought it to Paddy.

'How do you feel this morning?' she said when she entered the room.

'A lot aisier, thank God, a lot aisier.'

'Take this now and turn in and sleep. It'll do you good.'

Paddy took the warm bowl in his two hands, sipping slowly, and giving an odd cough as the strong whiskey caught his breath. Whenever he paused his eyes were on the window watching the mare on the hillside, and when he had finished, he sighed and lay back happily. His body felt deliciously warm and he smiled sweetly. Poor Kate; he misjudged her; she has a heart of corn and means well. Warm eddies of air flowed slowly through his head, stealing into every corner, filling him with a thoughtless ecstasy, and closing his eyes in sleep.

As he slept the dealer came, and the mare was sold. When he awakened he felt a queer emptiness in the room, as if something had been taken from it. Instinctively he turned to the window and looked out. The mare was nowhere to be seen and the stone-slap had been tumbled. He seized his stick and battered impatiently on the biscuit tin. He was about to get out of bed when Kate came into the room.

'The mare has got out of the field!'

'She has that and what's more she'll never set foot in it again.'

He waited, waited to hear the worst, that she was sick or had broken a leg.

'The dealer was here an hour ago and I sold her, and, let me tell you, I got a good penny for her,' she added a little proudly.

His anger roused him, and he stared at his sister, his eyes fiercely bright and his mouth open. Catching the rail of the bed he raised himself up and glared at her again.

'Lie down, Paddy, like a good man and quieten yourself. Sure we did it for your own good,' she said, trying to make light of it, and fixing the clothes up around his chest. 'What was she but a poor bit of a beast dying with age? And a good bargain we made.'

'Bargain, is it? And me after rearing her since she was a wee foal . . . No; he'll not get her, I tell you! He'll not get her!'

'For the love of God, man, have sense, have reason!'

But he wasn't listening. He brushed her aside with his arm, and his hands trembled as he put on his boots. He seized his stick and made for the door. They tried to stop him and he raised his stick to them. 'Don't meddle with me or I'll give you a belt with this!'

He was out, taking the short-cut down by the back of the house, across the hills that led to the quay. He might be in time; they'd hardly have her in the boat yet. Stones in the gaps fell with a crash behind him and he didn't stop to build them up, not caring where sheep strayed or cattle either. His eyes were fixed on the sea, on the mainland where Maggie was going. His heart hammered wildly, hammered with sharp stinging pains, and he had to halt to ease himself.

He thought of his beast, the poor beast that hated noise and fuss, standing nervous on the pier with a rope tied round her four legs. Gradually the rope would tighten, and she would topple with a thud on the uneven stones while the boys around would cheer. It was always a sight for the young, this shipping of beasts in the little sailing boats. The thought maddened him. His breath wheezed and he licked his dry, salty lips.

And soon he came on to the road that swept in a half circle to the quay. He saw the boat and an oar sticking over the side. He wouldn't have time to go round. Below him jutted a neck of rock near which the boat would pass on her journey out. He might be able to hail them.

He splashed his way through shallow sea-pools on to the rock, scrambled over its mane of wet seaweed, until he reached the furthest point. Sweat was streaming below his hat and he trembled weakly as she saw the black nose of the boat coming towards him. He saw the curling froth below her bow. A large wave tilted the boat and he saw the white side of his mare, lying motionless between the beams. They were opposite him now, a hundred yards from him. He raised his stick and called, but he seemed to have lost his voice. He waved and called again, his voice sounding strange and weak. The man in the stern waved back as he would to a child. The boat passed the rock, leaving a wedge of calm water in her wake. The noise of the oars stopped and the sail filled in the breeze. For a long time he looked at the receding boat, his spirit draining from him. A wave washed up the rock, frothing at his feet, and he turned wearily away, going slowly back the road that led home.

BRYAN MacMAHON
The Ring

I should like you to have known my grandmother. She was my mother's mother, and as I remember her she was a widow with a warm farm in the Kickham country in Tipperary. Her land was on the southern slope of a hill, and there it drank in the sun which, to me, seemed always to be balanced on the teeth of the Galtees. Each year I spent the greater part of my summer holidays at my grandmother's place. It was a great change for me to leave our home in a bitter sea-coast village in Kerry and visit my grandmother's. Why, man, the grass gone to waste on a hundred yards of the roadside in Tipperary was as much as you'd find in a dozen of our sea-poisoned fields. I always thought it a pity to see all that fine grass go to waste by the verge of the road. I think so still.

Although my Uncle Con was married, my grandmother held the whip hand in the farm. At the particular time I am trying to recall, the first child was in the cradle. (Ah, how time has galloped away! That child is now a nun in a convent on the Seychelles Islands.) My Uncle Con's wife, my Aunt Annie, was a gentle, delicate girl who was only charmed in herself to have somebody to assume the responsibility of the place. Which was just as well indeed, considering the nature of woman my grandmother was. Since that time when her husband's horse had walked into the farmyard unguided, with my grandfather, Martin Dermody, dead in the body of the car, her heart had turned to stone in her breast. Small wonder to that turning, since she was left with six young children – five girls and one boy, my Uncle Con. But she faced the world bravely and did well by them all. Ah! but she was hard, main hard.

Once at a race-meeting I picked up a jockey's crop. When I balanced it on my palm it reminded me of my grandmother. Once I had a twenty-two-pound salmon laced to sixteen feet of Castleconnell greenheart; the rod reminded me of my grandmother. True, like crop and rod, she had an element of flexibility, but like them there was no trace of fragility. Now after all these years I cannot recall her person clearly; to me she is but something tall and dark and austere. But lately I see her character with a greater clarity. Now I understand things that puzzled me when I was a boy. Towards me she displayed a certain black affection. Oh, but I made her laugh warmly once. That was when I told her of the man who had stopped me on the road beyond the limekiln and asked me if I were a grandson of Martin Dermody. Inflating with a shy pride, I had told him that I was. He then gave me a shilling and said, 'Maybe you're called Martin after your grandfather?' 'No,' I said, 'I'm called Con after my Uncle Con.' It was then my grandmother had laughed a little warmly. But my Uncle Con caught me under the armpits, tousled my hair and said I was a clever Kerry rascal.

The solitary occasion on which I remember her to have shown emotion was remarkable. Maybe remarkable isn't the proper word; obscene would be closer to the mark. Obscene I would have thought of it then, had I known the meaning of the word. Today I think it merely pathetic.

How was it that it all started? Yes, there was I with my bare legs trailing from the heel of a loaded hay-float. I was watching the broad silver parallels we were leaving in the clean after-grass. My Uncle Con was standing in the front of the float guiding the mare. Drawing in the hay to the hayshed we were. Already we had a pillar and a half of the hayshed filled. My grandmother was up on the hay, forking the lighter trusses. The servant-boy was

handling the heavier forkfuls. A neighbour was throwing
it up to them.

When the float stopped at the hayshed I noticed that
something was amiss. For one thing the man on the hay
was idle, as indeed was the man on the ground. My
grandmother was on the ground, looking at the hay with
cold calculating eyes. She turned to my Uncle Con.

'Draw in no more hay, Con,' she said. 'I've lost my
wedding ring.'

'Where? In the hay?' he queried.

'Yes, in the hay.'

'But I thought you had a keeper?'

'I've lost the keeper, too. My hands are getting thin.'

'The story could be worse,' he commented.

My grandmother did not reply for a little while. She
was eyeing the stack with enmity.

' 'Tis in that half-pillar,' she said at last. 'I must look
for it.'

'You've a job before you, mother,' said Uncle Con.

She spoke to the servant-boy and the neighbour. 'Go
down and shake out those couple of pikes at the end of
the Bog Meadow,' she ordered. 'They're heating in the
centre.'

'Can't we be drawing in to the idle pillar, mother?' my
Uncle Con asked gently.

'No, Con,' she answered. 'I'll be putting the hay from
the middle pillar there.'

The drawing-in was over for the day. That was about
four o'clock in the afternoon. Before she tackled the half-
pillar my grandmother went down on her hands and
knees and started to search the loose hay in the idle pillar.
She searched wisp by wisp, even sop by sop. My Uncle
Con beckoned to me to come away. Anyway, we knew
she'd stop at six o'clock. 'Six to six' was her motto for
working hours. She never broke that rule.

That was a Monday evening. On Tuesday we offered
to help – my Uncle Con and I. She was down on her
knees when we asked her. 'No, no,' she said abruptly.

Then, by way of explanation, when she saw that we were crestfallen: 'You see, if we didn't find it I'd be worried that ye didn't search as carefully as ye should, and I'd have no peace of mind until I had searched it all over again.' So she worked hard all day, breaking off only for her meals and stopping sharp at six o'clock.

By Wednesday evening she had made a fair gap in the hay but had found no ring. Now and again during the day we used to go down to see if she had had any success. She was very wan in the face when she stopped in the evening.

On Thursday morning her face was still more strained and drawn. She seemed reluctant to leave the rick even to take her meals. What little she ate seemed like so much dust in her mouth. We took down tea to her several times during the day.

By Friday the house was on edge. My Uncle Con spoke guardedly to her at dinner-time. 'This will set us back a graydle, mother,' he said. 'I know, son; I know, son; I know,' was all she said in reply.

Saturday came and the strain was unendurable. About three o'clock in the afternoon she found the keeper. We had been watching her in turns from the kitchen window. I remember my uncle's face lighting up and his saying, 'Glory, she's found it!' But he drew a long breath when again she started burrowing feverishly in the hay. Then we knew it was only the keeper. We didn't run out at all. We waited till she came in at six o'clock. There were times between three and six when our three heads were together at the small window watching her. I was thinking she was like a mouse nibbling at a giant's loaf.

At six she came in and said, 'I found the keeper.' After her tea she couldn't stay still. She fidgeted around the kitchen for an hour or so. Then, 'Laws were made to be broken,' said my grandmother with a brittle bravery, and she stalked out to the hayshed. Again we watched her.

Coming on for dusk she returned and lighted a stable lantern and went back to resume her search. Nobody crossed her. We didn't say yes, aye or no to her. After a time my Uncle Con took her heavy coat off the rack and went down and threw it across her shoulders. I was with him. 'There's a touch of frost there to-night, mother,' said my Uncle Con.

We loitered for a while in the darkness outside the ring of her lantern's light. But she resented our pitying eyes so we went in. We sat around the big fire waiting – Uncle Con, Aunt Annie and I. That was the lonely waiting – without speaking – just as if we were waiting for an old person to die or for a child to come into the world. Near twelve we heard her step on the cobbles. 'Twas typical of my grandmother that she placed the lantern on the ledge of the dresser and quenched the candle in it before she spoke to us.

'I found it,' she said. The words dropped out of her drawn face.

'Get hot milk for my mother, Annie,' said Uncle Con briskly.

My grandmother sat by the fire, a little to one side. Her face was as cold as death. I kept watching her like a hawk but her eyes didn't even flicker. The wedding ring was inside its keeper, and my grandmother kept twirling it round and round with the fingers of her right hand.

Suddenly, as if ashamed of her fingers' betrayal, she hid her hands under her check apron. Then, unpredictably, the fists under the apron came up to meet her face, and her face bent down to meet the fists in the apron. 'Oh, Martin, Martin,' she sobbed, and then she cried like the rain.

ANTHONY C. WEST
Not Isaac

Stephen Muir's father and the three men on the farm always considered that the boy was soft, especially about killing things. They often joked him, hoping to stiffen him, but only enraging him because he could not explain what he felt about taking an animal's life.

When he crossed sixteen the matter came to a head. And that autumn, when a large pig was being slaughtered for the domestic bacon supply, his softness was clearly demonstrated to all, save his gentle mother.

The three men – Bill Brady, John Conlan and Tommie Maguire – had driven the hog into an enclosed yard where it innocently nosed about, having had nothing but rough care and food from human beings till then. Two of the men had heavy sticks and Brady, a sort of untitled foreman, was armed with a seven-pound sledgehammer. He walked quietly up to the animal, measured it, set himself, and swung the hammer, intending to hit the beast squarely between the eyes and stun it till the throat could be slit.

But the pig moved its head slightly and took the blow on an ear. It fell, struggled, Brady roaring at the others to help him hold it down, Stephen knowing they were half scared of it. The beast got up, throwing the three men off, and staggered round in crazy circles, now knowing enough to mistrust completely Brady and his hammer. Falling and rising and shaking its head as if to dislodge the pain, it squealed in terror each time any of them approached it. Brady was annoyed and the others started to laugh hysterically.

Brady chased after it, the hammer ready for a more damaging blow. They united to drive it into a corner, but the animal seemed to have realised that corners were fatal things and, in spite of the urgent shouts and blows, it persisted in staggering wantonly about the middle of the yard.

Brady lost his temper completely and tried to deliver several random blows as the pig dodged about. One swipe struck the nose and another gashed the sound ear.

Stephen had been watching all this from an upstairs window. Normally, he never interfered with the men and the fact that he was his father's son gave him no authority over them. He felt Brady's hammer blows on his own head and desperately tried to think of a way to help the animal into an easier, quicker death.

Both parents were out and old Tilly Magee, the cook-cum-housekeeper, was deaf as an old oak post. Then he remembered that his father had a small old-fashioned revolver in a cupboard. He had often played with the weapon and knew how to use it even if he had never fired a shot.

He found the gun and one ancient shell and ran out with it to the yard. The maimed and bloody pig was snorting in fear and blindly seeking impossible escape, the three men now beside themselves with frustrated, tense rage, their three simple minds locked to the animal as if it must die so that they might continue to exist.

They paid no heed to the boy at first and he had to shout and hold Brady's coat before the man desisted in the crazy chase. He was so full of rage of a different kind that the tears came to his eyes.

The men stopped, self-consciously, their three pairs of eyes staring and bloodshot and, like the pig, breathing stertorously through open, frothy mouths, their lips mauve with anger and exertion. Brady swore coarsely at the animal as if it were at fault for not going quietly to death.

Stephen slipped the shell into the correct chamber in

the gun, handing it to Brady and telling him to hold the barrel close to the pig's head. Then he went away quickly and very soon heard the shot. From his window he saw them hurrying from the boiler house with pails of steaming water and knew that the selfless gun had done its duty.

Afterwards, the men probably felt embarrassed about the affair and to cover up they joked the boy more heavily as if their ferine brutality was all of manhood and Stephen's pale face and tears were weak and womanish. Conor Muir was ashamed of his son's apparent lack of pluck, taking it almost as a personal slight on blood and country breeding, as if the boy had stolen something or in some way had brought ill repute upon the house. And he bawled Stephen out for interfering with the old gun, saying it might have blown off Brady's hand.

Stephen said nothing about the pig. His father would have been angry, not in sympathy with the animal, but because the manhandling might have damaged the bacon.

Brady was Stephen's most articulate tormentor; he had an acrid wit and some self-importance. Conlan was his half-brother and Maguire was his cousin. As their fathers before them, they had worked on the farm since boyhood. The three of them were very alike. They had thick, strong bodies, heavy, red necks, long noses with hairy slits for nostrils, and high, narrow heads. Essentially they were brutal. Their lives had asked them for little learning or finesse. To them, as to Conor Muir, a cow was a thing on four legs with an udder for milk between the two hind ones and worth so many pounds.

Finally, to silence and satisfy everyone, Stephen volunteered to kill and dress the Christmas wether, which was always divided fairly between the Muirs and the men for the holiday. The event was to take place on the first wet afternoon of Christmas week as they had been busy with autumn cultivations made late by a stormy November.

For days the weather remained bright and dry and Stephen remembered looking for each sunrise and wishing the day would continue fine. He knew the gentle beast he

was to slay. He could remember it as a curly, playful lamb.
It was running with half a dozen others in a small field
behind the barn. They all had the white face and high
nose of the Cheviot and were pathetically harmless and
inoffensive. Always they bunched together in the far corner of the field when anyone came to the gate; standing
and gazing curiously and nodding their heads, not exactly
in fear, but in generic nervousness. When one moved
they all moved, seeming to abhor solitariness or isolation.

On the Thursday, four days before Christmas, rain fell
all day and at lunch-time Conor Muir said the sheep
would be killed. His wife said nothing, looking down at
her plate and covertly glancing at her son with a gleam
of sympathy in her grey eyes.

After the meal Stephen saw Brady sloping down the
fields with the dog, a sack over his shoulders to break the
rain and puttees of sacking wrapped around his legs. He
seemed to move with overt cockiness as if in anticipation
of a diversion.

Stephen went to the old larder with its high racks of
wicked hooks from ceiling to floor, reminding him of tales
about medieval torture chambers. Even as a child he had
always hated the place with its hooks and smells as if the
ghosts of the animals it had seen slaughtered had haunted
it.

Conlan and Maguire were waiting for the wether to
come, smoking their rank pipes and spreading odours of
wet, cow-smelling clothes. As Stephen took off his jacket
Conlan asked him how he felt, winking at his cousin.
Stephen did not answer and took up the little sticking
knife and commenced to sharpen it on the steel.

Whet-whet! Whet-whet! the steel said to the knife's
unseen edge almost like a bird call. There was a low,
strong table like a butcher's block, slightly cupped and
black in the cracks with old blood, and the whole larder
smelled slightly of rancid grease and carbolic.

They heard the dog bark and the chopping patter of
the wether's nervous hoofs. The collie rushed past the

beast, turning it back and holding it for Brady to drive into the small walled yard outside the larder door. Conlan and Maguire went out while Stephen waited, his mind now becoming dull and registering every move in slow motion.

There was a slight scuffle over the rain sounds on the roof as the sheep was caught and someone swore at the excited dog, telling it to go and lie down. Then the three men dragged in the victim, one at each shoulder and one at its rump, their big red hands buried deeply in the grey-white fleece. The wether did not bleat or struggle and only slid along the tiled floor on four stiff legs.

Stephen held the knife behind his back, ashamed to let the little animal see it, Abraham and thickets and ancient sacrifices running through his mind. As if the knife itself had bid him he felt his hand tighten on the haft.

The sheep panted with short silent pants, the slitted nostrils moving as the gills of a fish. And its head, its lovely antique head, was wise and beautiful with a terrible and uncomplaining wisdom aware of a long past through which its race had furnished food for knives, bellies, and altars and had heard the sonorous names of long-forgotten gods chanted in gloomy cave, tumulus, and lavish temple.

And its eyes were there, not seeing him nor knife more than another thing. That was the terrible part of it – the virgin, fearless, guiltless innocence. But still he held the knife, the blade against his wrist, for the eyes were grey with kindness, sleepy, and barred with long jewelled stones of beauty snared in honest opal fire.

'Up on the bench with her!' Brady was saying.

They lifted it with unnecessary roughness on to the block. It lay awkwardly on its side, the four very neat legs struck out, the neck and head thrown back as if in fatalistic readiness. It struggled a little and they held it down. It did not struggle against fear or hurt or death, but because it was uncomfortable.

Stephen's hand slowly bared the dull fang of knife and he looked down on it. Harlot it was to any man's hand;

a cruel, strong thing not made for kindness and healing. . . .

'Come on, me boy!' Maguire urged. 'What are ye waitin' for?'

The others laughed. Stephen looked up at them, balancing the knife in his hand, and he could only see three beings holding a fourth down.

Reaching forward his left hand he grasped the beast's satin throat, feeling for the windpipe, then edging his fingers back to the ear, his right hand hardening on the knife haft. Poising the blade just behind the jaw-root, he pressed firmly down without resistance.

The barred eye never changed nor challenged, showing neither fear nor blame. Nor did the body struggle against the mortal wounding. With rigid forearm he pressed the knife home, turning it and outcutting invisibly.

And still the beauty of the eye remained unchanged. Slowly the breathing weakened and blood snored in the lungs, the bright breath-blood dripping slowly from the twitching nostrils with astonishing brightness while the limbs impulsively protested a very little as a worm might curl when a spade touches it.

Stephen withdrew the knife, looking at it curiously, its moist, senseless blade having partaken of a mystery greater than any man might bear, and he was thinking whimsically it was a poor repayment for that first innocent witness so long ago when the barred eyes had gazed on beauty on a mother's knee, their body heat keeping the stable warm.

'Come on! Off with her skin!' Brady was goading, still looking slyly at the others. They had agreed between themselves not to help him, but he knew exactly what to do.

And for him now, the killing over, the beast was no more than an unfashioned stone or lump of unshaped clay.

But his hand was still hard on the knife and sheep smell oozed over his face as he wiped the sweat off with the back of his left hand. The knife locked rigid his forearm and he saw three similar throats, red-necked and slightly hairy with their protruding Adam's apples, arrogant and

ignorant, in minds subhuman and human only in form.
And he saw three pairs of guileful eyes half-smiling at his
lividness and still the ready knife held fast his hand, still
poised, greedy, insatiable, ireless.

He turned to the sheep as it moved comfortably and
sighed contentedly, the eye still barred in beauty's harmless death. Without direction from Brady, he flayed the
carcass and they helped him hang it, then watched him
paunch it. Gently the soft grey guts slipped out of the
gaping belly-slit, pathetic in the indecent exposure, and
still pulsing in their peristaltic action. The birthed, skin-
less form mightily like a man's, pink, marble-fatted flesh
– Death? No. No longer sheep, no longer anything.

For their benefit he even decorated the flanks with little
cuts that made an ash-leaf pattern on the warm elastic
flesh.

When he finished they were full of praise. Suddenly he
turned on them, holding the knife blade between his right
finger and thumb. Then slowly he raised his arm and
flung it with all his strength at the door, the point going
deeply, gladly, into the wood and shivering as with life.

Then he took his jacket and walked out quietly into the
soft clean evening on which the rain had ceased to fall
and a thrush was singing gaily in the sycamore tree over
the larder roof in faithful anticipation of the spring.

MARY LAVIN
Happiness

Mother had a lot to say. This does not mean she was
always talking but that we children felt the wells she
drew upon were deep, deep, deep. Her theme was happiness: what it was, what it was not; where we might
find it, where not; and how, if found, it must be guarded.
Never must we confound it with pleasure. Nor think
sorrow its exact opposite.

'Take Father Hugh.' Mother's eyes flashed as she
looked at him. 'According to him, sorrow is an ingredient
of happiness – a *necessary* ingredient, if you please!' And
when he tried to protest she put up her hand. 'There may
be a freakish truth in the theory – for some people. But
not for me. And not, I hope, for my children.' She looked
severely at us three girls. We laughed. None of us had had
much experience with sorrow. Bea and I were children
and Linda only a year old when our father died suddenly
after a short illness that had not at first seemed serious.
'I've known people to make sorrow a *substitute* for happiness,' Mother said.

Father Hugh protested again. 'You're not putting me
in that class, I hope?'

Father Hugh, ever since our father died, had been the
closest of anyone to us as a family, without being close
to any one of us in particular – even to Mother. He lived
in a monastery near our farm in County Meath, and he
had been one of the celebrants at the Requiem High
Mass our father's political importance had demanded.
He met us that day for the first time, but he took to

171

dropping in to see us, with the idea of filling the crater of loneliness left at our centre. He did not know that there was a cavity in his own life, much less that we would fill it. He and Mother were both young in those days and perhaps it gave scandal to some that he was so often in our house, staying till late into the night and, indeed, thinking nothing of stopping all night if there was any special reason, such as one of us being sick. He had even on occasion slept there if the night was too wet for tramping home across the fields.

When we girls were young, we were so used to having Father Hugh around that we never stood on ceremony with him but in his presence dried our hair and pared our nails and never minded what garments were strewn about. As for Mother – she thought nothing of running out of the bathroom in her slip, brushing her teeth or combing her hair, if she wanted to tell him something she might otherwise forget. And she brooked no criticism of her behaviour. 'Celibacy was never meant to take all the warmth and homeliness out of their lives,' she said.

On this point, too, Bea was adamant. Bea, the middle sister, was our oracle. 'I'm so glad he *has* Mother,' she said, 'as well as her having him, because it must be awful the way most women treat them – priests, I mean – as if they were pariahs. Mother treats him like a human being – that's all!'

And when it came to Mother's ears that there had been gossip about her making free with Father Hugh, she opened her eyes wide in astonishment. 'But he's only a priest!' she said.

Bea giggled. 'It's a good job he didn't hear *that*,' she said to me afterwards. 'It would undo the good she's done him. You'd think he was a eunuch.'

'Bea!' I said. 'Do you think he's in love with her?'

'If so, he doesn't know it,' Bea said firmly. 'It's her soul he's after! Maybe he wants to make sure of her in the next world!'

But thoughts of the world to come never troubled

Mother. 'If anything ever happens to me, children,' she said, 'suddenly, I mean, or when you are not near me, or I cannot speak to you, I want you to promise you won't feel bad. There's no need! Just remember that I had a happy life – and that if I had to choose my kind of heaven I'd take it on this earth with you again, no matter how much you might annoy me!'

You see, annoyance and fatigue, according to Mother, and even illness and pain, could coexist with happiness. She had a habit of asking people if they were happy at times and in places that – to say the least of it – seemed to us inappropriate. 'But are you happy?' she'd probe as one lay sick and bathed in sweat, or in the throes of a jumping toothache. And once in our presence she made the inquiry of an old friend as he lay upon his deathbed.

'Why not?' she said when we took her to task for it later. 'Isn't it more important than ever to be happy when you're dying? Take my own father! You know what he said in his last moments? On his deathbed, he defied me to name a man who had enjoyed a better life. In spite of dreadful pain, his face *radiated* happiness!' Mother nodded her head comfortably. 'Happiness drives out the pain, as fire burns out fire.'

Having no knowledge of our own to pit against hers, we thirstily drank in her rhetoric. Only Bea was sceptical. 'Perhaps you *got* it from him, like spots, or fever,' she said. 'Or something that could at least be slipped from hand to hand.'

'Do you think I'd have taken it if that were the case!' Mother cried. 'Then, when he needed it most?'

'Not there and then!' Bea said stubbornly. 'I meant as a sort of legacy.'

'Don't you think in *that* case,' Mother said, exasperated, 'he would have felt obliged to leave it to your grandmother?'

Certainly we knew that in spite of his lavish heart our grandfather had failed to provide our grandmother with enduring happiness. He had passed that job on to Mother.

And Mother had not made too good a fist of it, even when Father was living and she had him – and, later, us children – to help.

As for Father Hugh, he had given our grandmother up early in the game. 'God Almighty couldn't make that woman happy,' he said one day, seeing Mother's face, drawn and pale with fatigue, preparing for the nightly run over to her own mother's flat that would exhaust her utterly.

There were evenings after she came home from the library where she worked when we saw her stand with the car keys in her hand, trying to think which would be worse – to slog over there on foot, or take out the car again. And yet the distance was short. It was Mother's day that had been too long.

'Weren't you over to see her this morning?' Father Hugh demanded.

'No matter!' said Mother. She was no doubt thinking of the forlorn face our grandmother always put on when she was leaving. ('Don't say good night, Vera,' Grandmother would plead. 'It makes me feel too lonely. And you never can tell – you might slip over again before you go to bed!')

'Do you know the time?' Bea would say impatiently, if she happened to be with Mother. Not indeed that the lateness of the hour counted for anything, because in all likelihood Mother *would* go back, if only to pass by under the window and see that the lights were out, or stand and listen and make sure that as far as she could tell all was well.

'I wouldn't mind if she was happy,' Mother said.

'And how do you know she's not?' we'd ask.

'When people are happy, I can feel it. Can't you?'

We were not sure. Most people thought our grandmother was a gay creature, a small birdy being who even at a great age laughed like a girl, and – more remarkably – sang like one, as she went about her day. But beak and claw were of steel. She'd think nothing of sending

Mother back to a shop three times if her errands were not exactly right. 'Not sugar like that – that's *too* fine; it's not castor sugar I want. But *not* as coarse as *that*, either. I want an in-between kind.'

Provoked one day, my youngest sister, Linda, turned and gave battle. 'You're mean!' she cried. 'You love ordering people about!'

Grandmother preened, as if Linda had acclaimed an attribute. 'I was always hard to please,' she said. 'As a girl, I used to be called Miss Imperious.'

And Miss Imperious she remained as long as she lived, even when she was a great age. Her orders were then given a wry twist by the fact that as she advanced in age she took to calling her daughter Mother, as we did.

There was one great phrase with which our grandmother opened every sentence: 'if only'. 'If only,' she'd say, when we came to visit her – 'if only you'd come earlier, before I was worn out expecting you!' Or if we were early, then if only it was later, after she'd had a rest and could enjoy us, be *able* for us. And if we brought her flowers, she'd sigh to think that if only we'd brought them the previous day she'd have had a visitor to appreciate them, or say it was a pity the stems weren't longer. If only we'd picked a few green leaves, or included some buds, because, she said disparagingly, the poor flowers we'd brought were already wilting. We might just as well not have brought them! As the years went on, Grandmother had a new bead to add to her rosary: if only her friends were not all dead! By their absence, they reduced to nil all *real* enjoyment in anything. Our own father – her son-in-law – was the one person who had ever gone close to pleasing her. But even here there had been a snag. 'If only he was my real son!' she used to say, with a sigh.

Mother's mother lived on through our childhood and into our early maturity (though she outlived the money our grandfather left her), and in our minds she was a complicated mixture of valiance and defeat. Courageous

and generous within the limits of her own life, her simplest
demand was yet enormous in the larger frame of
Mother's life, and so we never could see her with the
same clarity of vision with which we saw our grandfather, or our own father. Them we saw only through
Mother's eyes.

'Take your grandfather!' she'd cry, and instantly we'd
see him, his eyes burning upon us – yes, upon *us*, although in his day only one of us had been born: me. At
another time, Mother would cry, 'Take your own father!'
and instantly we'd see *him* – tall, handsome, young, and
much more suited to marry one of us than poor bedraggled
Mother.

Most fascinating of all were the times Mother would
say, 'Take me!' By magic then, staring down the years,
we'd see blazingly clear a small girl with black hair and
buttoned boots, who, though plain and pouting, burned
bright, like a star. 'I was happy, you see,' Mother said.
And we'd strain hard to try and understand the mystery
of the light that still radiated from her. 'I used to lean
along a tree that grew out over the river,' she said, 'and
look down through the grey leaves at the water flowing
past below, and I used to think it was not the stream
that flowed but me, spreadeagled over it, who flew
through the air! Like a bird! That I'd found the secret!'
She made it seem there might *be* such a secret, just waiting
to be found.

Another time she'd dream that she'd be a great singer.

'We didn't know you sang, Mother!'

She had to laugh. 'Like a crow,' she said.

Sometimes she used to think she'd swim the Channel.

'Did you swim *that* well, Mother?'

'Oh, not really – just the breast stroke,' she said. 'And
then only by the aid of two pig bladders blown up by my
father and tied around my middle. But I used to throb –
yes, throb – with happiness.'

Behind Mother's back, Bea raised her eyebrows.

What was it, we used to ask ourselves – that quality that she, we felt sure, misnamed? Was it courage? Was it strength, health, or high spirits? Something you could not give or take – a conundrum? A game of catch-as-catch-can?

'I know,' cried Bea. 'A sham!'

Whatever it was, we knew that Mother would let no wind of violence from within or without tear it from her. Although, one evening when Father Hugh was with us, our astonished ears heard her proclaim that there might be a time when one had to slacken hold on it – let go – to catch at it again with a surer hand. In the way, we supposed, that the high-wire walker up among the painted stars of his canvas sky must wait to fling himself through the air until the bar he catches at has started to sway perversely from him. Oh no, no! That downward drag at our innards we could not bear, the belly swelling to the shape of a pear. Let happiness go by the board. 'After all, lots of people seem to make out without it,' Bea cried. It was too tricky a business. And might it not be that one had to be born with a flair for it?

'A flair would not be enough,' Mother answered. 'Take Father Hugh. He, if anyone, has a flair for it – a natural capacity! You've only to look at him when he's off guard, with you children, or helping me in the garden. But he rejects happiness! He casts it from him.'

'That is simply not true, Vera,' cried Father Hugh, overhearing her. 'It's just that I don't place an inordinate value on it like you. I don't think it's enough to carry one all the way. To the end, I mean – and after.'

'Oh, don't talk about the end when we're only in the middle,' cried Mother. And, indeed, at that moment her own face shone with such happiness it was hard to believe that her earth was not her heaven. Certainly it was her constant contention that of happiness she had had a lion's share. This, however, we, in private, doubted. Perhaps there were times when she had had a surplus of it – when she was young, say, with her redoubtable father, whose love blazed circles around her, making winter into summer and ice into fire. Perhaps she did have a brimming measure in her early married years. By straining hard, we could find traces left in our minds from those days of milk and honey. Our father, while he lived, had cast a magic over everything, for us as well as for her. He held his love up over us like an umbrella and kept off the troubles that afterwards came down on us, pouring cats and dogs!

But if she did have more than the common lot of happiness in those early days, what use was that when we could remember so clearly how our father's death had ravaged her? And how could we forget the distress it brought on us when, afraid to let her out of our sight, Bea and I stumbled after her everywhere, through the woods and along the bank of the river, where, in the weeks that followed, she tried vainly to find peace.

The summer after Father died, we were invited to France to stay with friends, and when she went walking on the cliffs at Fécamp our fears for her grew frenzied, so that we hung on to her arm and dragged at her skirt, hoping that like leaded weights we'd pin her down if she went too near to the edge. But at night we had to abandon our watch, being forced to follow the conventions of a family still whole – a home still intact – and go to bed at the same time as the other children. It was at that hour, when the coast guard was gone from his rowing boat off-shore and the sand was as cold and grey as the sea, that Mother liked to swim. And when she had washed, kissed, and left us, our hearts almost died inside us and we'd creep out of bed again to stand in our bare feet at the mansard and watch as she ran down the shingle, striking out when she reached the water where, far out, wave and sky and mist were one, and the greyness closed over her. If we took our eyes off her for an instant, it was impossible to find her again.

'Oh, make her turn back, God, please!' I prayed out loud one night.

Startled, Bea turned away from the window. 'She'll *have* to turn back sometime, won't she? Unless . . . ?'

Locking our damp hands together, we stared out again. 'She wouldn't!' I whispered. 'It would be a sin!'

Secure in the deterring power of sin, we let out our breath. Then Bea's breath caught again. 'What if she went out so far she used up all her strength? She couldn't swim back! It wouldn't be a sin then!'

'It's the intention that counts,' I whispered.

A second later, we could see an arm lift heavily up and wearily cleave down, and at last Mother was in the shallows, wading back to shore.

'Don't let her see us!' cried Bea. As if our chattering teeth would not give us away when she looked in at us before she went to her own room on the other side of the corridor, where, later in the night, sometimes the sound of crying would reach us.

What was it worth – a happiness bought that dearly?

Mother had never questioned it. And once she told us, 'On a wintry day, I brought my own mother a snowdrop. It was the first one of the year – a bleak bud that had come up stunted before its time – and I meant it for a sign. But do you know what your grandmother said? "What good are snowdrops to me now?" Such a thing to say! What good is a snowdrop at all if it doesn't hold its value always, and never lose it! Isn't that the whole point of a snowdrop? And that is the whole point of happiness, too! What good would it be if it could be erased without trace? Take me and those daffodils!' Stooping, she buried her face in a bunch that lay on the table waiting to be put in vases. 'If they didn't hold their beauty absolute and inviolable, do you think I could bear the sight of them after what happened when your father was in hospital?'

It was a fair question. When Father went to hospital, Mother went with him and stayed in a small hotel across the street so she could be with him all day from early to

late. 'Because it was so awful for him – being in Dublin!'
she said. 'You have no idea how he hated it.'

That he was dying neither of them realised. How could
they know, as it rushed through the sky, that their star
was a falling star! But one evening when she'd left him
asleep Mother came home for a few hours to see how we
were faring, and it broke her heart to see the daffodils
out all over the place – in the woods, under the trees, and
along the sides of the avenue. There had never been so
many, and she thought how awful it was that Father was
missing them. 'You sent up little bunches to him, you
poor dears!' she said. 'Sweet little bunches, too – squeezed
tight as posies by your little fists! But stuffed into vases
they couldn't really make up to him for not being able
to see them growing!'

So on the way back to the hospital she stopped her car
and pulled a great bunch – the full of her arms. 'They
took up the whole back seat,' she said, 'and I was so
excited at the thought of walking into his room and dump-
ing them on his bed – you know – just plomping them
so he could smell them, and feel them, and look and look!
I didn't mean them to be put in vases, or anything ridiculous like that – it would have taken a rainwater barrel to
hold them. Why, I could hardly see over them as I came
up the steps; I kept tripping. But when I came into the
hall, that nun – I told you about her – that nun came up
to me, sprang out of nowhere it seemed, although I know
now that she was waiting for me, knowing that somebody
had to bring me to my senses. But the way she did it!
Reached out and grabbed the flowers, letting lots of them
fall – I remember them getting stood on. "Where are you
going with those foolish flowers, you foolish woman?"
she said. "Don't you know your husband is dying? Your
prayers are all you can give him now!"

'She was right. I *was* foolish. But I wasn't cured.
Afterwards, it was nothing but foolishness the way I
dragged you children after me all over Europe. As if any
one place was going to be different from another, any

better, any less desolate. But there was great satisfaction in bringing you places your father and I had planned to bring you – although in fairness to him I must say that he would not perhaps have brought you so young. And he would not have had an ulterior motive. But above all, he would not have attempted those trips in such a dilapidated car.'

Oh, that car! It was a battered and dilapidated red sports car, so depleted of accessories that when, eventually, we got a new car Mother still stuck out her hand on bends, and in wet weather jumped out to wipe the windscreen with her sleeve. And if fussed, she'd let down the window and shout at people, forgetting she now had a horn. How we had ever fitted into it with all our luggage was a miracle.

'You were never lumpish – any of you!' Mother said proudly. 'But you were very healthy and very strong.' She turned to me. 'Think of how you got that car up the hill in Switzerland!'

'The Alps are not hills, Mother!' I pointed out coldly, as I had done at the time, when, as actually happened, the car failed to make it on one of the inclines. Mother let it run back until it wedged against the rock face, and I had to get out and push till she got going again in first gear. But when it got started it couldn't be stopped to pick me up until it got to the top, where they had to wait for me, and for a very long time.

'Ah, well,' she said, sighing wistfully at the thought of those trips. 'You got something out of them, I hope. All that travelling must have helped you with your geography and your history.'

We looked at each other and smiled, and then Mother herself laughed. 'Remember the time,' she said, 'when we were in Italy, and it was Easter, and all the shops were chock-full of food? The butchers' shops had poultry and game hanging up outside the doors fully feathered, and with their poor heads dripping blood, and in the windows they had poor little lambs and suckling pigs and

young goats, all skinned and hanging by their hindfeet.'
Mother shuddered. 'They think so much about food. I
found it revolting. I had to hurry past. But Linda, who
must have been only four then, dragged at me and stared
and stared. You know how children are at that age; they
have a morbid fascination for what is cruel and bloody.
Her face was flushed and her eyes were wide. I hurried
her back to the hotel. But next morning she crept into
my room. She crept up to me and pressed against me.
"Can't we go back, just once, and look again at that
shop?" she whispered. "The shop where they have the
little children hanging up for Easter!" It was the young
goats, of course, but I'd said "kids", I suppose. How we
laughed.' But her face was grave. 'You were *so* good on
those trips, all of you,' she said. 'You were really very
good children in general. Otherwise I would never have
put so much effort into rearing you, because I wasn't a
bit maternal. You brought out the best in me! I put an
unnatural effort into you, of course, because I was taking
my standards from your father, forgetting that his might
not have remained so inflexible if he had lived to middle
age and was beset by life, like other parents.'

'Well, the job is nearly over now, Vera,' said Father
Hugh. 'And you didn't do so badly.'

'That's right, Hugh,' said Mother, and she straightened
up, and put her hand to her back the way she sometimes
did in the garden when she got up from her knees after
weeding. 'I didn't go over to the enemy anyway! We
survived!' Then a flash of defiance came into her eyes.
'And we were happy. That's the main thing!'

Father Hugh frowned. 'There you go again!' he said.

Mother turned on him. 'I don't think you realise the
onslaughts that were made upon our happiness! The
minute Robert died, they came down on me – cohorts of
relatives, friends, even strangers, all draped in black,
opening their arms like bats to let me pass into their
company. "Life is a vale of tears," they said. "You are
privileged to find it out so young!" Ugh! After I stag-

gered onto my feet and began to take hold of life once more, they fell back defeated. And the first day I gave a laugh – pouff, they were blown out like candles. They weren't living in a real world at all; they belonged to a ghostly world where life was easy: all one had to do was sit and weep. It takes effort to push back the stone from the mouth of the tomb and walk out.'

Effort. Effort. Ah, but that strange-sounding word could invoke little sympathy from those who had not learned yet what it meant. Life must have been hardest for Mother in those years when we older ones were at college – no longer children, and still dependent on her. Indeed, we made more demands on her than ever then, having moved into new areas of activity and emotion. And our friends! Our friends came and went as freely as we did ourselves, so that the house was often like a café – and one where pets were not prohibited but took their places on our chairs and beds, as regardless as the people. And anyway it was hard to have sympathy for someone who got things into such a state as Mother. All over the house there was clutter. Her study was like the returned-letter department of a post-office, with stacks of paper everywhere, bills paid and unpaid, letters answered and unanswered, tax returns, pamphlets, leaflets. If by mistake we left the door open on a windy day, we came back to find papers flapping through the air like frightened birds. Efficient only in that she managed eventually to conclude every task she began, it never seemed possible to outsiders that by Mother's methods anything whatever could be accomplished. In an attempt to keep order elsewhere, she made her own room the clearing house into which the rest of us put everything: things to be given away, things to be mended, things to be stored, things to be treasured, things to be returned – even things to be thrown out! By the end of the year, the room resembled an obsolescence dump. And no one could help her; the chaos of her life was as personal as an act of creation – one might as well try to finish another person's poem.

As the years passed, Mother rushed around more hectically. And although Bea and I had married and were not at home any more, except at holiday time and for occasional weekends, Linda was noisier than the two of us put together had been, and for every follower we had brought home she brought twenty. The house was never still. Now that we were reduced to being visitors, we watched Mother's tension mount to vertigo, knowing that, like a spinning top, she could not rest till she fell. But now at the smallest pretext Father Hugh would call in the doctor and Mother would be put on the mail boat and dispatched for London. For it was essential that she get far enough away to make phoning home every night prohibitively costly.

Unfortunately, the thought of departure often drove a spur into her and she redoubled her effort to achieve order in her affairs. She would be up until the early hours ransacking her desk. To her, as always, the shortest parting entailed a preparation as for death. And as if it were her end that was at hand, we would all be summoned, although she had no time to speak a word to us, because five minutes before departure she would still be attempting to reply to letters that were the acquisition of weeks and would have taken whole days to dispatch.

'Don't you know the taxi is at the door, Vera?' Father Hugh would say, running his hand through his grey hair and looking very dishevelled himself. She had him at times as distracted as herself. 'You can't do any more. You'll have to leave the rest till you come back.'

'I can't, I can't!' Mother would cry. 'I'll have to cancel my plans.'

One day, Father Hugh opened the lid of her case, which was strapped up in the hall, and with a swipe of his arm he cleared all the papers on the top of the desk pell-mell into the suitcase. 'You can sort them on the boat,' he said, 'or the train to London!'

Thereafter, Mother's luggage always included an empty case to hold the unfinished papers on her desk. And years afterwards a steward on the Irish Mail told us she was a familiar figure, working away at letters and bills nearly all the way from Holyhead to Euston. 'She gave it up about Rugby or Crewe,' he said. 'She'd get talking to someone in the compartment.' He smiled. 'There was one time coming down the train I was just in time to see her close up the window with a guilty look. I didn't say anything, but I think she'd emptied those papers of hers out the window!'

Quite likely. When we were children, even a few hours away from us gave her composure. And in two weeks or less, when she'd come home, the well of her spirit would be freshened. We'd hardly know her – her step so light, her eye so bright, and her love and patience once more freely flowing. But in no time at all the house would fill up once more with the noise and confusion of too many people and too many animals, and again we'd be fighting our corner with cats and dogs, bats, mice, bees and even wasps. 'Don't kill it!' Mother would cry if we raised a hand to an angry wasp. 'Just catch it, dear, and put it outside. Open the window and let it fly away!' But even this treatment could at times be deemed too harsh. 'Wait a minute. Close the window!' she'd cry. 'It's too cold outside. It will die. That's why it came in, I suppose! Oh dear, what will we do?' Life would be going full blast again.

There was only one place Mother found rest. When she was at breaking point and fit to fall, she'd go out into the garden – not to sit or stroll around but to dig, to drag up weeds, to move great clumps of corms or rhizomes, or indeed quite frequently to haul huge rocks from one place to another. She was always laying down a path, building a dry wall, or making compost heaps as high as hills. However jaded she might be going out, when dark forced her in at last her step had the spring of a daisy. So if she did not succeed in defining happiness to our understanding, we could see that, whatever it was, she possessed it to the full when she was in her garden.

One of us said as much one Sunday when Bea and I had dropped round for the afternoon. Father Hugh was with us again. 'It's an unthinking happiness, though,' he cavilled. We were standing at the drawing-room window, looking out to where in the fading light we could see Mother on her knees weeding, in the long border that stretched from the house right down to the woods. 'I wonder how she'd take it if she were stricken down and had to give up that heavy work!' he said. Was he perhaps a little jealous of how she could stoop and bend? He himself had begun to use a stick. I was often a little jealous of her myself, because although I was married and had children of my own, I had married young and felt the weight of living as heavy as a weight of years. 'She doesn't take enough care of herself,' Father Hugh said sadly. 'Look at her out there with nothing under her knees to protect her from the damp ground.' It was almost too dim for us to see her, but even in the drawing room it was chilly. 'She should not be let stay out there after the sun goes down.'

'Just you try to get her in then!' said Linda, who had come into the room in time to hear him. 'Don't you know by now anyway that what would kill another person only seems to make Mother thrive?'

Father Hugh shook his head again. 'You seem to forget it's not younger she's getting!' He fidgeted and fussed, and several times went to the window to stare out apprehensively. He was really getting quite elderly.

'Come and sit down, Father Hugh,' Bea said, and to take his mind off Mother she turned on the light and blotted out the garden. Instead of seeing through the window, we saw into it as into a mirror, and there between the flower-laden tables and the lamps it was ourselves we saw moving vaguely. Like Father Hugh, we, too, were waiting for her to come in before we called an end to the day.

'Oh, this is ridiculous!' Father Hugh cried at last. 'She'll have to listen to reason.' And going back to the window he threw it open. 'Vera!' he called. 'Vera!' – sternly, so sternly that, more intimate than an endearment, his tone shocked us. 'She didn't hear me,' he said, turning back blinking at us in the lighted room. 'I'm going to her.' And in a minute he was gone from the room. As he ran down the garden path, we stared at each other, astonished; his step, like his voice, was the step of a lover. 'I'm coming, Vera!' he cried.

Although she was never stubborn except in things that mattered, Mother had not moved. In the wholehearted way she did everything, she was bent down close to the ground. It wasn't the light only that was dimming; her eyesight also was failing, I thought, as instinctively I followed Father Hugh.

But halfway down the path I stopped. I had seen something he had not: Mother's hand that appeared to support itself in a forked branch of an old tree peony she had planted as a bride was not in fact gripping it but impaled upon it. And the hand that appeared to be grubbing in the clay in fact was sunk into the soft mould. 'Mother!' I screamed, and I ran forward, but when I reached her I covered my face with my hands. 'Oh Father Hugh!' I cried. 'Is she dead?'

It was Bea who answered, hysterical. 'She is! She is!' she cried, and she began to pound Father Hugh on the back with her fists, as if his pessimistic words had made this happen.

But Mother was not dead. And at first the doctor even offered hope of her pulling through. But from the moment Father Hugh lifted her up to carry her into the house we ourselves had no hope, seeing how effortlessly he, who was not strong, could carry her. When he put her down on her bed, her head hardly creased the pillow. Mother lived for four more hours.

Like the days of her life, those four hours that Mother lived were packed tight with concern and anxiety. Partly conscious, partly delirious, she seemed to think the counterpane was her desk, and she scrabbled her fingers upon it as if trying to sort out a muddle of bills and correspondence. No longer indifferent now, we listened, anguished, to the distracted cries that had for all our lifetime been so familiar to us. 'Oh, where is it? Where is it? I had it a minute ago! Where on earth did I put it?'

'Vera, Vera, stop worrying,' Father Hugh pleaded, but she waved him away and went on sifting through the sheets as if they were sheets of paper. 'Oh, Vera!' he begged. 'Listen to me. Do you not know – '

Bea pushed between them. 'You're not to tell her!' she commanded. 'Why frighten her?'

'But it ought not to frighten her,' said Father Hugh. 'This is what I was always afraid would happen – that she'd be frightened when it came to the end.'

At that moment, as if to vindicate him, Mother's hands fell idle on the coverlet, palms upward and empty. And turning her head she stared at each of us in turn, beseechingly. 'I cannot face it,' she whispered. 'I can't! I can't! I can't!'

'Oh, my God!' Bea said, and she started to cry.

'Vera. For God's sake listen to me,' Father Hugh cried, and pressing his face to hers, as close as a kiss, he kept whispering to her, trying to cast into the dark tunnel before her the light of his faith.

But it seemed to us that Mother must already be looking into God's exigent eyes. 'I can't!' she cried. 'I can't!'

Then her mind came back from the stark world of the spirit to the world where her body was still detained, but even that world was now a whirling kaleidoscope of things which only she could see. Suddenly her eyes focussed, and, catching at Father Hugh, she pulled herself up a little and pointed to something we could not see. 'What will be done with them?' Her voice was anxious. 'They ought to be put in water anyway,' she said, and, leaning over the edge of the bed, she pointed to the floor. 'Don't step on that one!' she said sharply. Then, more sharply still, she addressed us all. 'Have them sent to the public ward,' she said peremptorily. 'Don't let that nun take them; she'll only put them on the altar. And God doesn't want them! He made them for *us* – not for Himself!'

It was the familiar rhetoric that all her life had characterised her utterances. For a moment we were mystified. Then Bea gasped. 'The daffodils!' she cried. 'The day Father died!' And over her face came the light that had so often blazed over Mother's. Leaning across the bed, she pushed Father Hugh aside. And, putting out her hands, she held Mother's face between her palms as tenderly as if it were the face of a child. 'It's all right, Mother. You don't *have* to face it! It's over!' Then she who had so fiercely forbade Father Hugh to do so blurted out the truth. 'You've finished with this world, Mother,' she said, and, confident that her tidings were joyous, her voice was strong.

Mother made the last effort of her life and grasped at Bea's meaning. She let out a sigh, and, closing her eyes, she sank back, and this time her head sank so deep into the pillow that it would have been dented had it been a pillow of stone.

BENEDICT KIELY
The Dogs
in the Great Glen

The professor had come over from America to search
out his origins and I met him in Dublin on the way to
Kerry where his grandfather had come from and where
he had relations, including a grand-uncle, still living.

'But the trouble is,' he said, 'that I've lost the address
my mother gave me. She wrote to tell them I was coming
to Europe. That's all they know. All I remember is a name
out of my dead father's memories: the great Glen of
Kanareen.'

'You could write to your mother.'

'That would take time. She'd be slow to answer. And I
feel impelled right away to find the place my grandfather
told my father about.

'You wouldn't understand,' he said. 'Your origins are
all around you.'

'You can say that again, professor. My origins crop up
like the bones of rock in thin sour soil. They come un-
wanted like the mushroom of merulius lacrimans on the
walls of a decaying house.'

'It's no laughing matter,' he said.

'It isn't for me. This island's too small to afford a place
in which to hide from one's origins. Or from anything
else. During the war a young fellow in Dublin said to me,
"Mister, even if I ran away to sea I wouldn't get beyond
the three-mile limit." '

He said, 'But it's large enough to lose a valley in. I

couldn't find the valley of Kanareen marked on any map
or mentioned in any directory.'

'I have a middling knowledge of the Kerry mountains,'
I said. 'I could join you in the search.'

'It's not marked on the half-inch ordnance survey map.'

'There are more things in Kerry than were ever dreamt
of by the Ordnance Survey. The place could have another
official name. At the back of my head I feel that once in
the town of Kenmare in Kerry I heard a man mention
the name of Kanareen.'

We set off two days later in a battered, rattly Ford
Prefect. Haste, he said, would be dangerous because
Kanareen might not be there at all, but if we idled from
place to place in the lackadaisical Irish summer we might,
when the sentries were sleeping and the glen unguarded,
slip secretly as thieves in to the land whose legends were
part of his rearing.

'Until I met you,' the professor said, 'I was afraid the
valley might have been a dream world my grandfather
imagined to dull the edge of the first nights in a new land.
I could see how he might have come to believe in it himself and told my father – and then, of course, my father
told me.'

One of his grandfather's relatives had been a Cistercian
monk in Mount Melleray, and we went there hoping to
see the evidence of a name in a book and to kneel, perhaps, under the high arched roof of the chapel close to
where that monk had knelt. But, when we had traversed
the corkscrew road over the purple Knockmealdowns and
gone up to the mountain monastery through the forest the
monks had made in the wilderness, it was late evening
and the doors were closed. The birds sang vespers. The
great silence affected us with something between awe
and a painful, intolerable shyness. We hadn't the heart
to ring a doorbell or to promise ourselves to return in the
morning. Not speaking to each other we retreated, the
rattle of the Ford Prefect as irreverent as dicing on the
altar-steps. Half a mile down the road the mute, single-

file procession of a group of women exercitants walking back to the female guest-house underlined the holy, unreal, unanswering stillness that had closed us out. It could easily have been that his grandfather never had a relative a monk in Mount Melleray.

A cousin of his mother's mother had, he had been told, been a cooper in Lady Gregory's Gort in the County Galway. But when we crossed the country westwards to Gort, it produced nothing except the information that apart from the big breweries, where they survived like birds or bison in a sanctuary, the coopers had gone, leaving behind them not a hoop or a stave. So we visited the woods of Coole, close to Gort, where Lady Gregory's house had once stood, and on the brimming lake-water among the stones we saw by a happy poetic accident the number of swans the poet had seen.

Afterwards in Galway City there was, as there always is in Galway City, a night's hard drinking that was like a fit of jovial hysteria, and a giggling ninny of a woman in the bar who kept saying, 'You're the nicest American I ever met. You don't look like an American. You don't even carry a camera. You look like a Kerryman.'

And in the end, we came to Kenmare in Kerry, and in another bar we met a talkative Kerryman who could tell us all about the prowess of the Kerry team, about the heroic feats of John Joe Sheehy or Paddy Bawn Brosnan. He knew so much, that man, yet he couldn't tell us where in the wilderness of mountains we might find the Glen of Kanareen. Nor could anybody else in the bar be of the least help to us, not even the postman who could only say that wherever it was, that is if it was at all, it wasn't in his district.

'It could of course,' he said, 'be east over the mountain.'

Murmuring sympathetically, the entire bar assented. The rest of the world was east over the mountain.

With the resigned air of men washing their hands of a helpless, hopeless case the postman and the football savant directed us to a roadside post office twelve miles away where, in a high-hedged garden before an old grey-stone house with latticed windows and an incongruous, green, official post office, there was a child, quite naked, playing with a coloured, musical spinning-top as big as itself, and an old half-deaf man sunning himself and swaying in a rocking-chair, a straw hat tilted forwards to shade his eyes. Like Oisin remembering the Fenians, he told us he had known once of a young woman who married a man from a place called Kanareen, but there had been contention about the match and her people had kept up no correspondence with her. But the day she left home with her husband that was the way she went. He pointed. The way went inland and up and up. We followed it.

'That young woman could have been a relation of mine,' the professor said.

On a rock-strewn slope, and silhouetted on a saw-toothed ridge where you'd think only a chamois could get by without broken legs, small black cows, accurate and active as goats, rasped good milk from the grass between the stone. His grandfather had told his father about those athletic, legendary cows and about the proverb that said, 'Kerry cows know Sunday'. For in famine times, a century since, mountain people bled the cows once a week to mix the blood into yellow maize meal and provide a meat dish, a special Sunday dinner.

The road twisted on across moorland that on our left sloped dizzily to the sea, as if the solid ground might easily slip and slide into the depths. Mountain shadows melted like purple dust into a green bay. Across a ravine, set quite alone on a long, slanting, brown knife-blade of a mountain, was a white house with a red door. The rattle of our pathetic little car affronted the vast stillness. We were free to moralise on the extent of all space in relation to the trivial area that limited our ordinary daily lives.

The two old druids of men resting from work on the leeward side of a turf-bank listened to our enquiry with the same attentive, half-conscious patience they gave to bird-cries or the sound of wind in the heather. Then they waved us ahead towards a narrow cleft in the distant wall of mountains as if they doubted the ability of ourselves and our conveyance to negotiate the Gap and find the Glen. They offered us strong tea and a drop out of a bottle. They watched us with kind irony as we drove away. Until the Gap swallowed us and the hazardous, twisting track absorbed all our attention we could look back and still see them, motionless, waiting with indifference for the landslide that would end it all.

By a roadside pool where water-beetles lived their vicious secretive lives, we sat and rested, with the pass and the cliffs, overhung with heather, behind us and another ridge ahead. Brazenly the sheer rocks reflected the sun and semaphored at us. Below us, in the dry summer, the bed of a stream held only a trickle of water twisting painfully around piles of round black stones. Touch a beetle with a stalk of dry grass and the creature either dived like a shot or, angry at invasion, savagely grappled with the stalk.

'That silly woman in Galway,' the professor said.

He dropped a stone into the pool and the beetles submerged to weather the storm.

'That day by the lake at Lady Gregory's Coole. The exact number of swans Yeats saw when the poem came to him. Upon the brimming water among the stones are nine and fifty swans. Since I don't carry a camera nobody will ever believe me. But you saw them. You counted them.'

'Now that I am so far,' he said, 'I'm half-afraid to finish the journey. What will they be like? What will they think of me? Will I go over that ridge there to find my grandfather's brother living in a cave?'

Poking at and tormenting the beetles on the black mirror of the pool, I told him, 'Once I went from Dublin to near Shannon Pot, where the river rises, to help an American woman find the house where her dead woman friend had been reared. On her deathbed the friend had written it all out on a sheet of notepaper: "Cross the river at Battle Bridge. Go straight through the village with the ruined castle on the right. Go on a mile to the crossroads and the labourer's cottage with the lovely snapdragons in the flower garden. Take the road to the right there, and then the second boreen on the left beyond the school-house. Then stop at the third house on that boreen. You can see the river from the flagstone at the door."

'Apart from the snapdragons it was exactly as she had written it down. The dead woman had walked that boreen as a barefooted schoolgirl. Not able to revisit it herself she entrusted the mission as her dying wish to her dearest friend. We found the house. Her people were long gone from it but the new tenants remembered them. They welcomed us with melodeon and fiddle and all the neighbours came in and collated the long memories of the townland. They feasted us with cold ham and chicken, porter and whiskey, until I had cramps for a week.'

'My only grip on identity,' he said, 'is that a silly woman told me I looked like a Kerryman. My grandfather was a Kerryman. What do Kerrymen look like?'

'Big,' I said.

'And this is the heart of Kerry. And what my grandfather said about the black cows was true. With a camera I could have taken a picture of those climbing cows. And up that hill trail and over that ridge is Kanareen.'

'We hope,' I said.

The tired cooling engine coughed apologetically when we abandoned it and put city-shod feet to the last ascent.

'If that was the mountain my grandfather walked over in the naked dawn coming home from an all-night card-playing then, by God, he was a better man than me,' said the professor.

He folded his arms and looked hard at the razor-cut edges of stone on the side of the mountain.

'Short of too much drink and the danger of mugging,' he said, 'getting home at night in New York is a simpler operation than crawling over that hunk of miniature Mount Everest. Like walking up the side of a house.'

He was as proud as Punch of the climbing prowess of his grandfather.

'My father told me,' he said, 'that one night coming home from the card-playing my grandfather slipped down fifteen feet of rock and the only damage done was the ruin of one of two bottles of whiskey he had in the tail-pockets of his greatcoat. The second bottle was unharmed.'

The men who surfaced the track we were walking on had been catering for horses and narrow iron-hooped wheels. After five minutes of agonised slipping and sliding, wisdom came to us and we took to the cushioned grass and heather. As we ascended the professor told me what his grandfather had told his father about the market town he used to go to when he was a boy. It was a small town where even on market days the dogs would sit nowhere except exactly in the middle of the street. They were lazy town dogs, not active, loyal and intelligent like the dogs the grandfather had known in the great glen. The way the old man had described it, the town's five streets grasped the ground of Ireland as the hand of a strong swimmer might grasp a ledge of rock to hoist himself out of the water. On one side was the sea. On the other side a shoulder of mountain rose so steeply that the Gaelic name of it meant the gable of the house.

When the old man went as a boy to the town on a market day it was his custom to climb that mountain, up through furze and following goat tracks, leaving his shiny boots, that he only put on, anyway, when he entered the town, securely in hiding behind a furze bush. The way he remembered that mountain it would seem that twenty minutes' active climbing brought him halfways to heaven. The little town was far below him, and the bay and the islands. The unkempt coastline tumbled and sprawled to left and right, and westwards the ocean went on for ever. The sounds of market-day, voices, carts, dogs barking, musicians on the streets, came up to him as faint, silvery whispers. On the tip of one island two tall aerials marked the place where, he was told, messages went down into the sea to travel all the way to America by cable. That was a great marvel for a boy from the mountains to hear about: the ghostly, shrill, undersea voices; the words of people in every tongue of Europe far down among monstrous fish and shapeless sea-serpents that never saw the light of the sun. He closed his eyes one day and it seemed to him that the sounds of the little town were the voices of Europe setting out on their submarine travels. That was the time he knew that when he was old enough he would leave the Glen of Kanareen and go with the voices westwards to America.

'Or so he said. Or so he told my father,' said the professor.

Another fifty yards and we would be on top of the ridge. We kept our eyes on the ground, fearful of the moment of vision and, for good or ill, revelation. Beyond the ridge there might be nothing but a void to prove that his grandfather had been a dreamer or a liar. Rapidly, nervously, he tried to talk down his fears.

'He would tell stories for ever, my father said, about ghosts and the good people. There was one case of an old woman whose people buried her – when she died, of course – against her will, across the water, which meant on the far side of the lake in the glen. Her dying wish was to be buried in another graveyard, nearer home. And there she was, sitting in her own chair in the chimney corner, waiting for them, when they came home from the funeral. To ease her spirit they replanted her.'

To ease the nervous moment I said, 'There was a poltergeist once in a farmhouse in these mountains, and the police decided to investigate the queer happenings, and didn't an ass's collar come flying across the room to settle around the sergeant's neck. Due to subsequent ridicule the poor man had to be transferred to Dublin.'

Laughing, we looked at the brown infant runnel that went parallel to the path. It flowed with us: we were over the watershed. So we raised our head slowly and saw the great Glen of Kanareen. It was what Cortez saw, and all the rest of it. It was a discovery. It was a new world. It gathered the sunshine into a gigantic coloured bowl. We accepted it detail by detail.

'It was there all the time,' he said. 'It was no dream. It was no lie.'

The first thing we realised was the lake. The runnel leaped down to join the lake, and we looked down on it through ash trees regularly spaced on a steep, smooth, green slope. Grasping from tree to tree you could descend to the pebbled, lapping edge of the water.

'That was the way,' the professor said, 'the boys in his time climbed down to fish or swim. Black, bull-headed mountain trout. Cannibal trout. There was one place where they could dive off sheer rock into seventy feet of water. Rolling like a gentle sea: that was how he described it. They gathered kindling, too, on the slopes under the ash trees.'

Then, after the lake, we realised the guardian mountain; not rigidly chiselled into ridges of rock like the mountain behind us but soft and gently curving, protective and, above all, noble, a monarch of mountains, an antlered stag holding a proud horned head up to the highest point of the blue sky. Green fields swathed its base. Sharp lines of stone walls, dividing wide areas of moorland sheep-grazing, marked man's grip for a thousand feet or so above sea-level then gave up the struggle and left the mountain alone and untainted. Halfways up one snow-white cloud rested as if it had hooked itself on a snagged rock and there it stayed, motionless, as step by step we went down into the glen. Below the cloud a long cataract made a thin, white, forked-lightning line, and, in the heart of the glen, the river that the cataract became sprawled on a brown and green and golden patchwork bed.

'It must be some one of those houses,' he said, pointing ahead and down to the white houses of Kanareen.

'Take a blind pick,' I said. 'I see at least fifty.'

They were scattered over the glen in five or six clusters.

'From what I heard it should be over in that direction,' he said.

Small rich fields were ripe in the sun. This was a glen of plenty, a gold-field in the middle of a desert, a happy laughing mockery of the arid surrounding moors and mountains. Five hundred yards away a dozen people were working at hay. They didn't look up or give any sign that they had seen two strangers cross the high threshold of their kingdom but, as we went down, stepping like grenadier guards, the black-and-white sheepdogs detached themselves from the haymaking and moved silently across to intercept our path. Five of them I counted. My step faltered.

'This could be it,' I suggested with hollow joviality. 'I feel a little like an early Christian.'

The professor said nothing. We went on down, deserting the comfort of the grass and heather at the side of the track. It seemed to me that our feet on the loose pebbles made a tearing, crackling, grinding noise that shook echoes even out of the imperturbable mountain. The white cloud had not moved. The haymakers had not honoured us with a glance.

'We could,' I said, 'make ourselves known to them in a civil fashion. We could ask the way to your grand-uncle's house. We could have a formal introduction to those slinking beasts.'

'No, let me,' he said. 'Give me my head. Let me try to remember what I was told.'

'The hearts of these highland people, I've heard, are made of pure gold,' I said. 'But they're inclined to be the tiniest bit suspicious of town-dressed strangers. As sure as God made smells and shotguns they think we're inspectors from some government department: weeds or warble-fly or, horror of horrors, rates and taxes. With equanimity they'd see us eaten.'

He laughed. His stride had a new elasticity in it. He was another man. The melancholy of the monastic summer dusk at Mount Melleray was gone. He was somebody else coming home. The white cloud had not moved. The silent dogs came closer. The unheeding people went on with their work.

'The office of rates collector is not sought after in these parts,' I said. 'Shotguns are still used to settle vexed questions of land title. Only a general threat of excommunication can settle a major feud.'

'This was the way he'd come home from the gambling cabin,' the professor said, 'his pockets clinking with winnings. That night he fell he'd won the two bottles of whiskey. He was only eighteen when he went away. But he was the tallest man in the glen. So he said. And lucky at cards.'

The dogs were twenty yards away, silent, fanning out like soldiers cautiously circling a point of attack.

'He was an infant prodigy,' I said. 'He was a peerless grandfather for a man to have. He also had one great advantage over us – he knew the names of these taciturn dogs and they knew his smell.'

He took off his white hat and waved at the workers. One man at a haycock raised a pitchfork – in salute or in threat? Nobody else paid the least attention. The dogs were now at our heels, suiting their pace politely to ours. They didn't even sniff. They had impeccable manners.

'This sure is the right glen,' he said. 'The old man was never done talking about the dogs. They were all black-and-white in his day, too.'

He stopped to look at them. They stopped. They didn't look up at us. They didn't snarl. They had broad shaggy backs. Even for their breed they were big dogs. Their long tails were rigid. Fixing my eyes on the white cloud I walked on.

'Let's establish contact,' I said, 'before we're casually eaten. All I ever heard about the dogs in these mountains is that their family tree is as old as the Red Branch Knights. That they're the best sheepdogs in Ireland and better than anything in the Highlands of Scotland. They also savage you first and bark afterwards.'

Noses down, they padded along behind us. Their quiet breath was hot on my calves. High up and far away the nesting white cloud had the security of heaven.

'Only strangers who act suspiciously,' the professor said.

'What else are we? I'd say we smell bad to them.'

'Not me,' he said. 'Not me. The old man told a story about a stranger who came to Kanareen when most of the people were away at the market. The house he came to visit was empty except for two dogs. So he sat all day at the door of the house and the dogs lay and watched him and said and did nothing. Only once, he felt thirsty and went into the kitchen of the house and lifted a bowl to go to the well for water. Then there was a low duet of a snarl that froze his blood. So he went thirsty and the dogs lay quiet.'

'Hospitable people.'

'The secret is touch nothing, lay no hand on property, and you're safe.'

'So help me God,' I said, 'I wouldn't deprive them of a bone or a blade of grass.'

Twice in my life I had been bitten by dogs. Once, walking to school along a sidestreet on a sunny morning and simultaneously reading in *The Boy's Magazine* about a soccer centre forward, the flower of the flock, called Fiery Cross the Shooting Star – he was redheaded and his surname was Cross – I had stepped on a sleeping Irish terrier. In retaliation, the startled brute had bitten me. Nor could I find it in my heart to blame him, so that, in my subconscious, dogs took on the awful heaven-appointed dignity of avenging angels. The other time – and this was an even more disquieting experience – a mongrel dog had come up softly behind me while I was walking on the fairgreen in the town I was reared in and bitten the calf of my leg so as to draw spurts of blood. I kicked him but not resenting the kick, he had walked away as if it was the most natural, legitimate thing in heaven and earth for a dog to bite me and be kicked in return. Third time, I thought, it will be rabies. So as we walked and the silent watchers of the valley padded at our heels, I enlivened the way with brave and trivial chatter. I recited my story of the four wild brothers of Adrigole.

'Once upon a time,' I said, 'there lived four brothers in a rocky corner of Adrigole in West Cork, under the mountain called Hungry Hill. Daphne du Maurier wrote a book called after the mountain, but divil a word in it about the four brothers of Adrigole. They lived, I heard tell, according to instinct and never laced their boots and came out only once a year to visit the nearest town which was Castletownberehaven on the side of Bantry Bay. They'd stand there, backs to the wall, smoking, saying nothing, contemplating the giddy market-day throng. One day they ran out of tobacco and went into the local branch of the Bank of Ireland to buy it and raised havoc because the teller refused to satisfy their needs. To pacify them the manager and the teller had to disgorge their own supplies. So they went back to Adrigole to live happily without lacing their boots, and ever after they thought that in towns and cities the bank was the place where you bought tobacco.

'That,' said I with a hollow laugh, 'is my moral tale about the four brothers of Adrigole.'

On a level with the stream that came from the lake and went down to join the valley's main river, we walked towards a group of four whitewashed, thatched farmhouses that were shining and scrupulously clean. The track looped to the left. Through a small triangular meadow a short-cut went straight towards the houses. In the heart of the meadow, by the side of the short-cut, there was a spring well of clear water, the stones that lined its sides and the roof cupped over it all white and cleansed with lime. He went down three stone steps and looked at the water. For good luck there was a tiny brown trout imprisoned in the well. He said quietly, 'That was the way my grandfather described it. But it could hardly be the self-same fish.'

He stooped to the clear water. He filled his cupped hands and drank. He stooped again, and again filled his cupped hands and slowly, carefully, not spilling a drop, came up the moist, cool steps. Then, with the air of a priest scattering hyssop, he sprinkled the five dogs with the spring-water. They backed away from him, thoughtfully. They didn't snarl or show teeth. He had them puzzled. He laughed with warm good nature at their obvious perplexity. He was making his own of them. He licked his wet hands. Like good pupils attentively studying a teacher, the dogs watched him.

'Elixir,' he said. 'He told my father that the sweetest drink he ever had was out of this well when he was on his way back from a drag hunt in the next glen. He was a great hunter.'

'He was Nimrod,' I said. 'He was everything. He was the universal Kerryman.'

'No kidding,' he said. 'Through a thorn hedge six feet thick and down a precipice and across a stream to make sure of a wounded bird. Or all night long waist deep in an icy swamp waiting for the wild geese. And the day of this drag hunt. What he most remembered about it was the way they sold the porter to the hunting crowd in the pub at the crossroads. To meet the huntsmen halfways they moved the bar out to the farmyard. With hounds and cows and geese and chickens it was like having a drink in Noah's Ark. The pint tumblers were set on doors lifted off their hinges and laid flat on hurdles. The beer was in wooden tubs and all the barmaids had to do was dip and there was the pint. They didn't bother to rinse the tumblers. He said it was the quickest-served and the flattest pint of porter he ever saw or tasted. Bitter and black as bog water. Completely devoid of the creamy clerical collar that should grace a good pint. On the way home he spent an hour here rinsing his mouth and the well-water tasted as sweet, he said, as silver.'

The white cloud was gone from the mountain.

'Where did it go?' I said. 'Where could it vanish to?'

In all the wide sky there wasn't a speck of cloud. The mountain was changing colour, deepening to purple with the approaching evening.

He grasped me by the elbow, urging me forwards. He said, 'Step on it. We're almost home.'

We crossed a crude wooden stile and followed the short-cut through a walled garden of bright-green heads of cabbage and black and red currant bushes. Startled, fruit-thieving birds rustled away from us and on a rowan tree a sated, impudent blackbird opened his throat and sang.

'Don't touch a currant,' I said, 'or a head of cabbage. Don't ride your luck too hard.'

He laughed like a boy half hysterical with happiness. He said, 'Luck. Me and these dogs, we know each other. We've been formally introduced.'

'Glad to know you dogs,' he said to them over his shoulder.

They trotted behind us. We crossed a second stile and followed the short-cut through a haggard, and underfoot the ground was velvety with chipped straw. We opened a five-barred iron gate, and to me it seemed that the noise of its creaking hinges must be audible from end to end of the glen. While I paused to rebolt it he and the dogs had gone on, the dogs trotting in the lead. I ran after them. I was the stranger who had once been the guide. We passed three houses as if they didn't exist. They were empty. The people who lived in them were above at the hay. Towards the fourth thatched house of the group we walked along a green boreen, lined with hazels and an occasional mountain ash. The guardian mountain was by now so purple that the sky behind it seemed, by contrast, as silvery as the scales of a fish. From unknown lands behind the lines of hazels two more black-and-white dogs ran, barking with excitement, to join our escort. Where the hazels ended there was a house fronted by a low stone wall and a profusion of fuchsia. An old man sat on the wall and

around him clustered the children of the four houses. He
was a tall, broad-shouldered old man with copious white
hair and dark side whiskers and a clear prominent profile.
He was dressed in good grey with long, old-fashioned
skirts to his coat – formally dressed as if for some formal
event – and his wide-brimmed black hat rested on the wall
beside him, and his joined hands rested on the curved
handle of a strong ash plant. He stood up as we approached. The stick fell to the ground. He stepped over
it and came towards us. He was as tall or, without a
slight stoop of age, taller than the professor. He put out his
two hands and rested them on the professor's shoulders.
It wasn't an embrace. It was an appraisal, a salute, a sign
of recognition.

He said, 'Kevin, well and truly we knew you'd come if
you were in the neighbourhood at all. I watched you
walking down. I knew you from the top of the glen. You
have the same gait my brother had, the heavens be his
bed. My brother that was your grandfather.'

'They say a grandson often walks like the grandfather,'
said the professor.

His voice was shaken and there were tears on his face.
So, a stranger in the place myself, I walked away a bit and
looked back up the glen. The sunlight was slanting now
and shadows were lengthening on mountain slopes and
across the small fields. From where I stood the lake was
invisible, but the ashwood on the slope above it was dark
as ink. Through sunlight and shadow the happy haymakers came running down towards us; and barking,
playing, frisking over each other, the seven black-and-
white dogs, messengers of good news, ran to meet them.
The great glen, all happy echoes, was opening out and
singing to welcome its true son.

Under the hazels, as I watched the running haymakers,
the children came shyly around me to show me that I also
was welcome. Beyond the high ridge, the hard mountain
the card-players used to cross to the cabin of the gambling

stood up gaunt and arrogant and leaned over towards us
as if it were listening.

It was moonlight, I thought, not sunlight, over the great
glen. From house to house, the dogs were barking, not
baying the moon, but to welcome home the young men
from the card-playing over the mountain. The edges of
rock glistened like quartz. The tall young gambler came
laughing down the glen, greatcoat swinging open, waving
in his hand the one bottle of whiskey that hadn't been
broken when he tumbled down the spink. The ghosts of
his own dogs laughed and leaped and frolicked at his heels.

JAMES PLUNKETT
Ferris Moore
and the Earwig

The long, thin, unmuscular body which lay supine in the
sunny field was, Mr Ferris Moore eventually conceded,
the property of Mr Ferris Moore. For the moment at any
rate. Mr Ferris Moore had been inhabiting the body for
close on sixty-two years. Or rather, Mr Ferris Moore
qualified (his eyes closed contentedly and his ears grate-
fully aware of the sound of the nearby river), a succession
of bodies not by any means similar in shape and health
had been inhabited for that period by a succession of
mysteriously related individuals who might be referred
to collectively, though unsatisfactorily, as Ferris Moore.
For instance, Ferris Moore pointed out to himself, the
brown-limbed boy whose sad little ghost had been haunt-
ing his thoughts for some moments past could only in the
most loose and general way be considered Ferris Moore.
The boy had once played cowboys and Indians in this
very meadow. He had climbed trees. He had, for a period
of now forgotten duration, owned a pet rabbit to which
he fed lettuce from the kitchen garden, something which
Aunt Emily, long since departed from the last body of all,
had expressly forbidden. If that remotely remembered
little being was also Ferris Moore, then it became necessary
to distinguish. He had been Ferris Moore Eight. The
long, thin body, presently conscious of the sun, the smell
of grass and the sultry hum of insects, was Ferris Moore
Sixty-two.

Ferris Moore should have been relieved at achieving

this little measure of clarification, but he was not. Something – an indisposition of the body juices perhaps – kept him melancholy. He raised himself into a sitting position and leaned over the river bank to see if the earwig was still there. It was. He had felt it would be. It clung to the steep, damp bank, its near pincers stiff and erect against the threat of its enemy. It clung to a small dry patch of the bank, encircled by the water which oozed in a thin stream on every side of it, so tiny a stream that it would hardly wet the top of the finger of Ferris Moore Sixty-two. But it would sweep the earwig away if it tried to crawl through. Plainly, the earwig was trapped.

Or rather, the earwig believed itself to be trapped. It could not know the thought in God's mind. It could not know that Ferris Moore (sixty-two) had determined, at some later moment still to be more precisely determined, to rescue the earwig. Not out of love or pity, but because Ferris Moore had decided to demonstrate that the will, in spite of the doctrine of Epicurus and the arguments of the Determinists, is free to choose. In other words, that he had the faculty of inward self-determination to action.

The last phrase required considerable formulation and for the moment it exhausted Ferris Moore's desire to concentrate. Relaxing, he began to speculate lazily about the earwig and its plight. How had it got there in the first place? Had a bird dropped it from its beak? Had it been questing along the bank for food or for ambulatory pleasure while, all unnoticed, the natural drainage increased and the banks began their deadly ooze? Ferris Moore decided that he could not say. He felt critical, however, of its general behaviour. There was no sense in offering a threat to, or trying to evoke terror in, a watery ooze. To raise the rear pincers in such circumstances was an unnecessary betrayal of the emotions. The sustained muscular tension it called for must have the effect, on such a day, of making the earwig uncomfortably warm. If earwigs suffered from that sort of thing. Ferris Moore was not sure.

It was undoubtedly a very beautiful day. Too beautiful.
Beauty, Ferris Moore had long observed, was conducive
to sadness. Perhaps it was not the indisposition of the
juices after all. He felt a gentle pleasure in the warmth of
the sun which seeped through his clothes, but underneath
that pleasure there was pain. In some dark cave of his
consciousness Death, he felt, was making preparations to
take over where Ferris Moore would be obliged to let go.
When he closed his eyes this deeper part of him seemed
to feel the silent spinning of the world on its tilted axis and
its simultaneous forward motion through the great void of
space. Searching for some expression of this mood, Ferris
Moore remembered poor Dick, of whom Housman had
written:

> Fall, winter, fall; for he,
> Prompt hand and headpiece clever,
> Has woven a winter robe,
> And made of earth and sea
> His overcoat for ever,
> And wears the turning globe.

Searching for a homelier expression of the mood, Ferris
Moore remembered the words of an old gardener who
returned at the age of eighty from the funeral of a friend
and, being asked how he had got on in the cemetery,
replied: 'The gravedigger shook his shovel at me.'

But these were unpleasant thoughts for so perfect an
afternoon. Tonight, at dinner, he would open another
bottle of wine, whatever his sister might have to say about
it. He had had some words with her at lunch. She was
older than he and although they had lived for years
together in the lonely house their parents had left to them,
they frequently had words. Not noisy words, but polite,
frigidly controlled expressions of ill-feeling.

He had been reading a book throughout the meal, in
order to avoid speaking to her.

'I wish you'd speak to me,' she had complained at last.

'I am reading, my dear.'

'You are always reading. Poetry, pamphlets, making-and-mending, philosophy, war diaries, detective novels, dictionaries.'

He had said nothing.

'Anyway,' she resumed, 'I don't believe you are reading at all.'

'You express yourself strongly, my dear.'

'Your book is upside down.'

Ferris Moore had not missed the note of triumph.

'Of course. Why not?'

'It seems unusual.'

Thinking quickly, Ferris Moore replied, 'It is recommended as a cure for astigmatism.'

'What is astigmatism?'

'An uneven tension in the muscles of the eye.'

'Is it very painful?'

'Only when one talks about it.'

At one time he had felt it might have been better to marry a wife, but now he realised that it would have amounted to the same thing. Unless, of course, there had been children and that would have been disastrous. Children trampled on flower beds and stole fruit. It was best to be as alone as one could. Life in itself was sufficiently unintelligible without additional complications. We came, we went. The sun rose. Things grew. Cold and emptiness enveloped this little blob on which there was action but no apparent purpose. Was there a God? Possibly. Did He care? Hardly.

It was that thought which first drove Ferris Moore to drink. Not to drink too much, but to drink at all. It happened at the age of fifty. He had never drunk up to then, but over the years the round of his life lost its flavour. It seemed senseless just to potter about the garden or walk to the village and back again; to read the papers at breakfast and sleep a little after lunch; to play string quartets on the gramophone (his was an old-fashioned house) or write articles of local historical interest which he never felt quite interesting enough to show to anyone.

His sister had objected to the drink and pointed out that he was bound by his promise to his dead father to abstain from powerful waters for life. He had felt himself a little bit guilty at first but eventually he worked it out in the form of a dialogue which ran so satisfactorily that now and then he still took it from his desk and read it.

A. Do you deny that you promised your dead father to abstain from powerful waters?

B. Most emphatically.

A. Your own diary asserts the contrary.

B. The diary is imprecise.

A. In what particular?

B. The diary is that of Ferris Moore Twenty-eight. I am Ferris Moore Fifty. I can hardly remember Ferris Moore Twenty-eight.

A. But he exists.

B. He does not exist. Any more than Ferris Moore Eight does.

A. Who was Ferris Moore Eight?

B. Simply someone I once knew. He used to chase butterflies and kept a pet rabbit. He also climbed trees. I am Ferris Moore Fifty and quite incapable, as you see, of climbing a tree or chasing a butterfly. This flesh is not the same flesh, this form is not the same form. This voice and the mind which directs it, they are not the same at all.

A. Then where are they? Where are Ferris Moore Twenty-eight and Ferris Moore Eight?

B. Why ask me? They have both gone away. They have left leaving no address.

A. Ah – but there is something else.

B. What else can there be?

A. Uniqueness. A uniqueness which is common to Ferris Moore Eight, Ferris Moore Twenty-eight, Ferris Moore Fifty. This uniqueness is constantly present in the arithmetical progression of bodies which is the physical manifestation of the journey of Ferris Moore through Time. From this we must imply a continuation of responsibility.

B. The philosophers, I know, speak of this uniqueness but I am not altogether convinced of it.

A. You will never shake us on Uniqueness. Without it there would be no responsibility, no culprit for any crime, no basis for law.

B. Does this uniqueness continue outside of Time?

A. Well-brought up people believe so. It is only fair, however, to rule that the question is beyond the competence of the present enquiry.

B. In that case I am free of my promise. If, for the sake of argument, I concede Uniqueness, I can maintain that the Uniqueness which was my father has moved out of Time. If I believed in a benevolent and personal God I might still hesitate. But I do not so believe. For me God died some years ago, quite suddenly. I was gardening at the time. I thought of my father. He had planted and his work surrounded me. I looked up into the blue sky. It was deep. It was worse than deep. It was empty. The heavens were blue and beautiful and empty. At that moment my father's uniqueness became a remote possibility. And even if it still Is, I argue that there can be no basis in law for a compact between a uniqueness which abides in a body and moves in Time and one which is pure spirit, remote, moving beyond Time. Death is unbridgeable. I am now going to have my first drink.

He did so. He had found it helped, too, despite his sister's disapproval. It softened the outlines of Reality. It blurred the menacing shapes of things without a Maker.

The doomed earwig on the steep side of the bank caught the attention of Ferris Moore more closely. As with it, so with him. He was surrounded on all sides by a flood from which there was no escape. He placed it in the order Orthoptera. Somewhere under its horny case there were wings. Why did it not use them? Probably, Ferris Moore conjectured, they were used only for the nuptial flight. If so it was a great waste of wings. Under the horny case too lurked a soul and an intelligence. The earwig Was. It knew that it Was. It was obviously uncertain, however, that it was going to continue to Be. Ferris Moore would attend to that presently. But only temporarily. That was the sad thing.

The realisation that he was sad about the earwig brought Ferris Moore into a sitting position once more. He had not been sad about another creature for a long time. During the middle twenties a vague sympathy for the lower classes had suggested itself to him because, despite their boorishness and their undeniably outrageous behaviour about which his sister had remarked adversely, it seemed unfortunate that so many should be hungry and hopeless. On another occasion, when a little boy smiled at him he had felt a strange pang of sympathy too – illogically this time since the child was happy and healthy. After that there was nothing to be moved about, except in a way when, listening to the Schubert Quintet, he felt it a pity the composer should have died before the work had been performed. Or again, when the King died and a pang of genuine regret pierced him. And now the plight of the earwig which he was about to rescue suggested once again the idea of inter-relationship or responsibility or, in so far as he could formulate the emotion, a sense of familyhood under an All-Fatherhood. Perhaps Love best expressed it, although it seemed extravagant to consider a trapped earwig and describe the resultant emotion as one of Love.

Ferris Moore stirred himself and searched around stiffly and painfully for a stick. Eventually he found one and returned to the edge of the bank. He sat for a while in a mood of recollection. It was really a very beautiful afternoon. At a distance from where he was sitting a belt of pine trees formed a semi-circle around the flower-scattered meadow. The blue sky above displayed here and there a small, fat, white cloud. It was a world which even God might condescend to walk in, always assuming of course that the idea of an intelligent and sympathetic God was compatible with the awe-inspiring irrationality of certain aspects of His Creation. Ferris Moore, his rejection of such an idea weakening under the benign assault of sunlight and scenery, found that he was no longer acting under his original impulse. The rescue would not be designed to demonstrate his possession of the faculty of inward self-determination to action. It would be an acknowledgment of kinship and brotherhood, an acceptance of universal inter-responsibility dictated by an All-Fatherhood, interested or disinterested, caring or uncaring, capable, if so desired, of being investigated more closely at a later date, if he so determined.

Ferris Moore leaned over the bank and found with relief that the earwig was still there. Very carefully Ferris Moore let down the stick. At first the earwig backed away from it. It was suspicious. It did not trust this strange arrival. But Ferris Moore had patience and intelligence. He let the stick hang perfectly still just about an inch from the earwig's head. In a few minutes, as Ferris Moore had cunningly anticipated, it crawled over slowly, made its necessary investigation, then crawled on to the end of the stick. Ferris Moore smiled with quiet triumph. The brown water below reflected the smile back at him. Ferris Moore saw his own face and for a moment allowed the smile to distract his attention. It startled him. He had not smiled at himself for quite a long time. Now it was his undoing. The stick jerked awkwardly. The earwig lost its grip. Ferris Moore realised what had happened when the small point of a splash dissipated his smiling image. He was thunderstruck. The earwig, a bright brown speck on a dark brown tide, drifted slowly downstream, until the failing eyes of Ferris Moore Sixty-two could no longer distinguish it. When it had gone and the shock had spent itself he shrugged sadly and dropped the stick into the river too. Then he lay back once more and stared into the blue sky. He was thinking . . .

Beyond the blue lay the darkness of outer space, and beyond the limits of outer space, at the remote point of

Infinity, without length or breadth or thickness, abided the mind of God, towards which all things travelled at an unreckonable speed; including Ferris Moore Sixty-two, his unloved sister, the King, the little boy with smiling eyes and the small, drowned earwig on the brown bosom of the waters.

VAL MULKERNS
You Must Be Joking

Morgan Judge, who had progressed from art to commerce and from wealth to blissful idleness, surveyed his early-morning kitchen with satisfaction. His cat lifted a blue and flattering eye from the warm depths of her basket, the sun seeped gently through yellow curtains, and as yet the tea-cosy had not been lifted from the telephone. Even if the instrument did ring it would be with a gentle far-away plea which could easily be disregarded if that moment's precise mood did not warrant lifting first the tea-cosy and then the receiver. Normally, of course, you marked the beginning of each day by unveiling the tele-phone. That was merely custom and not essential: this morning he might not unveil it at all.

Humming a strong passage from one of the Branden-burg Concertos, he flipped back the yellow curtains and surveyed the world. Spring. The unholy clamour of birds, the straight spears of tulips just about to burst into flower, the green moist lawn beautiful after its second mowing of the year. His magnolia tree was past its best and almost in leaf, but half way down the garden heavy lilacs made their promise. The buds were no more than pimple-size and dark purple, but the leaves had a tender and burgeon-ing richness. A week's sun would make blossoms and scent explode simultaneously, and by then the berberis would also be in bloom along the red-brick wall. There were, he conceded, less satisfying times of the year than late April.

Still humming, Morgan filled a miniature silver teapot

with water and put it to boil on an electric ring. Kettles he despised. While it boiled, he looked at the multitude of postcards and scribbled reminders which Mona had pinned to the wall behind the telephone.

'Thursday, 6 o'c. Hibernian,' he read aloud. 'Ask laundry about yellow pillow case, damn them.' And then, '8 o'c Ross, Wed.' Yes. That was last night. How are you this morning, Ross Amory? And how, Morgan wondered, is my wife? They didn't share the same bed any more now, and recently they had fixed up separate rooms, but this was merely a civilised arrangement best suited to their circumstances. There were certainly times when Mona irritated him, but on the whole she was the person whose company he found least demanding and most flattering in the world – or in his world, anyway, as he knew it.

When the water boiled he made weak China tea in the miniature teapot and then toasted two slices of rye bread. While it was still warm, he gently spread on the crisp surface about a spoonful of olive oil – not the common variety, but pure virgin olive oil from a large can, replaced twice a year by a most superior grocer. Each can cost seventy shillings, and it was cheap at the price.

As he nibbled, occasionally gyrating oddly to avoid getting a drip of oil on his crimson silk dressing-gown (which had a matching scarf) the cat rubbed herself affectionately against his legs as an indication that she would like her morning trip out of doors. He decanted her through the window, washed his hands carefully, and was returning with pleasure to his oily toast when the phone bubbled gently beneath the tea-cosy. It was more a vibration than an actual noise, and more a memory of one than an actual vibration happening at that moment. The reason was that Mona had thoughtfully sewn together two tea-cosies which had been faraway wedding presents, so that the depth of fluffy material between Morgan and the sound was considerable. In many ways he knew it woud be impossible to find another woman who suited him as well as Mona.

On a wild impulse – for this was normally Mona's job

– he tossed aside the cosy and picked up the receiver. It was, after all, a rather special day.

'Hello.'

'Hello, sir, Patrick Nelson Armstrong here.'

'Who?'

'Armstrong. The London *Clarion*, you know, sir. Wondering if on this propitious day I might speak to Mona Ambrose. About her plans for her *next* book, you know.'

'She is asleep,' Morgan said severely, 'celebrating the publication of her *present* book. I can't possibly waken her up at ten o'clock in the morning.'

'Of course not,' the wretched voice agreed, 'but I wonder if she – that is, I wonder if both of you could come along to my hotel – it's the Shelbourne, actually – and have dinner with me this evening? And later perhaps go on to Tony Tully's new play? It so happens I have been promised three tickets.'

'*Three tickets*,' said Morgan, impressed despite himself. The revered president of this island republic could hardly hope to be given more than three tickets for this starry first night. It was even rumoured that the play might go on tour to Belfast.

'You see, Tony knows I know something to his credit,' the confident voice explained, 'and if I let it out his reputation as a scoundrel would be ruined.'

'Tell you what,' Morgan offered, 'come to the publishers' reception at six o'clock in the Hibernian this evening and we'll see. You may even meet my wife there.'

'Wonderful. My predecessor told me how charming she is. Perhaps you would be kind enough to look out for a lanky blond fellow wearing a yellow waistcoat, whom the doorman will probably be in the process of evicting?'

'No need,' Morgan said handsomely, 'I'll have an invitation sent around to your hotel. Goodbye.'

'Thank you so much, sir.'

The voice vanished and Morgan returned to his toast and congealed pure virgin olive oil. Seeing the state it was

in, he cut off the bite marks and decided to take it upstairs
with a cup of tea to his wife. He emptied the tea-leaves
out of the silver teapot into the kitchen stove, and then
set about making a pot of Indian tea. Mona had some
depraved tastes even after twenty years of marriage to
him. She had been known, when staying with friends, to
drink coffee in the mornings, but never would she do that
in this house.

He generously added another slice of rye toast —
anointed rather less liberally with pure virgin olive oil —
to his wife's repast, and carried up the tray. He did not
knock at her bedroom door but, tray carefully balanced,
elbowed his way in, and as soon as his hands were free
drew back the curtains vigorously before looking towards
the bed.

Mona heaved herself and her yellow eiderdown in one
movement away from the bright sunlight and replaced her
face under the bedclothes. Only her short chopped hair
showed, and it reminded him of the knitted dolls one sees
sometimes in babies' prams. Once it had been silkily
brown and beautiful, but a series of expensive hair-
dressers had turned it first platinum blonde, then red,
then a sort of smoky grey, then black, and now brown
again. At times indeed, only for the extraordinary fairish
streaks (each quite distinct and not intended to blend
with the rest, it seemed, but put in at the staggering cost
of five shillings per streak) she reminded him of the old
Mona who used to write bad poetry, and who shattered
him on their wedding day by appearing with a cropped
boy's head, her romantic long hair having been left on the
floor of her first hairdresser the evening before. He smiled
as he remembered his first action as a husband: it had
been to drive her to the hairdresser's and demand back
the fallen switches of Mona's hair. Too dazzled by the
bridal irruption, and too surprised to refuse, the management had given them to him in an enormous paper bag
marked with their illustrious name. They had been going

to make a particularly fine hairpiece from Mona's shearings.

He waited for Mona's first wakening groan, and sat down on her dressing stool which was covered in yellow velvet. A big print of Botticelli's 'Venus and Mars' shone in the spill of light above the mantelpiece, and, as always, he pitied that poor bastard who had laboured and spent himself without taking so much as a feather out of the pert girl sitting up there in bed and shaking out her snake-curled hair. Distracted, he became aware to his annoyance that Mona was staring and half-smiling at him before he had noticed she was awake, and he thumped over with the tray.

'There, madam. Sit up and eat.'

She was never at her best at such times of the morning. Her night cream had sunk in and so she wasn't greasy now, but her brown eyes were so puffy that three hours later nobody would believe what he had seen. She licked her dry lips and smiled at him. From this angle it was obvious that she had two chins, both of them quite attractive. But nobody could say she had not successfully cherished her teeth, which were small and white and pretty as a cat's.

'Did I waken you?' she asked sweetly, reaching up to kiss him. It was a time-honoured opening gambit, at once a reminder of where she had been the previous evening and an expression of meaningless apology. As usual, he didn't answer.

'Happy publication day,' he said.

'Oh. God!' She crumpled her thin and still pretty shoulders and closed her eyes. 'I shall never get used to it. I know nothing will happen – nothing ever does. But I always feel the same way. That the publisher will realise his mistake and send over Alan to take all that lovely money away. That I shall be banned by my own countrymen on this very day – but they never ban you now, do they, until everyone has had time to buy up every copy in the bookshops? So why do I go on feeling – undefended, at somebody's mercy, abandoned, every single publication day?'

'Because you enjoy the contrast between that and the real thing,' Morgan said unfeelingly. 'You will be in the hands of your hairdresser in forty-five minutes. You and I and Signor Cicisbeo d'Amato will then have a champagne luncheon, at my expense, in your favourite dive overlooking the river – though indeed I can think of better places.'

'How can you call beautiful Ross such a beastly name?' she murmured. 'And *when* may I have just plain butter on my toast?'

'After that,' Morgan went on, ignoring her, 'we shall go on our customary tour of the bookshops to see which has the cutest display before we take you to Switzer's to sign autographs for all those depraved students and libidinous elderly Civil Servants. Then I shall take you home to your waiting bath, while Signor Cicisbeo departs for his, and then you will spend two hours preparing for the reception at which you will arrive (as usual) forty-five minutes late. Today, however, you'd better be a little sharper. Armstrong of the *Clarion* is over to see you, and he'll be there.'

'You're such a darling,' she said affectionately. 'What would I do without you? Any telegrams?'

'I left them – as usual – in the hall to encourage you to come down. One from your publishers – with love, no doubt. One from Signor Cicisbeo d'Amato – ditto, no doubt. And one from the milkman, like last time.'

'Ordinary people are so *sweet* to me,' she sighed emotionally, drinking the last of the tea and struggling to finish up one slice of oiled toast. She did not quite succeed, and handed up the tray apologetically, her lips greasy. Morgan took it away downstairs to give to his cat.

The reception, for which two enormous communicating Georgian rooms had been reserved, was much the same as last year's and all the years before. There were cascades of spring flowers on the buffet table (all of Mona's books had been launched in the spring), and champagne which the waiters had been instructed not to allow flow too freely, and cheese dip and smoked salmon and a boar's head which was probably made of plaster. Certainly it looked plaster, Morgan decided, no more real than most of the guests.

There was a huddle of poets, over beside the Bushmills – two successful homosexuals, one still-hopeful womaniser, and three irrefutably married, with large families. The three wives stood together, two of them very pretty and very pregnant, and one extremely large by nature. She was an authority on Charlotte Brooke, although few in the room could precisely recall who Charlotte Brooke had been.

There were novelists, rather more gregarious than the poets, all over the place. Some were dressed in open tartan shirts because this was traditionally a very dressy affair and it was a symbol of independence, universally respected, to wear no tie. Many of the tieless ones were better novelists whose own works quietly appeared in the bookshops without the aid of any ballyhoo like this, but some were television people who had come straight from the overheated studios. Above one of the Adam fireplaces was a large blown-up print of Mona prising open a crocus with two fingers, her tongue held between her teeth. Underneath stood Ross Amory, heavy dark head thrown back in a manner that recalled a film actor of the 'thirties. His spade-shaped black beard was very contemporary, however, and recalled that of Shakespeare: the most remarkable thing about it was that it was composed of a number of small tight curls, rather like Persian lamb. His finely preserved large white teeth flashed amiably around, while his dark and splendid eyes skimmed the entrances where Mona might at any moment appear. Once, as a student, Morgan remembered, he had published a tiny gilt-edged volume of translations from Ovid, at the expense of his mother, who had never read them but who still kept house for him and was still willing to pay for the publication of anything further he might ever add to his output. But he preferred to give public readings from Yeats, from which he made an amount of money.

Morgan kept an eye on him while chatting to a couple of female journalists who were concerned about the non-appearance of Mona. Damn it, Morgan told them, she had only left him for two minutes (she told him) to go to the powder room. Would she mind, the prettier of the two journalists asked Morgan, did he think she would mind being surprised in the powder room so that the material of her dress could be checked?

'I shouldn't do that,' Morgan advised. 'Your editor can't be in *that* much of a hurry. Let me get you another drink.'

He was leaving the two ladies just as a tall blond youth in a yellow waistcoat and the tightest trousers Morgan had ever seen went up to Ross. 'May I introduce myself, sir? Armstrong of the *Clarion*. I spoke to you on the telephone this morning, if you remember?'

'You spoke to *me* on the telephone this morning – I remember quite distinctly,' Morgan cut in. 'How do you do? Let me get you a drink.'

'How do you do, sir, I do beg your pardon. A tincture of Irish whiskey would be very pleasant if it's available.' He was bowing in apology to Ross when Morgan introduced them.

'This is the poet Ross Amory, a friend of ours.'

'How do you do, sir?'

Ross merely vouchsafed a flash of his beautiful teeth before turning away to speak to the female journalist who had been so anxious to get back to the office. His very deep yet honeyed voice kept her happy until Morgan returned with her drink, by which time the *Clarion* man had vanished. Annoyed, they glanced around for him until Ross (who could see around corners when he chose) picked him out at the far end of the room, in the process of kissing Mona's hand.

There was a sudden drift of people towards that end of the room, but Morgan banged the young man's drink down on the mantelpiece and decided to stay put. The disapproval on Ross Amory's face amused him. 'Very pleasant young fella, don't you think,' Morgan said wickedly, and affected surprise at Ross's reaction.

'I think he suffers from one of the worst defects of his class – a total unawareness of his own insignificance,' Ross murmured, and stared across the sea of heads to the tall blond one bent over Mona's. The fellow was even taller than he was, and Ross Amory was accustomed to looking down on most of the writers in Dublin.

He somehow contrived to look down at Patrick Nelson Armstrong when Mona brought him over, by directing his gaze down along the patrician length of his nose and examining only the newspaperman's top waistcoat button. The waistcoat itself, he noted, was of canary handwoven tweed and indescribably vulgar.

'Would you believe it, darling, *both* sets of Patrick's grandparents were Irish!' prattled Mona happily, squeezing an elbow of Ross and Morgan at the same time. 'He says he felt at home here right from the beginning. Did you know his children are called Devorgilla, Conall and Caitriona – isn't that sweet?'

'Charming,' Ross agreed, without lifting an eyebrow and smiling benignly at Mona.

'Something in me snaps back into place when I come over here,' Patrick offered eagerly. 'I feel as if they misplaced something when I was assembled over there, and it's only when I touch down on Irish soil that suddenly – whatever it is, rights itself.'

'Whereabouts on your person do you feel this error of assembly when you are over there?' Ross enquired slowly, lifting his eyes in apparent innocence to the younger man's face. But Mona was not deceived.

'Stop it, Ross,' she said.

'Where is your wife?' Morgan cut in peacefully. 'Forgive my enquiry, but nobody mentioned her.'

'Virginia isn't up to travel just at present,' Patrick said modestly.

'Poor thing,' Mona smiled. 'What will you call this one?'

'Stella if it's a girl – because of Swift, you know. I thought of Diarmuid if it's a boy.'

'Doesn't your wife have any say in the choice of names?' Ross asked insolently.

'Her father was Irish.' Patrick smiled. His good humour seemed unbreakable. 'The only people who object to the children's names are the teachers of the elder two, Devorgilla and Conall. The poor teachers can't pronounce them.'

'Nor can you, as a matter of fact.' Ross's coup de grace was delivered effectively just before he sauntered across the room to talk to a fellow-poet.

Mona cleared her throat nervously. 'Ross isn't feeling himself today – you must excuse him, Patrick. He's over-tired.'

'Of course. Poets are moody chaps.'

'Let me get you some more Irish,' Morgan said suddenly as though in amends. 'Bushmills?'

'Oh, if you please.'

'You, Mona?'

'Bushmills for me too, please.'

When Morgan returned with the drinks, Mona thanked him so profusely that he looked closely at her. 'Something awfully unfortunate has happened, darling,' she said, giving him her most radiant smile. 'Patrick was absolutely *promised* three seats for Tony's play tonight, and just after lunch they rang his hotel and said he could only have two. So *you* must go, darling.'

'Don't be silly.' Morgan knew her so well that this speech seemed to him not only delicious but touchingly funny. 'You know perfectly well that you wouldn't miss this for any money, and you know equally well that if I *did* decide to go, Patrick might find that he had, after all, only been allowed one ticket.'

'I assure you, sir, upon my honour – '

'I'm joking, of course,' Morgan said kindly. 'Naturally Mona will go.'

'You're sure you don't *mind*?' Mona insisted.

'Not a bit.'

'Then thank you, Patrick, I'll come.'

'The honour is entirely mine,' Patrick was solemnly assuring her as Morgan left them.

He was gathering up the scattered volumes of *Games My Father Taught Me* after most of the guests had gone, and had just checked that several copies were as usual missing, when Ross appeared with his dark face thunderstruck.

'Where has Mona gone?'

'To Tony Tully's first night with the troubadour son of St Patrick, of course.'

'Gone alone? You mean to say you let her . . .'

'She's gone to the theatre accompanied by that nice young fellow Irishman to whom you were exceedingly rude.'

'You can't mean it. You *must* be joking.'

'Of course I'm not joking. Didn't you hear he's safely married with children who have names of impeccable respectability? Don't you *know* the coverage he will give to Mona in next Sunday's *Clarion*? Have you any remotest idea of what that coverage will *mean* to Mona in terms of copies sold?'

'I think you're simply disgusting,' Ross burst out, 'thinking in terms of sordid royalties when the honour of your wife is at stake. I know his kind. He has the ferret's eyes of a rapist and he comes from the most depraved city in the world. How *could* you expose her to positive moral danger?'

As he raged, and Morgan, with the skill of long practice, patiently tried to soothe him down, Mona was settling contentedly into the dress circle with Patrick.

'You must call me Lisa,' she smiled.

'That's what I love about Irish people. You're so natural and unaffected,' said Patrick Nelson Armstrong.

WILLIAM TREVOR
Teresa's Wedding

The remains of the wedding-cake was on top of the piano in Swanton's lounge-bar, beneath a framed advertisement for Power's whiskey. Chas Flynn, the best man, had opened two packets of confetti: it lay thickly on the remains of the wedding-cake, on the surface of the bar and the piano, on the table and the two small chairs that the lounge-bar contained, and on the tattered green and red linoleum.

The wedding guests, themselves covered in confetti, stood in groups. Father Hogan, who had conducted the service in the Church of the Immaculate Conception, stood with Mrs Atty, the mother of the bride, and Mrs Cornish, the mother of the bridegroom, and Mrs Tracy, a sister of Mrs Atty's.

Mrs Tracy was the stoutest of the three women, a farmer's widow who lived eight miles from the town. In spite of the jubilant nature of the occasion, she was dressed in black, a colour she had affected since the death of her husband three years ago. Mrs Atty, bespectacled, with her grey hair in a bun, wore a flowered dress – small yellow and blue blooms that blended easily with the confetti. Mrs Cornish was in pink, with a pink hat. Father Hogan, a big red-complexioned man, held a tumbler containing whiskey and water in equal measures; his companions sipped Winter's Tale sherry.

Artie Cornish, the bridegroom, drank stout with his friends Eddie Boland and Chas Flynn, who worked in the town's bacon factory, and Screw Doyle, so called because he served behind the counter in Phelan's hardware shop. Artie, who worked in a shop himself – Driscoll's Provisions and Bar – was a freckled man of twenty-eight, six years older than his bride. He was heavily built, his bulk encased now in a suit of navy-blue serge, similar to the suits that all the other men were wearing that morning in Swanton's lounge-bar. In the opinion of Mr Driscoll, his employer, he was a conscientious shopman, with a good memory for where commodities were kept on the shelves. Customers occasionally found him slow.

The fathers of the bride and bridegroom, Mr Atty and Mr Cornish, were talking about greyhounds, keeping close to the bar. They shared a feeling of unease, caused by being in the lounge-bar of Swanton's, with women present, on a Saturday morning. 'Bring us two more big ones,' Mr Cornish requested of Kevin, a youth behind the bar, hoping that this addition to his consumption of whiskey would relax matters. They wore white carnations in the button-holes of their suits, and stiff white collars which were reddening their necks. Unknown to one another, they shared the same thought: a wish that the bride and groom would soon decide to bring the occasion to an end by going to prepare themselves for their journey to Cork on the half-one bus. Mr Atty and Mr Cornish, bald-headed men of fifty-three and fifty-five, had it in mind to spend the remainder of the day in Swanton's lounge-bar, celebrating in their particular way the union of their children.

The bride, who had been Teresa Atty and was now Teresa Cornish, had a round, pretty face and black, pretty hair, and was a month and a half pregnant. She stood in the corner of the lounge with her friends, Philomena Morrissey and Kitty Roche, both of whom had been bridesmaids. All three of them were attired in their wedding finery, dresses they had feverishly worked on to get finished in time for the wedding. They planned to alter the dresses and have them dyed so that later on they could go to parties in them, even though parties were rare in the town.

'I hope you'll be happy, Teresa,' Kitty Roche whispered. 'I hope you'll be all right.' She couldn't help giggling, even though she didn't want to. She giggled because she'd drunk a glass of gin and Kia-Ora orange which Screw Doyle had said would steady her. She'd been nervous in the church. She'd tripped twice on the walk down the aisle.

'You'll be marrying yourself one of these days,' Teresa whispered, her cheeks still glowing after the excitement of the ceremony. 'I hope you'll be happy too, Kit.'

But Kitty Roche, who was asthmatic, did not believe she'd ever marry. She'd be like Miss Levis, the Protestant woman on the Cork road, who'd never got married because of tuberculosis. Or old Hannah Flood, who had a bad hip. And it wasn't just that no one would want to be saddled with a diseased wife: there was also the fact that the asthma caused a recurrent skin complaint on her face and neck and hands.

Teresa and Philomena drank glasses of Babycham, and Kitty drank Kia-Ora with water instead of gin in it. They'd known each other all their lives. They'd been to the Presentation nuns together, they'd taken First Communion together. Even when they'd left the nuns, when Teresa had gone to work in the Medical Hall and Kitty Roche and Philomena in Keane's drapery, they'd continued to see each other almost every day.

'We'll think of you, Teresa,' Philomena said. 'We'll pray for you.' Philomena, plump and pale-haired, had every hope of marrying and had even planned her dress, in light lemony lace, with a Limerick veil. Twice in the last month she'd gone out with Des Foley the vet, and even if he was a few years older than he might be and had a car that smelt of cattle disinfectant, there was more to be said for Des Foley than for many another.

Teresa's two sisters, much older than Teresa, stood by the piano and the framed Power's advertisement, between the two windows of the lounge-bar. Agnes, in smart powder-blue, was tall and thin, the older of the two;

Loretta, in brown, was small. Their own two marriages, eleven and nine years ago, had been consecrated by Father Hogan in the Church of the Immaculate Conception and celebrated afterwards in this same lounge-bar. Loretta had married a man who was no longer mentioned because he'd gone to England and had never come back. Agnes had married George Tobin, who was at present sitting outside the lounge-bar in a Ford Prefect, in charge of his and Agnes's three small children. The Tobins lived in Cork now, George being the manager of a shoe-shop there. Loretta lived with her parents, like an unmarried daughter again.

'Sickens you,' Agnes said 'She's only a kid, marrying a goop like that. She'll be stuck in this dump of a town for ever.'

Loretta didn't say anything. It was well known that Agnes's own marriage had turned out well: George Tobin was a teetotaller and had no interest in either horses or greyhounds. From where she stood Loretta could see him through the window, sitting patiently in the Ford Prefect, reading a comic to his children. Loretta's marriage had not been consummated.

'Well, though I've said it before I'll say it again,' said Father Hogan. 'It's a great day for a mother.'

Mrs Atty and Mrs Cornish politely agreed, without speaking. Mrs Tracy smiled.

'And for an aunt too, Mrs Tracy. Naturally enough.'

Mrs Tracy smiled again. 'A great day,' she said.

'Ah, I'm happy for Teresa,' Father Hogan said. 'And for Artie, too, Mrs Cornish; naturally enough. Aren't they as fine a couple as ever stepped out of this town?'

'Are they leaving the town?' Mrs Tracy asked, confusion breaking in her face. 'I thought Artie was fixed in Driscoll's.'

'It's a manner of speaking, Mrs Tracy,' Father Hogan explained. 'It's a way of putting the thing. When I was marrying them this morning I looked down at their two faces and I said to myself, "Isn't it great God gave them life?" '

The three women looked across the lounge, at Teresa standing with her friends Philomena and Kitty Roche, and then at Artie, with Screw Doyle, Eddie Boland and Chas Flynn.

'He has a great career in front of him in Driscoll's,' Father Hogan pronounced. 'Will Teresa remain on in the Medical Hall, Mrs Atty?'

Mrs Atty replied that her daughter would remain for a while in the Medical Hall. It was Father Hogan who had persuaded Artie of his duty when Artie had hesitated. Mrs Atty and Teresa had gone to him for advice, he'd spoken to Artie and to Mr and Mrs Cornish, and the matter had naturally not been mentioned on either side since.

'Will I get you another glassful, Father?' inquired Mrs Tracy, holding out her hand for the priest's tumbler.

'Well, it isn't every day I'm honoured,' said Father Hogan with his smile, putting the tumbler into Mrs Tracy's hand.

At the bar Mr Atty and Mr Cornish drank steadily on. In their corner Teresa and her bridesmaids talked about weddings that had taken place in the Church of the Immaculate Conception in the past, how they had stood by the railings of the church when they were children, excited by the finery and the men in serge suits. Teresa's sisters whispered, Agnes continuing about the inadequacy of the man Teresa had just married. Loretta whispered without actually forming words. She wished her sister wouldn't go on so because she didn't want to think about any of it, about what had happened to Teresa, and what would happen to her again tonight, in a hotel in Cork. She'd fainted when it had happened to herself, when he'd come at her like a farm animal. She'd fought like a mad thing.

It was noisier in the lounge-bar than it had been. The voices of the bridegroom's friends were raised; behind the bar young Kevin had switched on the wireless. *Take my hand,* cooed a soft male voice, *take my whole life too.*

'Bedad, there'll be no holding you tonight, Artie,' Eddie Boland whispered thickly into the bridegroom's ear. He nudged Artie in the stomach with his elbow, spilling some Guinness. He laughed uproariously.

'We're following you in two cars,' Screw Doyle said. 'We'll be waiting in the double bed for you.' Screw Doyle laughed also, striking the floor repeatedly with his left foot, which was a habit of his when excited. At a late hour the night before he'd told Artie that once, after a dance, he'd spent an hour in a field with the girl whom Artie had agreed to marry. 'I had a great bloody ride of her,' he'd confided.

'I'll have a word with Teresa,' said Father Hogan, moving away from Teresa's mother, her aunt and Mrs Cornish. He did not, however, cross the lounge immediately, but paused by the bar, where Mr Cornish and Mr Atty were. He put his empty tumbler on the bar itself, and Mr Atty pushed it towards young Kevin, who at once refilled it.

'Well, it's a great day for a father,' said Father Hogan. 'Aren't they a tip-top credit to each other?'

'Who's that, Father?' inquired Mr Cornish, his eyes a little bleary, sweat hanging from his cheeks.

Father Hogan laughed. He put his tumbler on the bar again, and Mr Cornish pushed it towards young Kevin for another refill.

In their corner Philomena confided to Teresa and Kitty Roche that she wouldn't mind marrying Des Foley the vet. She'd had four glasses of Babycham. If he asked her this minute, she said, she'd probably say yes. 'Is Chas Flynn nice?' Kitty Roche asked, squinting across at him.

On the wireless Petula Clark was singing 'Downtown'. Eddie Boland was whistling 'Mother Macree'. 'Listen, Screw,' Artie said, keeping his voice low although it wasn't necessary. 'Is that true? Did you go into a field with Teresa?'

Loretta watched while George Tobin in his Ford Prefect turned a page of the comic he was reading to his children. Her sister's voice continued in its abuse of the town and its people, in particular the shopman who had got Teresa pregnant. Agnes hated the town and always had. She'd met George Tobin at a dance in Cork and had said to Loretta that in six months' time she'd be gone from the town for ever. Which was precisely what had happened, except that marriage had made her less nice than she'd been. She'd hated the town in a jolly way once, laughing over it. Now she hardly laughed at all.

'Look at him,' she was saying. 'I doubt he knows how to hold a knife and fork.'

Loretta ceased her observation of her sister's husband through the window and regarded Artie Cornish instead. She looked away from him immediately because his face, so quickly replacing the face of George Tobin, had caused in her mind a double image which now brutally persisted. She felt a sickness in her stomach, and closed her eyes and prayed. But the double image remained: George Tobin and Artie Cornish coming at her sisters like two farmyard animals and her sisters fighting to get away. 'Dear Jesus,' she whispered to herself. 'Dear Jesus, help me.'

'Sure it was only a bit of gas,' Screw Doyle assured Artie. 'Sure there was no harm done, Artie.'

In no way did Teresa love him. She had been aware of that when Father Hogan had arranged the marriage, and even before that, when she'd told her mother that she thought she was pregnant and had then mentioned Artie Cornish's name. Artie Cornish was much the same as his friends: you could be walking along a road with Screw Doyle or Artie Cornish and you could hardly tell the difference. There was nothing special about Artie Cornish, except that he always added up the figures twice when he was serving you in Driscoll's. There was nothing bad about him either, any more than there was anything bad about Eddie Boland or Chas Flynn or even Screw Doyle. She'd said privately to Father Hogan that she didn't love him or feel anything for him one way or the other: Father Hogan had replied that in the circumstances all that line of talk was irrelevant.

When she was at the Presentation Convent Teresa had imagined her wedding, and even the celebration in this very lounge-bar. She had imagined everything that had happened that morning, and the things that were happening still. She had imagined herself standing with her bridesmaids as she was standing now, her mother and her aunt drinking sherry, Agnes and Loretta being there too, and other people, and music. Only the bridegroom had been mysterious, some faceless, bodiless presence, beyond imagination. From conversations she had had with Philomena and Kitty Roche, and with her sisters, she knew that they had imagined in a similar way. Yet Agnes had settled for George Tobin because George Tobin was employed in Cork and could take her away from the town. Loretta, who had been married for a matter of weeks, was going to become a nun.

Artie ordered more bottles of stout from young Kevin. He didn't want to catch the half-one bus and have to sit beside her all the way to Cork. He didn't want to go to the Lee Hotel when they could just as easily have remained in the town, when he could just as easily have gone in to Driscoll's tomorrow and continued as before. It would have been different if Screw Doyle hadn't said he'd been in a field with her: you could pretend a bit on the bus, and in the hotel, just to make the whole thing go. You could pretend like you'd been pretending ever since Father Hogan had laid down the law, you could make the best of it like Father Hogan had said.

He handed a bottle of stout to Chas Flynn and one to Screw Doyle and another to Eddie Boland. He'd ask her about it on the bus. He'd repeat what Screw Doyle had said and ask her if it was true. For all he knew the child

she was carrying was Screw Doyle's child and would be
born with Screw Doyle's thin nose, and everyone in the
town would know when they looked at it. His mother
had told him when he was sixteen never to trust a girl,
never to get involved, because he'd be caught in the end.
He'd get caught because he was easy-going, because he
didn't possess the smartness of Screw Doyle and some of
the others. 'Sure, you might as well marry Teresa as anyone else,' his father had said after Father Hogan had
called to see them about the matter. His mother had said
things would never be the same between them again.

Eddie Boland sat down at the piano and played 'Mother
Macree', causing Agnes and Loretta to move to the other
side of the lounge-bar. In the motor-car outside the Tobin
children asked their father what the music was for.

'God go with you, girl,' Father Hogan said to Teresa,
motioning Kitty Roche and Philomena away. 'Isn't it a
grand thing that's happened, Teresa?' His red-skinned
face, with the shiny false teeth so evenly arrayed in it,
was close to hers. For a moment he thought he might
kiss her, which of course was ridiculous, Father Hogan
kissing anyone, even at a wedding celebration.

'It's a great day for all of us, girl.'

When she'd told her mother, her mother said it made
her feel sick in her stomach. Her father hit her on the side
of the face. Agnes came down specially from Cork to try
and sort the matter out. It was then that Loretta had first
mentioned becoming a nun.

'I want to say two words,' said Father Hogan, still
standing beside her, but now addressing everyone in the
lounge-bar. 'Come over here alongside us, Artie. Is there
a drop in everyone's glass?'

Artie moved across the lounge-bar, with his glass of
stout. Mr Cornish told young Kevin to pour out a few
more measures. Eddie Boland stopped playing the piano.

'It's only this,' said Father Hogan. 'I want us all to lift

our glasses to Artie and Teresa. May God go with you, the pair of you,' he said, lifting his own glass.

'Health, wealth and happiness,' proclaimed Mr Cornish from the bar.

'And an early night,' shouted Screw Doyle. 'Don't forget to draw the curtains, Artie.'

They stood awkwardly, not holding hands, not even touching. Teresa watched while her mother drank the remains of her sherry, and while her aunt drank and Mrs Cornish drank. Agnes's face was disdainful, a calculated reply to the coarseness of Screw Doyle's remarks. Loretta was staring ahead of her, concentrating her mind on her novitiate. A quick flush passed over the roughened countenance of Kitty Roche. Philomena laughed, and all the men in the lounge-bar, except Father Hogan, laughed.

'That's sufficient of that talk,' Father Hogan said with contrived severity. 'May you meet happiness halfway,' he added, suitably altering his intonation. 'The pair of you, Artie and Teresa.'

Noise broke out again after that. Father Hogan shook hands with Teresa and then with Artie. He had a funeral at half-past three, he said: he'd better go and get his dinner inside him.

'Good-bye, Father,' Artie said. 'Thanks for doing the job.'

'God bless the pair of you,' said Father Hogan, and went away.

'We should be going for the bus,' Artie said to her. 'It wouldn't do to miss the old bus.'

'No, it wouldn't.'

'I'll see you down there. You'll have to change your clothes.'

'Yes.'

'I'll come the way I am.'

'You're fine the way you are, Artie.'

He looked at the stout in his glass and didn't raise his eyes from it when he spoke again. 'Did Screw Doyle take you into a field, Teresa?'

He hadn't meant to say it then. It was wrong to come out with it like that, in the lounge-bar, with the wedding-cake still there on the piano, and Teresa still in her wedding-dress, and confetti everywhere. He knew it was wrong even before the words came out; he knew that the stout had angered and befuddled him.

'Sorry,' he said. 'Sorry, Teresa.'

She shook her head. It didn't matter: it was only to be expected that a man you didn't love and who didn't love you would ask a question like that at your wedding celebration.

'Yes,' she said. 'Yes, he did.'

'He told me. I thought he was codding. I wanted to know.'

'It's your baby, Artie. The other thing was years ago.'

He looked at her. Her face was flushed, her eyes had tears in them.

'I had too much stout,' he said.

They stood where Father Hogan had left them, drawn away from their wedding guests. Not knowing where else to look, they looked together at Father Hogan's black back as he left the lounge-bar, and then at the perspiring, naked heads of Mr Cornish and Mr Atty by the bar.

At least they had no illusions, she thought. Nothing worse could happen than what had happened already after Father Hogan had laid down the law. She wasn't going to get a shock like Loretta had got. She wasn't going to go sour like Agnes had gone when she'd discovered that it wasn't enough just to marry a man for a purpose, in order to escape from a town. Philomena was convincing herself that she'd fallen in love with an elderly vet, and if she got any encouragement Kitty Roche would convince herself that she was mad about anyone at all.

For a moment as Teresa stood there, the last moment before she left the lounge-bar, she felt that she and Artie might make some kind of marriage together because there was nothing that could be destroyed, no magic or anything else. He could ask her the question he had asked, while she stood there in her wedding dress: he could ask her and she could truthfully reply, because there was nothing special about the occasion, or the lounge-bar all covered in confetti.

BRIAN FRIEL
Foundry House

When his father and mother died, Joe Brennan applied
for their house, his old home, the gate lodge to Foundry
House. He wrote direct to Mr Bernard (as Mr Hogan
was known locally), pointing out that he was a radio-
and-television mechanic in the Music Shop; that although
he had never worked for Mr Hogan, his father had been
an employee in the foundry for over fifty years; and that
he himself had been born and reared in the gate lodge.
Rita, his wife, who was more practical than he, insisted
that he mention their nine children and the fact that they
were living in three rooms above a launderette.

'That should influence him,' she said. 'Aren't they
supposed to be one of the best Catholic families in the
North of Ireland?' So, against his wishes, he added a
paragraph about his family and their inadequate accom-
modation, and sent off his application. Two days later,
he received a reply from Mrs Hogan, written on mauve
scented notepaper with fluted edges. Of course she
remembered him, she said. He was the small, round-
faced boy with the brown curls who used to play with
her Declan. And to think that he now had nine babies
of his own! Where did time go? He could collect the
keys from the agent and move in as soon as he wished.
There were no longer any duties attached to the position
of gatekeeper, she added – not since wartime, when the
authorities had taken away the great iron gates that sealed
the mouth of the avenue.

'Brown curls!' Rita squealed with delight when Joe

read her the letter. 'Brown curls! She mustn't have seen you for twenty years or more!'

'That's all right, now,' was all Joe could say. He was moved with relief and an odd sense of humility at his unworthiness. 'That's all right. That's all right.'

They moved into their new house at the end of summer. It was a low-set, solid stone building with a steep roof and exaggerated eaves that gave it the appearance of a gnome's house in a fairy tale. The main Derry-Belfast road ran parallel to the house, and on the other side the ground rose rapidly in a tangle of shrubs and wild rhododendron and decaying trees, through which the avenue crawled up to Foundry House at the top of the hill. The residence was not visible from the road or from any part of the town; one could only guess at its location somewhere in the green patch that lay between the new housing estate and the brassiere factory. But Joe remembered from his childhood that if one stood at the door of Foundry House on a clear morning, before the smoke from the red-brick factories clouded the air, one could see through the trees and the undergrowth, past the gate lodge and the busy main road, and right down to the river below, from which the sun drew a million momentary flashes of light that danced and died in the vegetation.

For Joe, moving into the gate lodge was a home-coming; for Rita and the children, it was a changeover to a new life. There were many improvements to be made — there was no indoor toilet and no running water, the house was lit by gas only, and the windows, each made up of a score of small, diamond-shaped pieces of glass, gave little light — and Joe accepted that they were inevitable. But he found himself putting them off from day to day and from week to week. He did not have much time when he came home from work, because the evenings were getting so short. Also, he had applied to the urban council for a money grant, and they were sending along an architect soon. And he had to keep an eye on the children, who

looked on the grounds as their own private part and
climbed trees and lit fires in the undergrowth and played
their shrieking games of hide-and-seek or cowboys-and-
Indians right up to the very front of the big house itself.

'Come back here! Come back!' Joe would call after
them in an urgent undertone. 'Why can't you play down
below near your own house? Get away down at once
with you!'

'We want to play up here, Daddy,' some of them would
plead. 'There are better hiding places up here.'

'The old man, he'll soon scatter you!' Joe would say.
'Or he'll put the big dog on you. God help you then!'

'But there is no old man. Only the old woman and the
maid. And there is no dog, either.'

'No Mr Bernard? Huh! Just let him catch you, and
you'll know all about it. No Mr Bernard! The dog may
be gone, but Mr Bernard's not. Come on now! Play
around your own door or else come into the house
altogether.'

No Mr Bernard! Mr Bernard always had been, Joe
thought to himself, and always would be – a large, stern-
faced man with a long white beard and a heavy step and
a walking stick, the same ever since he remembered him.
And beside him the Great Dane, who copied his master
as best he could in expression and gait – a dour, sullen
animal as big as a calf and as savage as a tiger, according
to the men in the foundry. And Mrs Hogan? He supposed she could be called an old woman now, too. Well
over sixty, because Declan and he were of an age, and he
was thirty-three himself. Yes, an old woman, or at least
elderly, even though she was twenty years younger than
her husband. And not Declan now, or even Master Declan,
but Father Declan, a Jesuit. And then there was Claire,
Miss Claire, the girl, younger than Declan by a year. Fat,
blue-eyed Claire, who had blushed every time she
passed the gate lodge because she knew some of the
Brennans were sure to be peering out through the diamond windows. She had walked with her head to one

side, as if she were listening for something, and used to trail her fingers along the boxwood that fringed both sides of the avenue. 'Such a lovely girl,' Joe's mother used to say. 'So simple and so sweet. Not like the things I see running about this town. There's something good before that child. Something very good.' And she was right. Miss Claire was now Sister Claire of the Annunciation Nuns and was out in Africa. Nor would she ever be home again. Never. Sister Claire and Father Declan—just the two of them, and both of them in religion, and the big house up above going to pieces, and no one to take over the foundry when the time would come. Everything they could want in the world, anything that money could buy, and they turned their backs on it all. Strange, Joe thought. Strange. But right, because they were the Hogans.

They were a month in the house and were seated at their tea, all eleven of them, when Mrs Hogan called on them. It was now October and there were no evenings to speak of; the rich, warm days ended abruptly in a dusk that was uneasy with cold breezes. Rita was relieved at the change in the weather, because now the children, still unsure of the impenetrable dark and the nervous movements in the undergrowth, were content to finish their games when daylight faded, and she had no difficulty in gathering them for their evening meal. Joe answered the knock at the door.

'I'm so sorry to disturb you, Mr Brennan. But I wonder could you do me a favour?'

She was a tall, ungraceful woman, with a man's shoulders and a wasted body and long, thin feet. When she spoke, her mouth and lips worked in excessive movement.

Rita was at Joe's elbow. 'Did you not ask the woman in?' she reproved him. 'Come on inside, Mrs Hogan.'

'I'm sorry,' Joe stammered. 'I thought . . . I was about to . . .' How could he say he didn't dare?

'Thank you all the same,' Mrs Hogan said. 'But I oughtn't to have left Bernard at all. What brought me down was this. Mary – our maid, you know – she tells me that you have a tape-recording machine. She says you're in that business. I wonder could we borrow it for an afternoon? Next Sunday?'

'Certainly, Mrs Hogan. Certainly,' said Rita. 'Take it with you now. We never use it. Do we, Joe?'

'If Sunday suits you, I would like to have it then when Father Declan comes,' Mrs Hogan said. 'You see, my daughter, Claire, has sent us a tape-recording of her voice – these nuns nowadays, they're so modern – and we were hoping to have Father Declan with us when we play it. You know, a sort of family reunion, on Sunday.'

'Any time at all,' said Rita. 'Take it with you now. Go and get it, Joe, and carry it up.'

'No, no. Really. Sunday will do – Sunday afternoon. Besides, neither Bernard nor I know how to work the machine. We'll be depending on you to operate it for us, Mr Brennan.'

'And why wouldn't he?' said Rita. 'He does nothing on a Sunday afternoon, anyway. Certainly he will.'

Now that her request had been made and granted, Mrs Hogan stood irresolutely between the white gaslight in the hall and the blackness outside. Her mouth and lips still worked, although no sound came.

'Sunday then,' she said at last. 'A reunion.'

'Sunday afternoon,' said Rita. 'I'll send him up as soon as he has his dinner in him.'

'Thank you,' said Mrs Hogan. 'Thank you.' Her mouth formed an 'O,' and she drew in her breath. But she snapped it shut again and turned and strode off up the avenue.

Rita closed the door and leaned against it. She doubled up with laughter. 'Lord, if you could only see your face!' she gasped between bursts.

'What do you mean, my face?'

'All scared-looking, like a child caught stealing!'

'What are you raving about?' he asked irritably.

'And she was as scared-looking as yourself.' She held

her hand to her side. 'She must have been looking for the brown curls and the round face! And not a word out of you! Like a big, scared dummy!'

'Shut up,' he mumbled gruffly. 'Shut up, will you?'

Joe had never been inside Foundry House, had never spoken to Mr Bernard, and had not seen Declan since his ordination. And now, as he stood before the hall door and the evil face on the leering knocker, the only introductory remark his mind would supply him was one from his childhood: 'My daddy says here are the keys to the workshop and that he put out the fire in the office before he left.' He was still struggling to suppress this senseless memory when Father Declan opened the door.

'Ah, Joe, Joe, Joe! Come inside. Come inside. We are waiting for you. And you have the machine with you? Good man! Good man! Great! Great!'

Father Declan was fair and slight, and his gestures fluttering and birdlike. The black suit accentuated the whiteness of his hair and skin and hands.

'Straight ahead, Joe. First door to the right. You know – the breakfast room. They live there now, Father and Mother. Convenient to the kitchen, and all. And Mother tells me you are married and have a large family?'

'That's right, Father.'

'Good man! Good man! Marvellous, too. No, no, not that door, Joe; the next one. No, they don't use the drawing room any more. Too large and too expensive to heat. That's it, yes. No, no, don't knock. Just go right in. That's it. Good man! Good man!'

One minute he was behind Joe, steering him through the hallway, and the next he had sped past him and was standing in the middle of the floor of the breakfast room, his glasses flashing, his arms extended in reception. 'Good man. Here we are. Joe Brennan, Mother, with the tape recorder.'

'So kind of you, Joe,' said Mrs Hogan, emerging from behind the door. 'It's going to be quite a reunion, isn't it?'

'How many young Brennans are there?' asked Father Declan.

'Nine, Father.'

'Good! Good! Great! Great!'

'Such healthy children, too,' said Mrs Hogan. 'I've seen them playing on the avenue. And so . . . so healthy.'

'Have a seat, Joe. Just leave the recorder there. Anywhere at all. Good man. That's it. Fine!'

'You've had your lunch, Mr Brennan?'

'Yes, thanks, Mrs Hogan. Thank you all the same.'

'What I mean is, you didn't rush off without it?'

'Lucky for you, Joe,' the priest broke in. 'Because these people, I discover, live on snacks now. Milk and bananas – that sort of thing.'

'You'll find the room cold, I'm afraid, Mr Brennan.'

'If you have a power plug, I'll get this thing . . .'

'A power plug. A power plug. A power plug. A power plug.' The priest cracked his fingers each time he said the words and frowned in concentration.

'What about that thing there?' asked Mrs Hogan, pointing to the side of the mantelpiece.

'That's a gas bracket, Mother. No. Electric. Electric.' One white finger rested on his chin. 'An electric power plug. There must be one somewhere in the – ah! Here we are!' He dropped on his knees below the window and looked back exultantly over his shoulder. 'I just thought so. Here we are. I knew there must be one somewhere.'

'Did you find one?' asked Mrs Hogan.

'Yes, we did, didn't we, Joe? Will this do? Does your machine fit this?'

'That's grand, Father.'

'Good! Good! Then I'll go and bring Father down. He's in bed resting. Where is the tape, Mother?'

'Tape? Oh, the tape! Yes, there on the sideboard.'

'Fine! Fine! That's everything, then. Father and I will be down in a minute. Good! Good!'

'Logs,' said Mrs Hogan to herself. Then, remembering Joe, she said to him, 'We burn our own fuel. For economy.'

She smiled bleakly at him and followed her son from the room.

Joe busied himself with rigging up the machine and putting the new tape in position. When he was working in someone's house, it was part of his routine to examine the pictures and photographs around the walls, to open drawers and presses, to finger ornaments and bric-à-brac. But, here in Foundry House, a modesty, a shyness, a vague deference to something long ago did not allow his eyes even to roam from the work he was engaged in. Yet he was conscious of certain aspects of the room; the ceiling was high, perhaps as high as the roof of his own house, the fireplace was of black marble, the door handle was of cut glass, and the door itself did not close properly. Above his head was a print of horses galloping across open fields; the corner of the carpet was nibbled away. His work gave him assurance.

'There you are now, Mrs Hogan,' he said when she returned with a big basket of logs. 'All you have to do is turn this knob and away she goes.'

She ignored his stiff movement to help her with her load of logs, and knelt at the fireplace until she had built up the fire. Then, rubbing her hands down her skirt, she came and stood beside him.

'What was that, Mr Brennan?'

'I was saying that all you have to do is to turn this knob here to start it going, and turn it back to stop it. Nothing at all to it.'

'Yes?' she said, thrusting her lips forward, her mind a blank.

'That's all,' said Joe. 'Right to start, left to stop. A child could work it.' He tugged at the lapels of his jacket to indicate that he was ready to leave.

'No difficulty at all,' she repeated dreamily. Then suddenly alert again, 'Here they come. You sit there, Mr Brennan, on this side of the fire, Father Declan will sit here, I will sit beside the table. A real family circle.'

'You'll want to listen to this by yourselves, Mrs Hogan.
So if you don't mind . . .'

'Don't leave, Mr Brennan. You will stay, won't you?
You remember Claire, our lovely Claire. You remember
her, don't you? She's out in Africa, you know, and she'll
never be home again. Never. Not even for a death. You'll
stay, and hear her talking to us, won't you? Of course
you will.' Her finger tips touched the tops of her ears.
'Claire's voice. Talking to us. And you'll want to hear it
too, won't you?'

Before he could answer, the door burst open. Mr
Bernard had come down.

It took them five minutes to get from the door to the
leather armchair beside the fire, and Joe was reminded
of a baby being taught to walk. Father Declan came in
first, backward, crouching slightly, his eyes on his father's
feet and his arms outstretched and beckoning. 'Slow-ly.
Slow-ly,' he said in a hypnotist's voice. 'Slow-ly. Slow-ly.'
Then his father appeared. First a stick, a hand, an arm,
the curve of his stomach, then the beard, yellow
and untidy, then the whole man. Since his return to the
gate lodge, Joe had not thought of Mr Bernard beyond
the fact that he was there. In his mind there was a
twenty-year-old image that had never been adjusted, a
picture which was so familiar to him that he had long
since ceased to look at it. But this was not the image, this
giant who had grown in height and swollen in girth
instead of shrinking, this huge, monolithic figure that
inched its way across the faded carpet, one mechanical
step after the other, in response to a word from the black,
weaving figure before him. Joe looked at his face, fleshy,
trembling, coloured in dead purple and grey-black, and
at the eyes, wide and staring and quick with the terror of
stumbling or of falling or even of missing a syllable of
the instructions from the priest. 'Lift again. Lift it. Lift
it. Good. Good. Now down, down. And the right, up and
up and up – yes – and now down.' The old man wore an
overcoat streaked down the front with food stains, and

the hands, one clutching the head of the stick, the other limp and lifeless by his side, were so big they had no contour. His breathing was a succession of rapid sighs.

Until the journey from door to armchair was completed, Mrs Hogan made fussy jobs for herself and addressed herself to no one in particular. 'The leaves are terrible this year. Simply terrible. I must get a man to sweep them up and do something with the rockery, too, because it has got out of hand altogether . . .'

'Slow-ly. Slow-ly. Left. Left. That's it . . . up yet. Yes. And down again. Down.'

'I never saw such a year for leaves. And the worst of it is the wind blows them straight up against the hall door. Only this morning, I was saying to Mary we must make a pile of them and burn them before they smother us altogether. A bonfire – that's what we'll make.'

'Now turn. Turn. Turn. That's it. Right round. Round. Round. Now back. Good. Good.'

'Your children would enjoy a bonfire, wouldn't they, Mr Brennan? Such lively children they are, too, and so healthy, so full of life. I see them, you know, from my bedroom window. Running all over the place. So lively and full of spirits.'

A crunch, a heavy thud, and Mr Bernard was seated, not upright but sideways over the arm of the chair, as he had dropped. His eyes blinked in relief at having missed disaster once more.

'Now,' said Mrs Hogan briskly, 'I think we're ready to begin, aren't we? This is Mr Brennan of the gate lodge, Daddy. He has given us the loan of his tape-recording machine and is going to work it for us. Isn't that kind of him?'

'How are you, Mr Hogan?' said Joe.

The old man did not answer, but looked across at him. Was it a sly, reproving look, Joe wondered, or was it the awkward angle of the old man's head that made it appear sly?

'Which of these knobs is it?' asked Father Declan, his

fingers playing arpeggios over the recorder. ' "On." This
is it, isn't it? Yes. This is it.'

'The second one is for volume, Father,' said Joe.

'Volume. Yes. I see. Well, all set?'

'Ready,' said Mrs Hogan.

'Ready, Daddy?' asked Father Declan.

'Daddy's ready,' said Mrs Hogan.

'Joe?'

'Ready,' said Joe, because that was what Mrs Hogan
had said.

'Here goes then,' said Father Declan. 'Come in, Claire.
We're waiting.'

The recorder purred. The soft sound of the revolving
spools spread up and out until it was as heavy as the
noise of distant seas. Mrs Hogan sat at the edge of her
chair; Mr Bernard remained slumped as he had fallen.
Father Declan stood poised as a ballet dancer before the
fire. The spools gathered speed and the purring was a
pounding of blood in the ears.

'It often takes a few seconds – ' Joe began.

'Quiet!' snapped Mrs Hogan. 'Quiet, boy! Quiet!'

Then the voice came and all other sound died.

'Hello, Mammy and Daddy and Father Declan. This
is Sister Claire speaking to the three of you from St
Joseph's Mission, Kaluga, Northern Rhodesia. I hope you
are all together when this is being played back, because I
am imagining you all sitting before a great big fire in the
drawing room at this minute, Daddy spread out and taking
his well-earned relaxation on one side, and you, Mammy,
sitting on the other side, and Declan between you both.
How are you all? I wish to talk to each of you in turn –
to Declan first, then to you, Mammy, and last, but by no
means least, to my dear daddy. Later in the recording,
Reverend Mother, who is here beside me, will say a few
words to you, and after that you will hear my school choir
singing some Irish songs that I have taught them and some
native songs they have taught me. I hope you will enjoy
them.'

Joe tried to remember the voice. Then he realised that
he probably had never heard Claire speak. This sounded
more like reading than speaking, he thought – like a
teacher reading a story to a class of infants, making her
voice go up and down in pretended interest.

She addressed the priest first, and Joe looked at him –
eyes closed, hands joined at the left shoulder, head to the
side, feet crossed, his whole body limp and graceful as if
in repose. She asked him for his prayers and thanked him
for his letter last Christmas. She said that every day she
got her children to pray both for him and for the success
of his work, and asked him to send her the collection of
Irish melodies – a blue-backed book, she said, which he
would find either in the piano stool or in the glass book-
case beside the drawing-room window.

'And now you, Mammy. You did not mention your
lumbago in your last letter, so I take it you are not suffering so much from it. And I hope you have found a good
maid at last, because the house is much too big for you
to manage all by yourself. There are many young girls
around the mission here who would willingly give you a
hand, but then they are too far away, aren't they? However, please God, you are now fixed up.'

She went on to ask about the gardens and the summer
crop of flowers, and told of the garden she had beside the
convent and of the flowers she was growing. While her
daughter spoke to her, Mrs Hogan worked her mouth
and lips furiously, and Joe wondered what she was saying
to herself.

'And now I come to my own daddy. How are you,
Daddy? I am sure you were very sorry when Prince had
to be shot, you had him so long. And then the Prince
before that – how long did you have him? I was telling
Sister Monica here about him the other day, about the
first Prince, and when I said he lived to be nineteen and
a half, she just laughed in my face and said she was sure
I was mistaken. But he was nineteen and a half, wasn't
he? You got him on my sixth birthday, I remember, and

although I never saw the second Prince – you got him after I had entered – I am quite sure he was as lovely as the first. Now, why don't you get yourself a third, Daddy? He would be company for you when you go on your rambles, and it would be nice for *you* to have him lying beside you on the office floor, the way the first Prince used to lie.'

Joe watched the old man. Mr Bernard could not move himself to face the recorder, but his eyes were on it, the large, startled eyes of a horse.

'And now, Daddy, before I talk any more to you, I am going to play a tune for you on my violin. I hope you like it. It is the "Gartan Mother's Lullaby". Do you remember it?'

She began to play. The music was tuneful but no more. The lean, tinny notes found a weakness in the tape or in the machine, because when she played the higher part of the melody, the only sound reproduced was a shrieking monotone. Joe sprang to his feet and worked at the controls but he could do nothing. The sound adjusted itself when she came to the initial melody again, and he went back to his seat.

It was then, as he turned to go back to the fire, that he noticed the old man. He had moved somehow in his arm-chair and was facing the recorder, staring at it. His one good hand pressed down on the sides of his chair and his body rocked backward and forward. His expression, too, had changed. The dead purple of his cheeks was now a living scarlet, and the mouth was open. Then, even as Joe watched, he suddenly levered himself upright in the chair, his face pulsating with uncontrollable emotion, the veins in his neck dilating, the mouth shaping in preparation for speech. He leaned forward, half pointing toward the recorder with one huge hand.

'*Claire!*'

The terrible cry – hoarse, breathy, almost lost in his asthmatic snortings – released Father Declan and Mrs

Hogan from their concentration on the tape. They ran to him as he fell back into the chair.

Darkness had fallen by the time Joe left Foundry House. He had helped Father Declan to carry the old man upstairs to his bedroom and helped to undress him and put him to bed. He suggested a doctor, but neither the priest nor Mrs Hogan answered him. Then he came downstairs alone and switched off the humming machine. He waited for almost an hour for the others to come down – he felt awkward about leaving without making some sort of farewell – but when neither of them came, he tiptoed out through the hall and pulled the door after him. He left the recorder behind.

The kitchen at home was chaotic. The baby was in a zinc bath before the fire, three younger children were wrestling in their pyjamas, and the five elder were eating at the table. Rita, her hair in a turban and her sleeves rolled up, stood in the middle of the floor and shouted unheeded instructions above the din. Joe's arrival drew her temper to him.

'So you came home at last! Did you have a nice afternoon with your fancy friends?'

He picked his steps between the wrestlers and sat in the corner below the humming gas jet.

'I'm speaking to you! Are you deaf?'

'I heard you,' he said. 'Yes, I had a nice afternoon.'

She sat resolutely on the opposite side of the fireplace, to show that she had done her share of the work; it was now his turn to give a hand.

'Well!' She took a cigarette from her apron pocket and lit it. The chaos around her was forgotten.

'Well, what?' she asked.

'You went up with the recorder, and what happened?'

'They were all there – the three of them.'

'Then what?'

'We played the tape through.'

'What's the house like inside?'

'It's very nice,' Joe said slowly. 'Very nice.'

She waited for him to continue. When he did not, she said, 'Did the grandeur up there frighten you, or what?'

'I was just thinking about them, that's all,' he said.

'The old man, what's he like?'

'Mr Bernard? Oh, Mr Bernard . . . he's the same as ever. Older, of course, but the same Mr Bernard.'

'And Father Declan?'

'A fine man. A fine priest. Yes, very fine.'

'Huh!' said Rita. 'It's not worth your while going out, for all the news you bring home.'

'The tape was lovely,' said Joe quickly. 'She spoke to all of them in turn – Father Declan and then to her mother and then to Mr Bernard himself. And she played a tune on the violin for him, too.'

'Did they like it?'

'They loved it, loved it. It was a lovely recording.'

'Did she offer you anything?'

'Forced me to have tea with them, but I said no, I had to leave.'

'What room were they in?'

'The breakfast room. The drawing room was always draughty.'

'A nice room?'

'The breakfast room? Oh, lovely, lovely . . . Glass handle on the door and a beautiful carpet and beautiful pictures . . . everything. Just lovely.'

'So that's Foundry House,' said Rita, knowing that she was going to hear no gossipy details.

'That's Foundry House,' Joe echoed. 'The same as ever – no different.'

She put out her cigarette and stuck the butt behind her ear.

'They're a great family, Rita,' he said. 'A great, grand family.'

'So they are,' she said casually, stooping to lift the baby out of its bath. Its wet hands patterned her thin blouse. 'Here, Joe! A job for you. Dress this divil for bed.'

She set the baby on his knee and went to separate the wrestlers. Joe caught the child, closed his eyes, and rubbed his cheek against the infant's soft, damp skin. 'The same as ever,' he crooned into the child's ear. 'A great family. A grand family.'

JOHN MONTAGUE
An Occasion of Sin

About ten miles south of Dublin, not far from Blackrock, there is a small bathing place. You turn down a side road, cross a railway bridge, and there, below the wall, is a little bay with a pier running out into the sea on the left. The water is not deep, but much calmer and warmer than at many points further along the coast. When the tide comes in, it covers the expanse of green rocks on the right, lifting the seaweed like long hair. At its highest, one can dive from the ledge of the Martello Tower, which stands partly concealed between the pier and the sea wall.

Françoise O'Meara began coming there shortly after Easter of '56. A chubby, open-faced girl, at ease with herself and the world, she had arrived from France only six months before, after her marriage. At first she hated it: the damp mists of November seemed to eat into her spirit; but she kept quiet, for her huband's sake. And when winter began to wear into spring, and the days grew softer, she felt her heart expand; it was as simple as that.

Early in the new year, her husband bought her a car, to help her pass the time when he was at the office. It was nothing much, an old Austin, with wide running boards and rust-streaked roof, but she cleaned and polished it till it shone. With it, she explored all the little villages around Dublin: Delgany, where a pack of beagles came streaming across the road; Howth, where she wandered for hours along the cliffs; the roads above Rathfarnham. And Seacove, where she came to bathe as soon as her husband would allow her.

'But nobody bathes at this time of the year,' he said in astonishment, 'except the madmen at the Forty Foot!'

'But I *want* to!' she cried. 'What does it matter what people do. I won't melt!'

She stretched her arms wide as she spoke, and he had to admit that she didn't look as if she would; her breasts pushing her blouse, her stocky, firm hips, her wide grey eyes – he had never seen anyone look so positive in his life.

At first it was marvellous being on her own, feeling the icy shock of the water as she plunged in. It brought back a period of her childhood, spent at Etretat, on the Normandy coast: she had bathed through November, running along the deserted beach afterwards, the water drying on her body in the sharp wind. She doubted if she could do that at Seacove, but she found a corner of the wall which trapped whatever sun there was, and when the rain spat she went into the Martello Tower Café and had a bar of chocolate and a cup of tea. Sometimes it was so cold that her skin was goose-pimpled, but she loved it all; she felt she had never been so completely alive.

It was mid-May before anyone joined her along the sea wall. The earliest comer was a small fat man, who unpeeled to show a paunch carpeted with white hair. He waved to her before diving off the pierhead and trundling straight out to sea. When he came back, his face was lobster-red with exertion, and he pummelled himself savagely with a towel. He had surprisingly small, almost dainty feet, she noticed, as he danced up and down on the stones, blowing a white column of breath into the air. As he left, he always gave her a friendly wink or called (his words swallowed by the wind): 'That beats Banagher!'

She liked him a lot. She didn't feel as much at ease with the others. An English couple came down from the Stella Maris boarding house to eat a picnic lunch and read the *Daily Express*. Though sitting side by side, they rarely spoke, casting mournful glances at the sky which, even at its brightest, always had a faintly threatening aspect, like a chemical solution on the point of precipitation. And more and more local men came, mainly on bicycles. They swung to a halt along the sea wall, removing the clips from their trousers, removing their togs from the carrier, and tramping purposefully down towards the sea. One of them, who looked like a clerk (lean, bespectacled, his mouth cut into his face), carried equipment for underwater fishing, goggles, flippers and spear.

What troubled her was their method of undressing: she had never seen anything like it. First they spread a paper on the ground. Upon this they squatted, slowly unpeeling their outer garments. When they were down to shirt and trousers, they took a swift look round, and then gave a kind of convulsive wriggle, so that the lower half of the trousers hung limply. There was a brief glimpse of white before a towel was wrapped across the loins; gradually the full length of the trousers unwound, in a series of convulsive shudders. A further lunge and the togs went sliding up the thighs, until they struck the outcrop of the hipbone. A second look round, a swift pull of the towel with the left hand, a jerk of the togs with the right, and the job was done. Or nearly: creaking to their feet, they pulled their thigh-length shirts over their heads to reveal pallid torsoes.

At the beginning, this procedure amused her: it looked like a comedy sequence, especially as it had to be performed in reverse, when they came out of the water. But then it began to worry her: why were they doing it? Was it because there were women present? But there were none apart from the Englishman's wife, who sat gazing out to sea, munching her sandwiches: and herself. But she had seen men undressing on beaches ever since she was a child and hardly even noticed it. In any case, the division of the human race into male and female was an interesting fact with which she had come to terms long ago: she did not need to have her attention called to it in such an extraordinary way.

What troubled her even more was the way they watched her when she was undressing. She usually had her togs on under her dress; when she hadn't, she sat on the edge of the sea wall, sliding the bathing suit swiftly up her body, before jumping down to pull the dress over her head: the speed and cleanness of the motion pleased her. But as she fastened the straps over her back she could feel eyes on her every move: she felt like an animal in a cage. And it was not either curiosity or admiration, because when she raised her eyes, they all looked swiftly away. The man with the goggles was the worst: she caught him gazing at her avidly, the black band pushed up around his ears, like a racing motorist. She smiled to cover her embarrassment but to her surprise he turned his head, with an angry snap. What was wrong with her?

Because there was something: it just wasn't right, and she wanted to leave. She mentioned her doubts to her husband who laughed and then grew thoughtful.

'You're not very sympathetic,' he pointed out. 'After all, this is a cold country. People are not used to the sun.'

'Rubbish,' she replied. 'It's as warm as Normandy. It's something more than that.'

'Maybe it's just modesty.'

'Then why do they look at me like that? They're as lecherous as troopers but they won't admit it.'

'You don't understand,' he retreated.

It was mid-June when the clerical students appeared at Seacove. They came along the coast road from Dun Laoghaire on bicycles, black as a flock of crows. Their coats flapped in the sea-wind as they tried to pass each other out, rising on the pedals. Then they curved down the side-road towards the Martello Tower, where they piled their machines into the wooden racks, solemn-looking Raleighs and low-handled racers.

When they appeared, some of them had started undressing, taking off their coats and hard clerical collars as they came. Most already had their togs on, stepping out of their trousers on the beach, to create a huddle of identical black clothes. The others undressed in a group under the shadow of the sea wall, and then came racing down; together they trooped towards the pierhead.

For the next quarter of an hour the sea was teeming with them, dense as a shoal of mackerel. They plunged, they splashed, they turned upside down. One who was timid kept retreating to the shallow water, but two others stole up and ducked him vigorously, only to be buffeted, from behind, in their turn. The surface of the water was cut into clouds of spray. Far out the arms of the three strongest swimmers flashed, in a race to the lighthouse point.

When they came out of the sea to dry and lie down, they generally found a space cleared around their clothes, the people having withdrawn to give them more room. But the clerical students did not seem to observe, or mind, plumping themselves down in whatever space offered. One or two had brought books, but the majority lay on their backs, talking and laughing. At first their chatter disturbed Françoise from the novel she was reading, but it soon sank into her consciousness, like a litany.

'But Pius always had a great cult of the Virgin. They say he saw her in the Vatican gardens.'

'If Carlow had banged in that penalty, they'd be in the final Sunday.'

'Father Conroy says that after the second year in the bush you nearly forget home exists.'

While she was amused by their energy, Françoise would probably not have spoken to them, but for the accident of falling asleep one day, a yellow edition of Mauriac lying across her stomach. When she awoke, the students were settling around her. It was a warm day, and their usual place near the water had been taken by a group of English families with children, so they looked for the nearest free area. Although they pretended indifference, she could feel a current of curiosity running through them at finding her so close; now and again she caught a shy glance, or a chuckle, as one glanced at another meaningfully. Among their white skins and long shorts, she became suddenly conscious of her gay blue- and red-striped bathing suit, blazing like a flag in the sunshine. And of her already browning legs and arms.

'Is that French you're reading?' said one finally. Just back from a second plunge in the sea, he was towelling himself slowly, shaking drops of water over everyone. He had a coarse, friendly face, covered with blotches, and a shock of carroty hair, which stuck up in wet tufts.

She held up the volume in answer. *'Le Fleuve de Feu,'* she spelled; 'the river of fire, one of Mauriac's novels.'

'He's a Catholic writer, isn't he?' said another, with sudden interest. The other turned to look at him, and he flushed brick-red, sitting his ground.

'Well,' she grimaced, remembering certain episodes in the novel, 'he is and he isn't. He's very bleak, in an old-fashioned sort of way. The river of fire is meant to be,' she searched for the words, 'the flood of human passion.'

There was silence for a minute or two. 'Are you French?' said a wondering voice.

'Yes, I am,' she confessed, apologetically, 'but I'm married to an Irishman.'

'We thought you couldn't be from here,' said another voice, triumphantly. Everyone seemed more at ease, now that her national identity had been established. They talked idly for a few minutes before the red-haired boy, who seemed to be in charge, looked at his watch and said it was time to go. They all dressed quickly, and as they sailed along the sea wall on their bicycles (she could only see their heads, like moving targets in a funfair) they waved to her.

'See you tomorrow,' they called gaily.

By early July the meetings between Françoise and the students had become a daily affair. As they rode up on their bicycles they would call out to her, 'Hello, Françoise.' And after they bathed, they came clambering up the rocks, to sit around her in a semi-circle. Usually the big red-haired boy (called 'Ginger' by his companions) would start the conversation with a staccato demand; 'What part of France are you from?' or, 'Do ye like it here?' but the others soon took over, while he sank back into a satisfied silence, like a dog that has performed an expected trick.

At first the conversation was general: Françoise felt like a teacher as they questioned her about life in Paris. And whatever she told them seemed to take on such an air of unreality, more like a lesson than real life. They liked to hear about the Louvre, or Notre Dame, but when she tried to tell them of what she knew best, the student life around the Latin Quarter, their attention slid away. But it was not her fault, because when she questioned them about their own future (they were going on to the Missions), they were equally vague. It was as though only what related to the present was real, and anything else exotic; unless one was plunged into it, when, of course, it became normal. Such torpidity angered her.

'But wouldn't you like to see Paris?' she exclaimed.

They looked at each other. Yes, they would like to see Paris, and might, some day, on the way back from Africa. But what they really wanted to do was to learn French: all they got was a few lessons a week from Father Dundee.

Another day they spoke of the worker priests. Fresh from the convent, a *jeune fille bien pensante*, Françoise had plunged into social work, around the rue Belhomme and the fringes of Montmartre. And she had come to know several of the worker priests. One she knew had fallen in love with a prostitute and had to struggle to save his vocation: she thought him a wonderful man. But her story was received in silence; a world where people did not go to mass, where passion was organised and dangerous, did not exist for them, except as a textbook vision of evil.

'Things must be very lax in France,' said Ginger, rising up.

She could have brained him.

Still, she enjoyed their company, and felt quite disappointed whenever (because of examinations or some religious ceremony) they did not show up. And it was not just because they fulfilled a woman's dream to find herself surrounded by admiring men. Totally at ease with her, they offered no calculation of seduction or flattery, except a kind of friendly teasing. It reminded her of when she had played with her brothers (she was the only girl) through the long summer holidays; that their relationship might not seem as innocent to others never crossed her mind.

She was lying on the sea wall after her swim, one afternoon, when she felt a shadow move across her vision. At first she thought it was one of the students, though they had told her the day before that they might not be coming. But no; it was the small fat man who had been one of the first to join her at Seacove. She smiled up at him in welcome, shielding her eyes against the sun. But he did not smile back, sitting down beside her heavily, his usual cheery face set in an attempt at solemnity.

'Missing your little friends today?'

She laughed. 'Yes, a bit,' she confessed. 'I rather like them, they're very pleasant company.'

He remained silent for a moment. 'I'm not sure it's right for you to be talking to them,' he plunged.

'Lots of people on the beach' – he was obviously uncomfortable – 'are talking.'

'But they're only children!' Her shock was so deep that she was trembling: if such an inoffensive man believed this, what must the others be thinking?

'They're clerical students,' he said stubbornly. 'They're going to be priests.'

'But all the more reason: one can't,' she searched for the word, '*isolate* them.'

'That's not how we see it. You're giving bad example.'

'I'm giving what?'

'Bad example.'

Against her will, she felt tears prick the corners of her eyes. 'Do you believe that?' she asked, attempting to smile.

'I don't know,' he said seriously. 'It's a matter for your conscience. But it's not right for a single girl to be making free with clerical students.'

'But I'm not single!'

It was his turn to be shocked. 'You're a married woman! And you come – '

He did not end the sentence but she knew what he meant.

'Yes, I'm a married woman, and my husband lets me go to the beach on my own, and talk to whoever I like. You see, he trusts me.'

He rose slowly. 'Well, daughter,' he said, with a baffled return to kindliness, 'it's up to yourself. I only wanted to warn you.'

As he padded heavily away, she saw that the whole beach was watching her. This time she did not smile, but stared straight in front of her. There was a procession of yachts making towards Dun Laoghaire harbour, their white sails like butterflies. Turning over, she hid her face against the concrete, and began to cry.

But what was she going to do? As she drove back towards Dublin, Françoise was so absorbed that she nearly got into an accident, obeying an ancient reflex to turn on the right into the Georgian street where they lived. An oncoming Ford hooted loudly, and she swung her car up onto the pavement, just in time. She saw her husband's surprised face looking through the window: thank God he was home.

She did not mention the matter, however, until several hours later, when she was no longer as upset as she had been at the beach. And when she did come round to it, she tried to tell it as lightly as possible, hoping to distance it for herself, to see it clearly. But though her husband laughed a little at the beginning, his face became more serious, and she felt her nervousness rising again.

'But what right had he to say that to me?' she burst out, finally.

Kieran O'Meara did not answer, but kept turning the pages of the *Evening Press*.

'What right has anyone to accuse people like that?' she repeated.

'Obviously he thought he was doing the right thing.'

She hesitated. 'But surely *you* don't think . . .'

His face became a little red, as he answered. 'No, of course not. But I don't deny that in certain circumstances you might be classed as an occasion of sin.'

She sat down with a bump in the armchair, a dishcloth in her hand. At first she felt like laughing, but after repeating the phrase 'an occasion of sin' to herself a few times, she no longer found it funny and felt like crying. Did everyone in this country measure things like this? At a party, a few nights before, one of her husband's friends had solemnly told her that sex was the worst sin because it was the most pleasant. Another had gripped her arm, once, crossing the street: 'Be careful.' 'But you're in danger too!' she laughed, only to hear his answer: 'It's not myself I'm worried about, it's you. I'm in the state of sanctifying grace.' The face of the small fat man swam up before her, full of painful self-righteousness, as he told her she was 'giving bad example'. What in the name of God was she doing in this benighted place?

'Do you find me an occasion of sin?' she said, at last, in a strangled voice.

'It's different for me,' he said, impatiently. 'After all, we're married.'

It came as a complete surprise to him to see her rise from the chair, throw the dishcloth on the table, and vanish from the room. Soon he heard the front door bang, and her feet running down the steps.

Hands in the pockets of her white raincoat, Françoise O'Meara strode along the bank of the Grand Canal. There was a thin rain falling, but she ignored it, glad if anything for its damp imprint upon her face. Trees swam up to her, out of the haze: a pair of lovers were leaning against one of them, their faces blending. Neither of them had coats, they must be soaked through, but they did not seem to mind.

Well, there was a pair who were enjoying themselves, anyway. But why did they have to choose the dampest place in all Dublin, risking double pneumonia to add to their troubles? What was this instinct to seek darkness and discomfort, rather than the friendly light of day? She remembered the couples lying on the deck of the Holyhead boat when she had come over: she had to stumble over them in order to get down the stairs. It was like night-time in a bombed city, people hiding from the blows of fate; she had never had such a sense of desolation. And then, when she had negotiated the noise and porter stains of the Saloon and got to the Ladies, she found that the paper was strewn across the floor and that someone had scrawled FUCK CAVAN in lipstick on the mirror.

Her husband had nearly split his sides laughing when she asked what that meant. And yet, despite his education and travel, he was as odd as any of them. From the outside, he looked completely normal, especially when he left for the office in the morning in his neat executive suit. But inside he was a nest of superstition and stubbornness; it was like living with a Zulu tribesman. It emerged in all kinds of small things: the way he avoided walking under ladders, the way he always blessed himself during thunderstorms, the way he saluted every church he passed, a hand flying from the wheel to his forehead even in the thick of city traffic. And that wasn't the worst. One night she had woken up to see him sitting bolt upright in bed, his face tense and white.

'Do you hear it?' he managed to say.

Faintly, on the wind, she heard a crying sound, a sort of wail. It sounded weird all right, but it was probably only some animal locked out, or in heat, the kind of thing one hears in any garden, only magnified by the echo-chamber of the night.

'It's a banshee,' he said. 'They follow our family. Aunt Margaret must be going to die.'

And, strangely enough, Aunt Margaret did die, but several weeks later, and from old age more than anything else: she was over eighty and could have toppled into the grave at any time. But all through the funeral, Kieran kept looking at Françoise reproachfully, as if to say *you see*! And now the disease was beginning to get at her, sending her to stalk through the night like a Mauriac heroine, melancholy eating at her heart. As she approached Leeson Street Bridge, she saw two swans, a cob and a pen, moving slowly down the current. Behind them, almost indistinguishable because of their grey feathers, came four young ones. The sight calmed her: it was time to go back. Though he deserved it, she did not want her husband to be worrying about her. In any case, she had more or less decided what she was going to do.

The important thing was not to show, by the least sign, that she was troubled by what they thought of her. Swinging her togs in her left hand, Françoise O'Meara sauntered down towards the beach at Seacove. It was already pretty full, but, as though by design, a little space had been left, directly under the sea wall, where she usually sat. So she was to be ostracised as well! She would show them: with a delicious sense of her audience she hoisted herself up onto the concrete and began to undress. But she was only halfway through changing when the students arrived. In an ordinary way, she would have taken this in her stride, but she saw the people watching them as they tramped over, and the clasp of her bra stuck, and she was left to greet them half in, half out of her dress. And when she did get the bathing suit straightened she saw that, since they had all arrived more or less together, they were expecting her to join them in a swim. Laying his towel out carefully on the ground, like an altar-cloth, Ginger turned towards the sea: 'Coming?'

Scarlet-faced, she marched down with him to the pier-

head. The tide was high, and just below the Martello
Tower the man with the goggles broke surface, splutter-
ing, as though on purpose to stare at her. A little way out,
a group of clerical students were horse-playing: she wasn't
going to join in *that*. Without speaking to her companion,
she struck out towards the Lighthouse Point, cutting the
water with a swift sidestroke. But before she had gone far,
she found Ginger at her side: and another boy on the
other. Passing (they both knew the crawl), falling back,
repassing, they accompanied her out to the point, and back
again. Were they never to leave her alone?

And afterwards, when they lay on the beach, they kept
pestering her with questions. And not the usual ones, but
much bolder, in an innocent sort of way: what had got
into them? It was the boy who had asked about Mauriac
who began it, wanting to know if she had ended the book,
whether she knew any people like that, what she thought
of its view of love. And then, out of the blue:

'What's it like, to be married?'

She rolled over on her stomach and looked at him. No,
he was not being roguish, he was quite serious, gazing at
her with interest, as were most of the others. But how
could one answer such a question, before such an
audience?

'Well, it's very important for a woman, naturally,' she
began, feeling as ripe with clichés as a woman's page
columnist. 'And not just because people – society – imply
that if a woman is not married she's a failure: that's a
terrible trap. And it is not merely living together, though
– ' she looked at them: they were still intent ' – that's
pleasant enough, but in order to fulfil herself, in the process of giving. And that's the whole paradox, that if it's
a true marriage, she feels freer, just because she has given.'

'Freer?'

'Yes, freer after marriage than before it. It's not like an
affair, where though the feeling may be as intense, one
knows that one can escape. The freedom in marriage is the
freedom of having committed oneself: at least that's true

for the woman.' Her remarks were received in silence, but it was not the puzzled silence of their first meetings, but a thoughtful one, as though, while they could not quite understand what she meant, they were prepared to examine it. But she still could not quiet a nagging doubt in her mind, and demanded: 'What made you ask me that?'

It was not her questioner, but Ginger, who had hardly been listening, who gave her her answer. 'Sure, it's well known,' he said pleasantly, gathering up his belongings, 'that French women think about nothing but love.'

He pronounced it 'luve', with a deep curl in the vowel. Before she could think of a reply, they were half-way across the beach.

She was still raging when she got home, all the more so since she knew she could not tell her husband about it. She was still raging when she went to bed, shifting so much that she made her husband grunt irritably. She was still raging when she woke up, from a dream in which the experience lay curdled.

She dreamt that she was at Seacove in the early morning. The sea was a deep running green, with small waves hitting the pierhead. There was no one in sight so she took off her clothes and slipped into the water. She was half-way across to the Lighthouse Point when she sensed something beneath her: it was the man with the goggles, his black flippers beating the water soundlessly as he surged up towards her. His eyes roved over her naked body as he reached out for her leg. She felt herself being pulled under, and kicked out strongly. She heard the glass of his goggles smash as she broke to the surface again; where her husband was drawing the blinds to let in the morning light.

Today, she decided, she must end the whole stupid affair: it had gone on too long, caused her too much worry. After all, the people who had protested were probably right: the fact that the boys were getting fresh with her proved it. She toyed with the idea of just not going back to the beach, but it seemed cowardly. Better to face the students directly, and tell them she could not see them again.

So when they arrived at the beach in the mid-afternoon they found her sitting stiffly against the sea wall, a book resting on her knees. Saluting her with their usual friendliness, they got hardly any reply. At the time, they passed no remarks, but lying on the beach after their swim they found the silence heavy and tried to coax her with questions. But she cut them short each time, ostentatiously returning to her book.

'Is there anything wrong?' one of them asked, at last.

Keeping her eyes fixed on the print, she nodded. 'More or less.'

'It wouldn't have anything to do with us?' This from Ginger, with sudden probing interest.

'As a matter of fact, it has.' Shyness slowly giving way to relief, she told about her conversation with the little fat man. 'But, of course, it's really my fault,' she ended lamely. 'I should have known better.'

Waiting their judgement, she looked up. To her surprise, they were smiling at her, affectionately.

'Is that all?'

'Isn't it enough?'

'But sure we knew all that before.'

'You know it!' she exclaimed in horror. 'But how . . .'

'Somebody came to the College a few days ago and complained to the Dean.'

'And what did he say?'

'He asked us what you were like.'

'And what did you say?' she breathed.

'We said' – the tone was teasing but sincere – 'we said you were a better French teacher than Father Dundee.'

The casual innocence of the remark, restoring the whole heart of their relationship, brought a shout of laughter from her. But as her surprise wore off, she could not resist picking at it, suspiciously, at least once more.

'But what about what the people said? Didn't it upset you?'

Ginger's gaze seemed to rest on her for a moment, and then moved away, bouncing like a rubber ball down the steps towards the sea.

'Ach, sure some people would see bad in anything,' he said easily.

And that was all: no longer interested, they turned to talk about something else. They were going on their holidays soon (no wonder they were so frisky!) and wouldn't be seeing her much again. But they had enjoyed meeting her; maybe she would be there next year? She lay with her back against the sea wall, listening to them, her new book (it was Simone de Beauvoir's *Le Deuxième Sexe*) at her side. A movement caught her eye down the beach: someone was trying to climb on to the ledge of the Martello Tower. First came the spear, then the black goggles, then the flippers, like an emerging sea monster. Remembering her dream, she began to laugh again, so much so that her companions looked at her inquiringly. Yes, she said quickly, she might be at Seacove next year.

Though in her heart she knew that she wouldn't.

MAEVE KELLY

Lovers

A heavy, late-hanging chestnut, still inside its armoured car, hit Tom Conway on the nose when he lifted his head to stare at the threadbare branches above him. He rubbed his nose tenderly. Violence everywhere, he said to himself, lurking in men's hearts and even on tree tops. 'There's no end to it,' he said aloud. His wife heard him, coming from the pig pen, clanking buckets.

'You're a lovely sight,' he said bitterly.

'If it's beauty you're after,' she replied, 'you'll have to be content with yourself and the mirror.'

He watched her defiant back and nodded approvingly. 'Spunk is better than beauty,' he called after her. Her shoulders shrugged in mock contempt. She hadn't thought of a reply. He had her there. A late marriage was like a late autumn, full of the knowledge of recent summer and coming winter. Their words had to have fire in them to fend off old age, to substitute for youth's passion.

'Are you feeling all right?' he asked her when he followed her to the kitchen. 'Any tea in the pot?'

'Yes,' she said. 'No.'

'Are you making any?'

'For you I'll make it.'

There's beauty, he thought. 'Have some yourself,' he said.

'I haven't time to be sitting down gossiping.' Her voice was tart.

He pondered over it for a moment. 'Are you sure you are feeling all right?'

'I said yes.'

'Yes isn't enough.'

'It will do for now. There's cow dung on your nose.'

'That was a chestnut.'

'That's new,' she said mockingly, 'chestnuts wearing cow dung.'

'I don't know about it being new,' he said. 'Everyone wears cow dung nowadays. Didn't you know? The most plentiful product in Ireland. During the last war they made cigarettes out of it, so who knows? Perhaps it will be re-constituted meat soon.'

'What in God's name is that?' she asked and didn't wait for an answer. 'You're in a very talkative mood today? Did you get another bill?'

He was furious. 'You're a suspicious old hen,' he said and was satisfied to see her look guilty.

'I'll get you the tea,' she said placatingly. 'And you might like some apple cake.' Chalk one up to me, he thought. But it didn't do to overplay his hand. Self-righteousness was all right once in a while. Twice it was teetering on precipices. Three times it was a long drop into the valley of her contempt. 'Thank you,' he said graciously, and winced from her side-long look. But she swallowed it. She knew when to swallow.

'It's November,' he said.

'Well?'

'Doesn't it make you feel lonely?' He took her silence to be agreement. 'Sunshine gone,' he continued, 'and – '

'What sunshine?' she interrupted harshly.

He took a moment to recover. 'It's the idea of sunshine then,' he attempted, feebly.

'That's good,' she said. 'I like that. An idea. That's all it ever is.'

She slopped his tea carelessly into the cup.

'You're a terrible woman,' he said sadly, not caring. 'You've no nature in you. You've no heart.'

'You knew that when you married me.'

'I did not.'

' "Annie will make a great wife," ' she quoted with unexpected bitterness. ' "She's no beauty, not much nature, but a great worker." '

'Who said that?' he asked indignantly.

'The parish pulpit kisser, Donnelly.'

He relaxed. 'Who'd take notice of him?'

'You said it too.'

'You know I didn't mean it.'

'Once it isn't meant, twice it's established.'

'I didn't say it twice.'

'It doesn't matter who said it, as long as it's said.'

'It matters.'

'Look,' she said fiercely. 'Once, it's a prig's opinion, twice it's godalmighty dogma.'

'You're an awful woman,' he said bewildered. 'I don't know what to do with you.'

She smiled at him.

'Finish your tea,' she said.

It was lovely to sit in the kitchen, listening to the pots simmering and sighing. It was lovely to waken on a November morning and watch the mist strangle the rising sun and the sun tear the mist into shreds. It was lovely to see her in the bed beside him. It was comforting and exciting at the same time.

'You were carrying buckets this morning,' he accused. 'You know you're not supposed to carry weights.'

'Old wives' tales,' she said scornfully.

'You've lost three already,' he said angrily.

'I can count,' she said and the words dropped like stones into the spreading silence they created. I can count. One baby, two babies, three babies. All lost around the fatal three months. And last month was a near thing. 'I cannot stay still,' she said, as near to apology as he had ever known. 'I like to be doing things. I don't take chances. I just can't coddle myself.'

'It isn't just yourself,' he reproached her.

'I know,' she sighed. 'I suppose I'm too old. We're both too old. Nature's telling me I shouldn't be having children. I'll be over sixty by the time it's reared.'

She was right. There was no answer to that. The November day began to weigh more heavily on him. 'I'll get at the potatoes or the frost will get them for me.'

'I'll help you in a minute,' she shouted after him.

'You will not,' he said. 'You'll stay there.' He almost said in the kitchen where you belong, but saved himself in time. Doing a woman's work like other women, rearing babies, tidying up, preparing his meals, being around when he wanted her. But no, out she'd be in five minutes, cap pulled down over her ears, windcheater hiding the bump of her four months' pregnancy, wellingtons covering the first varicose veins. 'Watch the chestnut tree,' she shouted after him. 'There might be another one waiting for you.'

If women were trees, she said to herself when he had gone, how handy that would be, dropping your fruit so casually. But does the earth groan and heave when it is thrusting up a young tree? That chestnut tree was a miracle growing where it did in the corner of the stony old yard. Maybe I'll have a miracle too.

The wind lifted Tom's hair as he passed the stables. The sky had cleared suddenly, swept clean of scudding clouds. He wondered briefly where they had gone, if they huddled together in some stormy corner, building up moisture, threatening already flooded fields. A stable door banged suddenly and the wind died and even more suddenly a great silence covered the farm. Beside him, the sheepdog cringed, tucking its tail between its legs. Looking back at the chestnut tree he saw that the last precarious leaves hung motionless and he had an eerie feeling of impending danger. 'Get up, you fool dog,' he snarled, angry at his own weakness, and the dog whimpered and ran into a stable. At the cow-house Tom paused, listening to the faint rustle that seemed to be giving birth to heavier soughs. A great sigh of wind came through the chinks of the stone walls and a slate rattled down from the roof over him. 'A storm,' he said, enlightened. 'A storm.'

It hit him while he latched and bolted the half-door beside him, tearing at his coat, searing his cheeks to redness. It bludgeoned him while he staggered, gasping at its ferocity, dodging the next slate which missed decapitating him by inches. 'Christ,' he said, 'that's all I need. Slates for enemies.' The thought of battle was strangely exhilarating. He tried to yell defiantly, but his voice was sucked back into his throat, almost choking him. He turned his back and his trousers stung his legs, whipping into them like thongs. He stretched his arms out and leaning backwards yelled, 'Come on, big wind, come on, big wind. I can take you.' Vengefully the wind lashed his ears and he turned, facing into it again, arrowing his body forward to give less resistance. 'Brain against brawn,' he gasped. 'It's got to win or we might as well all lie down and give up.' His words hiccoughed back and he gasped and struggled for breath. 'Bastard wind,' he tried again. 'Bastard, no good, base-born out of some rotten hole in the universe.'

Annie laughed when she saw him weaving towards the kitchen window, his eyes screwed up against the airborne debris of the yard, his fists jabbing forward against some imagined punchbag. The hosts of the air might be arrayed against him but he would take them all on. She ran to open the door and he fell in, sprawling helplessly at her feet, while she slammed the door, locking it quickly. 'It's breezy out,' she said, looking down at him. 'You were always prone to exaggeration,' he said when he had caught his breath. She helped him pull off his boots. They moved to the window and stared out at the slates hurtling from the roof and splitting and scattering across the yard.

They thought of the cattle out in the fields but knew they would find shelter in the craggy places where the hawthorn trees sprouted and linked branches, forming tunnels where the animals could lie in wild weather. Tom worried about the heifer who was due to calve and Annie voiced his thoughts.

'We should bring up the heifer. She's due soon.'

'You're right,' he said. 'She'll be safer inside.'

'I'll go with you.' She rushed to get cap and wind-cheater and he did not protest. He took the rope looped on the hook of the back door and slung it over his left shoulder.

They linked arms at first and then held hands as they forced themselves over the fields, leaning against the wind. Their ears were battered by the whine and screeching around them. From the yard came the crashing of milk churns and cans sent flying from their habitual places and rolled backwards and forwards, banging against the stone walls. Annie had a strange sense of joy in their linked hands. They were two puny objects of no account to anyone, to be missed by no one if these delinquent air currents should lift them up and throw them into the estuary. Their cows would be milked by their part-time helper and someone else would walk their fields and don a new armour of hope. It was a strange and fearful thing to be able to walk almost upright against this challenge. She thought how fear imprisoned hearts while courage liberated them.

Tom pointed towards the river and they watched in wonder the great heaving mass cast itself helplessly in white foam against the banks. Below it their last field of hay, saved by inches, it had seemed, during the late days of the wet summer, was now irretrievable. The hay trams, left hopefully until the field might dry out, now tumbled into the pools around them. It was painful to have to accept again that one hour could so ravage the careful toil of many days. Whatever poet talked of the slow unfolding of seasons had been no farmer, Tom thought. But then, what poet could be a farmer? They hadn't the stomach for it. Spinning words and ideas was a queer way to spend a life, and he shut off with scorn the faintly remembered poetic dreams of his youth. It was difficult to think of anything with the distraction of a hurricane tugging at his sleeves. Better perhaps to surrender, to forgo the pleasure and effort of intellect, to unload from strained muscles the burden of labour, to lean on this mad dog of a wind and let it take over. What bruises could it give him if it whirled him into its vortex and sucked him into the silence of death?

Beside him, Annie pulled restlessly. 'Hurry, hurry. I don't see her with the others.' They searched along the hedges and by the sally trees, until they found her lying in a corner of the field, neck thrust up, legs splayed out, and heard her groan loudly.

'She's started,' Annie said. 'We'll never get her up to the house.'

'She might be better here,' Tom said. 'Healthier and cleaner.'

'But it's so cold,' Annie protested. 'And what if she takes too long?'

'We'll leave her alone for a while,' Tom said. 'Let her get on with it.'

Annie suddenly put her two arms protectingly across her stomach. 'I'll go up to the house,' she said.

Her unexpected meekness alarmed him and yet he could not bring himself to ask her was she all right or offer to accompany her, but he could not resist whispering, 'Be careful' when she had left him. He shouted it aloud then when it was too late for her to hear and the shrieking wind tore his words to tatters. He watched her all the way up the sloping field, lost her when she dipped into a hollow, followed her again with his streaming eyes as she neared the farm gate. Flying slates made the yard more dangerous than the open spaces, but she was out of sight then, and he could only hope that she was safely in the house.

He crouched under the hedge away from the heifer and tucked his head into his knees. He hated wind. Its irrationality depressed him. Like a mob or a cowardly bully, one never knew what to expect from it. The human skull was frail after all when it could be crushed by a casually falling tree or split by a slate. Perhaps open desert was the safest place. But they had sandstorms, clogging your nose, suffocating, burning eyes. And the sea was worse again, hands clawing for substance, an unnatural element. He smiled to himself and touched lovingly the earth at his feet. Worst of all was the rational violence of men, weapons discharged with accuracy, words and bombs and bullets all aimed to destroy and kill. For a moment he felt affection for the chaos around him, because it was irrational and without malice. He heard the heifer's bellow and lunged forward as if catapulted by the frantic appeal. She had probably been labouring for hours and was exhausted. The calf's forelegs were showing. 'Christ,' he said prayerfully as he tied the rope and began to pull.

Even in the cold the sweat oozed from his pores, trickling under his armpits, lodging freezing inside his shirt. The heifer's groans mingled with his own and with the wind so that he lived through an eternity of anguished noise, each second of effort a condensation of the labour of his whole life. Surrounded by primitive forces he was possessed of superstitious fear. If he failed in this, he failed in everything. If calf or mother died, what of his own child and its mother? 'Christ,' he said again, summoning the forces of good to his aid.

When the calf flopped onto the ground he fell beside it, panting and gulping. Then he began to clean the mucus from its mouth and nostrils, stretched its neck, forced open its mouth, pressed on its side to encourage oxygen to take root in its lungs. The air whistled around him and he cursed it and implored it to penetrate the limp animal under his hands. When it gave a little kick with its hind legs he worked harder, praying and cursing at the same time. The heifer stood up and came over to them, lowing softly. He stood back and watched while the calf moved more strongly in response to its mother's tongue. Around them the creaking hedges sieved air, loud, drunken, raucous and uncaring. He took off his coat, wrapped it around the calf and hoisted it onto his shoulders.

Annie saw them as they came over the rise of the land, man, calf and cow riding the wind.

EDNA O'BRIEN
Love-Child

I walked by the river and straightaway fell to thinking of
Hickey. The story of the goose was the obvious reason,
since he had shot one close to that very spot. Geese
cackled from the opposite bank, their cackles muted somewhat and almost melodious because of being issued
through a fine growth of rushes. He came to mind clearly
in his plus-fours, with his big appetite and his thieving.
All our own geese had been taken by a fox one year, but
directly across the river dwelt a family who had a fine
flock and he resolved to shoot one. He did it at dusk, but
it so happened that the goose he shot was a wild goose,
with scarcely a lick of meat on it, and my mother was
boiling and broiling it for four days to no avail. Even the
broth was insipid.

I think it was to make up for that fiasco that he stole the
cabbages. My mother came down to breakfast one morning to find a sack full of York cabbages on the floor, and
though Hickey wouldn't admit it, my mother knew he had
filched them from Mrs Minogue's garden. She was the old
woman with a little plot of ground behind the sweetshop.
The only woman whose cabbages had not been consumed
by slugs that year. Later in the day, my mother gasped
to see old Mrs Minogue hurrying up the drive with a
bundle held in front of her. The sack of cabbages was
hidden in the shoe closet, where I think it contracted a
permanent smell of must, and my mother was busy con-
cocting excuses when Mrs Minogue knocked both on the
window and on the door, as country people tend to do.

She refused to come in, being too shy, but out of her apron she dropped four heads of cabbage, starting crying, and said it nearly broke her heart to have only four to give us. She then told how some blackguard had robbed her during the night – said it must have been a tinker – and she went off hurriedly, muttering apologies about not being able to offer better. My mother never tasted any of those cabbages, and Hickey grew well and truly tired of them; like me, he maintained that the odours and sweat of the shoe closet had permanently impaired them.

The next thing he stole was a sword from the General's grave, directly after the General's burial, and a very fearsome affair it was in its leather scabbard. He boasted how he could have stolen a watch or a medal from the same source but that it was only weapons he was after. He kept it under his bed, along with sundry things like bicycle chains, pedals, and odd bits of scrap metal.

He stole from us, too, and the day he was leaving my mother asked him to kindly return the little teaspoon to make up the dozen, because there was a terrible gap in her velvet-lined box – a spoon-shaped gap where the missing spoon should be. He denied taking it, but afterwards we found the spoon on the cow-house window, stained yellow to make it seem that he had been using it for dosing cattle. We couldn't afford to pay him, so he went to England to take up work in a car factory. We heard that he kept up his agricultural skills and had an allotment, which served both as a pastime and as a means of earning extra money. We heard from a neighbour who worked in the same factory and who came home to his mad wife for three months of each year and begot another soft-headed child. It seemed that Hickey was prospering.

Whenever Hickey was mentioned, the same stories were told. He had been invited to a wedding and announced to my father that he wouldn't be available for milking on a certain day. He rose early, cooked himself three rashers and two eggs, and wakened everyone with his humming, so jubilant was he. The egg-shells askew on the table galled my mother, as did the dinner plate with the thick lodge of fat on it. He waited down at the wicker gate, probably whistling, thinking ahead to the largesse – the eighteen bottles of whiskey, ditto of brandy, champagne, and barrels of porter. He had heard the groom order from the publican the evening before, and even he was obliged to say perhaps it was too extravagant. The wedding was to be held some miles away in a lakeside town, where the couple had rented a banqueting suite. The lake and pleasure boats would provide an added excitement – as the groom said, it was more of an event to go elsewhere for a wedding than to stay at home.

Hickey waited seven hours in all, pacing back and forth, lighting a cigarette and then putting it out only to light it again and finally spit out the tobacco. The neighbour who obliged by taking the milk to the creamery said Hickey's nerves were a devil altogether – that he was like a jumping jack down there, or a flea in a matchbox. It was long past lunchtime when the postman told him how they had been fooling him – there was no wedding at all, and the big order of whiskey and porter was given only to substantiate the joke. Hickey was lepping. He came up home, went to bed, and refused to eat or speak, or do the evening milking.

The other story concerned a servant girl, Rosanna, who was six months pregnant, and how the doctor, who was also her employer, came to Hickey in the cornfield and told him that he was responsible. Hickey denied it, lost his head, and raised the pitchfork to the doctor, who escaped only because he was such a practised runner and very fit.

Soon after, Hickey left. I cried for several weeks and used to stay in his room, standing by the little window in order to smell him, feel him, hear him, in order to commune with him. Often I saw his tongue travelling over his verdigris teeth, and so many times saw his big frame come in at the gate below, and saw him run a few steps to work up the thrust to get his leg over the bar of his bicycle. Saw him as clearly as if he had been approaching, but in fact never saw him again.

He did come back to the neighbourhood one summer. He went to see his friend the publican, and although intending to come and pay us a visit he got drunk and was sent home stretched out in the back of a lorry. My mother took it badly, wondering why he had behaved so spiteful, saying England had ruined him, but I myself, still loving him, thought that perhaps our house and the driveway and his own little room, converted now into a bathroom, would sadden him and revive too many memories – the summers, the harvest, the threshing, the little ferret he had, the time he had fallen asleep down in the woods when supposed to be watching for foxes, the way he was scandalised in the local paper by having a skit written about him: 'Gunman Snores While Mr Reynard Steals Farmer's Fowl'. Also, in my most secret thoughts it occurred to me that his fury with the doctor must have meant he was responsible. There was no way of telling, because the maid had slept with everyone – the local men from the cottages whose wives were dead or having babies or in the asylum; the circus people who came a couple of times a year; the black doctor; in fact, anyone, and hence she was called the Bicycle.

At any rate, we never heard a word of Hickey until two days after my walk by the river, when the news came of his death. He died at fifty-seven after a long illness, had lost three stone, and was buried overseas.

I did what I had postponed doing for years. I made the journey to the factory town in England where he worked and to the house where he had lived with his sister. It was a small terraced house on a hill, adjacent to the country, and inside sat an invalid who I imagined was a cousin of his. She looked both very old and very young, and her little hands were like a china doll's; I shuddered at shaking one of them. I have never seen a creature whose eyes moved so much. They literally danced in her head, and I decided that, because of her inactivity otherwise, she must have over-developed these eye muscles to do her travelling for her.

There were various ornaments in the room, too, that stirred or rattled or chimed, and coloured liquid in a glass tube that constantly kept trickling into different shapes creating different formations. As if that were not enough, there were birds in cages – canaries all busy, twittering and agitating and singing. His sister told me that Hickey had bought them and trained them to sing, and even left their cage doors open to let them taste their freedom. She added that after his death the canaries also went silent.

She insisted on showing me his bedroom. It was a cheerless little room, with a patch of damp on the flowered wallpaper; the window looked out onto the hill behind. She gave me his mortuary card and I read the verse about ashes and dust, and she stood watching and sniffling, and then for want of something to do she spread her hand over the satin coverlet to smooth it, although it was not in need of smoothing, and she was telling me, almost against my will, of his last days and the way he raved about our house and the bog, and his old friends, and how he was trying to get cabbages to them, and then she listed off the names of all the people: my mother, my father, the doctor, Rosanna the maid, Jacksie his friend, the publican, my sisters – especially my sisters. There was not a word about me. I asked. 'He never mentioned you.' I said that was impossible, since I was his favourite, since he was in the house at my birth, since he taught me the time and boiled pullets' eggs for me, and brought me to hurling matches and often gave me Turkish delight. I lost my head, rather, and related some of our daft prattle and our promises to wed one day.

She lit into me, lost her composure, saying he never forgave me – saying she would never forgive me, either – because it was my fault he had stayed so long in our house and for little or no remuneration. Wasted himself out of love for me. Converted me into the daughter he never had, could never afford to have. My fault that he hadn't told the truth! It seems the creature downstairs was his daughter, the love-child, whom he had sought out and taken from the orphanage in London where her mother had put her.

I wanted to cry out to say love puts ridiculous bonds on people, I wanted to go downstairs and look into her eyes and see if they were a shiny periwinkle grey like his, but instead of that I ran out of there clutching the mortuary card, rebuking him for having been so feeble as to hide from us, from me, the truth, and all the love that he had borne me seemed no more than a ridiculous pretence. As ridiculous as the second verse on the mortuary card that said, 'A devout life came to an end. He died as he lived, everyone's friend.' A sham of a life. No one's friend. I cursed him. I dared him to speak up for himself. But it is not good to repudiate the dead because then they do not leave you alone, they are like dogs that bark intermittently at night.

JULIA O'FAOLAIN
The Knight

'A drop for the inner man.'

'For the road.'

Condon budged a heel and his spur tinkled. He
knocked an elbow against the wooden partition. The snug
must have been all of five feet by two. Drinks were served
through a hatch. It would not have done to be seen drinking in full regalia in the public bar.

'Like sitting in your coffin,' Condon said gloomily.

'Or in a confessional.'

It was embarrassing, Condon felt. Here was Hennessy
who had driven four miles to fetch him to the meeting so
that Elsie might have the car for her own use all week-end.
The least she might have done was ask the man in for a
drink. 'A wee toisheen,' thought Condon with Celtic
graciousness – and a chat. She could have made that effort,
God knew. In common courtesy. Hennessy had got him
into the Knights. But no: she'd had to pick tonight to
have one of her tantrums. He'd been afraid to let
Hennessy as much as see her! Bitch! Angrily, he blew
down his nose.

He was a choleric man with a face of a bright meaty
red, rubbery as a pomegranate rind, a face which looked
healthy enough on the bicycling priests who abounded in
his family but on him wore a congested gleam. It had a
fissile look and may have *felt* that way too, judging by
Condon's habit of keeping himself hemmed in. He had
certainly bound himself by a remarkable number of controls: starched collar, irksome marriage, rules of all the

secular sodalities open to him – most recently the Knights
– even, for a while, the British army which must have
been purgatory. He had been in it for – in his own words
– 'a sorrowful decade' and, on being demobbed, married
an Englishwoman in whom he detected and trounced
beliefs and snobberies beneath which he had groaned
during his years of service. He was currently a Franciscan
tertiary, a member of two parish sodalities, of the –
secretive – Opus Dei and of a blatant association of
Catholic laymen recently founded in Zürich with the aim
of countering creeping radicalism within the Church.
Each group imposed duties on members: buttressings so
welcomed by Condon that one might have supposed him
intent on containing some centrifugal passion liable to
blow him up like a bomb if he failed to keep it hedged.
Other members looked on his zeal with a dose of suspicion. He was aware of this and made efforts at levity. He
made one now.

'A bird never flew on wan wing.' The brogue, eroded
in England, renascent on his return, warmed like a marching tune. 'Have the other half of that.' He nodded at
Hennessy's glass.

'A small one, so.'

Condon rapped on the wood. 'Same again, Mihail,' he
told the bar-curate confidentially.

'Your wife's in poor health?' Hennessy commented.

Condon sighed. 'The Change.'

'Ah,' said Hennessy with distaste.

'Shshsh.' Condon put a finger to his lips. There were
voices in the public bar:

'Bloody Gyppos . . .' An Anglo-Irish roar. 'Regular
circus. At least the Yids can fight.'

'. . . died in the frost,' cried a carrying female version
of the same. 'I've started more under glass.'

'Well, here's to old Terry then. Chin-chin and *mort aux
vaches*.'

'What'd you join, Terry? French Foreign Legion?'

'No, we're . . .'

'Make mine a Bloody Mary.'

Condon dug an elbow into Hennessy's side. 'Tell me,' he whispered in agitation, 'why am I whispering? Why do fellows like that roar and you and me lower our voices in public? It's our country, isn't it?'

Hennessy shrugged. 'Rowdies,' he said contemptuously.

But that wasn't it. Hennessy hadn't lived with the English the way Condon had and couldn't know. It was all arrogance: the roars, the titters. All and always. Condon knew. Wasn't he married to one? Old Hennessy was looking at him oddly. A soapy customer. Don't trust. Think, quickly now, of something soothing. Right. His Knight's costume tonight in the bedroom pier-glass. Spurs, epaulets, his own patrician nose: mark of an ancient race. The image, fondly dandled, shivered and broke the way images do. Ho-old it. Patrician all right. A good jaw. Fine feathers – ah no, no. More to it than that. The *spirit* of the Order was imbuing him. Mind over matter. Condon believed in that order of things. Like the Communion wafer keeping fasting saints alive over periods of months. He was a reasoning man – trained in the law – but not narrow, acknowledged super-rational phenomena. More things, Horatio – how did it go? Membership in an ancient religious Order *must* entail an infusion of grace. Tonight was the ceremony to swear in new members. Condon being one. An important, significant moment for him, as he tried to explain to Elsie. But she was spiritually undeveloped.

'A sort of masonry then?' she'd asked when he'd told her how all the really influential Dublin businessmen . . . Certainly NOT or, anyway, not only. Why, the Order dated back nine hundred years. But the English cared only for their own pageantry: Chelsea pensioners, their bull-faced queen. Circuses! Ha! He hated their pomps, had been personally colonised but had thrown off the yoke, his character forming in recoil. Did she *know*, he wondered now as often, how thoroughly he had thrown it off? Did she? He saw himself, two hours ago, coming down the

stairs, waiting, one flight up, knee arched, for her admiration. She was in the kitchen.

'Elsie.'

'What?'

'Come here.'

'Come here yourself. I'm not a dog.'

'I want to show you something.' That spoiled the sur-
prise but she wouldn't come if he didn't beg. 'Please,
Elsie.' He thought he might be getting pins and needles.
Hand on the pommel of his sword, he waited.

'Huwwy then, because the oven . . .' She bustled into
the hall, wiping her hands on a cloth. A lively, heavily
painted woman in her forties, sagging here and there but
still ten times quicker than himself in movements. 'Ho!'
she checked and roared. 'Tito Gobbi, no less! Or is it
Wichard Tucker. You're not going *out* in it?'

Envy!

He walked down the stairs, minding his cloak. 'What's
for dinner?'

'Steak and kidney pie.'

'My ulcer!'

'You haven't a nerve in your body. How could you
have an ulcer?'

Her cooking still undermined him – the first thing he
had dared notice when he'd attended those parties of hers
in Scunthorpe. He'd been a filler-in then: the extra
bachelor asked to balance the table. The tight velvet of her
evening trousers had drawn his attention and the display of
Sheffield plate. It was on his own sideboard now. ('Mr
Condon likes his gwub,' she'd noted.) The 'w' she put in
'Patrick' when she began to use his name impressed him.
He thought for a while it might be upper-class. ('I sweat
bwicks when Patwick tells a joke!') It was a relief as well
as a diappointment when she turned out to be a house-
keeper who had married her ageing employer. When the
old man died within a year of marriage, Condon rallied
round. Mourning enhanced her attractiveness but sat lightly
on her. She was quick – giddy, he thought now – and he

couldn't keep up with her, seemed to get heavier when he
tried. Even her things turned hostile. He remembered the
day her electric lawn-mower ran off with him. Weeping
with rage, he had struggled to hold it as it plunged down
the area slope and crashed through the kitchen window –
with himself skidding behind: Handy Andy, Paddy-the-
Irishman! The servants were in stitches. He didn't dare
ask her not to mention it, could still hear her tell the
story – how many times? – to neighbours over summer
drinks on the wretched lawn: 'And away it wan with
pooah Patwick!' They had neighed, hawhawed, choked
themselves. He hated them. Buggers to a man. Bloody
snobs in their blazers with heraldic thingamybobs on the
pockets. Always telling him off. ('In England, people don't
say "bloody"!' ' "Bugger" is rather a strong term over here,
old man!' So well it might be!) What he'd put up with!
And if you *didn't* put up with it you had no sense of
humour. Well, their day was done. India, Ghana, Cyprus,
even Rhodesia . . . Little Ireland had shown the way. Let
England quake! The West's awake! The West, the East –
which of them cared for England now?

'Ah Jesus, that stuff's out of date,' Patrick's cousin told
him when he came back to live in Ireland. 'Our economy
is linked to England's. Let the dead bury the dead! And
isn't your wife English?'

Her! He looked at her scraping out the remnants of
pastry from the dish. Greedy! But she kept her figure.
People admired her. 'A damn fine woman,' they told
Patrick, who was half pleased and half not. He had never
forgiven her evasion of his embrace in the car coming
from the church ceremony and the way she had lingered
in the hotel bar before making for their bedroom. He had
lingered too but, damn it, that was understandable. *He* was
chaste, whereas she – decadent product of a decadent
country. Bloomy and scented like a hot-house flower
warmed by the trade winds of the Empire.

'Why are you looking at me like that?'

'I was thinking,' Patrick said, 'we Irish are a spiritual

people! All that about the Celt having one foot in the grave, you know? Well, the older I get, the truer I know it to be.'

She hooted.

'I suppose you don't want pudding?'

'What?'

'Apple charlotte.'

He held out his plate. 'No cream?'

'Oh Patwick! Your waist bulge!'

'I *want* cream.'

He scattered sugar on the brown cliffs of his charlotte. Brown, crumbly hills and crags such as the Knights must have defended against Turks and Saracens. The Irish branch to which Patrick belonged, lacking aristocratic quarterings, had a merely subsidiary connection, but Patrick managed to forget this and anyway *she* would never know. He took and ate the last brown bastion of charlotte from his plate.

She was fidgeting with hers. Afraid of carbohydrates. Her contaminated beauty excited him and sometimes, when she was asleep beside him, he would lean over and, between the ball of finger and thumb, fold the wrinkles into uglier grooves. Smoothing them, he could almost restore her to her peak, a time when men used to look after her and draw, with final cocks of the head in his direction, interrogation marks in the air: how, their wonder grilled him, had *she* come to marry *him*? How? Mmpp! Small mystery there when you came down to brass tacks. Widow's nerves. She wanted a man. Anything – he lambasted himself – in trousers. *Much* more to the point was the question: why had *he* married her? He was a man given to self-query. Pious practices – meditation, examination of conscience – imposed by the various rules he had embraced had revealed to Condon the riches of his own mind. It was theatre to him who had rarely been to a theatre if not to see a panto at Christmas. The first plushy swish of the curtain – he kept his thoughts sealed off in social moments lest one surface and reveal itself – the first

dip into the accurately spotlit darkness, when he had a
spell of privacy, was as stimulating as sex. How, today's
Mind demanded of yesterday's, had it made itself up?
Why? What if it had it to do over again? Any regrets?
Any guidelines for the future? Doppel-ganging Condons
stalked his own mental boards. *Why had he married?*
was a favoured theme to ponder on drives down the arteries
of Ireland – frequent since Elsie, despite his work being in
Dublin, had insisted on buying a 'gentleman's residence'
in County Meath. 'Why?' he would ask himself, as the
tyres slipped and spun through wintery silt or swerved
from a panicky rabbit. 'Why? Why? – Ah, sure I suppose
I was a bit of a fool! Yes.' Marriage had looked like a
ladder up. It had proved a snake. 'A bit of a fool in those
days, God help us.' Better to marry than to burn – but
what if you burned within marriage?

Condon still awoke sweating from nightmare re-enact-
ments of that First Night. 'Saint Joseph,' he still muttered,
as he fought off the dream, 'Patron of Happy Families, let
me not lose respect for her!' ('Patwick', she used to say,
'is a tewwible old Puwitan! Of course that makes things
such fun for him! It's being Iwish!') He had gone to
complain and confess to an English priest who reassured
him. It was all natural, an image of Divine Love. Condon
knew better, but let himself be swayed. Hours after she
had said good night he, stiffened by a half-bottle of port
from her former husband's stock, would mount the stairs,
stumble briefly about in the bathroom and, to a gurgle of
receding water, in darkness and with a great devastation
of springs, land on the bed of his legal paramour.
('Patwick! You make me feel like Euwo-o-opa!') So let
her. Who'd turned whom into an animal? If this is natural,
natural let it be! Her cries were smothered, her protests
unheeded. The swine revenged themselves on Circe:
multiplied, enormous, he snuffled, dug, burrowed, and
skewered ('Patwick, you might *shave!*'), flattening, tearing, crushing, mauling, then rolling away to the other end
of the bed to remark, 'I see the hedge needs clipping.

Have to see to it. Sloppy!' For his spirit refused to follow
where his flesh engaged. He felt embarrassed afterwards,
preferred not to breakfast with her and took to slipping
out to a hotel where he was able, as a bonus, to eat all he
wanted without hearing remarks about calories.

Tonight he would be taking a vow of Conjugal Chastity,
promising 'to possess his vessel in sanctification and
honour'. (Ha! Put a stop to *her* gallop!) Formerly,
Knights' wives had been required to join in the oath –
imagine Elsie: a heretic – but that practice had been
abolished. Fully professed Knights took vows of celibacy.

Condon had long concluded that Elsie's appeal for himself had lain in her Protestantism. Bred to think it perilous,
he had invested her and it with a risky phosphorescence.
Which had waned. Naturally enough. Marooned, the
buoyant Medusa clogs to the consistency of gelatine, and
what had Protestantism turned out to be but a set of rules
and checks? More etiquette than religion. Elsie got the
two mixed up. He doubted that she saw a qualitative
difference between adultery and failure to stand up when
a woman came into the room.

'A bahbawwian,' she'd start in, the minute some poor
decent slob like Hennessy was well out the door. 'The
man's a bahbawwian! You've buwwied me among the
beastly Hottentots!'

His people.

'No, Patwick! They are *not* fwiendly! It's all a fwaud!
They're cold and sniggering and smug! Bahbawwians!'

Well, there was no arguing with prejudice. And he
knew right well what it was she missed in Ireland: smut
and men making passes at her. What she'd have liked
would be to hobnob with the Ascendancy. Hadn't she
wanted to follow the hunt tomorrow?

'The foliage will be glowious! Amanda's keeping two
places in her jeep. I'd have thought you'd have wanted to
see the countwy. You *talk* enough about Ireland.'

He didn't. He hated land untamed by pavements, had a
feeling it was cannibalic and out to get him. Explicable:

his ancestors had been evicted *off* it after toiling and starving *on* it. He'd got his flinty profile from men pared down by a constant blast of misfortune.

'Please, Patwick. I told the Master we'd follow.'

'No.'

The word 'Master' embarrassed him. He hated hunts: the discomfort of Amanda Shand's jeep rattling his bones over frozen fields and withered heaps of ragweed. Booted and furred, the women would squeal and exchange dirty jokes as they followed the redcoats ('Pink, Patwick! Please') on their bloody pursuit down lanes like river-beds where brass bedsteads served as slatternly gates, and untrimmed brambles clawed.

'I'm spending the night at the club. I can't make it.'

She pouted.

He shrugged.

She made little enough effort with *his* friends, so why should *he* put up with Miss Amanda Shand of Shand House, a trollopy piece, louse-poor but with the Ascendancy style to her still: vowels, pedigree dogs? The dogs she raised for a living, and was reputed to have given up her own bed to an Afghan bitch and litter. But, until the roof fell in on them, those people kept up the pretence. Elsie could have helped consolidate his position – he'd hoped for this – if she'd been the hostess here that she'd been in Scunthorpe. He needed friends. He was a briefless barrister and had been too long abroad. She could have increased his support so easily if she'd turned her charm on his clerical relatives. But no. *They* didn't stand up when she came into a room.

'A priest in this country takes precedence over a woman, Elsie.'

'You've buwwied me among the beastly Hottentots!'

And tears. And accusations. Why did he leave her to moulder here? She'd given him the best years of her life. Why shouldn't she come to his meeting tonight? Even Masons had a women's night.

Masons!

'The military monks, to whose Order I have the honour to belong, were celibate. There is no place for women in our ceremonies.'

More tears. He stayed on guard. In a long war, victory can be short-lived and tears a feint. When she said, 'Don't you care for me any more?' he answered, 'I love nobody but Jesus.'

'Oh!' Her mouth fell open unguardedly and showed her fillings. 'Jesus!' she repeated. 'Jesus!' She used a little scream and ran out of the room.

In the old days, she used to flatten him with humour. But then, on her own ground, she'd had a gallery. Without one, Jesus became invincible.

Patrick, beginning to feel sorry for her, was pouring her a drink when the doorbell rang. Hennessy. Patrick put down the glass and ran to head him off. He mustn't come in. A guest would resurrect Elsie who could make him her sounding-board, stooge, straight man and microphone to funnel God knew what bad language and hysteria to the clubs and pubs of half Dublin.

Condon bundled Hennessy down the stairs and back into his car.

'Right you are,' Hennessy kept acquiescing. 'Right, right, Condon. We'll have a drink in the local. I love pubs. Nice and relaxed. Fine, don't give it a thought.'

Voices from the public bar:

'Remember that time the U.N. took a contingent of Paddies to the Congo? No, dear, *not* the Irish Guards, the Free State Army. All dressed in bullswool. *That's* what they call it, cross my heart. No, of course *I* don't know is it from bulls, but it *is* as thick as asbestos and thorny as a fairy rath. And off they went dressed up to their necks in it to the Congo. Left, right, left, right, or whatever *that* is in Erse.'

'To the tropics.'

'Must have been cooked to an Irish stew.'

'Ready for the cannibals.'

'Which reminds me, Amanda, where are we dining?'

'Not with me, dears, I haven't a scrap in the place.'

So Amanda Shand was there. Patrick drank morosely. Hennessy stood and said he had to go where no one could go for him. Patrick reflected that Hennessy was a bit vulgar sometimes all right. A bit of a Hottentot.

'. . . hear the one about the two old Dublin biddies discussing the Congo. One says a neighbour's son has been "caught by the Balloobas". "By the Balloobas, dija say, Mrs?" says her crony. "Oh *that* musta been terrible painful!" '

Laughter.

'And the one about . . .'

Patrick closed his ears. Hear no, see no, think no evil. Difficult. It wormed its way everywhere, sapped the most doughty resistances.

He thought of a visit he had made that morning to a clerical cousin confined in a home for mad priests – a disagreeable duty but Patrick had felt obliged. Blood was thicker than water and he had promised his aunt he'd go. He'd come away feeling tainted. Weakness flowed like a contagion from Father Fahy. A mild fellow, shut up because of his embarrassing delusions, he thought himself the father of twelve children with a wife expecting a thirteenth.

'I don't mind the number,' he had confided to Condon, 'I'm not superstitious about such matters. As a priest . . .' The smile flicked off and on. It was not impressive, for his teeth fitted badly and there were no funds to get inmates new ones. As long as he stayed shut up here, ecclesiastical authority saw little point in throwing good money after bad. 'Poor Anna is worn out, tense, you know, frayed. She worries about our eldest, Brendan, who's up in the College of Surgeons and . . .' The priest had names and occupations for every member of his imagined brood. 'You know yourself, Patrick, women . . .'

Fahy confided doubts about the Holy Father's policy with regard to birth-control. 'Poor Anna is a literal be-

liever,' he groaned, 'a simple woman.' He must have been
a bad priest, a shirker. Wasn't he trying to shift anxieties,
which had sifted through the confessional grating, on to
Patrick himself, the confessor's confessor? Distasteful that
a priest should imagine a wife for himself with such
domestic clarity! How far, one tried to wonder, *did* the
imaginings go? Bad times. Our Blessed Lady had fore-
told as much in 1917 to the children at Fatima. 'My Son,'
she had said, 'has drawn back His hand to smite the world.
I am holding it back but my arm grows tired.' It must be
numb by now. Well, Patrick was doing his bit, joining the
Knights: a warrior against the forces of darkness. War.
The language of the Church was heady with it but practice dampeningly meek. St George had been struck off the
register of saints.

'No, no and no, I won't be beaten down!' Amanda
Shand's voice rose in a flirtatious shriek. 'The doggies are
my bread and butter! Damn it all, Terry, I'm a single girl
and . . ."

Girl, thought Condon. Forty if she was a day. Selling
one of her hounds. That sort lived by myth: distressed
lady, *morya*. Couldn't take a *real* job because if she worked
from nine to five as a secretary, she would *be* a secretary.
Dabbling in dog-breeding she could live off the smell of an
oil rag and be a lady still. He doubted she saw meat more
than once a week. Patrick had no patience with the like.
Where was Hennessy? Bit of prostatic trouble there.
What were we but future worm-food?

'Seriously . . .' Terry's voice now. 'It's the youth. I hope
I'm no old fogy. I'm thirty-nine and like my bit of fun.
I don't mind long hair or free love or any of that, but I
think they've lost sight of some jolly important matters,
what with all this fraternising with nigs and . . .'

'*Who's* going out to fight for nig-nogs, Terry? Bet you
don't even know which side you'll be on!'

'Right! You're absolutely right. I don't give a damn
which side I'm on. They're all black to me, haha. No, but I
do have a purpose. I think the next great war will be with

the coloureds. Don't laugh! I mean *they'll* be attacking
us. Look at South Africa, Rhodesia, the U.S. They've got
the message. It's easy for us to sit on our bums in Southern
Ireland – the last country where a gentleman is recognised
as such, by the way, which is why I like it here – to sit here
on our bums and disapprove of the white supremacists.
Much too easy. It may be less so in the future. Look at
China. Count them up. They want what we've got, right?
Right. I don't say I blame the poor buggers but every
man's got to fight his own corner. And there isn't enough
to go round, right? Besides, a lot of decent things would
go down the drain if the West went under. . . . Well, the
long and the short of it is I'm going out to fight *for* the
nigs in order to train myself to fight *against* them.'

'And for the lolly.'

'And for the lolly.'

'Upon this battle depends the survival of Christian civ.,
what?'

'Right.'

'. . . all that we have known and cared for will sink . . .'

Someone, not Terry, began to deliver in tones wavering
between drunken parody and drunken sentiment a speech
which slipped through Condon's defences. With astonishment, he realised that he and the rowdies in the bar had
something in common. There was that fellow, in his literal,
simple way, heeding the call of the times and assuming
the military part of the knightly mission at the very
moment when Condon himself was shouldering its
spiritual side. They complemented each other. Well and
why not? Hadn't Protestant volunteers fought the Turk
with Catholic Knights at the siege of Malta? Patrick stood
up. He was thinking of going into the bar when he heard
Amanda say:

'Hey, what about giving Elsie a tinkle?'

'Elsie who?'

'Elsie Condom or Condon or whatever. She's got a
soft spot for old Terry here and she's sure to produce
sandwiches. Her lord and master's almost certain to be off

the premises. Bet she'd like to light your fire, Terry, on your last night.'

'Got her number?'

'In the book. Listen, it'd be doing a good deed in a naughty world to poke old Elsie. Seriously. She doesn't get much and . . .'

'What about yourself, Amanda . . . ?'

'Oh *well*, if . . .'

Patrick collided with Hennessy who was finally returning and pushed him, for the second time that evening, backwards out the door and into his own car. A yellow Austin Healey with a GB on its rump was drawn up beside it. Patrick resisted an impulse to give it a passing kick. His mind jumbled thoughts like a washing-machine throwing about soiled linen and, above it, he managed to chat about how time-was-getting-on-sorry-Hennessy-but-better-be-hitting-the-road-slippery-as-well-be-off-betimes. The man must think he was mad.

Patrick felt a thrust of humiliation knife him. He felt almost tearful. An unskinned part of himself had been reached. He had thought he and Elsie had something, a . . . union . . . a solidarity which . . . In his own head he groped sadly, reaching an unexplored place. Hennessy's voice came to him but he couldn't distinguish the words. He felt exposed, mutilated. Hennessy's Volkswagen funnelled down the hedgy roads. Briars scraped the windows and squeaked.

'There should be a quorum,' Hennessy was saying. 'We should hold out for that.'

'Yes,' managed Condon.

'And what's your position on the other matter?'

What matter? Which? Had Hennessy *heard*?

'I . . . what?'

'Are you feeling all right?'

'No. I had a dizzy spell. I'm afraid I missed . . .'

'Oh well, it doesn't matter.' Hennessy sounded miffed. But Condon had to know. 'No, no, *tell* me.'

'I've *been* telling you! Corcoran wants selection of the

ambulance corps to be left up to him and his henchmen. A matter of getting the strings into his own hand and . . .'

'Ah.'

Condon's mind drifted again. Didn't she *care* for him at all then, if she . . . Oh, and that was what *she* had asked him! He groaned.

'Are you in pain?'

'No, no, slight twinge. My ulcer. . . . Nothing serious.'

He *must*, would, pull himself together. Mind over matter. Yes.

The Knights' ceremony was being held in a Dublin hotel. An entire floor had been taken over, but members spilled into corridors and stairs and lobby where, cloaked and armed, they drew the eye, impressing the serf-grey citizenry with their spiritual and temporal pelf. A drunken poet got into the lift with Condon and Hennessy. Pink and pendulous, his nose (Condon reproved himself for thinking) resembled a skinned male organ. The poet fixed the Knights with his tight, urine-yellow goat's eyes and grinned. A notorious lecher, he was not the sort of man with whom either would choose to associate, but they were, as always in Dublin, on nodding terms with him.

'How are things, Ian?'

'A wet old night.'

'Ha,' roared the poet in a peasant brogue, assumed, as all Dubliners knew, to make them feel effete, urban and far from the loamy roots of things. 'How are our Knights T-T-Templarss? Still as r-r-andy-d-dy and roistering as when they were burnt at the stake by Philippe le Bel? Burnt,' he hissed, 'b-b-burrrrntt and their goods confiscated, ha! Not that *that's* likely to happen again. There's a rising tide of p-p-permiss-ssiveness, as they call it now. Still secret, still underground but about to oo-ooz-z-z-ze up and submerge us all in a f-f-f-foam of s-s-sperm! The age of Eros is upon us. I've just c-come back from the cu-cu-cunty counthrrry where they've been enjoying a spell of warm weather, and yez-d never credit the goings on I witnessed under hedges and d-d-ditches.'

'I'm sure we wouldn't,' Hennessy told him. 'This is our floor.' He stepped out with a gelid nod. 'Be seeing you.' But the poet followed them.

'Maids and matrons,' he roared. 'Wedded wives f-f-fu-fuck-ck-cking in the f-f-fields. Cuckoo eggs in every nest. Maybe your own spouses are . . .'

Condon hit him. Before he knew it his fist had shot out and caught the pink, wettish – he felt it wet on his knuckles – nose. Or was the wetness blood? It was. His knuckles were stained with it. The poet had been put on a couch and his collar loosened.

'He's O.K. Just a nose-bleed.'

'Head back, Ian, hold your head back.'

'No, better not. The blood makes you sick. Indigestible. Spit it out. Get us a glass. Thanks. Mind the carpet now.'

'Hold his nose over the glass. In, man, in. Poke it in.'

'Get him to a bathroom.'

'Good thing it happened on this floor. No scandal. How did he get in?'

'Gate-crasher.'

A Knight walked up to Condon. 'Come and wash your hands too. He's all right, drunk, deserved what he got. Do him a world of good.'

Other voices joined in.

'What was it he said about . . . Condon's wife?'

'Shush!' And loudly: 'Someone should have done it long ago. A foul-mouthed fellow, a gurrier.'

'A fine lesson for him. A low type. You're a hard man, Condon, A true Knight, haha!'

Surrounded by his fellows, Condon felt his agitation abate into a lapping tide of excitement. Someone must have given him a brandy because, as the ceremony began, a manservant in cotton gloves tapped him on the arm to recover the empty glass. He gave it to the man and himself to rituals he had been studying for some weeks. This was to be a brief and worldly affair because of the hour and place. Mass would be celebrated in the Order's chapel next morning. Would he stay? He had intended to but now

was not so sure. The panoply of the differing ranks of
Knights and monks confused him. All wore crosses recall-
ing the crusades on which Knights had gone leaving
wives locked in chastity belts. Or was that myth? Had the
first Knights been celibate? And had such contraptions
been widely used? Very unsanitary, if so. He had seen
one once in a museum. Was it the Cluny museum in Paris?
He wasn't sure, reproached himself for not achieving a
prayerful mood. *Oh my God, I am heartily sorry for having
offended Thee, and I detest my sins above every other
evil* . . . Did he? He did not! He was glad he had pucked
that obscene fellow on the gob. Watch what's happening.
You'll miss your cue. The oath of conjugal chastity brought
back figures crouching in a corner of his brain: Terry-
the-nig-killer and Elsie. Niggers for that sort began at
Liverpool. No holds barred with wives of nigs or Papists.
No holds barred with any wives in profligate England.
Adultery winked at. Since Henry the Eighth. Ruin seize
thee, ruthless king, Confusion on thy banners wait . . .
That was some other . . . *Would* she? NO. Ah no, she was
forty-four – still dirty-minded, though, had violated his
privacy in talk with Amanda Shand. Don't trust, you can't
trust her. Ah God, his knightly honour was a joke, be-
smirched in advance. Maybe, at this very . . .

He made to leap up but a hand pulled him back, recall-
ing him to the time and place. 'Not yet,' whispered
Hennessy, thinking Condon had mistaken the cues printed
on the slips of paper which had been handed out. 'Not
till after the hymn.'

Nigs. Knicks. Patrick sank back on his knees. To think
she should spoil a moment of such spiritual significance,
dragging his soul down to the level of her own. A stain
on one Knight's honour must affect the Order as a whole.
Every man responsible for his woman. He had read in the
National Geographic about adultresses somewhere in
Africa being impaled *per vaginam*. Punished whereby
they had – but the idea was repugnant. Better punish the
lover like in *The Cask of Amontillado*. Brick him up. By

God if he came home this night and found them at it!
Jesus, let them not, because if they . . . Please, Jesus. He'd
have no choice. But. Universally recognised. *Crime
passionnel.* Juries let off the husband. And the heavenly
jury? *Veni creator spiritus* . . . The hymn ended and the
Knights rose creakily. Not one was under fifty. Patrick's
head reeled and whirled. Pounded.

'Well now, let's toast our new Knight of Honour and
Devotion.' Hennessy led him off.

There was no slipping away. They drank fast and gar-
rulously. At one point Condon was sick. He threw up
with decorum, in the lavatory, unknown to any. He ate a
peppermint to sweeten his breath. Coming back, he
brought the conversation round to Parnell and Kitty
O'Shea.

'The woman was an adulteress.'

'But was it fair to punish her lover and the millions who
depended on him? The course of Irish history might . . .'

'You're forgetting the scandal! The scandal to the souls
of those same millions! How could the Church . . .'

Rounds of drinks waited, marshalled like skittles. Four
brandies had been bought for Patrick. The bar was closing
but every man wanted to stand his round. Honour obliged.

Suddenly, Condon said he needed to get home. Urgently.
His wife was unwell, subject to giddy spells, and might
not hear the phone.

'Can I borrow your car?' he asked Hennessy. 'I'll get it
back to you tomorrow.'

Hennessy gave him the keys.

Patrick took them and rushed out of the hotel, started
the car without warming the engine and raced hell-for-
leather out of Dublin and into the hedgy embrace of
country roads. Here he was forced by an attack of nausea
to pull in and found himself, out of the car, weeping in a
ditch and embracing a thorn tree. 'Elsie,' he groaned, to
his astonishment, 'Elsie!' He began to roar and bellow
like a bull, filling and emptying his lungs with desolate,
twanging air. After some minutes he got back into the car,

feeling wet and so paralytic with cold he could hardly
touch his fingers around the stick-shift. He put on the
heater and drove in shivering sobriety back across the
mountains, concentrating on the road and reciting prayers
to calm his nerves. '. . . disease of desire,' he whispered
mechanically, 'to possess his vessel in sanctification and
honour, not in the disease of desire as do the Gentiles
who know not God . . .'

As he turned into his own winding drive, darkly flanked
by rhododendrons, he got a glimpse of Elsie's lighted
window and her silhouette, heavier than he had remembered it, closing the curtains. He rounded the last curve
and came on the battered yellow Austin Healey which had
been parked earlier in the public-house yard. Standing by
its nose – he must have been looking at the motor, for the
bonnet was raised – like a moth in the glare of Patrick's
headlights, was a man in a check sports coat: Terry.
Patrick drove straight for him, as though following a
traffic signal in the man's gullet. He could see into the
pulsing throat and even the flap on the uvula glistening
against the dark interior. There was a thump. Patrick's
head hit the headrest behind him. The man fell forward on
to the Volkswagen, then, on the rebound, into the unbon-
neted engine of his own car. Heels up, arms flopping, he
was carried backwards as the two cars pursued their course
into a tree. The Austin Healey buckled, the man's limbs
crunched within the integument of his clothes. Patrick –
although he was to prove to be suffering from minor
concussion – felt nothing.

Moments later, Elsie found his cloaked figure, bending
over the wreckage, howling in the elated, almost musical
accents of dogs on a moonlit night: 'I *did* it. Jesus, I did
it.'

That version never got out.

Connections rallied. Witnesses testified that the Englishman had been drinking heavily in the pub. They surmised
he must have lost his way and strayed up Condon's drive-

way in search of the cross-roads. In all likelihood, he would have neglected to turn on his lights. That Condon should round the bend of his own driveway at an incautious speed was understandable at so late an hour in a gentleman tired after a long drive and eager to get home to his bed. A regrettable accident.

Terry's friends waked him jovially, pleased with the excuse for a little extra drinking. 'After all,' said Amanda Shand, 'he was only a bird of passage.' The Condons, she had heard, were getting on together as never before. He had taken her for a change of scene to Malta and *she* had sent Amanda a card saying she was 'having a whale of a time'.

TOM MacINTYRE
The Dogs of Fionn

Eyes on some high ditch she'd flown yesterday on the heels of the hounds, enter the Lady of the Manor. The scatter of customers parted – baggy matrons, a snuff-coloured pensioner, two or three youngsters – and fell back as she stepped up to the counter.

'A hawf pound of hawm,' cried the Lady of the Manor.

If I was fresh to the village, I was still certain who it was. You don't mistake Cromwell's breed. Demeaned by solid ground, those well-shod feet fidgeted to find the stirrups again; the tweed skirt, thighs and rump betrothed to the saddle; square-chested, and, above, the long leathery features of the tribe.

'A hawf pound of hawm.'

Her brown fingers rained on the counter.

'Certainly, m'lady.'

Two young ones supported the shopkeeper as he hurried to serve. Ham, slicer, careful now –

'Wretched weathaw, Mallon.'

'Desperate, m'lady, desperate,' said Johnny Mallon, fussy over the slicer. *Whirrisssh, whirrisssh,* pink white-streaked slivers curled from the bone.

'Lot of fat there, Mallon' –

Panic.

'Sorry, m'lady.' Johnny jumped to it, switched the ham about, drove back his assistants, started again.

M'lady! Scrapings of the Ascendancy bucket and acting as if nothing had changed for the last three hundred years. The customers hung there, blurring as my astonishment thickened to humiliation.

'How's that now?'

'Bettah, Mallon.'

Johnny wrapped the purchase. I watched her. Straight-backed, eyes on another approaching ditch.

'Now, thank you very much.'

Handing over the ham, crouched for a pat on his shop-keeper poll.

She never saw him, never saw anybody as, flick of the reins, she turned and strode, rode from the shop.

Business picked up again, casually. Already, she'd crossed the footpath, and was sitting in her car. Before starting up, she glanced into the shop. From that cluttered dusk I raised a hand, one finger crooked. She saw my signal. She waited.

I don't think anyone noticed me leave. My eyes were on that Munnings' face behind the car window. She was lowering the glass. I stopped about a yard short of the car.

I'd no idea what I was going to say. She had bad eyebrows. stubby, smudged.

'Woman, a thought struck me.'

Pause. A hundred wars sabred between us.

'Yes?'

'All that,' I said, my tongue lithe metal, 'stopped about forty years ago.'

She gaped up at me, wheeled for an answer.

I turned away. 'You should remember that.'

Her car rasped from the kerb, and sped off.

You read the history books, and they tell you – nothing. But now, walking down the street, I thought, my God, that's why they went out to fight – because they'd ride you down. And this is what it felt like, the clash, the aftermath. . . .

Crossing the bridge on my way home, the oldest bridge in Ireland, some said. Norman stone spliced at its layered foundations. Bulging from late-summer rain, the river cut noisily through four squat eyes below. I turned right, and up the road which, topping the bluffs, sat on the southern bank. A dash of sun. Opposite, a line of sallies held the light, rusting it. Fragilely, the small leaves peeled and distributed fantastic bloom.

Then, not far ahead, I saw a woman I knew by sight. Young, fair-complexioned, with child, her face the opening corolla of pregnancy, neat smock, slacks, sandals. I was thinking how well she carried her child – when the barrage of whistles and catcalls and semi-articulated jeers struck, and she faltered. Embarrassed, she looked at me, bravely came on.

We both guessed, almost instantly, the source. I could look. Across the river, up the grey windowed wall of that sometime workhouse which served now as a boot-factory. In the far top line of windows, anonymous heads bobbed. The jeering started afresh, with more relish this time, savouring the target – 'Whittoo. . . . Any chance, Mrs . . . night . . . Yeeippeee. . . . Give us a . . . Hi, Ma'am . . . How's your . . . Psst . .' – spurting down, livid on the breeze. My blood spat. Must be my day for war. She was beside me.

'I'm – sorry, I' –

My apologies failed. She stood there, her back to the river. Hands pathetically shielding, she said something but another burst spewing from above took her words. And decided me.

'I'll be back' –

Turning, half-running, I back-tracked, and recrossed the bridge. They were moving fast too. The jeering had stopped. The distant windows showed blank, inoffensive. The possibility that – nameless – they could escape with such facility rowelled me. Veering left, hurrying under the massive walls, I could hear – sieved by stone – the machines. I came to the great arched gateway, and entered.

ENQUIRIES . . .

In the small office, the air was mucilage. At the table-desk in front of me, a thin girl idled over a typewriter.

'May I see the Manager?'

'Of course, sir.'

Curiously registering the impetus about me, she took my name, and, within seconds, the Manager appeared. Confronted by the office, I'd experienced a premonition of dismay, and now, echoing that, his presence dented something in me. Still, my complaint rushed out. When I was through, he spoke civilly.

'Damned glad you came round,' he said – the accent, his red pavilion-cheery moustached face no lie, was Yorkshire. 'Fact is we've had a lot of trouble with them. Rough crowd mostly, I'm afraid. This gives me a chance. I'll take care of them. Thank you' –

I'd have gone then, but it was too late. The rictus of camaraderie on his big face loosened for one second, purred sympathy, set stiff again.

Next, companionably gabbing, he was guiding me to the door. Together, we stood outside. The flagged yard, pale, sloped down from us to the jail façade of the main building. At our appearance, heads ducked in the high windows. We must meet for a drink some time, was he saying? Looking up at the windows, he buttoned his jacket, slapped me on the shoulder, and moved off across the yard, his supple hand-made shoes swingeing the stones.

JOHN McGAHERN
The Wine Breath

If I were to die, I'd miss most the mornings and the evenings, he thought as he walked the narrow dirt-track by the
lake in the late evening, and then wondered if his mind
was failing, for how could anybody think anything as
stupid: being a man he had no choice, he was doomed to
die; and being dead he'd miss nothing, being nothing.
And it went against everything in his life as a priest.

The solid world, though, was everywhere around him.
There was the lake, the road, the evening, and he was
going to call on Gillespie. Gillespie was sawing. Gillespie
was always sawing. The roaring rise-and-fall of the two-
stroke stayed like a rent in the evening. And when he got
to the black gate there was Gillespie, his overalled bulk
framed in the short avenue of alders, and he was sawing
not alders but beech, four or five tractorloads dumped in
the front of the house. The priest put a hand to the black
gate, bolted to the first of the alders, and was at once
arrested by showery sunlight falling down the avenue. It
lit up the one boot holding the length of beech in place,
it lit the arms moving the blade slowly up and down as it
tore through the beech, white chips milling out on the
chain.

Suddenly, as he was about to rattle the gate loudly to see
if this would penetrate the sawing, he felt himself (bathed
as in a dream) in an incredible sweetness of light. It was
the evening light on snow. The gate on which he had his
hand vanished, the alders, Gillespie's formidable bulk,
the roaring of the saw. He was in another day, the lost

day of Michael Bruen's funeral nearly thirty years before. All was silent and still there. Slow feet crunched on the snow. Ahead, at the foot of the hill, the coffin rode slowly forward on shoulders, its brown varnish and metal trappings dull in the glittering snow, riding just below the long waste of snow eight or ten feet deep over the whole countryside. The long dark line of mourners following the coffin stretched away towards Oakport Wood in the pathway cut through the snow. High on Killeelan Hill the graveyard evergreens rose out of the snow. The graveyard wall was covered, the narrow path cut up the side of the hill stopping at the little gate deep in the snow. The coffin climbed with painful slowness, as if it might never reach the gate, often pausing for the bearers to be changed; and someone started to pray, the prayer travelling down the whole mile-long line of the mourners as they shuffled behind the coffin in the narrow tunnel cut in the snow.

It was the day in February 1947 that they buried Michael Bruen. Never before or since had he experienced the Mystery in such awesomeness. Now as he stood at the gate there was no awe or terror, only the coffin moving slowly towards the dark trees on the hill, the long line of mourners, and everywhere the blinding white light, among the half-buried thorn bushes, and beyond Killeelan on the covered waste of Gloria Bog, on the sides of Slieve an Iarainn.

He did not know how long he had stood in that lost day, in that white light, probably for no more than a moment. He could not have stood the intensity for any longer. When he woke out of it the grey light of the alders had reasserted itself. His hand was still on the bar of the gate. Gillespie was still sawing, bent over the saw-horse, his boot on the length of beechwood, completely enclosed in the roaring rise-and-fall of the saw. The priest felt as vulnerable as if he had suddenly woken out of sleep, shaken and somewhat ashamed to have been caught asleep in the actual day and life, without any protection of walls.

He was about to rattle the gate again, feeling a washed-out parody of a child or old man on what was after all nothing more than a poor errand: to tell the Gillespies that a bed had at long last been made available in the Regional Hospital for the operation on Mrs Gillespie's piles, when his eyes were caught again by the quality of the light. It was one of those late October days, small white clouds drifting about the sun, and the watery light was shining down the alder rows to fall on the white chips of the beechwood strewn all about Gillespie, some inches deep. It was the same white light as the light on snow. As he watched the light went out on the beech chips, and it was the grey day again around Gillespie's sawing. It had been as simple as that. The suggestion of snow had been enough to plunge him in the lost day of Michael Bruen's funeral. Everything in that remembered day was so pure and perfect that he felt purged of all tiredness and bitterness, was, for a moment, eager to begin life again.

And, making sure that Gillespie hadn't noticed him at the gate, he turned back on the road. The bed wouldn't be ready for another week. The news could wait a day or more. Before leaving he stole a last look at the dull white ground about the sawhorse. The most difficult things seem always to lie closest to us, to lie always around our feet.

Ever since his mother's death he found himself stumbling into these dead days. Once, crushed mint in the garden had given him back a day he'd spent with her at the sea in such reality that he had been frightened, as if he'd suddenly fallen through time; it was as if the world of the dead was as available to him as the world of the living. It was also humiliating for him to realise that she must have been the mainspring of his days. And now that the mainspring was broken the hands were weakly falling here and falling there. Today there had been the sudden light on the bits of white beech. He'd not have noticed it if he hadn't been alone, if Gillespie had not been so absorbed in his sawing. Before there must have been some such simple trigger that he'd been too ashamed or bewildered to notice.

Stealthily and quickly he went down the dirt-track by the lake till he got to the main road. To the left was the church in a rookery of old trees, and behind it the house where he lived. Safe on the wide main road he let his mind go back to the beech chips. They rested there around Gillespie's large bulk, and paler still was the line of mourners following the coffin through the snow, a picture you could believe or disbelieve but not be in. In idle exasperation he began to count the trees in the hedge along the road as he walked: ash, green oak, whitethorn, ash, the last leaves a vivid yellow on the wild cherry, empty October fields in dull wet light behind the hedges. This, then, was the actual day, the only day that mattered, the day from which our salvation had to be won or lost: it stood solidly and impenetrably there, denying the weak life of the person, with nothing of the eternal other than it would dully endure, while the day set alight in his mind by the light of the white beech, though it had been nothing more than a funeral he had attended during a dramatic snowfall when a boy, seemed bathed in the eternal, seemed everything we had been taught and told of the world of God.

Dissatisfied, and feeling as tired again as he'd been on his way to Gillespie's, he did not go through the church gate with its circle and cross, nor did he call to the sexton locking up under the bellrope. In order to be certain of being left alone he went by the circular path at the side, round to the house, for a high laurel hedge hid the path from the graveyard and church. There he made coffee without turning on the light. Always when about to give birth or die cattle sought out a clean place in some corner of the field, away from the herd.

Michael Bruen had been a big kindly agreeable man, what was called a lovely man. His hair was a coarse grey. He wore loose-fitting tweeds with red cattleman's boots. When young he had been a policeman in Dublin. It was said he had either won or inherited money, and had come home to where he'd come from, to buy the big Crossna farm, to marry and grow rich.

He had a large family, and men were employed on the farm. The yard and its big outhouses with the red roofs rang with work; cans, machinery, raillery, the sliding of hooves, someone whistling. And within the house, away from the yard, was the enormous cave of a kitchen, the long table down its centre, the fireplace at its end, the plates and pots and presses along the walls, sides of bacon wrapped in gauze hanging from hooks in the ceiling, the whole room full of the excitement and bustle of women.

Often as a boy the priest had gone to Michael Bruen's on some errand for his father, a far smaller farmer than Michael. Once the beast was housed or the load emptied Michael would take him into the kitchen.

He remembered the last December evening well. He had driven over a white bullock. The huge fire of wood blazed all the brighter because of the frost.

'Give this man something,' Michael had led him. 'Something solid that'll warm the life back into him.'

'A cup of tea will do fine,' he had protested in the custom.

'Nonsense. Don't pay him the slightest attention. Empty bags can't stand.'

Eileen, the prettiest of Michael's daughters, laughed as she took down the pan. Her arms were white to the elbows with a fine dusting of flour.

'He'll remember this was a good place to come to when he has to start thinking about a wife.' Michael's words gave licence to general hilarity.

It was hard to concentrate on Michael's question about his father, so delicious was the smell of frying. The mug of steaming tea was put by his side. The butter melted on the fresh bread on the plate. There were sausages, liver, bacon, a slice of black-pudding and sweetest grisceens.

'Now set to,' Michael laughed. 'We don't want any empty bags leaving Bruen's.'

Michael came with him to the gate when he left. 'Tell

your father it's ages since we had a drink in the Royal.
And that if he doesn't search me out in the Royal the next
Fair Day I'll have to go over and bate the lugs off him.'
As he shook his hand in the half-light of the yard lamp
it was the last time he was to see him alive. Before the
last flakes had stopped falling, and when old people were
searching back to 'the great snows when Count Plunkett
was elected' to find another such fall, Michael Bruen
had died, and his life was already another such poor water-
mark of memory.

The snow lay eight feet deep on the roads, and dead
cattle and sheep were found in drifts of fifteen feet in the
fields. All of the people who hadn't lost sheep or cattle
were in extraordinary good humour, their own ills buried
for a time as deep as their envy of any other's good
fortune in the general difficulty of the snow. It took days
to cut a way out to the main road, the snow having to be
cut in blocks breast-high out of a face of frozen snow. A
wild cheer went up as the men at last cut through to the
gang digging in from the main road. Another cheer greeted
the first van to come in, Doherty's bread van, and it had
hardly died when the hearse came with the coffin for
Michael Bruen. That night they cut the path up the side of
Killeelan Hill and found the family headstone beside the
big yew just inside the gate and opened the grave. They
hadn't finished digging when the first funeral bell came
clearly over the snow the next day to tell them that the
coffin had started on its way.

The priest hadn't thought of the day for years or of
Michael Bruen till he had stumbled into it without warning by way of the sudden light on the beech chips. It did
not augur well. There were days, especially of late, when
he seemed to be lost in dead days, to see time present as a
flimsy accumulating tissue over all the time that was lost.
Sometimes he saw himself as an old man that boys were
helping down to the shore, restraining the tension of their
need to laugh as they pointed out a rock in the path he
seemed about to stumble over, and then they had to lift

their eyes and smile apologetically to the passersby while he stood staring out to sea, having forgotten all about the rock in his path. 'It's this way we're going,' he felt the imaginary tug on his sleeve, and he was drawn again into the tortuous existence of the everyday, away from the eternal of the sea or the lost light on frozen snow across Killeelan Hill.

Never before though had he noticed anything like the beech chips. There was the joy of holding what had eluded him for so long, in its amazing simplicity: but mastered knowledge was soon no knowledge, unless it opened, became part of a greater knowledge, and what did the beech chips do but turn back to his own death.

Like the sudden snowfall and Michael Bruen's burial his life had been like any other, except to himself, and then only in odd visions of it, as a lost life. When it had been agreeable and equable he had no vision of it at all.

The country childhood. His mother and father. The arrival at the shocking knowledge of birth and death. His attraction to the priesthood as a way of vanquishing death and avoiding birth. O hurry it, he thought. There is not much to a life. Many have it. There is not enough room. His father and mother were old when they married, and he was 'the fruit of old things', he heard derisively. His mother had been a seamstress. He could still see the needle flashing in her strong hands, that single needle flash composed of thousands of hours.

'His mother had the vocation for him,' perhaps she had, perhaps all the mothers of the country had, it had so passed into the speech of the country, in all the forms of both beatification and derision; and it was out of fear of death he became a priest, which becomes in its time the fear of life, and wasn't it natural to turn back to the mother in this fear: she was older than fear, having given him his life, and who would give a life if they knew its end. There was then his father's death, the father accepting it as he had accepted all poor fortune all his life long, as his due, refusing to credit the good.

And afterwards his mother sold the land to 'Horse' McLaughlin and came to live with him, and was happy. She attended all the Masses and Devotions, took messages, and she sewed, though she had no longer any need, linen for the altar, soutanes and surplices, his shirts and all her own clothes. Sometimes her concern for him irritated him to exasperation but he hardly ever let it show. He was busy with the many duties of a priest. The fences on the past and future were secure. He must have been what is called happy, and there was a whole part of his life that without his knowing had come to turn to her for its own expression.

He discovered it when she began her death. He came home one summer evening to find all the lights in the house on. She was in the livingroom, in the usual chair. The table was piled high with dresses. Round the chair was a pile of rags. She did not look up when he entered, her still strong hands tearing apart a herring-bone skirt she had made only the year before.

'What on earth are you doing, Mother?' He caught her by the hands when she didn't answer.

'It's time you were up for Mass,' she said.

'What are you doing with all your dresses?'

'What dresses?'

'All the dresses you've just been tearing up.'

'I don't know anything about dresses,' and then he saw there was something wrong. She made no resistance when he led her up the stairs.

For some days she seemed absent and confused but, though he watched her carefully, she was otherwise very little different from her old self, and she did not appear ill. Then he came home one evening to find her standing like a child in the middle of the room, surrounded by an enormous pile of rags. She had taken up from where she'd been interrupted at the herring-bone skirt, and had torn up every dress or article of clothing she had ever made. After his initial shock he did the usual and sent for the doctor.

'I'm afraid it's just the onset of senility,' the doctor said.

'It's irreversible?'

The doctor nodded, 'It very seldom takes such a violent form, but that's what it is. She'll have to be looked after.' And with a sadness that part of his life was over, he took her to the Home and saw her settled there.

She recognised him when he visited her there the first year, but without excitement, as if he was already far away; and then the day came when he had to admit that she no longer knew who he was, had become like a dog kennelled out too long. He was with her when she died. She'd turned her face toward him. There came what seemed a light of recognition in the eyes like a last glow of a match before it goes out, and then she died.

There was nothing left but his own life. There had been nothing but that all along, but it had been obscured, comfortably obscured.

He turned on the radio.

A man had lost both legs in an explosion. There was violence on the night-shift at Ford's. The pound had steadied towards the close but was still down on the day.

Letting his fingers linger on the knob he turned it off. The disembodied voice on the air was not unlike the lost day he'd stumbled into through the light on the beech chips, except it had nothing of its radiance – the funeral during the years he must have carried it around with him had lost the sheltered burden of the everyday, had become light as the air in all the clarity of light. It was all timeless, and seemed at least a promise of the eternal.

He went to draw the curtain. She had made the red curtain too with its pale lining but hadn't torn it. How often must she have watched the moonlight on the still headstones beyond the laurel, as it lay evenly on them this night. She had been afraid of ghosts: old priests who had lived in this house, who through whiskey or some other ill had neglected to say some Mass for the dead – and because of the neglect the soul for whom the Mass should have been offered was forced to linger beyond its

319

time in Purgatory – and the priest guilty of the omission could himself not be released until the living priest had said the Mass, and was forced to come at midnight to the house in all his bondage until that Mass was said.

'They must have been all good priests, Mother. Good steady old fellows like myself. They never come back,' he used to assure her. He remembered his own idle words as he drew the curtain, lingering as much over the drawing of the curtain as he had lingered over the turning off of the radio. He would be glad of a ghost tonight, be glad of any visitation from beyond the walls of sense.

He took up the battered and friendly missal, which had been with him all his adult life, to read the office of the day. On bad days he kept it till late, the familiar words that changed with the changing year, that he had grown to love, and were as well his daily duty. It must be surely the greatest grace of life, the greatest freedom, to have to do what we love because it is also our duty. But he wasn't able to read on this evening among the old familiar words for long. An annoyance came between him and the page, the Mass he had to repeat every day, the Mass in English. He wasn't sure whether he hated it or the guitar-playing priests more. It was humiliating to think that these had never been such a scourge when his mother had been alive. Was his life the calm vessel it had seemed, dully setting out and returning from the fishing grounds. Or had he been always what he seemed now. 'Oh yes. There you go again,' he heard the familiar voice in the empty room. 'Complaining about the Mass in the vernacular. When you prefer the common names of flowers to their proper names,' and the sharp, energetic, almost brutal laugh. It was Peter Joyce, he was not dead. Peter Joyce had risen to become a bishop at the other end of the country, to become an old friend that he no longer saw.

'But they are more beautiful. Dog rose, wild woodbine, buttercup, daisy. . . .'

He heard his own protest. It was in a hotel that they

used to go to every summer on the Atlantic, a small hotel
where you could read after dinner without fear of a rising
roar from the bar beginning to outrival the Atlantic by
ten o'clock.

'And, no doubt, the little rose of Scotland, sharp and
sweet and breaks the heart,' he heard his friend quote
maliciously. 'And it's not the point. The reason that names
of flowers must be in Latin is that when flower lovers
meet they know what they are talking about, no matter
whether they're French or Greeks or Arabs. They have a
universal language.'

'I prefer the humble names, no matter what you say.'

'Of course you do. And it's parochial sentimentalists
like yourself who prefer the *smooth sowthistle* to *Sonchus
oleraceus* that's the whole cause of your late lamented
Mass in Latin disappearing. I have no sympathy with you.
You people tire me.'

The memory of that truculent argument dispelled completely his annoyance, as its simple logic had once taken
his breath away, but he was curiously tired after the vividness of the recall. It was only by a sheer act of will, sometimes having to count the words, that he was able to
finish his office. 'I know one thing, Peter Joyce. I know
that I know nothing,' he murmured when he finished. But
when he looked at the room about him he could hardly
believe it was so empty and dead and dry, the empty chair
where she should be sewing, the oaken table with the
scattered books, the clock on the mantel. And wildly and
aridly he wanted to curse. But his desire to curse was as
unfair as life. He had not wanted it.

And then, quietly, he saw that he had a ghost all right,
one that he had been walking around with for a long
time, a ghost he had not wanted to recognise – his own
death. He might as well get to know him well, he would
never leave now. He was in the room, and had no mortal
shape. Absence does not cast a shadow.

All there was was the white light of the lamp on the
open book, on the white marble; the brief sun of God on

beechwood, and the sudden light of that glistening snow, and the timeless mourners moving towards the yews on Killeelan Hill almost thirty years ago. It was as good as any, if there ever could be a good day to go.

And somewhere, outside this room that was an end, he knew that a young man not unlike he had been once stood on a granite step and listened to the doorbell ring, smiled as he heard a woman's footsteps come down the hallway, ran his fingers through his hair, and turned the bottle of white wine he held in his hands completely around as he prepared to enter a pleasant and uncomplicated evening, feeling himself immersed in time without end.

GILLMAN NOONAN
A Sexual Relationship

If Sean Kenny were to admit the truth about why he
thought he was attractive to women he would probably
skip, lightly and winningly, over all the more obvious
reasons – such as his tall, athletic figure, his gravity that
belied his twenty-five years, or his sense of humour com-
bined with just the right mixture of interest in external
things and those of the spirit – and set most store by his
carefully cultivated manner of not appearing to give a
damn about them. If this was cynicism, it worked. Quite
enough things, he felt sure, would not work out later in
life, but right now if they were working like this, well,
why interfere? He was enjoying himself. If a girl was prepared to go along with his non-committal way and sleep
with him, wasn't that her affair? And if afterwards – perhaps with her eye on the ring – she called him conceited
and inaccessible, or even a fraud, she was quite entitled
to do so once she didn't annoy him further. For once a
girl began to dig below the skin it didn't work anymore
and Kenny put a speedy end to it. He had no intention of
marrying for some time, so love and tantrums were
definitely out.

His nonchalant approach seemed to work too in the case
of Helga Liebig, his German teacher. He wasn't especially
attracted to her as a person – at least to the extent that he
knew her from class and intermittent conversations in the
tea breaks – but her body was superb. The first evening he
came to the language institute she ascended the stairs
before him displaying the most exquisite legs he had ever

seen. Her thighs were long and tanned with just the right amount of flesh on them, and as far as he could see the other parts attached to them were of equally fine proportions. True, he was a bit disappointed in her face when he sat down and had a chance to study her. She had a kind of lopsided Barbra Streisand face, only funnier. And it seemed too small for her body. It also had its own peculiar sense of humour. There were times when she stood with the chalk in her hand chuckling away idiotically while the class looked on wondering where the joke was. But that body made up for a lot of foolishness. Kenny saw it dimly outlined in a bedroom door, softly tense, provocatively akimbo in a whisper of lace, murmuring 'Kommst du, Liebling?'

Needless to say, in those intermittent conversations over tea Kenny gave no hint of harbouring any such visions of sensual dalliance. She was a sophisticated woman of about twenty-seven who spoke fluent English and would obviously be unimpressed by any amateurish posturing. So while other male members of the class made animated conversation with Helga Liebig and playfully shouted invitations to each other to have *noch eine Tasse Tee* or *noch einen Kuchen* (it is *einen*, is it, Fräulein Liebig?'), Kenny stood slightly apart, of the group yet not of it, and quietly sipped his tea. He was not a snob, certainly not a pipe and cravat type, but he liked reserve, and found that women liked men who had reserve. Sometimes he felt Helga regarding him and then, as though he had just happened to look at her, he ventured a throwaway boyish grin that tactfully fell short of a wink. And if he did approach her with a question, he made sure it reflected the higher echelons of management into which he was steadily climbing.

It was working, but when after a couple of months it came to actually asking her out she beat him – to his immense satisfaction – by a head. She had these two tickets to a recital of German music. Would he like to come? Love to. Great. Where did she live? Herbert Road?

Better still. On his way from Blackrock. Pick her up what time? Great. See you then, Helga.

He was very pleased with himself. Perhaps there would be problems, perhaps she had set her mind on marrying a cultured (yes he was, well-read and quite nifty on the fiddle) young Irishman with a future, perhaps deep down she was full of German fundamentalism, perhaps she was even a virgin (he doubted it very much) – but whatever she was he would play the game long enough for them to have a pleasant time together. He would enjoy himself, she would enjoy herself. Wasn't that what it was really all about? Then, when the relationship looked like settling into too definite a mould, *basta*. Even if it meant giving up classes to avoid further embarrassment. He doubted in any case if he would have the fortitude to get much beyond 'May I borrow you ball point pen, my own is *kaput*.'

Her manner on their first night out was the blend of idiosyncratic vagueness and intense analysis that characterised her teaching methods. In the little place where they had a meal after the recital her mood shifted rapidly from that strange raptness in which she did a lot of tongue-clicking to herself to acute observation when she would fix her attention on a part of his face other than his eyes and hold forth on contentious issues. Kenny was not happy with any of her moods – she was not an *easy* person to talk to and he was sure now that as a person she didn't really appeal to him – but at least, within a couple of hours, she had reassuringly disposed of the more obvious hurdles in the way of spirited bed play. Many of them were swept aside in such a headlong rush that he had difficulty in keeping up with her. Was he religious? Certainly not. These mediaeval superstitions. Neither was she. She hated people who talked about God. Such a vague individual. She considered herself a feminist but of the good sort. Did he approve of . . . ? He did? He approved of liberated women? He certainly did. They didn't put him off with their occasional intellectualising and so? They certainly didn't. She didn't think that marriage worked. Did he? Possibly. But he wasn't going to put it to the test for several years (that was *that* anyway!). Basically, she didn't approve at all of the nuclear family. Of the what? The nuclear family. You know, the . . . Oh, yes. No, no. He was all for nuclear disarmament. Ha ha. You didn't have divorce in Ireland, did you? No. Her parents were divorced. Really? So were one sister and a brother. Quite a batting average, what? Yes. But of course that wasn't what really influenced her in her views on marriage. She just valued her freedom to do as she pleased. (Excellent!) And to commit herself as she pleased. Yes, that's the ticket. Live, love and be happy for tomorrow . . . Oh, no, no, she didn't quite believe in *that* philosophy. Philosophy. Pardon? I said, philosophy. What philosophy?

Phew!

Then would come another lengthy period of vague looking into the distance while he (she didn't seem to care whether he spoke or not) rummaged around for things to say, twiddling his wine glass. It was as if whatever sun of intellect shone in her occasionally took a dive into impenetrable German mists out of which it had to struggle to emerge. A few times he caught himself drifting off with her, becoming transfixed to some ethereal point on the ceiling beyond the realm of the familiar. It worried him not a little because if her sexual nature revealed similar periods of on-off activity he would have to be quick off the mark to beam in on the current while it flowed, as during a strike of the Electricity Supply Board. A two hours on, two hours off affair in which there would be a lot of dark fumblings and mutterings. Vaguely he wondered if there was a manic-depressive strain in the family.

Twice more they went out, and though the pattern of communication remained the same with Kenny allowing himself to be picked up like a leaf and spun around in little whirlpools of conversation only to be deposited then, suddenly and flatly, in some obscure corner of his experience, at least their physical intimacy increased to his satisfaction. On their second night out they danced and she pressed her long firm body to his with an unmistakable promise of greater things to come. Indeed, on the way home he thought the time was ripe when, having recovered from one of her spells of near cataleptic indifference, she again radiated willingness. But: reserve, reserve. Kenny was not a messer. Also, she had invited him to spend a quiet evening at her place on the morrow, a Saturday. Fit and relaxed with the whole evening in front of them: what better time for dalliance!

The next evening he complimented himself on his good sense when, tapping gently on the flat door, he found it on the snib and entered to hear water sloshing in the bath and a voice, redolent, it seemed, of essence of pine and rosewood, say, 'I am there in a minute, Sean. Please serve yourself to a drink.' Through the slightly open door he caught a glimpse of naked shoulders. Yes, this was it. With a touch of class. In fact, it was straight out of one of his favourite sexual fantasies. He stood for a moment in the middle of the floor indulging it. The flat was comfortable, luxurious almost, with a lot of pillows and poufs and sheepskins lying about. Gentle baroque music came from the speakers on each side of the deep coal fire. Great. He helped himself to a liberal gin from a row of bottles on the sideboard.

'Any tonic?' he sang.

'Yes, in the fridge.'

Indeed, Irish girls had a lot to learn. No half-empty bottles of red biddy hidden in the loo after boozy parties. No towels and panties lying about with their hint of habitual slovenliness. Instead, the languid splash of scented water mingling with the sensuous rhythms of old music. He picked a volume of Nietzsche from the shelf and settled himself in a deep armchair. He read: 'To the despiser of the body will I speak a word. That they despise is caused by their esteem.' Great stuff.

'This Nietzsche guy is great stuff,' he called out.

'What?'

'Nietzsche. I like him.'

'Oh, *ja*! He has never really been understood. You know? The freedom he wanted.'

'The physical freedom.'

'*Ja*! That is also a good translation.'

'Excellent,' he agreed. Kenny, the great judge of Nietzsche translations.

Quietly he read aloud, enjoying his deep rich voice: 'With the creators, the reapers, and the rejoicers will I associate.' Marvellous stuff! 'For higher ones I wait, spake Zarathustra. Stronger ones, triumphanter ones, merrier ones, for such as are built squarely in body and spirit; laughing lions must come.' *Laughing lions must come!*

Kenny leant back and yielded to a fantasy of tawny strength prowling through the forests of her nerves and sinews, a smooth vibrant force waiting for release into exultant passion. And she would give him release, this tall creature now emerging, trailing aromas of the fresh pine grove, her long gown clinging to her firm scented flesh. 'Laughing lions must come,' he said to her by way of greeting. She smiled. The power was *on*! What a body! Only a genuine, lean-hipped, ho-ho-ho bacchanalian (Falstaffian!) lion could satisfy it, carry it along in an easy lope of passion over the mysterious mental obstacles in its path. He had held that body and knew its response. Her waffle he would ignore and be a laughing lion! As she bent down groping for cigarettes under the chair a perfectly moulded breast opened to his view with its jutty rutty pinky nipple. His passion stirred and he shifted in his chair. Down, Fido. Wait for the word. She still groped, talking away. What a body! Beautiful nipple. Hi, Nipple. I'm Laughing Lion. I'd like to meet your sister. Sure, Laughing Lion, any time. . . .

She was looking at him, waiting.

He blushed. 'I'm sorry,' he said. 'What were you saying?'

'My tubes.'

'Oh.' *Tubes?* 'Having trouble?' he added faintly.

'I've just told you,' she said rather accusingly, looking at his left ear.

'Are they very bad?' he said, staring at her right nostril as though he expected one of them to appear and explain its condition. A little intestinal disorder shouldn't be too difficult to overcome, however. 'Have you any Rennies in the house?'

'Rennies? It's the eggs.'

'Very good for the indigestion.' *Eggs?*

'Do you have indigestion?'

'No, no. I thought maybe for you.'

'Did I say I had indigestion?'

He looked into her eyes. The mists were descending. He felt their cloying chill. *Laugh*, Kenny! Be a laughing lion!

'Well, Helga, tubes or no tubes you're a treat to look at. Grrr! Ho-ho! The first time I saw you I said to myself . . .'

'Sean, you must listen. You see, the tubes won't carry the eggs much longer. That's why.'

He looked at her closely. Yes, the power was definitely off, and this time it looked like a long strike of the inner light. Jesus, Kenny, you do pick 'em. E.S.B. sex, intestines all screwed up, and now galloping obfuscation. The best thing was to humour her. Maybe he would hit the right switch again.

'What's going to carry them then?'

'What?'

'The eggs.'

'That's just it. There's nothing.'

'Nothing at all, at all, to carry your little eggs?'

'No, that's why, you see, I wanted to have a baby before it's too late.'

He sat up. *A baby?* Suddenly he began to see the light, but a different light. 'What tubes?' he almost shouted.

'My Fallopian tubes, of course.'

'What do you mean, "of course"? Do you think I know one bloody female tube from another?'

'They're the ones that carry the eggs! I've been telling you!'

'And they're breaking down?'

'One has already and the other is shaky. I can only conceive every second month.'

'And you want to have a *baby*?'

He felt the blood coming to his face and she glared at him, her nostrils flared as though she were only now getting his real spoor. The air was electric. No strike on now. Except in passion. He felt it trickling down his belly like a lump of melting ice.

'Yes, as soon as possible.'

'And that's why you want *me*?'

'Yes.'

'You mean . . . you mean, you want me as a stud?' His upper lip was beginning to twitch. Very bad sign.

'A stud?'

'A stallion.'

'I don't understand these words.'

'You mean, you want me to . . . to service you?'

At this she went off into a peculiar kind of chuckle that never rose to the surface but seemed to slop around in her endlessly like water in a bilge. Perhaps she was seeing herself as a long sleek automobile driving into a garage where Kenny in neat overalls and a peaked cap would stick a length of tube into her tank, squirt her full and then send her on her way with a hearty slap on the rear mudguard.

'No, Sean,' she said then, becoming very serious. 'I want you to make love to me. I want to have a satisfying sexual relationship with you. But I want it to result in a baby because right now I want a baby. I want to have one before I'm thirty. I just thought it only fair to tell you because some people just do not approve of having babies. They think there are enough in the world. And if you saw me going around in a few months with a big belly you might feel responsible and everything. I don't want that.'

He sat and gaped at her. But he hardly saw her. All he

saw was a thick mane of blonde hair and somewhere in the middle were the small eyes of a calculating lioness. Oh, sweet Christ, Kenny. All this time you were gently stalking through the undergrowth you were being stalked yourself. The monkeys in the trees were jabbering with delight. Snakes were wrapping themselves into tiny knots with laughter. Kenny, the laughing lion. Look at him sniffing the air, dropping his sexual cruds, giving the odd low magnificent growl. Only to fade now with humiliating abruptness like that ridiculous animal on the screen. Kenny, the *instant* laughing lion.

'Let's get this straight,' he said, tossing off his gin and trying to control the twitch in his lip. 'You want to have a sexual relationship with me but only if I consent to try and make it result in a baby. Is that it?'

'Yes.'

'Otherwise, no?'

'What do you mean?'

'No baby, no fuckie?'

'Well, I have little time to waste.' (Did she have a stop-watch?) 'Maybe in a few months it will be too late. And it is important to have sexual rapport because it may be difficult for me to conceive.' (If he wasn't a good co-driver, like, she'd have to reconsider his contract.) 'So we should start having sex as soon as possible.' (On your marks!)

One flap of her gown had slipped down revealing the long curve of her thigh. She was leaning forward intently and he could see all of her breasts. But for all she did for Kenny at that moment she might as well have been the one-buttock old woman in Voltaire's story.

'You do realise,' he said gravely, rising from the chair (he had to take his eyes off those two lumps of flesh), 'the responsibility of bringing a child into the world that has no father?'

'Oh, you mustn't worry about that,' she said. 'I may marry sometime, and anyway in Germany we think differently about unmarried mothers, particularly those who *want* their babies. Also, I shall be reasonably well off soon. So I have no real problems.'

'But the point I'm making is . . .' He fingered the air in distaste as though it were suddenly soiled and sticky. 'The point I want to make is that if I refuse to become a father you will just say, "All right, Sean, good-bye. I must find another man".'

'I hope you won't refuse,' she said. 'I like you. You like to appear dignified but underneath I think you are a nice sensitive boy. You also have a fine body.'

Good God! How the bitch had vetted him!

'And what a nice family I come from! Was that why you were asking me all about the artistic vein in my family and so on?'

'Well, naturally I wanted to know as much about you as possible. I mean, be fair. I could hardly have gone up to you in the tea room and said to you, "Sean, I want to sleep with you because I want to make a baby." But you cannot say that I asked you any questions about your health or the health of your family. I mean there is a limit. There I must take it as if we are lovers.'

'*Love?* You just want to use me!'

'And you?' she said, sharply now, her colour suddenly rising. 'What were you thinking of before I came out of the bathroom? You were thinking of having sex with me, were you not?'

'Yes, but for the sheer enjoyment of sex, with no object in mind.'

'No object but your own pleasure.'

'And yours.'

'We can still have that. I would like a gentle tender relationship with you. It's just that I want you to know that if I conceive a baby I will have it.'

'Yes, but you planned . . .'

'Of course! Did you not plan? Did you not start planning to strip me naked and put me into bed the first time you saw me? I know when a man is looking like that.'

'You've experience, I'm sure.'

'As you have, I'm sure.'

'But what it boils down to is that you w
around every so often, especially in the ri
bang you in the hope of giving you a baby.'

'Is that any different from you coming a
then and banging me because *you* feel the ne... ... ...'

'It's not the same.'

'Why not?'

'Because . . . because it's not . . . functional. It's spon-
taneous.'

'Yes, while it lasts. Then you say good-bye, Helga.
Maybe you never ring me again. I think of my pleasure
too of course but in this case I'm using it for an end. That
is all. And I'm trying to be honest. After all, we decided
already that we did not want to fall in love or anything
like that.' She added, rather smugly, he thought, 'I remember you being almost adamant about that.'

'You're a shrewd one, aren't you?'

'No shrewder than you seem to be.'

A polar air had entered their exchange. She had
gathered her gown tightly about her, folding her arms
across her stomach as though the baby were already in
there and she were determined to defend it. He was dis-
liking her intensely.

'Why don't you go back to your own country where it
might be easier to find a good stud?' He failed to keep the
sneer out of his voice.

'Why should it be difficult here? I mean, men are men.'

'Go on!'

'And I like Irishmen. Some of them. Some of them are
rather *too* masculine for my taste.' She was very angry
now. Her tongue was clicking away like mad. Kenny
walked about, flapping his arms. He had no roar left but
he felt like roaring.

'I chose you because I liked you,' he said, suddenly
leaning over her. 'I liked *you*, you understand? I desired
you. I didn't desire a bloody womb.'

'Do you think I thought of a bloody sperm count when

oked at *you*? No, if I hadn't liked *you* (she was giving the word the same contemptuous curl) would I have chosen *you* to be the father of my child?'

'Yes, but if I refused the first fence *you* had ten other stallions champing at the bit waiting to take *my* place, hadn't you? You just wanted prick.'

'And what did you want?' She shook his hand from her shoulder. 'Eternal love?'

'You chose me at random.'

'Yes, I stuck a pin in you.'

'I knew it. Like a bloody race-horse.'

'Exactly.'

They were almost nose to nose now.

'You have your race card too, haven't you?' she said. 'If one winner doesn't come up the next one will.'

'It's still not like yours.'

'No, it's more sophisticated, is it? The motives are pure, are they? Beautiful, pure, unselfish sex. But *you* must have the whip, *you* must do the riding. The purpose must be *yours*.'

'I did not want to just *service* you!' he roared.

'No, you wanted to fuck me.'

'Yes! A good old-fashioned Irish fuck with froth on it, on the basis of mutual agreement.'

'That is exactly what I wanted with you. A good sexual relationship. Passionate and tender and all the rest. Plus, if possible, a baby.'

'Oh, but with what cold, cunning, German calculation!'

'With what cold, cunning, sneaky Irish calculation were you planning to fuck me?'

They outnosed each other for a little longer. Then Kenny wheeled in fury and stalked out of the flat.

He drove straight to Blackrock, parked his car and set out to look for drinking friends. He found a few but after a while they bored him. Then he drank alone in a place where a shouting match seemed to be in progress between a mob and a television set. It just suited his mood. Until ten o'clock all he could think of was how he had been

334

neatly roped in, broken and led to the mating paddock before he knew what was up. By half-past ten he was getting drunk and suggesting to another unsteady individual with a black coalman's face that 'by Jesus, all we need in Dublin now is a Dial-a-Daddy service.' He wondered if such an amenity would be subject to VAT. The coalman thought he was suggesting a Dial-a-Prayer service under Vatican guidance. He expressed the view that while that kind of thing would be all right for Americans and other people contemplating suicide there were enough people on the phone to God in Ireland. By eleven o'clock Kenny, drunk now, was beginning to think that there were still some aspects of the situation they hadn't discussed to his satisfaction. At closing time he was on the phone to her, but there was no reply.

At eleven o'clock the following evening Kenny was sitting in his car on Herbert Road waiting for her to appear. He had phoned her earlier in the day and she had told him that she would be out, that in fact there was little point in him calling around because she had obviously misjudged him, that he was behaving in just the kind of emotional way she had wanted to avoid, that it was better they forget all about it. He said he would still call. She said she could not stop him from doing so but she might not be alone. At which, she had hung up.

When she finally appeared it was in the company of several others including, he saw to his intense chagrin, Mick Ryan, another member of the class. He was one of these intellectual types who acted in plays and spoke six languages. 'Another Call Daddy,' Kenny said with venom into the smoke-filled interior. 'When the business world fails her she resorts to the university.' You couldn't be up to them. He would go in and screw the ass off her. If she resisted he would rape her. Then he never wanted to see her again.

There was a brief embarrassed silence after she had introduced him to the company. As a casual friend he would hardly be calling on her at that hour. Ryan threw

him a smile that was like a sour swallow. Kenny showed
him all his fine teeth. The hound had probably been looking forward to a pleasant nightcap with his hostess when
the others had left. He probably thought he could screw in
six languages too.

Conversation languished. Kenny said little, and it was
apparent to all that there was some kind of tension between him and Helga. They avoided each other's eyes and
conversation. A lovers' tiff, no doubt. There's nothing like
a lovers' tiff to make people nervous, so about midnight
there was a hushed exodus with smiles all round, leaving
Kenny, strong and silent, sipping his drink beside the fire.
When Helga returned she looked at him, shook her head
and set about clearing things away. When everything was
tidy she said, 'Well, I'm going to bed.'

'Well,' said Kenny, not to be outdone, 'I'm going to
bed too.' He followed her into the bedroom. But as he
went he felt that the power was definitely off again. This
time in him.

She undressed quickly and hopped between the sheets.
He disrobed with gravity, folding his clothes over a chair
and laying out his change and key-rings and things in
perfect order. He glimpsed her smirk in the mirror and it
maddened him.

'That fellow Ryan . . .' he began. How she had whispered
with him in the hall!

'What about him?'

He leisurely slipped out of his trousers. 'He's a little
runt.'

'I don't think so.'

'That fellow would take advantage of you.'

'In what way?'

'Oh, he'd want to fall for you and marry you and all
that muck.'

'I'm glad I have a strong unromantic man to protect
me.'

What was she smirking at? His endowment? Well, she

336

should have thought of that before she opened the paddock gate.

With this thought he climbed in beside her, stretching
down his legs and lying very still. She didn't care if he
never had a name. He was an instrument. They lay still
and silent for a while.

'You're a funny man,' she said then, moving closer to
him.

'Why so?'

She touched his shoulders with the tips of her fingers.
He was rigid.

'Well, here we are lying naked beside each other and it
doesn't seem as if you're going to make love to me.'

'You're in a great hurry, aren't you?'

They looked at each other defiantly. Then, tight-lipped,
she flicked down the bed clothes exposing him, and firmly
held them down. Leaning on her elbow, she observed his
sad lack of enthusiasm. Still resting her arm on the clothes,
she squeezed the limp penis between thumb and fore-
finger. He started.

'Leave it,' he said between his teeth.

'Like a little sausage.'

'What did you expect him to look like? A little leg of
mutton?' He was trembling. 'Don't touch him.'

'A *klitzekleine Bockwurst.*'

'Leave it, I said!' He roughly brushed her aside and
snatched back the clothes. She turned away from him on
her side.

'Go home, Sean.'

'Am I dismissed?'

'Oh, *lieber Gott*, go home!' She seemed close to tears.
'You only mean to humiliate me.'

'*I* humiliate *you*?' He mustered a nasty laugh. 'You
paw me all over and then . . .'

'Go home, please!' She shook her head against the
pillow. 'God, how I hate men!' Then, drily: 'You're probably impotent anyway.'

'Very probably. And sterile.'

'I've no doubt.'

'Out of 100 million sperm cells I probably have 395.'

'Yes, and 394 of those would be on crutches.'

It was a good line. She loved it. She loved it so much she went off into uncontrolled spasms of mirth. Kenny endured the quivering bed for a long time until it got too much. He bounded out of it and grabbed his clothes. For the second time in forty-eight hours he stalked out of the flat.

He had walked about for an hour in the cold blustery night, fuming. Then he found that he had left his key-ring behind and spent another hour looking for a second flat key he had buried in the garden in a foolproof spot. With chattering teeth he drank several hot whiskeys and went to bed, but sleep eluded him. Towards dawn he slipped into a shallow dream in which there were a lot of sausages hiding under rashers from a German Flying Fork. But one of the sausages was his prick and it was having trouble appearing to be as natural as the other sausages all huddled together. Overhead the Flying Fork was escorted by two Messerschmitt nipples. An evil, guttural German voice came over the air: 'Nipple vun to Flying Fork. Enemy Wurstprick sighted. Avait instrukshuns to destroy protective rasher.' 'Flying Fork to Nipples vun and two. Go ahead.' The nipples zoomed down and his prick began to scream, 'No, no! I'm a sausage! I tell you, I'm a sausage! A neutral Irish sausage!' To no avail. With a crash the rasher was split apart by bullets. All the sausages wriggled away under other rashers, leaving the prick exposed and squirming like a worm. Then it began to distend into a huge tottering erection, while he shouted at it, 'Get down, you bastard! Get down! Do you want to get us all killed?' He awoke, gasping for air, as the glittering prongs were streaking down. . . .

He was indeed gasping. He found he could hardly breathe. When he tried to clear his throat it was a dry rasp. He swore but nothing came. His voice was completely gone. At half-past eight he intercepted a neighbouring flatdweller and gave him written instructions to call his office. Then he crawled back into bed and dosed himself on aspirin and hot honey drinks. Something had gone wrong with the flat's central heating and he was very cold.

At twelve o'clock the door opened and Helga walked in. 'You forgot your key,' she said. 'I rang your office and they told me you were sick.' He opened and closed his mouth like a stranded fish. 'Have you lost your voice?' Brilliant. That girl would go places. 'Can I get you anything?' He shook his head but she had turned to the door. 'There's a chemist next door.'

She brought him all sorts of things and then cooked him an omelette. He felt powerless. He wanted to tell her that she had herself to blame for all this, but as she handed him things all he could do was abjectly nod his thanks. She seemed to forget at times that he could at least hear and went on with a lot of idiotic mime, looking at him inquiringly as she touched her throat and made a face like she was swallowing gravel. He leant back in disgust and closed his eyes. Jesus Christ, Kenny, you do pick 'em.

At five she left for her classes but was back again at eight. She made him grog and had some herself. She soon got quite merry and her laughter began to sound like bilge water chuckling. He never thought he could hate anyone so much. Close to nine Phyllis Cronin arrived. She was a tall gawky girl who had been banged by most fellows in the office. Things went wrong with her, too. The last time Kenny was banging her in her own home her mother had arrived back unexpectedly and in the panic of dressing, sans mislaid underpants, he had jammed his foreskin in his zip. While the mother was wandering around the house calling, 'Phy-llis, are you ho-ome?' he was dancing around in agony trying to get his penis free. But now he clasped her hands in his and gazed up at her as though she were the very embodiment of romance. Helga, smiling her crooked smile, played her game and tut-

tutted over him, patting his pillow and talking about him as though she had been nursing him for years.

'But he has himself to blame,' she confided to the wide-eyed girl for whom such facts about the grave Kenny were indeed news. 'Last night he insisted on dancing around the flat in the nude. I told him he'd catch cold.'

Kenny grinned at Phyllis and gestured to Helga, touching his forehead. But Phyllis was believing every word.

'How are you, my ho-ho-ho laughing lion?' Helga smiled, leaning towards him.

Dancing in the nude, ho-ho-ho laughing lion! Would he ever live it down at the office? By the time Phyllis left Helga was almost planning the honeymoon.

Then it struck him that that was just what she *was* planning. A woman of genius! All this nonsense about the baby and her tubes was just a ploy to arouse his interest and concern. She was luring him into persuading her to marry *against* her will! Look at her now tidying up the place as though she already owned it. And preparing the couch for herself without as much as a by your leave. Perfidious woman! He made a fist at her and pointed to the door. 'Oh, shut up,' she said, shaking out a blanket. He subsided on the pillows. Had he said a word?

At two he was still awake, cold, feeling very sorry for himself. He saw himself as a ridiculous toy lion being kicked around the city by laughing urchins. All his dignity was gone. Or whatever he wanted to call his dignity. In her own corner Helga was sniffling. Suddenly he was sorry for both of them. He with his notions of freedom, she reaching out from some grim isolation of her own for a creature she could possess and love. Whatever they were after they were both in a bit of a mess right now. He cleared his throat and said, 'Helga?' It was only a whisper but she heard him. He heard her getting up, and then she was climbing into the bed beside him all rough and hairy in her sweater and jeans. She turned on her side and he hugged into her, feeling that for the first time their touch was human, feeling her warmth. And he wasn't touching her at all. Her body was buried beneath layers of clothes, soft warming layers. There couldn't be enough of them. He closed his eyes. Tomorrow could take care of babies and tubes and sexual relationships. Now all he wanted was to sleep. Eventually he did. And so did she.

MAURA TREACY

A Minor Incident

The Army truck had passed them earlier on the road.
The driver had kept close to the edge, forcing them to pull
the prams onto the grass verge, to press back against the
hedge until the briars pricked their shoulders. The covered
truck passed so close to them, looming above them, that
the children cried with fright. Then it was gone. Shaken,
they stepped out into the road again. From the back of the
truck the soldiers grinned.

Captain barked as he raced along on the other side of
the hedge. He had broken away from them earlier and
now he rushed back to the sound of the motor, scrambling
through a gap to shake himself and bark at the truck. But
it was too far off by then and when Sara shouted to him,
he gave up and came back to her. He squatted in front of
her, still panting, his pink tongue rippling between the
white rows of spiky teeth, his bushy tail swishing clouds of
dust off the road. He blocked her way until she patted him
and talked to him, and then he fell in behind and followed
tamely for another while.

They had walked too far in the heat and now on the way
home Sara lagged behind the others. Her mother and Mrs
Martin walked on in front, pushing their prams. Mrs
Flynn stooped to lift up her child. He had stumbled again
and dropped his bottle of milky tea and she would have to
carry him the rest of the way. She was going to have
another baby soon. Her leg was bandaged. Her hair kept
on falling in around her face and when she was out of
earshot Mrs Martin would whisper about her until she

caught up with them again. When their own baby awoke, Sara's mother sat him up and lifted Mrs Flynn's child onto the end of the pram.

As they walked on, back over the bridge and around the turn, they hurried towards the shade of the tall trees that grew on either side of the road, the branches meeting overhead. Here they lingered, feeling kinder towards each other. The river slurped against the arch of the bridge and when they moved on they could hear inside the walls of the estate the sharp rap back and forth of a tennis ball. They followed the staccato rhythm of the game and heard the voices of the Corbetts and their friends who were spending the summer there. As they passed the green door in the wall through which they might see the lawns, the tennis court, the shrubbery and the glasshouses, Mrs Flynn winked at Sara to come and peep too, but her mother had turned around and was beckoning her to come on. They were out on the open road again, with low banks on either side topped by barbed wire fences, when they heard the distant sound of an engine on the road behind them. Sara's mother and Mrs Martin looked at each other.

'They're coming back,' Mrs Flynn said. 'Come on, quick, we'll be as far as your house.'

'Oh, it might not be them at all,' Sara's mother said. But she reached back and grabbed Jamie's hand and he trotted along beside her, looking back, and stumbling. 'Sara!' She turned to her and smiled. 'That dog, is he gone again? Oh well, he's probably home by now.'

They were hurrying towards Martin's house when the truck came roaring down the road behind them and Captain reappeared, darting out under the wire. They had just reached the front of the house from the road and were walking in single file on the grassy margin.

The truck drove up beside them, the wheels spewing clouds of dust, and Captain came running after it, barking at the rolling wheels and at the men in the back of the truck who were yelling at him. Mrs Flynn called Captain to come back. The truck braked suddenly and Captain too skidded to a halt behind it. He crouched there, yapping at the jeering men as they pelted him with small stones and pellets of hardened mud they picked off the floor of the truck. He whimpered when they hit him and would cower for a moment. But he would not stay away. Mrs Flynn and Sara caught him between them and tried to coax him and lead him away. And all the time the engine churned the stillness of the day to shreds. Mrs Flynn held him back, her arms binding him against her legs while he struggled, quivering and panting with excitement, to escape. Mrs Martin whispered to Sara's mother that they should all go into the house. 'Maybe they won't mind us,' she said. But her mother shook her head and stayed there. She was trying to soothe Jamie and Mrs Flynn's child who had begun to cry.

'Come on, let him out, Missus,' one of the men shouted to Mrs Flynn. He was sitting nearest to the opening, facing them. He held his rifle across his knees. Mrs Flynn tightened her arms around the dog and looked to the other women. 'Come on, Missus, let him off.' He swivelled around, resting on one knee, the rifle against his shoulder. The other soldiers looked on, and the driver rested his elbow on the ledge of the window and adjusted the mirror.

Then another soldier poised his rifle, grinned and said, 'Leave him to me, I can take him where he is.' But the first soldier pushed him aside with his elbow. He shrugged his shoulders and sat back. Sara searched all their faces. There was one soldier, a thin pale man with a dark moustache, who sat there with his hands clasped between his knees. He looked on with none of the anticipation of the others, but neither with impatience, as if all this had been bound to occur and he must bide while it lasted.

'Ah, what do you want with the poor dog,' Mrs Flynn said. She smirked as she glanced at the other women to see what they thought, and to blame their presence if her tactics were not the most effective she might have used. 'He belongs to the little one here. Sure you wouldn't harm him.'

The soldier with the moustache stretched his leg, turned away and looked across the flat countryside. It was to him Sara felt they should have appealed to stop it. Now she too turned away. She stood there waiting, her head bowed, her fingers twisting the fringe of the baby's sunshade. She heard the soldier saying, in his alien accent, 'Maybe you'd rather I'd shoot him where he is . . . take two birds. . . .' She heard them whispering and someone laughed, 'Three birds, aye. What do you say, Missus?'

Mrs Flynn's arms went limp. The truck began to trundle away from them. Captain slipped from her arms. He stood still for a moment, unsure of his freedom. But as the truck picked up speed, he streaked away after it again, barking excitedly, flurries of dust in his wake. The soldier aimed and fired, and fired and fired again until the barking stopped. And when Sara looked up, the truck was near the top of the hill, clouded in dust as it gathered speed. The soldier was still shooting, into the air now, every shot puncturing the fragile blue shell of the day. Frightened birds flew squawking out of the hedges and trees, and in Martin's paddock a mare and her foal left their grazing and ran to the far side and the stamping of their hooves vibrated along the hard ground. And when the noise had stopped and the dust cleared she saw Captain lying on the road at the foot of the hill, unbelievably still as they approached him. Blood oozed through his brown and white coat in darkening patches and trickled onto the road and was absorbed in the dust.

KATE CRUISE O'BRIEN
The Glass Wall

The push-chair broke. It was as simple as that. The vomiting world decided not to get sick after all. And I grabbed the baby, righted the push-chair and took my son home. Before I reached home I had stopped shaking and the symptoms of panic – they call it agoraphobia, fear of open spaces – had ceased.

It was, and possibly always will be *my* agoraphobia. I don't use that 'my' with pride. No, not like 'my period'. Ah yes, what an achievement, what a little woman and, finally, there's another to suffer. No. It's not like that. There is no community of abnormal suffering, and what does such suffering produce except fear? *My* agoraphobia is a source of shame, a crippling thing, even a disgusting thing. I shake, I tremble and I'm afraid of my Judgement. The judgement for smoking forty cigarettes a day and drinking an amount that I can never remember is eternal death, or fear of it, which is worse. Fear of darkness and the unknown.

With one dear small fat hand clinging to mine I decided to defer fear of that darkness till later and hang on.

The fear had been riding me, clinging to me, my old man of the sea, for years. Two, to be precise.

It started in Sheffield. I had gone shopping with a friend. I was attempting to buy two pairs of black pants (large) in Marks and Spencers when it happened. Well, it didn't *happen*. I did it to myself. Much comfort. I was walking across a large shiny tiled floor, which, believe it or not, was warm. It looked cold. It should have been cold but my foot left damp steaming imprints on the cool white glaze. Then the flickering lights started to bother my eyes. I mean my eyes felt as if someone had fired a handful of salt into them. I didn't connect the stinging in my eyes with the flickering of the lights. My body was a jammed switchboard, each signal registering ALARM. Out of my control. I knew with no doubt whatsoever that I was going to die then. Right there on Marks and Spencers' shining hot plastic floor. Fall down dead in front of innumerable embarrassed shop assistants (all clad in plastic and possibly hot).

I looked for my friend frantically but my eyes wouldn't focus. I was afraid to look at any one point for very long. I was afraid that heaps of cheap underwear might dissolve and melt as my senses failed me, as I died. God knows I'd read enough accounts of the signs of death. Blindness, deafness, all at the last minute. I might hoodwink death by not looking or hearing, by not trying to anyway since death might see to it that I couldn't.

I ran towards the nearest person who might hold out a hand and stop me from dying. I felt that ladies in plastic coats could help. It wasn't the white plastic hospital coat I sought. It was just, at that time, that dying seemed abnormal and ladies in plastic coats beautifully normal. I felt that such ladies couldn't be witnesses to anything as terrible as my death. Well, I was wrong. They took my fear calmly, those ladies. As soon as they saw me they recognised me. On the other side. Sick, ill, imagined or otherwise, we don't want to know. They brought me water as I sat on a hot plastic seat. I gulped and gulped. One of them said, 'Don't drink it so fast. It's two flights up.'

'What is?'

'The tap.'

Well, they were probably right. The tap, the wear and the tear, the baby that cries in the night, the one person you have to be nice to because you couldn't bear to be uncharitable. Those demands, accepted, add up to a person who can't, won't and is too embarrassed to ask for any help. Except by making themselves so sick that sheer fear of that sickness will drive them beyond the limits of ordinary good manners. I rushed beyond those limits. It was as if I'd been awaiting my moment to knock down a few barriers here and there for years.

Marks and Spencers' white plastic ladies had alerted my friend. The water had failed. I just kept drinking it. So Marks and Spencers alerted the wine of friendship.

'Anne,' I said, as she held my water glass, willingly relinquished by the white plastic brigade. 'I'm having a heart attack.'

She knew I wasn't. She told me to relax, to lie down, come home, have tea. In the end she took me in a taxi (I wanted an ambulance) to hospital.

The doctor in the out-patients department recognised me instantly. He deserted the woman bitten by a dog (her hand was still throbbing and it had happened three weeks ago) and said he'd take me. I was desperate by then and indignant. I mean, I was dying, wasn't I? The nurses, incredibly, had told me to take my turn.

The doctor was kind or interested. It was as if he saw me across the palpitating glass wall that had come between me and the outside world. As if he understood that die today or die in thirty years, the fear of it is the same. He examined me most patiently. He was brave because the nurse was quite cross with him and kept on telling him about the lady who was bitten by the dog.

'Yes, I know,' he said. 'But this is interesting.'

It was good to be interesting but I wonder what I would have felt like if I hadn't been.

After a few moments of sounding and pressing and feeling he said, 'Why are you nervous? What are you afraid of?'

Well, if you must know, of dying, that first. After that I'm afraid of being found out. My husband's bound to find me out. I'm not anything. I've nothing to give. In fact, (with a hideous leer) there's a lot I'd like to *take*.

Well, I didn't say any of that. I said, and it was true, 'Of bombs.'

Then he looked at me and said in a sad voice, 'Of course, you come from Ireland.'

I admitted it. My hands started to shake again and the easy endless tears began. I'd found something, something that couldn't possibly be my fault or blame. Oh if they'd made thirty odd people into corpses couldn't they have crippled me in my mind?

Half Dublin claimed, with some pride, that it had missed death by inches. It wasn't difficult to make such a claim. Three evil cars in narrow streets. A bus strike and a horde of weary innocent commuters trying to make their way to the trains.

A loud bang from a place some space away. I ran towards it and I saw a man, a large man, being carried by two others. The man's trousers were torn and his hairy legs were bleeding. Then I saw a car burning in high merry flames. Those flames were quite busy, just like an ordinary fire. Crackling away. I asked a woman what had happened and she said, 'That car blew up.'

She said it grimly, as if it had been the car's fault.

I looked around and I saw a black leather boot on the ground. Above the boot there was a thick woolly rug. The boot was new. I'd wanted a pair like that yesterday.

That was the trouble, it could have been me.

The push-chair, however, did break down and I had to take that fat hand in mine and walk its dear owner home. It wasn't his fault, after all.

DESMOND HOGAN
Two Women Waiting

The coffee shop was as many you'd find in Dublin now,
burgeoning on a wave of good taste. It had gainly pictures
by Irish artists; it possessed a picturesque range of cakes.

She sat there, the high expectancy of rain in her, an
urgency such as the one that hangs over Dublin before
clouds burst. She was forty-eight, exactly thirty-one years
after having last seen Marion. Her fate, she realised, had
narrowed; her heart trembled. This moment was as rain
crashing in her or bombs falling. And it occurred to her
that bombs had broken from the sky shortly before they'd
parted, causing conflagration in Dresden, place from which
much of the convent china had originated, pale blues on
dark blues and the dark blues reflective of summer skies.

Marion.

The name crystallised and shaped itself when a woman
of Nora's acquaintance walked in.

There were brief words. She was buying a cheese-cake.
The accent was akin to an English accent. Nora realised
how far she'd waned from youthful idealism, dwelling on
Shelley's words to Dublin proletariat to middle-class
ennui, brittle dinner parties, toasts, literary acquaintances,
children who were remanded on drug charges yet inevitably, if they weren't to be on their most scrupulous guard,
would end up where their parents had put themselves,
milking the slender goat of Irish society. Carl, her son in
his leather jacket, Marilyn, her daughter, both going to
school, coming and going from Turkey or Montreal, for
the moment without care.

Nora for a moment looked closer at the image she had of herself in a mirror, a mirror at the back of her mind.

Once that face had been healthy and beautiful and strong as the hills about their school.

Once she'd had a red ribbon in her hair and the brown of her curls had fallen mirthfully once she had walked.

Once she walked through the blond and glowing fields about the school on Ireland's westernmost edge with Marion, hand in hand, white nylon blouses embracing, fluttering in the breeze.

Cadbury's chocolate had been the richest thing they'd known during the war until they kissed one day on a hill with one tree upon it, a kiss of peace, of adolescence, of pledging.

Cold blew through the door, the last minutes had relaxed Nora, the gesture of waiting, the simplicity of sentences she was uttering to herself. 'I remember Marion in a grove of trees repeating the Song of Solomon or the Ecclesiastes. I remember Marion in a church talking of Saint Catharine of Siena or of Theresa of Avila or of John of the Cross.

'I remember these names, sacred, inviolate names against a time of war, of intense desecration.'

Marion walked in, unchanged or at least that was the adjective which later caught Nora's breath. Her face for all of middle age was as beautiful as ever.

They kissed, lip upon lip, the message of the years carried, Nora's marriage, Marion's twenty-five years as a nun in an English convent.

'How are you?'

Marion had not lost that tough west of Ireland accent, an accent local to Galway city. Her face had not lost that pensive west of Ireland quality, a slowness in the eyes, a heaviness in the mouth.

Tea was renewed, cheese-cake appeared.

There were flustered questions.

'You will stay with us, won't you?'

'I'm staying with my sister.'

'You must come to Wexford with us. We have a summer house there.'

Marion's eyes stared; Nora was speaking as one of Ireland's rich.

Marion stared so intensely that Nora was forced to reconsider, leaving convent, marrying early, honeymooning in Florence, living a high life of social gatherings as her son sped into the Wicklow mountains on a motor-bike and her daughter led an uncelibate life in other young people's flats.

'Did you ever reconsider our relationship?' Marion's question was so direct; Nora fingered her tea-cup more closely.

'Yes.'

Yes, there'd been times in Wexford, poppies growing in summer, when I thought of you.

Nora didn't utter this thought.

Instead she answered, 'I often thought of you.'

In the toilet for a moment she considered her body without its fur coat, sparse – like an eagle's.

How am I going to say certain things, she wondered?

How can I tell Marion it has been close to forgetfulness, close to an oblivion bought with good clothes, good living?

In a pub over whiskey Marion talked of her time in the convent, a sort of autism, locked away in shadow and light.

'I was drawn to the convent,' she said, 'in an observation that life passes hastily, that each of us is endowed with something, a gift of life, a soul which we're rarely aware of. I came to understand my soul. I suppose on that realisation I left.'

A soul. Long time ago Marion had spoken of Byron with some tenderness; never of souls.

She'd quoted Keats and observed geese flying north in April.

'Have you ever heard the clanking of wild geese?' she said once. 'Doesn't it make you feel like flying?'

'I suppose I have sometimes considered my soul a flight,' Marion continued in the pub, 'a flight towards God.'

Hadn't there been times Nora considered flight, in a café in Paris, in a bistro in Berlin; inside herself, despite years of marriage and an offshoot of children, there'd been an area which registered flight, an area close as a sun-dial at school which had registered the tracks of the mid-day sun.

There'd been times when she'd walked into her suburban garden to feed robins in winter, to sit in summer or lie down and wish not to be young again but to be lying among a field of daisies as the one in Mayo where she'd gone to school.

'I will not go with you to Wexford,' Marion said, 'but I'd like to spend some time with you in Dublin.

'Next week I'll be going back to London. I'm working in a student cafeteria. I'm manageress.'

It was winter in Dublin. Therefore the odd snowflake. It had been a year harsh on the poor, much unemployment, but evidence in Dublin was of Europeanisation, many cafés opening, ice-cream parlours, wine being consumed in gross amounts, evidence everywhere of youth; on closer inspection one saw Dublin was a city which never tired of its youth.

After all, as Marion remarked, there was a statue of a debonair Robert Emmet outside Stephen's Green, a perennial symbol of the armed lover, young men loaded with ideas, with idealism, with fate.

Each step they took over leaves abandoned by Stephen's Green was a step over leaves rejected in Mayo long ago, each step was a step backwards, an uncovering of a beautiful apple. That apple symbolised the prosperity of innocence both had enjoyed and, as Nora considered, everyone must experience.

Her children joined Marion and herself and her husband for dinner one evening; roast lamb, roast potatoes.

Candles hung in an air of expectancy; outside snow, carefully threatening for weeks, merged with dusk. It was her daughter Marilyn's birthday. There was a cake. The cake was white.

Marilyn was twenty-one. An ordered birthday party would be held.

There was silence. Again inside Nora it was Mayo and bombs were whisking through the air in Dresden and snow was tumbling in Mayo. How gaunt Marion's face had looked against the sea then.

Time had passed, yet in another sense there had merely been a shift of mood; in Dublin now the same tremor made itself known, the tremor, the uncertainty of feeling, the mysterious and frightening disposition of the universe which had probably brought Marion into a convent.

Marion spoke. 'I've often wondered really why I left the convent. Now I realise it was because I renegued on life.'

She rose, like a lady in a dreadful Victorian novel, determined on getting to the window.

It was ghostly outside, a sense of beauty lulled all present, the young as well as the old.

'It was for reasons like this I left the convent,' Marion said, lifting her arms. 'Snow.

'Where Nora and I went to school,' she said as though continuing a mere cocktail conversation, 'there was one stained glass window created by a unique Irish woman artist. That glass fascinated me as much as March daisies. I knew somewhere I was destined to know the nature of creativity.

'So I searched.' She turned about.

'Nora was partial to my quest. We'd roam and delight on small wonders together. Our paths sharply divided when she married, I became a nun.

'I became a nun for all the wrong reasons.

'Twenty years I spent in a convent.

'For those years I bear no regret.

'However, I'll say something.' She stared at the young people and now it was known what she'd begun apparently as a soliloquy was actually a homily to the young on the

occasion of birthdays, December, snow. 'There's one thing
in life that's important.

'Not quest. No. God? No, not God even.

'Something deeper. Our relationships one to the other.
That's where we know God, life, the rest.

'I'll spend the rest of my life searching cafés for secrets.

'I'll spend the rest of my life delving a knowledge which
the secrecy of a convent could no longer give me. I'll look
for the relationship, passing or otherwise, with people.'

Marilyn was transfixed.

'So many young people think relating is sex, is profusion, is talk. Maybe.

'But there's a grain of truth missing from all this; one
must rediscover – for oneself – the knowledge, lost from
modern society, of God.'

She was staring at Nora. She'd drunk much wine but
the atmosphere was now one of sobriety, of listening.
Carl was the first to act. He put on a record. Brahms.
Laughter rose, snow fell, it clouded and puffed and disturbed.

Wine flowed; an image went unrequited, girls in white
blouses walking long ago through fields imminent with
spring and the end of the war and the beginning of lives.

NEIL JORDAN
Night in Tunisia

That year they took the green house again. She was there
again, older than him and a lot more venal. He saw her
on the white chairs that faced the tennis-court and again
in the burrows behind the tennis-court and again still
down on the fifteenth hole where the golf-course met the
mouth of the Boyne. It was twilight each time he saw
her and the peculiar light seemed to suspend her for an
infinity, a suspended infinite silence, full of years somehow. She must have been seventeen now that he was fourteen. She was fatter, something of an exhausted woman
about her and still something of the girl whom adults
called mindless. It was as if a cigarette between her fingers
had burnt towards the tip without her noticing. He heard
people talking about her even on her first day there, he
learnt that underneath her frayed blouse her wrists were
marked. She was a girl about whom they would talk anyway since she lived with a father who drank, who was
away for long stretches in England. Since she lived in a
green corrugated-iron house. Not even a house, a châlet
really, like the ones the townspeople built to house summer visitors. But she lived in it all the year round.

They took a green house too that summer, also made of
corrugated iron. They took it for two months this time,
since his father was playing what he said would be his
last stint, since there was no more place for brassmen
like him in the world of three-chord showbands. And this
time the two small bedrooms were divided differently,

his sister taking the small one, since she had to dress on her own now, himself and his father sharing the larger one where two years ago his sister and he had slept. Every night his father took the tenor sax and left for Mosney to play with sixteen others for older couples who remembered what the big bands of the forties sounded like. And he was left alone with his sister who talked less and less as her breasts grew bigger. With the alto saxophone which his father said he could learn when he forgot his fascination for three-chord ditties. With the guitar which he played a lot, as if in spite against the alto saxophone. And with the broken-keyed piano which he played occasionally.

When it rained on the iron roof the house sang and he was reminded of a green tin drum he used to have when he was younger. It was as if he was inside it.

He wandered round the first three days, his sister formal and correct beside him. There was one road made of tarmac, running through all the corrugated houses towards the tennis-court. It was covered always with drifts of sand, which billowed while they walked. They passed her once, on the same side, like an exotic and dishevelled bird, her long yellow cardigan coming down to her knees, covering her dress, if she wore any. He stopped as she passed and turned to face her. Her feet kept billowing up the sand, her eyes didn't see him, they were puffy and covered in black pencil. He felt hurt. He remembered an afternoon three years ago when they had lain on the golf links, the heat, the nakedness that didn't know itself, the grass on their three backs.

'Why don't you stop her?' he asked his sister.

'Because,' she answered. 'Because, because.'

He became obsessed with twilights. Between the hour after tea when his father left and the hour long after dark when his father came home he would wait for them, observe them, he would taste them as he would a sacrament. The tincture of the light fading, the blue that seemed to be sucked into a thin line beyond the sea into what the maths books called infinity, the darkness falling like a stone. He would look at the long shadows of the burrows on the strand and the long shadows of the posts that held the sagging tennis-nets on the tarmac courts. He would watch his sister walking down the road under the eyes of boys that were a little older than him. And since he hung around at twilight and well into the dark he came to stand with them, on the greens behind the clubhouse, their cigarette-tips and their laughter punctuating the dark. He played all the hits on the honky-tonk piano in the clubhouse for them and this compensated for his missing years. He played and he watched, afraid to say too much, listening to their jokes and their talk about girls, becoming most venal when it centred on her.

He laughed with them, that special thin laugh that can be stopped as soon as it's begun.

There was a raft they would swim out to on the beach. His skin was light and his arms were thin and he had no Adam's apple to speak of, no hair creeping over his togs, but he would undress all the same with them and swim out. They would spend a day on it while the sun browned their backs and coaxed beads of resin from the planks. When they shifted too much splinters of wood shot through their flesh. So mostly they lay inert, on their stomachs, their occasional erections hidden beneath them, watching on the strand the parade of life.

It galled his father what he played.
'What galls me,' he would say, 'is that you could be so good.'
But he felt vengeful and played them incessantly and even sang the tawdry lyrics. Some day soon, he sang, I'm going to tell the Moon about the crying game. And maybe he'll explain, he sang.

'Why don't you speak to her?' he asked his sister when they passed her again. It was seven o'clock and it was getting dark.

'Because,' she said. 'Because I don't.'

But he turned. He saw her down the road, her yellow cardigan making a scallop round her fattening buttocks.

'Rita,' he called. 'Rita.'

She turned. She looked at him blankly for a moment and then she smiled, her large pouting lips curving the invitation she gave to any boy that shouted at her.

He sat at the broken-keyed piano. The light was going down over the golf-links and his sister's paperback novel was turned over on the wooden table. He heard her in her room, her shoes knocking off the thin wooden partition. He heard the rustling of cotton and nylon and when the rustles stopped for a moment he got up quickly from the piano and opened the door. She gave a gasp and pulled the dress from the pile at her feet to cover herself. He asked her again did she remember and she said she didn't and her face blushed with such shame that he felt sorry and closed the door again.

The sea had the movement of cloth but the texture of glass. It flowed and undulated, but shone hard and bright. He thought of cloth and glass and how to mix them. A cloth made of glass fibre or a million woven mirrors. He saw that the light of twilight was repeated or reversed at early morning.

He decided to forget about his sister and join them, the brashness they were learning, coming over the transistors, the music that cemented it. And the odd melancholy of the adulthood they were about to straddle, to ride like a Honda down a road with one white line, pointless and inevitable.

His father on his nights off took out his Selmer, old loved

talisman that was even more shining than on the day he bought it. He would sit and accompany while his father stood and played 'That Certain Feeling', 'All the Things You Are', the names that carried their age with them, the embellishments and the filled-in notes that must have been something one day but that he had played too often, that he was too old now to get out of. And to please his father he would close his eyes and play, not knowing how or what he played, and his father would stop and let him play on, listening. And he would occasionally look and catch that look in his listening eyes, wry, sad and loving, his pleasure at how his son played only marred by the knowledge of how little it meant to him. And he would catch the look in his father's eyes and get annoyed and deliberately hit a bum note to spoil it. And the sadness in the eyes would outshine the wryness then and he would be sorry, but never sorry enough.

He soon learnt that they were as mistrustful of each other as she was of them and so he relaxed somewhat. He learnt to turn his silence into a pose. They listened to his playing and asked about his sister. They lay on the raft, watched women on the strand, their eyes stared so hard that the many shapes on the beach became one, indivisible. It made the sand-dunes and even the empty clubhouse redundant. Lying face down on the warm planks, the sun burning their backs with an aching languor. The blaring transistor, carried over in its plastic bag. Her on the beach, indivisible, her yellow cardigan glaring even on the hottest days. He noticed she had got fatter since he came. Under them on the warm planks the violent motions of their pricks. She who lived in the châlet all the year round.

The one bedroom and the two beds, his father's by the door, his by the window. The rippled metal walls. The moon like water on his hand, the bed beside him empty. Then the front door opening, the sound of the saxophone case laid down. His eyes closed, his father stripping in the darkness, climbing in, long underwear and vest. The body he'd known lifelong, old and somewhat loved, but not like his Selmer, shining. They get better with age, he said about instruments. His breath scraping the air now, scraping over the wash of the sea, sleeping.

The tall thin boy put his mouth to the mouth of the french letter and blew. It expanded, huge and bulbous, with a tiny bubble at the tip.

'It's getting worked up,' he said.

He had dark curling hair and dark shaven cheeks and a mass of tiny pimples where he shaved. The pimples spread from his ears downwards, as if scattered from a pepper-canister. His eyes were dark too, and always a little closed.

'We'll let it float to England,' he said, 'so it can find a fanny big enough for it.'

They watched it bobbing on the waves, brought back and forwards with the wash. Then a gust of wind lifted it and carried it off, falling to skim the surface and rising again, the bubble towards the sky.

He had walked up from the beach and the french letter bound for England. He had seen her yellow cardigan on the tennis-court from a long way off, above the strand. He was watching her play now, sitting on the white wrought-iron seat, his hands between his legs.

She was standing on the one spot, dead-centre of the court, hardly looking at all at her opponent. She was hitting every ball cleanly and lazily and the sound that came from her racquet each time was that taut twang that he knew only came from a good shot. He felt that even a complete stranger would have known, from her boredom, her ease, that she lived in a holiday town with a tennis-court all the year round. The only sign of effort was the beads of sweat round her lips and the tousled blonde curls round her forehead. And every now and then when the man she was playing against managed to send a shot towards the sidelines, she didn't bother to follow it at all. She let the white ball bounce impotent towards the wire mesh.

He watched the small fat man he didn't recognise lose three balls for every ball won. He relished the spectacle of a fat man in white being beaten by a bored teenage girl in sagging high-heels. Then he saw her throw her eyes upwards, throw her racquet down and walk from the court. The white ball rolled towards the wire mesh.

She sat beside him. She didn't look at him but she spoke as if she had known him those three years.

'You play him. I'm sick of it.'

He walked across the court and his body seemed to glow with the heat generated by the slight touch of hers. He picked up the racquet and the ball, placed his foot behind the white line and threw the ball up, his eye on it, white, skewered against the blue sky. Then it came down and he heard the resonant twang as his racquet hit it and it went spinning into the opposite court but there was no one there to take it. He looked up and saw the fat man and her walking towards a small white car. The fat man gesturing her in and she looked behind at him once before she entered.

And as the car sped off towards Mornington he swore she waved.

The car was gone down the Mornington road. He could hear the pop-pop of the tennis-balls hitting the courts and the twang of them hitting the racquets as he walked, growing fainter. He walked along the road, past the tarmac courts and past the grass courts and past the first few holes of the golf-course which angled in a T round the tennis-courts. He walked past several squares of garden until he came to his. It wasn't really a garden, a square of sand and scutch. He walked through the gate and up the path where the sand had been trodden hard to the green corrugated door. He turned the handle in the door, always left open. He saw the small square room, the sand fanning across the line from the doorstep, the piano with the sheet-music perched on the keys. He thought of the midday sun outside, the car with her in the passenger seat moving through it, the shoulders of the figure in the driver's seat. The shoulders hunched and fat, expressing something venal. He thought of the court, the white tennis-ball looping between her body and his. Her body relaxed, vacant and easeful, moving the racquet so the ball flew where she wished. His body worried, worrying the whole court. He felt there was something wrong, the obedient ball, the running man. What had she lost to gain that ease? he wondered. He thought of all the jokes he had heard and of the act behind the jokes that none of those who told the jokes experienced. The innuendos and the charged words like the notes his father played, like the melodies his father willed him to play. The rich full twang as the ball met her racquet at the centre.

He saw the alto saxophone on top of the piano. He took it down, placed it on the table and opened the case. He looked at the keys, remembering the first lessons his father had taught him when it was new-bought, months ago. The keys unpressed, mother-of-pearl on gold, spotted with dust. He took out the ligature and fixed the reed in the mouthpiece. He put it between his lips, settled his fingers and blew. The note came out harsh and childish, as if he'd never learnt. He heard a shifting movement in the inside room and knew that he'd woken his father.

He put the instrument back quietly and made for the tiny bathroom. He closed the door behind him quietly, imagining his father's grey vest rising from the bed to the light of the afternoon sun. He looked into the mirror that closed on the cabinet where the medicine things were kept. He saw his face in the mirror looking at him, frightened, quick glance. Then he saw his face taking courage and looking at him full-on, the brown eyes and the thin fragile jawline. And he began to look at his eyes as directly as they looked at him.

'You were playing,' his father said, in the living-room, in shirtsleeves, in uncombed afternoon hair, 'the alto – '
    'No,' he said, going for the front door, 'you were dreaming.'

And on the raft the fat asthmatic boy, obsessed more than any with the theatre on the strand, talking about 'it' in his lisping, mournful voice, smoking cigarettes that made his breath wheeze more. He had made classifications, rigid as calculus, meticulous as algebra. There were girls, he said, and women, and in between them what he termed lady, the lines of demarcation finely and inexorably drawn. Lady was thin and sat on towels, with high-heels and suntan-lotions, without kids. Woman was fat, with rugs and breasts that hung or bulged, with children. Then there were girls, his age, thin, fat and middling, nyloned, short-stockinged –

He lay on his stomach on the warm wood and listened to the fat boy talking and saw her walking down the strand. The straggling, uncaring walk that, he decided, was none of these or all of these at once. She was wearing flat shoes that went down at the heels with no stockings and the familiar cardigan that hid what could have classified her. She walked to a spot up the beach from the raft and unrolled the bundled towel from under her arm. Then she kicked off her shoes and pulled off her cardigan and wriggled out of the skirt her cardigan had hidden. She lay back on the towel in the yellow bathing suit that was too young for her, through which her body seemed to press like a butterfly already moulting in its chrysalis. She took a bottle then and shook it into her palm and began rubbing the liquid over her slack exposed body.

He listened to the fat boy talking about her – he was local

too – about her father who on his stretches home came back drunk and bounced rocks off the tin roof, shouting, 'Hewer.'

'What does that mean?' he asked.

'Just that,' said the asthmatic boy. 'Rhymes with "sure".'

He looked at her again from the raft, her slack stomach bent forward, her head on her knees. He saw her head lift and turn lazily towards the raft and he stood up then, stretching his body upwards, under what he imagined was her gaze. He dived, his body imagining itself suspended in air before it hit the water. Underwater he held his breath, swam through the flux of tiny bubbles, like crotchets before his open eyes.

'What did you say she was?' he asked the fat boy, swimming back to the raft.

'Hewer,' said the fat boy, more loudly.

He looked towards the strand and saw her on her back, her slightly plump thighs towards the sky, her hands shielding her eyes. He swam to the side of the raft then and gripped the wood with one hand and the fat boy's ankle with the other and pulled. The fat boy came crashing into the water and went down and when his head came up, gasping for asthmatic breath, he forced it down once more, though he didn't know what whore meant.

His father was cleaning the alto when he came back.

'What does "hewer" mean?' he asked his father.

His father stopped screwing in the ligature and looked at him, his old sidesman's eyes surprised, and somewhat moral.

'A woman,' he said, 'who sells her body for monetary gain.'

He stopped for a moment. He didn't understand.

'That's tautology,' he said.

'What's that?' his father asked.

'It repeats,' he said, and went into the toilet.

He heard the radio crackle over the sound of falling water and heard a rapid-fire succession of notes that seemed to spring from the falling water, that amazed him, so much faster than his father ever played, but slow behind it all, melancholy, like a river. He came out of the toilet and stood listening with his father. 'Who is that?' he asked his father. Then he heard the continuity announcer say the name Charlie Parker and saw his father staring at some point between the wooden table and the wooden holiday-home floor.

He played later on the piano in the clubhouse with the dud notes, all the songs, the trivial mythologies whose significance he had never questioned. It was as if he was fingering through his years and as he played he began to forget the melodies of all those goodbyes and heartaches, letting his fingers take him where they wanted to, trying to imitate that sound like a river he had just heard. It had got dark without him noticing and when finally he could just see the keys as question-marks in the dark, he stopped. He heard a noise behind him, the noise of somebody who has been listening, but who doesn't want you to know they are there. He turned and saw her looking at him, black in the square of light coming through the door. Her eyes were on his hands that were still pressing the keys and there was a harmonic hum tiny somewhere in the air. Her eyes rose to his face, unseeing and brittle, to meet his hot, tense stare. He still remembered the rough feel of the tartan blanket over them, three of them, the grass under them. But her eyes didn't, so he looked everywhere but on them, on her small pinched chin, ridiculous under her large face, on the yellow linen dress that was ragged round her throat, on her legs, almost black from so much sun. The tiny hairs on them glistened with the light behind her. He looked up then and her eyes were still on his, keeping his fingers on the keys, keeping the chord from fading.

He was out on the burrows once more, he didn't know how, and he met the thin boy. The thin boy sat down with him where they couldn't be seen and took a condom from his pocket and masturbated among the bushes. He saw how the liquid was caught by the antiseptic web, how the sand clung to it when the thin boy threw it, like it does to spittle.

He left the thin boy and walked down the beach, empty now of its glistening bodies. He looked up at the sky, from which the light was fading, like a thin silver wire. He came to where the beach faded into the mouth of a river. There was a statue there, a Virgin with thin fingers towards the sea, her feet layered with barnacles. There were fishermen looping a net round the mouth. He could see the dim line of the net they pulled and the occasional flashes of white salmon. And as the boat pulled the net towards the shore he saw how the water grew violent with flashes, how the loose shoal of silver-and-white turned into a panting, open-gilled pile. He saw the net close then, the fishermen lifting it, the water falling from it, the salmon laid bare, glutinous, clinging, wet, a little like boiled rice.

He imagined the glistening bodies that littered the beach pulled into a net like that. He imagined her among them, slapping for space, panting for air, he heard transistors blare Da Doi Run Run, he saw suntan-lotion bottles crack and splinter as the Fisher up above pulled harder. He imagined his face like a lifeguard's, dark sidelocks round his muscular jaw, a megaphone swinging from his neck, that crackled.

He saw the thin band of light had gone, just a glow off the sea now. He felt frightened, but forced himself not to run. He walked in quick rigid steps past the barnacled Virgin then and down the strand.

367

'Ten bob for a touch with the clothes on. A pound without.'

They were playing pontoon on the raft. He was watching the beach, the bodies thicker than salmon. When he heard the phrase he got up and kicked the dirt-cards into the water. He saw the Queen of Hearts face upwards in the foam. As they made for him he dived and swam out a few strokes.

'Cunts,' he yelled from the water. 'Cunts.'

On the beach the wind blew fine dry sand along the surface, drawing it in currents, a tide of sand.

His sister laid the cups out on the table and his father ate with long pauses between mouthfuls. His father's hand paused, the bread quivering in the air, as if he were about to say something. He looked at his sister's breasts across a bowl of apples, half-grown fruits. The apples came from monks who kept an orchard. Across the fields, behind the house. He imagined a monk's hand reaching for the unplucked fruit, white against the swinging brown habit. For monks never sunbathed.

When he had finished he got up from the table and idly pressed a few notes on the piano.

'Why do you play that?' his father asked. He was still at the table, between mouthfuls.

'I don't know,' he said.

'What galls me,' said his father, 'is that you could be good.'

He played a bit more of the idiotic tune that he didn't know why he played.

'If you'd let me teach you,' his father said, 'you'd be glad later on.'

'Then why not wait till later on and teach me then?'

'Because you're young, you're at the age. You'll never learn as well as now, if you let me teach you. You'll never feel things like you do now.'

He began to play again in defiance and then stopped. 'I'll pay you,' his father said.

His father woke him coming in around four. He heard his wheezing breath and his shuffling feet. He watched the grey, metal-coloured light filling the room that last night had emptied it. He thought of his father's promise to pay him. He thought of the women who sold their bodies for monetary gain. He imagined all of them on the dawn golf-course, waking in their dew-sodden clothes. He imagined fairways full of them, their monetary bodies covered with fine drops of water. Their dawn chatter like birdsong. Where was that golf-course, he wondered? He crept out of bed and into his clothes and out of the door, very quietly. He crossed the road and clambered over the wire fence that separated the road from the golf-course. He walked through several fairways, across several greens, past several fluttering pennants with the conceit in his mind all the time of her on one green, asleep and sodden, several pound notes in her closed fist. At the fourteenth green he stopped and saw that the dull metal colour had faded into morning, true morning. He began to walk back, his feet sodden from the dew.

He went in through the green corrugated door and put on a record of the man whose playing he had first heard two days ago. The man played 'Night in Tunisia', and the web of notes replaced the web that had tightened round his crown. The notes soared and fell, dispelling the world around him, tracing a series of arcs that seemed to point to a place, or if not a place, a state of mind. He closed his eyes and let the music fill him and tried to see that place. He could see a landscape of small hills, stretching to infinity, suffused in a yellow light that seemed to lap like water. He decided it was a place you were always in, yet always trying to reach, you walked towards all the time and yet never got there, as it was always beside you. He opened his eyes and wondered where Tunisia was on the atlas. Then he stopped wondering and reached up to the piano and took down the alto saxophone and placed it on the table. He opened the case and saw it gleaming in the light, new and unplayed. He knew he was waking his father from the only sleep he ever got, but he didn't care, imagining his father's pleasure. He heard him moving in the bedroom then, and saw him come in, his hair dishevelled, putting his shirt on. His father sat then, while he stood, listening to the sounds that had dispelled the world. When it had finished his father turned down the volume controls and took his fingers and placed them on the right keys and told him to blow.

He learned the first four keys that day and when his father took his own instrument and went out to his work in Butlin's he worked out several more for himself. When his father came back, at two in the morning, he was still playing. He passed him in the room, neither said anything, but he could feel his father's pleasure, tangible, cogent. He played on while his father undressed in the bedroom and when he was asleep he put it down nad walked out the door, across the hillocks of the golf-course onto the strand, still humid with the warmth of that incredible summer.

He forgot the raft and the games of pontoon and the thin boy's jargon. He stayed inside for days and laboriously transferred every combination of notes he had known on the piano onto the metal keys. He lost his tan and the gold sheen of the instrument became quickly tarnished with sweat, the sweat that came off his fingers in the hot metal room. He fashioned his mouth round the reed till the sounds he made became like a power of speech, a speech that his mouth was the vehicle for but that sprang from the knot of his stomach, the crook of his legs.

As he played he heard voices and sometimes the door knocked. But he turned his back on the open window and the view of the golf-course. Somewhere, he thought, there's a golf-course where bodies are free, not for monetary gain –

He broke his habit twice. Once he walked across the fields to the orchard where the monks plucked fruit with white fingers. He sat on a crumbling wall and watched the darkening and fading shadows of the apple trees. Another night he walked back down the strand to where it faded into the river mouth. He looked at the salmonless water and imagined the lifeguard up above calling through his megaphone. He imagined childhood falling from him, coming off his palms like scales from a fish. He didn't look up, he looked down at his fingers that were forming hard coats of skin at the tips, where they touched the keys.

And then, ten days after it had started, his face in the mirror looked older to him, his skin paler, his chin more ragged, less round. His father got up at half-past three and played the opening bars of 'Embraceable You' and, instead of filling in while his father played, he played while his father filled in. And then they both played, rapidly, in a kind of mutual anger, through all his favourites into that area where there are no tunes, only patterns like water, that shift and never settle. And his father put his instrument away and put several pound notes on the table. He took them, put the case up above the piano and went out the green door.

It was five o'clock as he walked down the road by the golf-course, squinting in the sunlight. He walked down by the tennis-court onto the strand, but it was too late now and the beach was empty and there was no one on the raft.

He walked back with the pound notes hot in his pocket and met the fat boy with two racquets under his arm. The fat boy asked him did he want to play and he said, 'Yes.'

They had lobbed an endless series of balls when the fat boy said, 'Did you hear?' 'Hear what?' he asked and then the fat boy mentioned her name. He told him how the lifeguard had rescued her twice during the week, from a part of the beach too near the shore to drown in by accident. He hit the ball towards the fat boy and imagined her body in the lifeguard's arms, his mouth on her mouth, pushing the breath in. Then he saw her sitting on the iron-wrought seat in a green dress now, vivid against the white metal. The pound notes throbbed in his pocket, but he hadn't the courage to stop playing and go to the seat. Her eyes were following the ball as it went backwards and forwards, listless and vacant. The light gradually became grey, almost as grey as the ball, so in the end he could only tell where it fell by the sound and they missed more than half the volleys. But still she sat on the white chair, her eyes on the ball, following it forwards and back. He felt a surge of hope in himself. He would tell her about that place, he told himself, she doesn't know. When it got totally dark he would stop, he told himself, go to her. But he knew that it never gets totally dark and he just might never stop and she might never rise from the white seat.

He hit the ball way above the fat boy's head into the wire meshing. He let the racquet fall on the tarmac. He walked towards her, looking straight into her eyes so that if his courage gave out he would be forced to say something. Come over to the burrows, he would say. He would tell her about that place, but the way she raised her head, he suspected she knew it.

She raised her head and opened her mouth, her answer already there. She inhabited that place, was already there, her open mouth like it was for the lifeguard when he pressed his hand to her stomach, pushed the salt water out, then put his lips to her lips and blew.

Biographical Notes

GEORGE MOORE (1852–1933): Born in Co. Mayo, the son of a wealthy, landowning M.P., he went to Paris in 1873 to paint but, failing as an artist, returned to Ireland in 1879. He was associated with Yeats and Lady Gregory in the founding of the Abbey Theatre, wrote three volumes of short stories, many novels and a celebrated autobiography, *Hail and Farewell*. Lived in London from 1911 until his death.

E. Œ. SOMERVILLE (1858–1949) and MARTIN ROSS (1862–1915): Edith Somerville was born in Corfu where her father was stationed, but the following year she was brought home to the family seat in Co. Cork where she spent most of her life. Violet Martin, her cousin, was born in Co. Galway, and they first met in 1886. The literary partnership commenced with *An Irish Cousin* in 1889 and three celebrated collections of *Irish R.M.* (Resident Magistrate) stories were published in 1899, 1908 and 1915. Violet Martin died in 1915 but Edith Somerville, believing that death had not ended their collaboration, continued to publish all her subsequent writings under their joint names.

LYNN DOYLE (1873–1961): Born in Co. Down, he started as a bank clerk in Belfast at the age of 16 and was a bank manager in Co. Dublin when he retired in 1934. A prolific novelist, poet and playwright, he is most famous for his many volumes of short stories about the mythical

Northern Ireland border village of Ballygullion, the first
of which was published in 1908 and the last in 1957.

SEAMUS O'KELLY (1875–1918): Born in Co. Galway,
he worked as a journalist in Ireland before moving to the
Saturday Evening Post in New York in 1912. For health
reasons he returned to Ireland in 1915 and in May, 1918,
died of a heart attack after the offices of a political paper
he was editing were raided by British forces. His plays
were performed in the Abbey Theatre and in London and
he wrote two novels and some half-dozen collections of
short stories, *The Rector* being from the second of these,
Waysiders, published in 1918.

DANIEL CORKERY (1878–1964): Born in Cork, he was
an important influence on many Irish writers, notably
Sean O'Faolain and Frank O'Connor. Professor of English
at University College, Cork from 1931–1947, his own
work was intensely nationalistic and in the latter part of
his life he abandoned English as a means of literary expression. *Joy* is from *A Munster Twilight*, the first of his
four volumes of short stories, published in 1916.

JAMES STEPHENS (1880–1950): Born in Dublin, he
lived in London from 1924 until his death. His best
known work is his novel *The Crock of Gold* (1912), which
won him an international reputation, but he also published
a number of poetry collections and two volumes of short
stories, *Here Are Ladies* (1913) and *Etched in Moonlight*
(1928), from the latter of which *Desire* is taken.

JAMES JOYCE (1882–1941): Generally regarded as the
most important and influential English-language prose
writer of the twentieth century. Apart from some poems
and a play, he wrote one collection of stories, *Dubliners*
(1914), and three novels, *A Portrait of the Artist as a
Young Man* (1916), *Ulysses* (1922) and *Finnegans Wake*

(1939). From 1904 until his death he lived abroad, mostly in Zürich and Paris. His last visit to Dublin was in 1912.

LIAM O'FLAHERTY (1896–1984): Born in the Aran Islands, he is one of the giants of the Irish short story. Apart from stories, he wrote many novels and three autobiographical books. He served in the British Army in the First World War and then fought in the Irish Revolution. He spent many years in the U.S., but lived mainly in Dublin from 1946 until his death in 1984.

ELIZABETH BOWEN (1899–1973): Born in Dublin, her family home was Bowen's Court, Co. Cork. She divided her time mostly between London and Ireland, and her international reputation as a writer is based on a succession of distinguished novels and short stories.

SEAN O'FAOLAIN (1900–   ): Born in Cork, he fought on the Republican side in the Irish Civil War. Probably the most distinguished all-round man of letters in the Irish cultural scene since Yeats. Playwright, novelist, poet, translator, essayist, biographer, and editor, he is best known as a short story writer with many collections to his name. *The Kitchen* is from *The Talking Trees* (1971).

FRANK O'CONNOR (1903–1966): Born in Cork. Largely self-educated, he worked as a librarian until 1938 and thereafter devoted all his time to writing. His first collection of stories, *Guests of the Nation*, was published in 1931. Among his other books are some half-dozen further short story collections, two novels, many translations from Irish poetry, biography, two volumes of autobiography, criticism, and a book on Shakespeare. He was a Director of the Abbey Theatre (where he had two plays produced) 1936–39 and a brilliantly persuasive lecturer and broadcaster.

PATRICK BOYLE (1905–   ): Born in Co. Antrim, a retired bank manager, he has written one novel and three collections of short stories. *At Night All Cats Are Grey* is the title story of his first collection, published in 1966.

MICHAEL McLAVERTY (1907–   ): One of Northern Ireland's most distinguished writers, he spent most of his life teaching in Belfast where he now lives in retirement. He wrote eight novels and many short stories.

BRYAN MacMAHON (1909–   ): Born in Co. Kerry where he taught for most of his life. He has written two volumes of short stories, novels, plays and pageants, and has also been active in the field of translating from the Irish.

ANTHONY C. WEST (1910–   ): One of the most neglected of Northern Ireland's writers, he has published one volume of short stories, *River's End* (1960), and some half-dozen novels. He lived for many years in Wales and is now living in London.

MARY LAVIN (1912–   ): Born in the U.S.A. but came to Ireland as a child and was educated at University College, Dublin. She has written two novels but her worldwide reputation rests firmly on her short stories, eleven collections of which have so far appeared. *Happiness* dates from 1969.

BENEDICT KIELY (1919–   ): Born in Northern Ireland, where he grew up, he subsequently spent many years teaching in the U.S., and now lives in Dublin. He has written many novels and three collections of short stories and is also a distinguished critic, biographer, journalist and broadcaster. *Nothing Happens in Carmincross*, a brilliant evocation of Ireland, came out in 1985.

JAMES PLUNKETT (1920–   ): Born in Dublin, he was a Trades Union official for some time but most of his working life has been in Irish radio and television. He has written one collection of short stories, and two novels of Dublin in the earlier years of this century which have gained him an international public.

VAL MULKERNS (1925–   ): Born in Dublin, she wrote two novels in the early 1950's and then, after many years' silence, published a collection of short stories, *Antiquities*, in 1978.

WILLIAM TREVOR (1928–   ): Born in Co. Cork, he won the Hawthornden Prize in 1965 with his novel, *The Old Boys*. He has continued to turn out either a novel or a short story collection almost every year as well as many TV plays and is widely considered to be one of the best living short story writers. *Fools of Fortune* appeared in 1983 and won the coveted Whitbread Award for Fiction.

BRIAN FRIEL (1929–   ): Born in Co. Tyrone, Northern Ireland, he has been a full-time writer since 1960 when he gave up teaching. He wrote two distinguished collections of stories early in his career but has since then devoted himself exclusively to the theatre.

JOHN MONTAGUE (1929–   ): Though best known as one of Northern Ireland's leading poets, in 1960 he published a significant short story collection, *Death of a Chieftain*. He taught in Paris and the U.S. for long spells and is now on the staff of University College, Cork.

MAEVE KELLY (1930–   ): Born in Co. Louth, she has written one short story collection, *A Life of her Own* (1976).

EDNA O'BRIEN (1932–   ): Born in Co. Clare, she achieved immediate success with her first novel, *The Country Girls* (1960), and followed this with a succession of novels and short story collections which have consolidated her high reputation. She has lived in London since 1958.

JULIA O'FAOLAIN (1933–   ): Born in London, the daughter of Sean O'Faolain, she has written novels and collections of short stories and commutes between London and the U.S. where her husband is a Professor of History in the University of California.

TOM MacINTYRE (1933–   ): Born in Co. Cavan, he has written one novel, one collection of short stories (1970), poetry and plays, and has recently been resident writer for the Calck Hook Dance Theatre in Paris.

JOHN McGAHERN (1935–   ): He was a schoolteacher in Dublin, his birthplace, from 1957 to 1964 until losing his job as a result of the banning of his second novel, *The Dark* in 1966. Since then he has been a fulltime writer with frequent teaching spells in the U.S. His latest work, a collection of short stories called *High Ground*, came out in 1985.

GILLMAN NOONAN (1937–   ): Born in Co. Cork, he has worked in Germany and Switzerland. He has published one collection of stories, *A Sexual Relationship* (1976).

MAURA TREACY (1946–   ): Born in Co. Kilkenny, she has published one collection of stories, *Sixpence in her Shoe* (1977).

KATE CRUISE O'BRIEN (1948–   ): Born in Dublin, the daughter of Conor Cruise O'Brien, she has published one collection of stories, *A Gift Horse* (1978).

DESMOND HOGAN (1951–   ): Born in Co. Galway, he has published three novels and two collections of short stories, including *Diamonds at the Bottom of the Sea* (1978), and has had plays produced in Dublin's Peacock Theatre. He lives in London. His latest novel, *A Curious Street*, received widespread acclaim on its publication in 1984.

NEIL JORDAN (1951–   ): Born in Dublin, he was for some time active in children's theatre and also in the founding of the Irish Writers' Co-Operative, which published his first collection of short stories, *Night in Tunisia,* in 1976. The collection was brought out in Britain in 1979 and shared the *Guardian* Fiction Prize for that year. He is also a successful film director, with *Angel* and *A Company of Wolves* to his credit. *The Dream of a Beast*, a compelling novella, came out in 1983.

LIAM O'FLAHERTY

THE INFORMER

Widely regarded as one of the classics of Irish fiction, THE INFORMER is a work of outstanding realism and understanding. Its pages blaze with the determined patriotism of an oppressed people locked in the struggle for freedom.

'A little masterpiece of its kind . . . O'Flaherty's portrait of the brutish informer is so marvellously vivid, and his whole narrative, with its slowly increasing atmosphere of terror, so perfectly unfolded that the book must be ranked very high indeed . . . a quite unforgettable story'

The Sunday Times

NEW ENGLISH LIBRARY

LIAM O'FLAHERTY

SHORT STORIES

Liam O'Flaherty was acclaimed by many as the master of the short story, and these pieces, representing a lifetime's work, live up to his reputation. He describes with an accuracy and feel that only an insider has, the mores and habits of the Irish. In loving detail and splendidly evocative prose, O'Flaherty's stories are a tribute to all that is essentially Irish. It will keep readers enthralled for years.

'I do not hesitate to compare his work with that of the most expert writers of the short story'

The Spectator

'O' Flaherty goes deeply into the situation with a mind joyously full of intelligence and original sin'

Rebecca West,
The Daily Telegraph

NEW ENGLISH LIBRARY

GOOD READING FROM NEL

E. R. BRAITHWAITE
☐ 00085 0 To Sir With Love   £1.95

LAURIE COLWIN
☐ 05727 5 Family Happiness   £1.95

ALAN FRANKS
☐ 05627 9 Boychester's Bugle   £1.50

T. N. MURARI
☐ 05897 2 Taj: A Novel of Mughal India   £2.95

LIAM O'FLAHERTY
☐ 04965 5 The Informer   £1.50
☐ 39499 9 Short Stories   £3.50

All these books are available at your local bookshop or newsagent, or can be ordered direct from the publisher. Just tick the titles you want and fill in the form below.

Prices and availability subject to change without notice.

___

NEL BOOKS, P.O. Box 11, Falmouth, Cornwall.

Please send cheque or postal order, and allow the following for postage and packing:

U.K. – 55p for one book, plus 22p for the second book, and 14p for each additional book ordered up to a £1.75 maximum.

B.F.P.O. and EIRE – 55p for the first book, plus 22p for the second book, and 14p per copy for the next 7 books, 8p per book thereafter.

OTHER OVERSEAS CUSTOMERS – £1.00 for the first book, plus 25p per copy for each additional book.

Name ....

Address ....

....